John Kernow was born in Cornwall and immigrated to Australia as a child. He was unspectacular academically. More impressive than his academic record was his ability to survive his western Sydney school physically unscathed. At university, he discovered that he had chosen one of the most boring subjects on the curriculum and that another was forcing him to read a well-known female author, most of whose characters he wanted to strangle. It was too much just to meet girls and he left university without graduating. He fell into engineering out of desperation and despite well intentioned warnings to avoid it like the plague. He managed both to stay sane and avoid discovery as a fraud by changing employers on a regular basis. Through that simple ploy he obtained employment in Australia, UK, the Middle East, and Asia. He now lives in Queensland with his wife and superannuated cat. His stated object as a writer is to amuse as many as possible and pay the cat's vet bill.

To my daughter Meg, without whom I'd probably never have begun, for keeping me at it and for her constant encouragement.

Also to Barbara for her praise and in particular for revealing her amusing 'bed shaking' incident which encouraged me to publish.

John Kernow

THE HAUNTING OF GASPARD FEEBLEBUNNY

AUSTIN MACAULEY PUBLISHERS™

LONDON * CAMBRIDGE * NEW YORK * SHARJAH

A CIP catalogue record for this title is available from the British Library.

ISBN 9781528928595 (Paperback)
ISBN 9781528932141 (ePub e-book)

www.austinmacauley.com

First Published 2023
Austin Macauley Publishers Ltd®
1 Canada Square
Canary Wharf
London
E14 5AA

1

Constable Feeblebunny was on the graveyard shift. In the light of what was to follow, that was irony indeed.

Gaspard had joined the police force (currently undergoing a name change to make it seem less threatening to the criminal element and appease those politically left of batty), in order to satisfy both his yearning for adventure and his sense of civic responsibility. Perhaps somewhere in there was also the vain hope it would stop people laughing at his name.

So far, the adventure side of things was a bit of a flop and he was beginning to wonder if he hadn't seen just a few too many detective series. Now, here he was, standing alone at the side of a deserted road manning a radar unit and hoping desperately for something to allay the boredom. Gaspard didn't really care whether or not it was a speeding driver, although that would at least give him a small feeling of usefulness, it might just as well be a sedate village parson chugging along at well under the limit. He just wanted the brief satisfaction of knowing his presence here had some point because up until now the closest he had come to fulfilling his duty was to consider charging a hedgehog for proceeding without due caution. Instead, he'd picked the creature up and carried it off the road. As a reward for his consideration several fleas transferred themselves to his uniform and the hedgehog peed on him. That should have taught him not to go soft on the criminal element but he really wouldn't be aware of the hedgehog's lack of gratitude or remorse until after he'd gone to bed and by then the source of the insects would have been argued successfully by any half decent brief.

His level of frustration had little to do with duties but a lot to do with his personality and need for achievement because despite his common sense telling him that he was still really dangerously inexperienced, he had an overwhelming need for immediate adventure. Luckily or otherwise, it was on its way.

It was one thirty a.m. when the unit pinged and the camera operated. Strangely, there seemed to be no sign of a vehicle approaching. He glanced at the screen which told him that something was passing at a speed of ninety-four miles an hour. There clearly being no car in sight, he did what nine out of ten males would do in the circumstances and gave the unit a hefty thump. The rest of the shift passed uneventfully with the unit apparently functioning as the manufacturer had intended. Nonetheless and despite some misgivings he mentioned the possible malfunction to his superiors. Fortunately for his credibility the unit did have a recording capability and when the records were accessed, they verified his story. Something had registered a speed well in excess of the limit and though the camera had operated nothing appeared in the photo except a small strange luminescence. After much head shaking and speculation as to whether he may have done something, nobody could think what, that may have induced the error, a backup unit was brought out of mothballs for the next night.

The following evening, he was on the same stretch of road in the same location. It was one thirty a.m. when the unit pinged and the camera operated. The unit registered a speed of ninety-four miles an hour but there was no vehicle in sight. For five nights in a row, the same event occurred. The offending machines were checked and rechecked, calibrated and recalibrated and theories examined and rejected. Soon, even those most cynically attempting to write the whole thing off with facile explanations gave up pushing theories of high speed and very punctual owls and the like and did what we all do in such circumstances. They threw up their hands, said it was gremlins and left the whole mess to Gaspard who was instructed to write a comprehensive report for the manufacturer. Under the circumstances the comprehensive bit took all of two lines. While deliberations were going on, Gaspard said little other than the occasional 'yes sir'. It was hard enough being saddled with the surname Feeblebunny without pushing his luck.

On night six, Gaspard was in position on the dark, lonely stretch of road. He was scratching vigorously as he awaited the phantom speeder, as he now thought of the phenomenon. He was not normally of a nervous disposition but the ominously leaden sky and the wind whistling and moaning as it haunted the tree branches was beginning to give him a fair dose of the willies. It sounded way too much like his grandfather after he'd fallen asleep and his dentures came loose. Somewhere a fox with either great timing or an amazing knowledge of English television shows emitted an eerie shriek. At least, Gaspard hoped it was a fox, or if not a fox then at any rate, something of this world. Standing on dark lonely country roads with shrieking foxes and howling winds will do that to anyone so we can't think less of him for having a touch of them. A director of Hollywood suspense dramas couldn't have done better. Or maybe he could because it was then the young policeman saw what he at first took to be a shadowy figure crouching in the bushes across the road.

He strained his eyes and came to the unnerving conclusion that what he was really seeing was an impenetrable blackness superimposed upon the normal night-time blackness. Or perhaps that should be what he was not seeing. It seemed to be a blackness not of the normal absence of light type of darkness but something almost palpable. It was the sort of darkness that any sensible ordinary darkness would do its best to distance itself from. He shook his head to clear his vision and aroused the pathetic hope that the perception it was a crouching figure was merely a trick of his optics. Being a relatively normal human, his brain then did its best to have him believe just that and denied any responsibility for the eventual outcome.

He mulled over the proposition that a dark figure would be lurking in bushes, in a position crouched or otherwise, on a lonely stretch of highway miles from anywhere and came to the conclusion that at any time of night, that would be unlikely. It was a trick of the light, or rather a lack of the light that was playing his eyes for mugs. That decided he then did his utmost not to look in that direction again. As the hour approached one thirty, Gaspard steeled himself. What happened next was both totally expected and totally unexpected. At one twenty-nine and fifty-five seconds, a dark figure rushed from the bushes and hurled itself into the centre of the carriageway. That was the unexpected bit. In the split seconds available for him to make sense of what was happening, Gaspard concluded that the figure was a man, impossibly tall, very thin and clad from head to toe in a black, hooded robe. The camera registered (the expected bit) and at that very instant the figure was bowled base over apex by some invisible force. As it somersaulted through the air there was a puzzling and brief flash of white that his brain decided was best not considered at this time. To add to things best not thought about, the figure landed with a sort of clatter, rather than the healthy thud (or perhaps unhealthy thud depending on the eventual outcome for the thudee.)

One would have been prepared for at least a 'bugger!' but other than the clatter there was nothing. Seeing someone bowled over by an invisible object tends to stun one somewhat and for a while Gaspard hovered indecisively, too shocked to move. During that time, the figure arose, seemingly none the worse for wear. It stooped briefly, picked up a long thin white object from the roadway, and inserted it within the folds of its cloak. After a deal of struggle, there was an audible click and the figure trudged back to the roadside bushes. It fished about for a second or two and eventually pulled from the brush what appeared to be a long pole. Gaspard's first reaction was the one which most of a healthily cautious disposition would have chosen. He decided it would, on the whole, all things considered, be best to appreciate what had happened from a safe distance. Soon alas, his policeman's instinct to render aid, freed him from his inaction and putting caution aside, he rushed to the man's aid.

O.K., to be truthful, he sort of ambled reluctantly but he did what was expected of one of his calling, albeit a little nervously. For 'little', read 'very'. "Are you alright? That was quite a tumble," he called as he moved towards the victim. He thought it best to give advance warning of his approach because it gave him the possibility of a head start should things go pear shaped. It was only as he reached the gloomy figure that he realised the object that it was carrying appeared to be a scythe.

"Quite, thank you. Thought I had the bugger that time. It's turning out to be trickier than I thought. I suppose I really should have thought things through a little better."

"Umm, sir, I think you should put down the scythe," said Gaspard nervously, trying vainly to see the man's face in the folds of the hood.

"Oh, don't worry, nothing for you to fear. Yet."

Gaspard experienced a moment of mental confusion. What had he been saying? Oh, yes. "Are you all right, sir?"

"Perfectly thank you. No need to trouble yourself, constable."

"Umm, might I ask what you were attempting to do sir?"

"No, I think not." Still experiencing a degree of befuddlement, Gaspard looked the figure up and down. There was a lot of up and come to think of it a lot of down as well. His face was hidden within the cowl and most of his body was well cloaked but the fingers around the scythe…ye gods, they looked like bones. His brain immediately began to do what brains do when confronted by the unreasonable which is either to reason it away or run like hell. Luckily it decided to stick around and fight it out and came up with possibly the most obvious answer which was that the man was wearing a Halloween costume. Satisfied it had found an explanation, his brain told him to stop looking at the hands just in case it might have cocked things up.

Gaspard's senses were telling him that the man's response had been completely faultless although he couldn't exactly remember what it was. He smiled by way of thanks. "And, ah, the clothing sir? It's a long way to Halloween, might I enquire…?"

"Suit's at the cleaners."

"I see, of course."

"Good lord, a badger!"

The figure raised an arm, exposing a long bony finger and pointed to a spot behind Gaspard who automatically turned, his training in the 'what's that behind you' school of diversion having been somewhat perfunctory. He was half into the turn when his survival instincts cut in and he did a rapid reversal. It was a partial save of face that did nothing to stop him feeling like an absolute pillock, accompanied by a partial sprain resulting from the sudden reversal. It was therefore fortunate in a way that the figure had vanished, although Gaspard couldn't help thinking that wherever the miscreant was he was thinking that he, Gaspard, was a twit.

Somehow, he was not surprised that there were no sounds of running footsteps, no sounds of bracken being trampled, not even a distant cry of 'up yours copper'. He knew without knowing why that there was absolutely no sense in trying to find the man, concluding that it would probably be stupid and almost certainly dangerous. Perhaps, he suddenly realised, it was that he had not actually heard the sinister individual's words. They had just somehow found their way into his head.

Then there was the sepulchral quality. And the bones. He quite sensibly resolved that this incident would not find its way into his report of the night's activities. Although it would almost certainly find its way into his nightmares.

Death was perplexed. The young policeman should not have been able to see him. As a mortal, there was only once in his lifetime that should have been possible. Well…not really in a lifetime. More at the junction. Death did a hasty check of his records. Feeblebunny, Gaspard H. No appointment for some time yet. Bugger. That meant that the copper was a prescient. There was always the

11

odd mortal that had the powers. Just his bloody luck to run into one on a difficult job.

Percival Pargeter was a man you couldn't get too close too, at least in the personal relationship sense. He was a man who kept to himself.

In the physical sense, it was best not to get too close either, certainly when he was introducing himself. The spray from those plosives could be quite distressing for most and many a bespectacled victim had had to surreptitiously wipe their glasses. Those suffering the introduction generally blessed their foresight in carrying a handkerchief. Percival was an individual of the type generally referred to by the psychiatric industry as an anal retentive, a term which implies a tightly clenched anus which is how most people tended to think of him, though not necessarily in such polite terms. He was one of those people who lives life by the philosophy of 'a place for everything and everything in its place'. A philosophy that was extremely unfortunate and bloody annoying for almost anyone who knew him, particularly as it included emotion. Percival began each day at precisely the same time, always ate the same breakfast in the same allotted time frame, dressed in the same manner and left for work at precisely the same hour.

Regardless of weather, traffic, civil disturbance or act of God, he was invariably punctual and had the uncanny ability to always walk through the factory door at the same hour and minute every day of his working life. This latter ability was such that it was a frequent discussion point among his workmates, particularly after one or several had dragged themselves in hours late having suffered train derailments, traffic accidents, hurricane force winds or a wet leaf on the rail line outside Tunbridge Wells. The only conclusion they managed to reach in years of agonising was that he would never be delayed by an act of God because the Almighty wouldn't have the nerve.

Management loved Percival because he was a model employee who did his job assiduously. That meant that in keeping with the universal laws of competence he would never be promoted because he was just too good at doing what he did, whatever it was. It didn't do to think too much about the activities of a man who performed such sterling duty at the scale rate of pay. Under the system the inept clods around him flourished while he rusted in place. For his part, Percival didn't care because promotion would have meant a change in routine although naturally, he often fulminated about the incompetent buggers who tried to tell him what to do. That was unfortunate for everybody around him. Perhaps more unfortunate for them, what Percival Pargeter did even better than his job was to annoy the crap out of everyone. It wasn't so much what he did as what he didn't do; which was to live.

Percival liked working the night shift because there were fewer distractions and fewer people about. It also meant that he could sleep most of the day, thus avoiding any chance of personal contact. It also gave the occasional opportunity to complain to his neighbours about noise, which was a great comfort.

It was the first evening of the strange radar incident. Percival Pargeter awoke at the side of the road in the presence of a sinister looking individual clad all in black and clutching a scythe. He had the distinct feeling that despite the other's bizarre appearance he knew him. He was struggling to make an association when the man spoke; or did he? "It is time. Come."

The creature, as Percy was immediately beginning to think of it, beckoned in a decidedly bony sort of way. Although struggling to come to terms with the fact that the voice seemed to be inside his head, Percival answered in the only way possible considering that he was late for work. "Piss off, I'm late." With that, he drove off at high speed leaving both his wrecked car and corporeal remains in the keeping of the awesome figure. Ironically, this was the moment that Percival, who had never really lived when he was alive; began to live.

"But you're dead," Death called after him, before finishing lamely, "you can't do this." He could do it of-course and Death knew it. He just didn't want to admit that there were occasionally those too stubborn, obsessed or what have you to admit they were dead. This was going to be a troublesome one, he could just feel it in his bones which was a real bugger considering that was all he was. He sighed. It was a sound of wind-blown dry leaves and as old as the world. Death and Santa Claus have the one thing in common. They are omnipresent. It doesn't take too much thinking to realise that's the only way it could work. The big difference between the two is that Santa is a gift giving, jolly old soul while Death is quite a bit less jolly and takes souls. Being omnipresent meant that the odd escapee from Death shouldn't be too much of a bother. All he had to do was be everywhere simultaneously and the miscreant would have to turn up but somehow it didn't work out that way. The laws of the universe aren't quite as immutable as scientists would have people believe which is why there are so many unquiet spirits hanging about in castles.

It would have been a pain in the bum if Death had one. In the phantom vehicle, Percival put his foot down. He could still make it on time if he broke the rule of a lifetime and exceeded the speed limit. It may have been of some comfort to him that he wasn't actually breaking the rule of lifetime, he being dead. When Percival passed Constable Feeblebunny's radar at one thirty a.m., he was doing precisely ninety-four miles an hour and more alive than at any time in his existence.

Although technically he no longer had an existence. Let's not split hairs. The following evening, Percival awoke at the side of the road with a sinister figure hovering over him and a distinct sense of déjà vu. The figure leaped. Percival shrieked and drove off at high speed. He was late for work. On the sixth evening following his premature demise, Percival awoke at the side of the road. He looked about warily. Something seemed to be missing. That thought entertained him for only the briefest moment because he was late for work. What the hell had he been thinking napping here under this tree? He took off at high speed, simultaneously castigating himself for speeding and forgiving himself on the grounds that he couldn't break a perfect eighteen year attendance record. Never in his life had he ever been late for anything and he wasn't going to start now. He'd probably have been mortified had he known that strictly speaking he was late for his own afterlife and on the attendance front he was off to a rocky start.

When the cloaked figure suddenly appeared in front of the car, Pargeter didn't even touch the brakes. He knew that he should stop. He knew that he should be feeling immense guilt but all he could really feel was an odd sense of triumph as the figure looped soundlessly through the air. He had not the slightest sense of remorse when he strolled through the factory door. How could he; he was on time.

"Constable!"

"Yes Sarge."

"The Super wants to see you. Something about last night's shift. Best shift your bum. Chop-chop." Gaspard felt the inevitable flash of fear up the passage. Not the one he was walking along either.

"Thanks, Sarge. Any idea?"

"None at all. Off you hop." The last words were followed by an involuntary snigger which was rapidly followed by a crushing sense of shame, nonetheless real for having been born of a fear of being done for insensitivity. "Umm, sorry about that last bit constable. Didn't mean to…you know…umm…well, off you go before himself gets impatient."

"Ah, Feeblebunny, come in. We've not met before I think. I'm Superintendent Fish. Like it says on the door, what?"

"Pleased to meet you sir," replied Gaspard, hoping desperately that his reaction on seeing his superior for the first time hadn't betrayed him. Fish was well named, with the bug-eyed look of a startled grouper. His bald, mottled head and slightly snaggled toothed appearance did nothing to enhance the image.

"Yes, yes. Now then, there's been a query about last night's shift. This phantom speeder thing." He narrowed his eyes as he looked Gaspard up and down. "Seems there's an anomaly on the photo." He paused for a moment to let the news sink in. "Any idea what?"

The pause had been a blessing for Gaspard who had now had sufficient time to rid himself of the effects of another unpleasant lightning bolt up the rectum.

"Well, no sir, none at all. Was there something unusual, sir?" he enquired a little warily. He'd been around long enough to understand that seemingly innocent questions from superiors often held a concealed barb.

"Yes and no constable. Very odd thing you see. The chap who first looked at the photo swears it shows a black robed figure somersaulting through the air. Can't shift him on it. Some others agree but then various people see various things. Some see nothing at all while others see a black smear or the like. Very odd. Take a look and tell me what you see." He proffered the photo.

"Umm, I'm afraid I must be listed amongst those who see nothing sir. Just the usual funny flash of light." Gaspard hoped his eyes weren't betraying his lie as the figure of last night's robed stranger was revealed upside down in mid-air. He tried to ignore what looked a lot like a skeletal foot emerging from the fabric and now that he looked closer, something bearing a suspicious resemblance to a free flying rib bone slightly above the soaring figure.

"Mm, like most of the others. Can't say I can see anything either. Now…can you remember anything unusual occurring? Something you may have forgotten to report. Strangely clad men flying upside-down in the carriageway, for instance?" He chuckled. "No, no, shouldn't jest. It's become a rather serious matter unfortunately. One of the chaps who swears it's a man is in Professional Standards and is insisting on a full investigation. Won't be put off. They'll want to talk to you later."

The Super bestowed a look of genuine sympathy on Gaspard, who was beginning to sweat and hoping it didn't show.

"Can't say I remember anything at all unusual sir, other than the phantom speeder that is. Quite a mystery that. I've spoken to the manufacturer's tech people and they're as baffled as anyone."

"Yes, quite. Well, that's about it constable. Expect a call from Professional Standards. Search your brain in the meantime for anything you may have forgotten. Be sure to look under the rug, ha-ha. Best not to discuss it with anyone, eh? Mum's the word."

"Very good, sir."

"Oh, one last thing lad. Apropos of nothing at all, your last name. Can't help but ask…unusual and all that…any idea of its origins?"

"None at all sir. I've tried of course. The best I can come up with is that it may be a corruption of a Norman French name but it's just supposition. It's either that or I must have had some unusual forebears for them to be saddled with it. I don't mind telling you sir that it can be a bit of a trial."

"Yes, I can see that. I suppose you have to exercise a bit of forebear…ance, what?" The super chortled at his own witticism.

"Quite so sir. I suppose you must have had a little experience yourself sir," ventured Gaspard, emboldened by the superintendent's attack of bonhomie and feeling a little fellow sympathy for one he thought must be a kindred spirit in the name department.

"Good Lord man, why would you think that?" fired back Fish acerbically.

"Umm, well, ah…no particular reason, please forgive my stupidity," replied Gaspard nervously, immediately realising that either Fish was in denial or more likely of such an exalted status that none would dare ridicule him openly.

"Yes, yes, of course, perfectly understandable, stress and all that. Anyway, keep up the good work, lad, there have been complementary reports."

"Thank you sir." The super's response to Gaspard's patronym had been milder than most although people were generally kind about it after an initial snigger or uncontrollable expression of shock or disbelief. He was inured by now to having to repeat his name after most first introductions. The worst part about it was that it made it difficult for people to take him seriously. Gaspard was pretty well set up physically without being one of the huge coppers of yesteryear so still should have had a reasonably intimidatory presence for the average villain but one look at his name tag had most offenders giving him lip. That sometimes led to unfortunate outcomes. Often of a physical nature. The effect on his workaday interaction with the public was bad enough but perhaps his greatest regret with regard to his name was in the romance area.

Even though he was attractive physically and of pleasant, even alluring personality, immediately after learning his name females seemed to find the idea of a relationship with him unappealing. His lack of success was such that he had all but given up.

Sergeant Hardcastle could have selected a more pleasant interview room but it was the mark of the man that he had chosen the only one yet to be refurbished in the 19th century wing of the police headquarters. It was windowless, dank and chill which was partially due to the sergeant having purposely shut off the heating well in advance of the meeting. The walls were covered in a peeling brown and cream institutional finish that wouldn't have been out of place in Bedlam. The floor was covered, if that was the word, in a thread bare and ancient industrial carpet, badly stained in places and with the floor boards showing through in others.

Most of the stains had been added artificially in order to put the wind up villains and many a young constable had been instructed to put nose bleeds or cut fingers to good use. The sole items of furniture were a battered, stained and scarred metal table that looked as though it would be more at home in a world war two Nissan hut, accompanied by chairs of a similar age and lack of appeal. The only one available to Gaspard had a split vinyl seat cover and a wobbly leg.

In typical fashion, Hardcastle began on an aggressive note. "Feeblebunny? What sort of a bloody name is that? No, wait, it's one of those bloody hoity toity names isn't? Like Cholmondeley being pronounced Chumley or St John being Sinjin. I bet you pronounce it something like Philby don't you?"

"Uh, no sergeant, although I'm surprised nobody ever thought of that. It's just as spelled. Feeblebunny."

"Christ, not even…I don't know…Febblerbunet or some such?"

"Uh, uh. Plain old Feeblebunny Sarge."

"Hell's bells, no wonder you became a copper. I suppose it was either that or a hit man. Only way you could be sure as few people as possible would take the piss. To be frank though if it were me, I would have opted for the latter." The sergeant gave one of those humourless smiles so often seen to adorn the mugs of born bastards.

"Alright Feeblebunny, enough of the pleasantries" said Hardcastle in a tone so icy that it could have sunk a dozen Titanics, "time to come clean. What happened up there last night that you're trying to hide?" Detective Sergeant Hardcastle was glaring at the unfortunate constable with his most intimidating glare. It was one he kept at the back of the closet and only trotted out on special occasions. As glares went it was pretty hard to ignore and even intimidated the other glares he kept in reserve.

Gaspard trembled. "I'm sorry sergeant but nothing happened, if it had it would have been in my report."

"Unless of course you have something to hide or screwed up somehow, eh? I've seen the photo. How do explain it?" Hardcastle had a bad reputation as a terrier when it came to worrying a subject to death. He was also a martinet of the old school and disliked by everyone. Like most bullies he prided himself on being frank. The word 'frank' as we all know is a perfect example of an irregular English verb. That being: I am frank; you are rude; he is a vicious bastard. Behind his back his name was altered slightly to begin with 'hard' but then something that only rhymed approximately with 'castle'.

"Well, I can't sergeant and from what I understand neither can anyone else. The super said everyone sees the photo differently. It's weird."

"Weird it may be boy but I know what my eyes tell me and I have to stick with that. Wouldn't be doing my job otherwise and what I see is a bloke being knocked arse over tit. So, I ask you again to explain it."

"Afraid I can't Sarge, I only know what I know and that's that there's nothing to know because to the best of my knowledge there's…ah…nothing to know." Gaspard shook his head, uncomfortably aware that he was close to babbling.

"Asleep eh?"

"No sergeant. Believe me, when you're waiting for the phantom to appear, sleep is the last thing that you feel like. It really winds you up sitting there and wondering whether it'll happen again. Nobody has the foggiest what's going on and you have to start thinking about whether or not it's something supernatural. To be frank it's a bit scary."

"Yeh, I've read all the bumf around it. Doesn't explain the photo though, does it, constable?"

"No Sarge. And nothing explains why everyone sees it differently either."

Hardcastle gave Gaspard the benefit of one of his better glares. "Alright, I can see you're going to stick with your story, so you might as well bugger off."

Gaspard's shoulders which had been creeping steadily up towards his ears with the tension of the situation dropped with relief. A little prematurely as it happened because Hardcastle was playing games. "Umm, I don't suppose your story would be any different if I were to tell you we're getting a forensics team up there to check things out?" Hardcastle grinned triumphantly.

"No sergeant," replied Gaspard, a little more casually than he felt. "It's as I said. Nothing untoward happened. I can't explain why you see what you see in the photo but if you feel you must investigate then you must."

The sergeant's triumphant grin slunk off with its tail between its legs. It did not make Hardcastle happy at all so he replaced it with a glower but he was only too aware that it was a poor substitute. The loss of face made him even angrier. "Alright you little turd but if I find the merest scrap of evidence, I'll nail you to a wall. You understand? In the meantime, you're suspended from duty pending the results of the enquiry." He gave Gaspard the benefit of his best evil grin before adding grudgingly: "On full pay of course."

Hardcastle found himself grinding his teeth in frustration. Not only was he suspicious of the recorded events but the officer about whom they revolved was one of the worst of sorts. In other words, he was young, pleasant and attractive. Just the sort that needed to be brought to heel. He gathered up his papers and looked cautiously about. He was sure they were still watching him.

Death scratched his head. How to deal with the Pargeter situation? He really did have more than enough to handle without chasing after wretches who refused to believe that they were dead. Wars, catastrophes, plagues, morons experimenting with drugs, supermarket heat and eat dinners, they all kept him on the bones of his toes. It really was too bad that there was a growing predilection amongst the mortals to challenge the ultimate inevitability. Those meeting their ends in the more traditional ways generally accepted their fate once he'd explained it to them but the modern self-centred, Facebook posting lifestyle had led a growing number to a certain bolshiness. He supposed it was something to do with the refusal to accept that they were not the centre of everything after all or that they'd been done in by a frozen tofu burger. What to do?

2

At precisely midnight by the atomic clock, there was a knock on the door.

Alright, to be really precise it was the merest part of a nanosecond out but nobody was going to notice. Well, alright, if we're going to be picky, Death was going to notice because by his reckoning the atomic clock was a trifle fast. As a demigod of sorts, you tend to notice things like that. Gaspard certainly didn't notice because of the three actual time pieces in his possession none's hands pointed even approximately to the same place on the dial. Of those flashy digital things built into everything from his fridge to his toilet roll holder none had been set with any great attention to GMT because Gaspard found the task difficult to master but mainly because most of the time, he really didn't give a bugger. In this instance, the actual time mattered not in the least because as we all know, anything within sixty minutes or so of the witching hour is technically midnight if one is irritated by callers.

This allows one to mutter darkly about it being bloody midnight which sounds so much more inconvenient than, say, eleven twenty. Gaspard wasn't actually inconvenienced in any way since having been on night shift for ages his day was just beginning. It was just that midnight knocks on the door, whether or not in strict accord with the atomic clock, did not presage anything good. A very wise man or to be more precise a clod who happened to say a wise thing, once said that nothing good happens after midnight and it was a philosophy with which Gaspard was in the heartiest of agreement. Being a copper on the streets at that time of night and dealing with the lady's formation vomiting teams and worse, tends to lead one quite hastily to that particular point of view. He therefore opened the door very warily.

Shortly thereafter he emitted a piercing shriek and slammed the door. It was probably not the bravest of things for a policeman to do but then one could forgive his reaction, owing as it did to being confronted by Death incarnate. "I'm sorry did I startle you?" Gaspard did a rapid volte face to discover the hooded figure from the previous evening standing in the middle of his living room. He managed to stifle the shriek this time but backed up against the door. The scythe might look very old and worn but it also looked very sharp and lethal.

Death stood saying nothing, his head cocked quizzically to one side. At length, Gaspard found his voice, although judging by the initial squeaky tone some part of it was still in hiding, probably in the region of his scrotum and very reluctant to emerge. "What...how...I mean..."

"Ah, you're wondering how I managed to get in when I was only just outside a locked door?"

"You could say that," quavered Gaspard.

"How does Santa get in?"

"What?"

"Not saying I'm anything much like Santa of course. It's just that we're both capable of being where we want, when we want. Wouldn't work otherwise don't you see. I mean I couldn't wait for my customers to let me in, could I? Knock, knock; who's there? Death. Bugger off. You see my point?"

"Then why did you knock in the first place?" queried Gaspard, his mind racing at the disclosure that he was talking to Death itself. There'd been a suspicion of course but it seemed just too fanciful. Now to have it confirmed. Well...

"Social call. Only polite. If I'd just appeared at your bedside, which is my usual modus operandi, you'd no doubt have had quite a turn. People have been known to...best not say what they've been known to but no doubt you can guess."

"Ah, thank you for your solicitude," croaked Gaspard, who had not the slightest doubt what people had been known to do as he strongly suspected that he may have just done it himself. Concomitant with that thought, he was wondering whether he should save time and have himself committed immediately or wait for somebody, no doubt his boss, to have him carried off in the giggle wagon.

"My pleasure," Death responded primly, obviously not a fan of sarcasm for all his years. Or maybe because of it.

"So, might I ask what this social call is all about? I should imagine it's not something you do on a regular basis. Correct me if I'm wrong."

"I am in need of your assistance." That little bit of information did a lot to rock Gaspard on his foundations for all its brevity. He pretty quickly computed that being asked for assistance by an omnipresent and for all he knew, very nearly omnipotent creature, was not going to end in anything good. "How?" he managed to wheeze at last.

"Before we discuss it perhaps, you'd like to make yourself a nice cup of tea or something? I believe it has a salubrious effect on mortals in times of stress and I can see that you're a trifle ill at ease."

Death gestured in the direction of the kitchen and Gaspard wasn't about to argue. The last thing he needed was tea, unless it was well laced with Scotch but he did need time to collect himself as various critical parts seemed to have gone into hiding and needed to be rounded up and made to behave themselves. As far as being ill at ease it wasn't so much a trifle as a whole dessert buffet.

"Umm, can I get you a cup?" He asked querulously and realised immediately that it was a stupid question to ask of an immortal being in the form a skeleton.

"Thank you, two sugars, no milk." Death paused for a brief moment before adding in a slightly embarrassed tone, "I don't suppose you have anything to pep it up a bit, do you? Drop of rum or such? It's been a bugger of a week."

"Of course. I just might join you," replied Gaspard, doing his best to avoid imagining how his unwanted guest might accomplish the feat of imbibing.

"And maybe a biscuit if you have one?" Gaspard immediately began to have serious doubts that Mister Death here was the real article. A biscuit eating, booze swilling skeleton? Not bloody likely. The doubts lasted only until Death spoke again. Or to be perfectly correct, some seconds after. "Look, I don't want to make you uncomfortable but would you mind if I take this bloody hood off? It's a real swine trying to eat with it on and I tend to get crumbs in the cassock. They get into all sorts of places, it can get quite irritating. Have to get the vacuum out sometimes."

"Not at all," croaked Gaspard, aware that if this character was some sort of loon who'd worked a clever trick at the door, he would have him dead to rights. If not, he would have him just dead and he, Gaspard would be a step closer to one of those funny jackets.

"Thank you. Please try not to be shocked."

That was an easy thing for Death to say but for the recipient it wasn't quite so easy to be suddenly presented with a skull peering from out a robe and maintain his equilibrium, no matter how well prepared mentally. The fact that the skull was sporting eyeballs didn't make it any easier. Somehow it just didn't seem right. It was somehow even worse that the skull was munching on a biscuit and daintily sipping tea. How the hell did he do it without a tongue for starters? And where the hell did it all go? Did he need to pass it? Gaspard found himself staring in horrified fascination. That and also in envy of Death's perfect set of teeth.

Many thoughts were jockeying for position but the preeminent one was why in the hell Death needed eyeballs? They had no optic nerve and no physical brain to process the signals. He could hear without ears and eat without stomach or tongue, so why eyeballs? The thought had almost finished its crossing when it suddenly came to a shambling halt and reversed direction. This way led to madness.

In the circumstances, Gaspard felt the need for several cups of tea, although to be brutally frank the tea portion of the beverage came in homeopathic quantities and was even more so with each cup. Death didn't seem to mind and in fact appeared to be enjoying himself. After the pair had come close to demolishing a bottle of particularly fine single malt, he didn't seem such a bad bloke.

"So Gaspard…hope you don't mind the familiarity…I am in need of your assistance as I have previously indicated. I need you to track down one Percival Pargeter for me." Death chuckled a little tipsily. "Just try saying that without any lips," he giggled. "What do you say?"

"Hang on. I don't understand. With all your powers, you want me to go chasing after some twerp?"

"Didn't make myself clear. Pargeter is no longer among the living. He is one of those obsessive bastards…pardon the French…who has been so single-mindedly attached to his routines that he refuses to admit he's dead. Most distressing. Get them from time to time."

"But hell's bells, I'm in no position to chase after spooks. We have names for people who do that and most have something to do with being a certifiable loon. They'll put me away." He cast about desperately for a winning argument. As casting went it was not about to land a big one. "Anyway, with all your powers surely…" In the realm of winning arguments that was not about to receive a podium finish but it was the best he could come up with on the spur of the moment because his line was tangled in a tree.

"Ah, yes, very busy man. You know the sort of thing, floods, famines, TV dinners, salmon mousse. And just in case you're under the typical illusion that humans constitute the body of my work, if you'll forgive a well-worn little jest;

allow me to disillusion you. I also do bunnies." Here he paused and Gaspard had the distinct feeling that Death was feeling a little morose at that disclosure. "I like bunnies," he said rather mournfully. "Do everything else too of course and let me tell if you're under the misapprehension that I have it easy, fish can be a right bugger, especially those down in the pelagic depths. Have you seen any of those things?" He gave a distinct shudder. "All bloody spines and eyeballs. You on the other hand are a policeman, it's your job to track down miscreants, simple as that."

"But he's not a miscreant. The last time I looked being dead wasn't on the books and...and you have powers for God's sake" shot back Gaspard, not convinced by the somewhat shifty nature of Death's tone and also slightly surprised that even though Death was not actually speaking the shiftiness was still evident. "Surely...I mean, what can I do that you can't?"

"Take a lot of time. Oh, I know that for all intents and purposes I have eternity, omnipresence, blah, blah, blah but being in thousands of places at once takes a lot of concentration. Fair gives me a headache at times, I'm a very busy being and it's not getting any easier. More people now than have ever lived did you know that? That means more deaths. Then there's factory fishing and farming...you get the picture I'm sure. To be frank, recalcitrant buggers like this one take it out of me. Lot of capital for little return. Now, you might say that it's my job and that I'm supposed to be able to get my man, or fish if it comes to that but none of us is perfect and I have to confess to having a bit of a weakness here and there. Concentration slips for a nanosecond and whoops there's another one gone. Then there's Castles. Something about the places seems to lead the recently departed to be difficult. They seem to think that *droit de seigneur* extends to life and death. And once they're away...well. I mean, have you ever spent the night in an English castle? All the screeching and gibbering even gives me the willies and it's a lot worse when they're dead believe me. Quite frankly there are some situations that just aren't worth the bloody effort and this Pargeter business is one of them."

"I wouldn't even know where to start," whined Gaspard. "And if I did find him what would I do?" He finished despairingly. "How do I convince someone who won't believe they're dead that they are?"

"You see what I have to deal with? Now here are the details, you can start first thing in the morning."

The details were neither spoken nor written but they were immediately burned into Gaspard's brain and possibly as a result his face took on a stubborn set that Death could not fail to notice. "But hang on. I've never seen a ghost. How can I catch someone I can't see?" Gaspard enquired cagily. Got you. "That's all up to me. Don't worry, a bit of hocus pocus on my part and you'll see more phantoms than is good for you. You have the aptitude. I mean, you saw me when few others can, at least while breathing. Now. You will do it. For one thing, you don't want me hanging about. I can make myself pretty obvious if I wish. Perhaps I could have a word with that nice Sergeant Hardcastle? Tell him how you left me alone and injured in the roadway? That bloody rib is still giving me pain. Wouldn't be surprised if I ended up with a touch of arthritis. I can be very convincing you know." Gaspard knew when he was beaten. Going up against a being that was close to all powerful was never going to end well.

"Very well. Perhaps you could give me a few ideas?" conceded Gaspard with a world-weary reluctance.

"Delighted. Any chance of another cup?"

"But what I still don't understand," slurred Gaspard companionably, having discovered an unopened bottle, "is this; if there are so many spooks lurking about, why are you going after this one in particular?"

"Good question," said Death. He hiccupped several times before continuing. "As you know, my job is not merely to sever the life force; I'm expected to bring in the souls. That includes having to bring in the difficult buggers who defy the rules but...and here's the point, I don't have to keep after them indefinitely. It's all a matter of expectation. The boys in Time and Motion recognise that there's a law of diminishing return and for all my powers, if I keep chasing people it affects my other work. They're willing to accept that there has to be a cut off and that sometimes the recently departed are just too stubborn or stupid to bother with."

Death nodded his head dreamily and appeared somewhat the worse for drink. Gaspard thought he may have been smiling but with a death's head it's rather hard to tell.

"So why not just go through the motions and then leave him be?" Gaspard queried, giving it one last good old college try. "Why involve me?"

"To be frank that wasn't my idea. While I was trying to figure out how to catch the bugger someone in Time and Motion dreamed up the idea of outside contracting. New boy. You know the type; all bright ideas; trying to impress the bosses. Won't listen to the voice of experience. Anyway, the big nobs decided it was worth a try to contract out the irritating stuff and leave me free to get on with what I'm really employed for."

He leaned forward conspiratorially. "I might say that if the trial succeeds there could well be something in it for you. They may even offer you a full-time post. Probably have to do a basic literacy and numeracy test but nothing that should bother a man of your abilities. There's a hell of a lot out there, so more than enough to keep you busy." He touched a finger bone to his face in a gesture that would have been tapping the side of his nose if he had one.

"And a word to the wise, some are a lot closer than you may think." Gaspard sat goggled eyed, a state that was only partly due to the booze. He was trying to imagine what a future as Death's deputy might be like and had the uneasy feeling that the position wouldn't be a voluntary one. For the last minute or so, something had been nagging at the back of his mind. In his befuddled state, he'd had a hard time putting his finger on it but at last the light dawned in a flash of mixed metaphor. "Umm, Time and Motion Department? You have a Time and Motion Department?"

"Unfortunately yes," replied Death. He cocked his head slightly and turned his bony palms upwards in a 'what are you going to do?' sort of gesture. "Have to keep up with the times, or so they tell me. Bunch of bloody whizz kids if you ask me."

Gaspard said nothing but the stunned expression on his face was more than sufficient to put his thoughts across. "So there you have it. I won't take up your time any further, I have a serious salmonella outbreak in an American hamburger chain on the books. They will insist on eating the bloody things…well…bloody. So…things to do for both of us eh and you mortals have little enough as it is. One last thing though, don't want to teach you how to do your job but you might want to start at the factory where Pargeter worked. He's work obsessed so that's a fair bet."

Gaspard nodded dumbly. "Right, so I'll check in in a day or two to see how you're getting on. Remember, impress the powers that be and there could be benefits you've never dreamed of. How does immortality sound for starters?" At the moment it didn't sound like much of a prize if it meant spending eternity tracking down recalcitrant spooks. Gaspard couldn't help thinking that the potential benefits may not be so much a dream as a nightmare.

Death paused and shuffled his feet in a slight show of embarrassment. "And maybe next time you could get in some Hobnobs? You know, the ones with the chocolate top."

"Ah, sure," said Gaspard distractedly, his mind racing with visions of celestial work standards units, "you said something about 'the powers that be', could that...ah...you know...ah, mean that...?"

"You're going to ask me the God question aren't you? Is He, or isn't He? Does He, or doesn't He? He or She? Sorry but against the rules. Something you have to sort out for yourself." The robed figure shrugged sympathetically with a faint clattering noise. That was disappointing but there was something else wasn't there? What had he said earlier? Santa! That was it. Surely not..."Umm, you said something earlier about Santa...you don't really mean that there is a Santa Claus?"

"Santa? Don't get me bloody started."

While Gaspard had been entertaining Death, Sergeant Hardcastle had been waiting at the roadside for the phantom speeder. He'd insisted that the unit go out again with a different operative so that he could see for himself what was happening. Hardcastle was a deeply suspicious type, (a trait which actually went very nicely with his paranoid schizophrenia) and couldn't help thinking that Feeblebunny was up to something. He had no idea what that might be but that didn't mean some jiggery pokery wasn't going on. So convinced was the sergeant that something was awry, he'd placed bets around the station that nothing untoward would happen on his watch.

At one thirty a.m. precisely, the camera registered. Hardcastle saw nothing but distinctly heard a cry of; 'up yours copperrrr' fading into the distance. He was not to know it of course but Percival was really beginning to enjoy himself. Sergeant Hardcastle was not enjoying himself because not only had he been made to look a twit but he was out thirty quid.

Constable Feeblebunny would suffer the consequences if the sergeant had any say in the matter. Unfortunately for Gaspard, he did.

Far too drunk to begin his investigations tonight, Gaspard was making himself a much-needed coffee when he heard the voice. "Has he gone?"

It was the parchment dry voice of an elderly female. Gaspard spun about to see an elderly woman, clad only in a dramatically soiled night gown perched on the end of his sofa. He was surprised of course but being half blotto the extent was limited and beginning to fall into the realms of bafflement which is the drunks usual state of being when they're not being bloody obnoxious. "Mrs D'Unstable?"

The bafflement was palpable because Mrs Maud D'Unstable had been dead for three years at least. There were two things about Mrs D'Unstable that usually surprised. The first was that she'd never actually been married or even in a relationship, the second was her surname which had originally been Dunstable. Maud in her early years had decided to add a bit of class by giving it what she thought to be a French touch. She hadn't thought a great deal about it however, a fact that was immediately apparent to anyone who'd seen it written. She had been known to all as Mrs Unstable ever since which was a pretty fair assessment of her personality.

"That's right dear. Is he gone?" The lips may have said 'dear' but the tone said 'you miserable bastard'.

"Who?" enquired Gaspard, although he had a pretty fair idea. He just didn't want to let the cat out of the bag in case he'd got it wrong. "That bony bastard of course. Cheek of him, making himself at home in my own flat after all he did to me."

"Umm, what would that be Mrs D'Unstable?"

"Tried to take me off of course. Not enough he killed me," she all but spat, rather unfairly thought Gaspard. Death could hardly be blamed if her time was up, could he?

"Bugger couldn't just leave me to be dead in peace, kept on pestering me to go with him. Said it was the rules. Bloody cheek. When I asked him where he would take me, he said he wasn't allowed to say. Well that did it. I wasn't born yesterday. Oblivion, that's why he wouldn't tell me. Obvious. Anyway, I fixed him, he never got me, did he? I might have killed myself but that doesn't mean I want to be dead." Maud was positively fuming and being worked up decided to get a few other things off her chest while she was at it. "And while we're on the subject of cheek, what the hell are you doing making yourself at home in my flat? I see you, swanning about the place like Lord Muck. Eating all that foreign rubbish from the takeaway and stinking the place up. It's my home, for chrissake. And don't get me started on some of the things you get up to. I see you. Bloody embarrassing for a woman of my age. A woman of any age. I'd heard of what you young fellows get up to sometimes but I never thought I'd see it. You should be bloody ashamed."

Gaspard's cheeks were burning with embarrassment as he frantically searched his memory to discover what it was she could have seen. To his horror he realised it was everything he'd ever done since moving in and he was pretty sure she wasn't referring to his burning the toast. He tried to put it all out of his mind and be reasonable. No point worrying about what an unquiet spirit may or may not have seen. Mrs D'Unstable grinned evilly. "Can't hide that flush from me my boy. Well may you blush. I've seen you in the bathroom." She paused long enough for Gaspard to feel himself sinking into the floor before adding cruelly, "poking your finger into your belly button and sniffing it."

The cackle that followed left no doubt that there was a lot more she could have said. For all his humiliation, Gaspard summoned what outrage he could. "I'm sorry Mrs D'Unstable but you're dead. It's my flat by rights. (Oh God, even on the loo?) If anyone should be miffed it's me. You've been invading my privacy. (Even that time…oh shit!) I'll thank you to leave."

"You what? Dream on boy. If that bony sod couldn't get rid of me, don't think you can. Just try it, that's all, just bloody try it." Gaspard emitted a shuddering, heartfelt sigh. He'd not known Mrs D'Unstable well before her untimely demise but he'd known her well enough to be aware that she had been disturbed, cantankerous and bloody minded. She was the sort of person who complained about the noise of cat paws in the neighbour's flat. He had little hope that death would have improved her personality. For the time being at least, they'd need to get along. When all this business with Pargeter was settled he'd have time to think about having her exorcised or whatever it was they did with ghosts.

"Alright Maud, may I call you that? I mean, in the circumstances, you know? You having had the advantage of me in…well, let's not go into that and you being in a night gown. If that doesn't put us on a first name basis, I don't know what does."

Maud merely hissed in response.

"Uh, alright Mrs D'Unstable, if that's what you prefer but neither of us has much alternative at the moment other than to get along, so let's not get off to a bad start eh? What say we stay out of each other's way as much as we can and make the most of a bad deal? After all, we've been sharing all this time, haven't we? It's just that I wasn't aware of the fact until a few moments ago. I promise

I'll do nothing to upset you if you promise to give me a bit of privacy. Who knows, it may work out better for both of us?"

"I know what that privacy business means. The very thought. Still, I suppose you're right. We'll give it a try but don't go inviting that robe wearing gobshite back again."

"I'm sorry but he turns up unannounced. He wants me to work for him. I'm afraid you'll just have to be careful and hide when he's around. Probably best if you stay in the spare room until it's all been sorted."

"Oh, bloody charming. I may as well be in a bloody tomb as locked away all hours."

"Sorry, Mrs D'Unstable but it's not in my power to control things. You can have the telly in there if that would help." That seemed to appease her a little judging by the cracks that appeared around her mouth. "Now, how about a nice cup of tea?"

"Cup of tea? Are you bloody daft? You think I'm one of them hoity toity bloody Asian ghosts what can absorb the essence or something? Last time I had a cup of tea sonny Jim was the day I died three years ago." Gaspard wished she hadn't said that because it forced him to remember the unpleasant aspects of her death. Not that there were many pleasant bits to death of any sort, it had just been a little nastier than some. She'd committed suicide with an overdose of sleeping pills washed down with a quantity of tea…not too unpleasant unless one considered that it had been a laxative tea of formidable potency which no doubt explained those stains on the night dress.

It hadn't been a pleasant end for Mrs D'Unstable and that was saying something. It hadn't been very pleasant for those finding her either. Particularly the end. Neighbours had been drawn to her body by the smell emanating from the flat but the smell hadn't been one of putrefaction. There had been a great deal of…well, there'd been a great deal. As a result, he'd managed to get a great deal on the flat because there weren't too many willing to live in a place with its unpleasant history. And pervasive odour. At least initially and pending the liberal application of various heavily scented cleansing products. The cleaning job had been both onerous and odorous and meant living in a place that transitioned olfactorily from a third world public loo to an oriental house of ill repute. Things were largely normal now after three years but there were still times, especially in damp weather when (appropriately enough) the ghosts of those earlier odours would emerge from the fabrics. "I'm sorry, force of habit" said Gaspard, tearing his thoughts away from past horrors while attempting to suppress a shudder. He was less successful in trying to pull his eyes away from the stains on the nighty (Oh God, she's sitting on the arm of the couch).

He summoned up his courage. "Umm, Mrs D'Unstable, in the interests of togetherness, I don't suppose you could…ah…you know…not to be critical you understand…but maybe you could, ah, change your nightgown?" Gaspard instinctively cringed.

"Oh, change the nightgown is it?" Maud enquired in a voice dripping in sarcasm. "Alright, let me just grab my purse and I'll pop down to M and S because I don't think there's much in the ghost closet at the moment." The glare that followed these words would have haunted Gaspard if he were not already being haunted. "You think I like the idea of spending eternity looking like something out of bloody Bedlam? Who do you think you are you bloody jumped up little wanker?" Mrs D'Unstable fixed the trembling young man with a meaningful look that somehow contrived to be simultaneously hurtful and accusatory.

"I'm sorry Maud…Mrs D'Unstable. I was only thinking of you really," stammered Gaspard.

"Yes, right, because you're such a kind hearted soul. Bugger off and sort out the telly sonny Jim before I lose my temper and give a good old-fashioned haunting. Oh, and now that you know I'm here, you might want to start picking up your underwear." While this exchange had been going on, a single lost and lonely thought had been attempting to fight its way through the confusion of metal shrubbery while desperately attempting to avoid the drunks rampaging about the place. It now managed to burst into the light. "Wait a minute! We've been together for three years and you've never spoken to me before. How did you know I'd be able to hear you?"

"Blessed if I know. I just did. All of a sudden like…" She paused briefly. "It's got to be him hasn't it? He made you see me so he let me know you could see me. Bugger's having us for mugs. You'd better be careful my young friend. He'd got something up his sleeve more than just bones."

Gaspard just wanted to leave the flat and be rid of his unwelcome house guest but being far too drunk to drive had little choice but to stay. Grudgingly he set about moving the television into the spare room. He never really watched much tele so the grudging was mainly brought about by the effort possibly reinforced by hating to do the vitriolic old bat any favours. The little chore had the effect of focussing his thoughts somewhat and he began to wonder why it was that he'd never felt the presence of Maud. If he could see Death, it was a bit odd that the close proximity of a spectre had never registered. It was only then that he remembered those sudden chills. Chills that were totally at odds with the ambient temperature. Chills that were experienced at times when one would least hope to experience them, such as when certain intimate bits were exposed. Now that he thought further on the matter, almost exclusively when certain intimate bits were exposed. Even in his intoxicated state the thought of chilly spectral hands had the adrenalin surging.

Constable Feeblebunny was not much of an imbiber of the demon drink. He was at best a tippler and one of amateur status at that. Up until tonight therefore, he had missed out on one of the great rites of passage. Never before had he experienced lying in a bed that stubbornly refused to remain static nor had he previously felt the need to stagger from that bed and spend lengthy periods clutching the toilet bowl and praying for death. When he wasn't sitting on it, that is. That innocent state was to alter alarmingly and with maximum discomfort. Those mandatory states reached and functions performed he finally managed to cling onto the bed long enough for sleep to claim him. Act three was yet to come.

Shakespeare said that drink is amongst other things a great provoker of sleep. While that may be the case, he neglected to mention that the sleep is often disturbed at best and frequently results in a condition known to the less fortunate as the midnight horrors. For those mercifully unfamiliar with the condition, it is a period resulting from a plunge in blood sugars when one awakens with a pounding heart, a tongue that feels like a piece of Axminster, a raging thirst and little black spots zooming about before the eyeballs. The additional nausea is more a case of the booze having stripped the lining off the stomach. What it doesn't usually include but what Gaspard was to experience when he succumbed to the terrible reality of mild alcohol poisoning, was a beshitten spectre sitting on the end of the bed like some very down market and incontinent Lady Macbeth.

His already racing heart managed to up the tempo as a shot of adrenalin hit him like a speeding bus and followed up with the dreaded flash of fear up the keester. He tried to leap from the bed but succeeded only in tangling a foot in the sheets and sprawling arse up onto the floor. "Charming," drawled Maud in her most censorious tone, "if I'd known I'd be spending my time with a drunk, I'd have killed myself somewhere else."

"Bloody hell, Maud, you frightened the crap out of me," groaned Gaspard, getting shakily to his feet via his hands and knees. He stood for a second or two before dropping onto the bed with a moan. "Yes, I'd noticed. I hope you've got something to clean up that bathroom. And your pyjamas. And it's Mrs D'Unstable to you when you're in this appalling state." Maud finished off the statement with a sniff of disapproval just in case she hadn't made it quite obvious enough that she was disgruntled. "What do you want Maud? I thought we had an agreement. Absolute privacy."

"Well, there was that but it doesn't cover matters of urgency does it?"

"What can be so bloody urgent at this godforsaken hour?" Gaspard exclaimed testily.

"I can't change the channel on the tele. All that's on is some dreadful horror film. Don't think I'd have sat here watching you snore and scratch your arse if I could do it myself. I know there's some manage it but I've never got the knack."

"You woke me up to change the flaming channel?" Gaspard groaned incredulously.

"Correction Vomitus Maximus. Can't do that either as it turns out. I had to wait for you to wake up. I don't mind telling you it wasn't a very edifying experience, whoever designed those pyjamas of yours should have thought a bit harder about coverage is all I'll say."

"Please Maud…Mrs D'Unstable, go away and let me die."

"You can do all the dying you want once you've changed the channel. Just promise me that when you do, you'll bugger off and leave me in peace."

"Alright, alright" mumbled Gaspard, grudgingly rising and shambling roughly in the direction of the spare room. He eventually made it across the bedroom relatively unscathed and walked into the door. Simultaneously muttering and fumbling with the door knob he was unaware for some seconds that he was pushing on a door that opened inwards. When he eventually realised his error, he pulled viciously on the door and hit himself on the toe.

"Hell and damnation!" roared Gaspard, although to be truthful the roar was more of a croak.

"What a display," clucked Mrs D'Unstable, "you should be ashamed. I'll tell you something else for free too young fella, you smell about as appealing as a turd sandwich. When you've done your duty by me, you should really think about a long bath." She paused for effect. "Either that or smear yourself in cowshit. They'd both be an improvement." She cackled.

Ever since falling out of bed, Gaspard's gorge had been rising. It was now overtaken by his ire in a photo finish. He snapped. "You're a great one to talk you sanctimonious old prune. I'll not be lectured to by someone who's happy to spend eternity covered in shit," he half panted. "What I don't understand is why you'd kill yourself and then decide to hang about the place making life miserable for those of us who can stand our own company. Why don't you just take our bony friend's offer and piss off." The tirade finished he felt first relieved and then dreadfully ashamed. "I'm sorry Mrs D'Unstable, it's the grog talking. What channel do you want?" Maud glowered but said nothing.

3

"Ay, he'll be right well missed" said Bertie, the factory owner. "Could have done wi' a chap like him down t' pits when I were lad. Hard working, single minded, don't get many o' them to the pound these days." He shook his head ruefully. "Bunch o' right spongers we have nowadays. All want soomit for nout. Ay, he'll be missed right enough."

Bert Postlethwaite liked to call himself a Yorkshireman of the old school. That was only true if the old school he was talking about was Eton. Bertram Postlethwaite-Arbuckle-ffinch had been born in Huddersfield when his mother went into premature labour on her way back from a shooting holiday at an estate in the Scottish Highlands. His growing up had been done in Kensington in that peculiarly upper crust English manner that meant he was at home only at times when his parents couldn't in good conscience dump him on someone else. The rest of his time, which was the majority of it, was spent at various high-priced boarding establishments for the sons of gentlefolk. Like many of his class and upbringing the lack of adult affection left him only able to truly relate to other males and young males at that. It was a defect that would eventually lead to a shameful and embarrassing series of events.

To family and friends, he was good old Bertie ffinch, a thorough going posh lad. To employees and suppliers, he was Bert Postlethwaite, a bluff ex miner and self-made man, partly educated at one of the poorer comprehensive schools. Luckily for the pretence there was a wealth to choose from. The belief was partly true in that Bert had built the business from scratch, aided only by a loan of five million pounds from his father. The bluff Yorkshireman persona was his own concept and worked very well in persuading his employees that he was a working-class man who would look after their interests as well as fooling the big end of town into underestimating him. It worked a treat and enabled him to fleece almost everybody.

35

When it later came to light what he been up to with certain young men, it would prove a hell of a surprise to those who knew him as Bert the factory owner but only bring a wry smile from those who knew him as posh Bertie.

"So, what is it I can do you for constable? I hope there was nothing untoward in his departure from this vale of tears?" Sometimes Bertie overdid things a little.

"No, just a tragic accident, oil on the road, hit a tree. Just a minor query unrelated to the accident…can't speak of it…confidential…hoping you could perhaps point me to his work station."

Gaspard had no idea how to explain his interest or even why he was asking if it came to that. He just had a vague hope that Percy would be by his post and amenable to a little friendly persuasion. It hadn't yet crossed his mind how he'd explain conversing with thin air. "Oh ay," said Bert, a trifle suspiciously. He hadn't managed to get where he was by being easily persuaded of others' motives. He gave it a quick mulling over before reaching the conclusion there was little to be lost in pointing out Pargeter's machine. He did so.

"That one there constable, third row, second from the back. Another lad on it now, of course as would be even were he alive. Percy were permanent night shift. Liked it that way. Marvellous bloody worker but not the sociable type. Often find that. Best workers are often loners. More focus you see." He eyed Gaspard off. "You know, if it's information of a personal nature you're after, you'd best talk to his sister. She's living in his dwelling at the moment. Doing a bit of a spruce up before it goes on t' market. You'd find her there now right enough."

To Gaspard that seemed the ticket. There was little to be gained in wandering about the factory if Percy wasn't likely to turn up any time soon. He thanked Bert and headed for Percy's home.

"Call me Deidre" said Deidre Pargeter, ushering him into the little cottage, lately the home of Percy and now the home of the late Percy. As cottages went it was perfectly acceptable if but sparsely furnished and completely lacking in all decoration. It was the sort of place that would have any decorator rushing out to purchase a chandelier from which to hang himself. "I must say that everyone has been so kind. What did you say you were wanting constable?" What Gaspard was really wanting was ideas but he bravely carried on. "Ah…well…it's just one or two minor things to check on…nothing to concern yourself with. I was just hoping I might have a quick look at Mr Pargeter's room?" He flushed slightly, never being very good at dissembling.

"Umm, well I suppose so," she replied, a slight note of uncertainty creeping into her voice. She led him a little reluctantly down a short corridor. "This one here," she announced, opening the door. The room was as sterile as the rest of the place containing only the bare necessities as long as one ignored the ghost of Percival Pargeter which was reclining on the bed. Percy had been wiling away the hours until he went to work by staring at the ceiling and counting the cracks, it really was a pest not being able to sleep, a fact he was having difficulty coming to terms with, it didn't fit in with his routine at all. When the door opened, he turned his head and glared at the intruders.

Gaspard jumped slightly and hoped that the spectre had not noticed his reaction. "As you can see, there's little enough here constable," offered Deidre with growing unease. Percy pulled a face at her and poked out his tongue. His gaze shifted to Gaspard and fixed on him warily. "No, just me, what the bloody hell is going on?" Percy spat peevishly.

"Ah, yes, thank you. Perhaps you wouldn't mind if I had a quick look around?" Gaspard enquired, desperately attempting to ignore the disgruntled ghost.

"What are you asking her for? It's my bloody room," interjected the late Mr Pargeter, now thoroughly agitated.

"It would have to be quick. There's nothing here," she responded attempting to keep it light.

"No, only me!"

She fixed Gaspard with a studied expression. "Look constable, I think perhaps you should tell me what you're looking for."

Percy sat up on the bed. "Better yet," he said clearly, "why don't you both just piss off and leave me in peace?" Gaspard did his best to ignore the rudeness. He did not yet want his quarry knowing that he was aware of his presence.

Even less did he want Miss Pargeter to know. It might result in some awkward moments. "Umm, well...you see..."

"Why aren't you in uniform?"

"What?"

"I think you should show me your warrant card," she exclaimed with an icy edge to her voice. "Umm...well, I left it home actually. I suppose I should confess that I'm not actually on duty today. My day off you see but I thought I might just clear this up while I had the chance."

"Clear what up? I think you need to tell me what is going on."

"Small matter, nothing to concern yourself about. As I was saying, bit bored at home, thought I'd tie up the loose ends, you understand." He was only too aware that he was sounding decidedly shifty. His dissembling was beginning to disassemble.

"No, I don't think I do. And now that I do think, I think that Feeblebunny is the silliest made up name ever and you smell of drink. I'll have to ask you to leave or I'll call the police."

"But I am the police."

"That is highly doubtful Mr Feeblebunny, if that's who you are." By now, her voice was dripping with venom. "Please leave now."

"That's right, sod off" shouted Percy. "And take her with you." He poked out his tongue again. "Bloody cheek of you pair."

"I really am a policeman," whined Gaspard as he was shown the door. He slunk out guiltily. Had he been a dog his tail would have been tucked firmly between his legs. A tail was something that he would have welcomed at the moment because his tender parts were feeling distinctly vulnerable to an assault from the rear. "And don't think I won't check," came the reply milliseconds before the door was slammed behind him.

Gaspard prayed fervently that no such course would be taken but just in case, he began desperately trying to think of a feasible reason for his visit. Off hand, he couldn't think of a single one.

He tried on hand but that didn't work either.

"So, what's your next move?" enquired Death from the passenger seat. Gaspard started, slammed on the brakes and narrowly avoided being rear ended by a following car. He waved an apology to the irate driver and pulled to the kerb. "Bloody hell, you scared the life out of me."

"Nice to know I'm not losing my touch," Death quipped.

"Ha bloody ha. What are you doing here?"

"Had a few spare moments, thought I'd drop by and see how things are progressing."

"Not well. His sister chucked me out and I might be in trouble at the station. If bloody Hardar…Hardcastle finds out I'll be in the shite well and truly."

"Unfortunate but I'm sure you'll cope. We have faith in you."

"Great, that makes me feel so much better. Anyway, I reckon my only hope is to wait for him at the factory, that's if he's still going to work. Surely, he must have realised by now that he's dead?"

"I do believe he's beginning to have doubts. I saw him at the funeral. It's still not enough to change his routine however. He's a creature of habit, much as I am," chortled Death, pulling on his robe to emphasise his joke.

"Oh, marvellous, you're a bloody comedian now. Why the hell didn't you grab Percy since you were there? Could have saved all this palaver."

"Out sourcing remember? I warned them. Told them it would have consequences but they're too smart to listen to me. I'm one of the old brigade and too entrenched in my ways if I remember their reasoning correctly. Bloody accountants," grumbled Death bitterly.

"Tell them to go to buggery for me, will you? I didn't consent to being a subcontractor" muttered Gaspard. "Anyway, now that I'm lumbered, I suppose I'll hang about his factory and try and talk to him there, can't think of anything else. Your approach of waiting at the death scene didn't have any success and as for flagging down his car…"

"That sounds like a plan," said Death, jumping in rapidly before anything more could be mentioned of his spectacular failure and clearly embarrassed by the whole sad affair. "Keep me informed. Oh, and don't forget the Hobnobs. Chocolate tops mind."

With that, Death simply vanished. Well, it was simple for Death, a bit of a chore for anyone else. Except maybe Santa. "What? No badgers?" shouted Gaspard bitterly in a futile and terribly uninspired attempt at a dig.

Sergeant Hardcastle was not one to give up easily. Especially when he had money riding on the outcome. Just before the usual hour of the phantom's arrival, he took up his position. As usual the road was deserted. No problem then. He stepped into the middle of the carriageway. As he had thought, there was nothing to be seen. What the hell had Feeblebunny been up to? It was then the radar pinged. An icy current of air washed over him and a voice that seemed to be inside him yelled, "out of the way you twerp!"

When he did not return to the station or answer any radio calls, a car was despatched to discover the reason. The officers who arrived at the scene found him sitting at the roadside trembling and muttering to himself.

A little later Gaspard was standing chilled and morose near the factory door when a small saloon with Percy at the wheel screamed into a nearby space. The odd thing was that there was already a car in that space. It certainly didn't bother Percy who leaped from the phantom vehicle and ran towards the employee entrance where Gaspard was waiting. "Mr Pargeter, could I have a quick word?" In the circumstances that seemed a bit inadequate but the police manual didn't really cover the situation. "I'm running late, sod off," panted the ghost petulantly.

'How the hell did a ghost get out of breath?' Gaspard wondered, though he figured it probably had something to do with him being a slave to his previous existence. Alive he would have been breathless so he carried that over into the afterlife. "I'll be quick I promise." Percy pulled up briefly and gave Gaspard a searching look. He was suddenly ill at ease.

"How…? You're that bugger at the house, aren't you? I had a feeling you could see me. How come you can when suddenly no one else seems to be able to? My sister walked right through me this morning. Bloody weird." He looked the unhappy constable up and down. "Doesn't matter; late for work and you've no right to be here. Leave or I'll call security."

He immediately headed for the door. "You might have a hard time doing that Mr Pargeter. You're dead. I'm sure you must realise that by now."

Percy turned at the door, a canny look on his features. "I figured it was something like that. Sister arranging my funeral and all," he said sarcastically.

"And you know what? It's bloody marvellous. I don't have to talk to anyone and that goes double for gobshites like you." With that, he gave what is commonly known as a rude gesture and slipped through the door. Literally. Gaspard had wanted to point out the one thing he felt may have convinced Pargeter, that being the inescapable fact he would never be truly alone ever again. Soon, people would buy his house and make death intolerable. They would belch, scratch and fart in his immediate vicinity without regard for his presence and he'd be locked in a world of other's dark secrets and sometimes disgusting behaviour. That much Gaspard had learned from Maud and he could never help but blush at the thought that all his foibles were known to the merest detail.

The unhappy fact that Maud had seen his foibles was something he didn't like to dwell upon. He scratched his head and trudged across the windswept car park where the wind was doing a rather half-arsed job of the task and seemed determined to deposit most of the sweeping down Gaspard's shirt front. For once, he was oblivious to the discomfort being in deep contemplation. He concluded that perhaps it would take bitter experience to convince his quarry that he would be better off truly dead, whatever that meant. How to convince Death and his masters of that though? Gaspard had a distinctly sinking feeling that his answer would not be good enough. Although even at this time of self-doubt, a germ of an idea was forming. There are a few perks to living alone, the premier one being that you can do pretty much what you want without censure.

Take breaking wind for example. Not the sort of thing most of us do in company unless we think we can get away with it by blaming the dog or someone who looks a bit different. At home alone, though we can simply let rip and hope we can escape any unfortunate side effects. We can sing in the shower no matter how bad our delivery, we can scratch where it itches, even pick our noses if that way inclined. Gaspard was living alone but wasn't. He now had Maud to think about and Maud was not one to suffer anything that displeased her on even the smallest scale. A wayward sniff, a gargle after tooth brushing, an unfortunate and unavoidable bathroom noise, all of these things and more would commence her sharp tongue wagging.

It would have been bad enough had she and Gaspard only just moved in together but she'd had over three years of suffering in silence and she was now determined to make the most of her opportunities. In short, she was rapidly making Gaspard bloody miserable. If it had been a ploy to force him out, it would have been a good one. In fact though, it was just that Maud was an intolerant, evil tempered old cow. That being the case Gaspard was happy when he received the call to come into the station even though he was still under temporary suspension which meant that whatever the reason it was probably not good tidings.

His thoughts flew immediately to Deidre Pargeter.

"This is really very unfortunate Feeblebunny." The super sucked his teeth and shuffled a few papers distractedly. "It seems a Deirdre Pargeter has been asking questions about you. She says you turned up at her house acting suspiciously and claimed to be investigating a case involving her late brother. From what I gather, she doubted that you were who you said you were. Mollified her a bit when we told her you were the real McCoy so to speak but she still wants to know what it's all about. From what I can see, we have two problems here. Firstly, you are under suspension and therefore not empowered to investigate anything and secondly, there is no case involving one Percival Pargeter who if my information is correct was a road accident victim."

Fish said no more, relying on the age-old inquisitor's ploy of studied silence to get his victim gabbling. He stared fixedly at the unfortunate constable who had not the slightest idea of what to say. "Well sir…umm…it's true that I did go to her house sir…er…and it was when I was suspended sir. I just hoped that I might try to get to the bottom of something…ah, you know sir, the funny business with the radar sir. It was more curiosity than anything. I didn't mean to make it official." Gaspard figured that this was about all he could say in the circumstances. He could hardly say that he was subcontractor to Death.

If he had any hope that the super would not ask the obvious question, it was a vain one. "We'll deal with the two matters separately. First the reason for the visit. I must admit to being at a loss as to how visiting the Pargeter's home could assist in any way constable. Perhaps you be so kind as to enlighten me?"

"Well sir," replied Gaspard, desperately searching for a way out but finding the emergency exit door locked and chained, "I confess I didn't really know. I'd seen the report of Pargeter's accident and noticed it was a short way from where I was set up and also close to the time of the phenomenon. I just had a weird feeling that there may be some sort of connection."

The question had been asked and Gaspard found wanting. It was now time for the coup de grace. "And you hoped to find the reason in his bedroom?" Gaspard slumped. Never very good at falsehood he could see that he was going to talk himself into a corner unless he opted for the truth. As a policeman he believed fervently that it was always the best policy with the possible exceptions of owning up to unfortunate odours and carpet stains. It was time to hazard all regardless of the consequences. That should give you some idea of the depth of his naivety. He took a deep breath to steady himself. "Do you believe in ghosts sir?" He enquired timorously.

"Did you say ghosts, constable?" Asked the Super cautiously with a note of disbelief. The wretched Gaspard nodded. A strange light came into the superintendent's eyes. "Umm, things in sheets, go around saying 'boo' a lot? That sort of ghost?"

"Yes sir, although that image doesn't quite fit the reality sir."

"Really? So, let me see if I have this right. You are proposing that the problem with your radar is that the ghost of Percival Pargeter is speeding down the queen's highway and setting off your device?"

"Yes sir. I know it sounds far-fetched sir."

"That would be one way of putting it, Feeblebunny." There was a short silence as Fish pursed his lips in thought, not an edifying spectacle considering his resemblance to his namesake. "Can ghosts really travel that fast I wonder?"

"Oh, he's in his car sir. He could hardly be capable of reaching ninety-four miles an hour on his own."

"Quite, quite" responded the super somewhat dazed by the direction of the conversation. "That would be absurd what? You know constable, I was totally unaware that cars could also have ghosts."

"It's complicated sir. I'm not quite sure myself how it works."

"See a lot of ghosts do you constable?"

"Oh no sir. Only Percy, oh and Maud of course."

"Maud?"

"Yes sir, she lives in my flat." There was another brief hiatus as the super wondered what the hell to say to that.

"Hardly lives if she's a ghost what?" ventured Fish at last. "Perhaps, haunts would be a more apposite term?" he concluded, wondering whether he should just end the interview now and send for the men in white jackets.

"I suppose. But she doesn't really do what you'd think of as haunting. She just hangs around and makes a nuisance of herself."

"I see. That must be most...er, inconvenient." The super was beginning to find the conversation fascinating despite his survival instincts telling him to flee before the loon before him went on a rampage.

"You don't know the half of it sir. She's a very irritating individual and now that I can see her, she spends all her time watching television. Frankly sir I dread the next electricity bill."

"Yes, most distressing. You say, 'now that I can see her,' Gaspard" began Fish, deciding that a first name basis might defuse any possible feelings of intimidation and reduce the threat level, "how long exactly have you been seeing these um...spectres."

"Oh, not long at all sir. Only a few days in fact. That's why I'm sure the whole thing has been sparked by the radar incident."

"Mm. I can see how you may feel that," replied Fish kindly, thinking that stress could do funny things to the mind.

"So now, assuming you're correct, how may I ask did you hope to prove your remarkable supposition?"

43

"By seeing his ghost sir. In his bedroom," he replied wretchedly.

"And why in the name of the devil his bedroom in particular?"

"Umm...he's on permanent nightshift sir." Superintendent Fish looked startled by this reply. "You're saying he still goes to work? Even though he's dead?" Fish was now beginning to adopt the sort of tone usually used when one suspects he's talking to someone both disturbed and possibly dangerous.

"Yes sir. It seems he refuses to believe he's dead sir. Or at least that's what we thought at first but it's more the case that he knows he's dead but just refuses to go quietly. He told me that he's enjoying the solitude it affords sir."

"He told you that? In his bedroom?"

"No sir. I couldn't speak to him in his bedroom, his sister would have thought I was mad sir. You know, gabbling on to thin air. I spoke to him at the factory where he works. Unfortunately, he was afraid of being late so I didn't get much of a chance but I'm sure he's the reason for the radar anomaly. You see sir, I believe he experiences the accident over and over again, always with the same result, that he believes he'll be late for work and then speeds off. I'm hoping though that now he's accepted the fact he's dead things may change for the better."

"And that would solve the problem with the machine wouldn't it? Yes, I can see that constable. Well done." Fish was at the point where the wise man realises that humouring the deluded is the best and safest form of action. "Umm...I believe you said 'we' earlier when speaking of the ghost. 'We thought' I believe you said? Might I enquire after this third party?"

"Oh, just someone with a belief in the afterlife that I consulted unofficially. He's an expert sir."

"An expert you say? In the afterlife. A medium, is he?"

"No sir, more an extra-long," responded Gaspard now beginning to lose his equanimity. He recovered quickly enough that Fish had no time to take umbrage. "Sorry sir, not attempting to be flippant, just misunderstood for a moment. Not exactly a medium sir, more a specialist in death and what comes afterwards."

"Interesting. And is he also a ghost?"

"Oh no sir. Nothing like that." Gaspard didn't need to be told that informing the super he'd been sipping tea with the embodiment of death was not a good career move. Not that the rest of it was any great shakes.

"Well, something to be grateful for I suppose. Now constable, I think that will be all for the time being. Let's just hope the Pargeter woman doesn't decide to lodge an official complaint. In the meantime, you'd best go home and get some rest. I think you probably need it after all the stress you've been under. I was hoping that Sergeant Hardcastle would have finished his investigation in short order but he's on sick leave. Poor chap has come down with a bad case of the shakes. Some sort of fever no doubt. Off you go now and mind you take it easy. And no contacting that bloody woman again, you hear me?"

"Yes, sir. Thank you. Umm…might I ask if…"

"No constable. That will be all for the time being" Fish said sympathetically. "We'll be in touch when Hardcastle has completed his investigation. Shouldn't be long now. In the meantime, just take it easy. Perhaps somewhere away from…Maud was it?"

"Yes sir. A good suggestion sir."

"Well then, that settles it. Just remember to leave details of any change of address with the sergeant." Fish smiled benignly.

Immediately upon Gaspard's departure Fish reached for the internal phone directory and shaking his head sadly went to the section headed with the letter 'p'.

"Doctor Coombs, I think we have a job for you."

"Alright Feeblebunny, it's time to come clean." The words were pure Hardcastle but the attitude was anything but. To Gaspard he seemed decidedly out of sorts. His face was drawn and he'd lost weight. The fact that his hair appeared to have turned grey overnight didn't help.

"You had something to do with the Pargeter accident, didn't you?"

"No Sarge. How could you ask that? I was at my station miles down the road. Surely you've seen the radar logs?"

"Of course I have," growled Hardcastle, "but I'm sure there are ways you could have got around that. Come on man. Take responsibility."

"Sarge, look, I know you can't get past that photo but I can't explain it and no matter how much you want me to be guilty of something, everything is just as I've said. Weird things happening to the camera, some sort of phenomenon, I've no more idea than anybody else. There's nothing more than that. Whatever that is."

As a defence this was pretty inadequate, although about as much as he could say in the circumstances. Gaspard knew that mentioning ghosts would be a disaster and hoped that the sergeant hadn't been informed of his discussion with the super. "Have you spoken to the accident investigation team? Surely they can clear this up?"

"Yes," murmured Hardcastle, clearly not happy at the direction things had taken. "And?"

"They say he hit a patch of oil and skidded into a tree." He tried to summon up his trademark glare but it seemed to have gone into hiding. "But that doesn't mean you weren't involved somehow," he finished unconvincingly. Gaspard was already cognisant of the facts, having obtained them from the desk sergeant. The reverend and Mrs Ball had been travelling nearby when the accident occurred, had witnessed everything and immediately summoned the police. The sergeant had been at pains to point out, with just the merest hint of a snicker, how lucky Pargeter had been in being pulled out by the police. "And the forensics from the radar site?"

"Nothing," growled Hardcastle.

"Please Sarge. It was just a bloody glitch with the radar. Why are you trying to make more of it than the facts support. You've found nothing that gives credence to your suppositions. Please, Sarge, let it drop."

"There's something not right about all this constable. We both know it. I've felt it in my waters from day one and I will prove it somehow." Hardcastle paused and shook his head, suddenly overwhelmed by the memory of his ghostly encounter. "In the meantime, however, you're free to return to duty. The super wants it wound up."

"That's it?"

"Yes. Well...not exactly. You're to report to Dr Coombs this afternoon at four. He has to clear you before you can officially return."

"Dr Coombs?"

"Staff headshrinker. Whatever you know, the super seems to think it may have affected you adversely in the mental stability department." He frowned. "For God's sake Feeblebunny, we both know that there's something weird happening up there. You have to tell me."

"Like I said Sarge, I don't know any more than you," responded Gaspard, feeling guilty in not sharing what he knew despite his dislike of the sergeant.

"The superintendent has filled me in on his conversation with you, Gaspard" said Dr Coombs in his most oleaginous manner. "Perhaps you'd like to tell me in your own words."

Now that he had a professionally sympathetic ear Gaspard was more in control. He gave an accurate account of his interview with the super but made sure that in addition he emphasised the stress under which he'd been placed by the radar incidents and most particularly by Hardcastle's hounding and insistence that he was guilty of some despicable act.

"I see. Apart from your problems with Professional Standards, is there anything else worrying you? You're otherwise happy in the job?"

"Oh yes. All I've ever wanted to be was a policeman."

"And it's living up to your expectations?"

"Mostly sir. It's early days and I've still got a lot to learn." He was a trifle disappointed if truth be told but he genuinely believed that things would become more interesting with time and experience.

They certainly would but not in any way he could imagine.

"Good, good. And your personal life? OK is it? No relationship troubles?"

"None at all. No relationship," replied Gaspard as lightly as he could manage.

"Does that trouble you, constable?"

"Not really sir. To be frank I've never really had much opportunity. Went to an all-boys school. Was in an all-male college at university and naturally fraternisation in the ranks is frowned upon. A good policy, I think. Never does to crap on one's own doorstep if you'll forgive the language."

"You regard having a relationship at work in those terms?"

"Sorry, probably a bad choice of words. What I mean is that work relationships can lead to strain if they're not successful," explained Gaspard hurriedly, suddenly wishing he'd not used the word strain in connection with crapping on doorsteps.

"Quite, quite. And you're not lonely? Not feeling any frustrations of a physical nature?"

"No sir. If I was lonely, I'd get a cat," joked Gaspard.

"Really? And the physical side? There are some needs a cat may find difficult to fulfil. Don't feel the need for a partner? Lady friend, boyfriend, friend of a gender-neutral persuasion?"

"Sometimes doctor, naturally but to be honest I'm a bit reticent when it comes to approaching people I'm attracted to. People tend not to take me seriously. It's the name you see? Most girls can't get past it."

"And that troubles you?" Coombs steepled his fingers and peered over them in an inquisitorial manner.

"One gets used to it doctor. These days I take the position that when I find someone who can take me seriously, then I'll have found someone who looks beyond the trivial to the real person." He smiled openly.

"A very healthy attitude, constable. But in the meantime, you see the ghost of a lady?"

"An elderly and very unpleasant lady, doctor. Believe me, she is not the stuff of a young man's fantasy."

The eventual result was predictable and Coombs found that, ironically enough, Constable Feeblebunny was suffering from stress resulting from the unprofessional actions of the Professional Standards Unit and the mystery surrounding the radar malfunctions. He recommended two weeks stress leave under mild medication followed by a return to light desk duties after a further assessment.

"Two weeks! That's marvellous." Death made as though to clap his hands with delight but then thought better of it and picked up a biscuit. "Now your job won't get in the way of your work."

Gaspard knew with certainty that had he been capable of it Death would be smiling hugely. "Oh yes, bloody fantastic. Just what my career needs. I'm sure nobody will hold it against me in the promotion stakes" answered Gaspard bitterly. "Now then, this Feeblebunny, right chap for promotion I think, has tea with ghosts but who doesn't, what?" He brayed, mimicking the superintendent. "Bloody hell!"

"Now, now, don't be like that. You have to think of the bigger picture."

"If there is a bigger picture, it probably looks like something done by Bosch," muttered Gaspard in frustration. "It certainly won't be any bloody Rembrandt I'm sure of that."

"Cheer up, things have a way of sorting themselves out. Now, to the business at hand, how are things going with our friend? Making any progress?"

"As I'm sure you're already aware," began Gaspard with a slight edge to his voice, "no I'm bloody not." He knew that he wasn't going to win any arguments but that didn't mean he had to sound pleased about it. "In fact, I'm getting nowhere. Why don't you fire me?"

Death said nothing. He took a sip of his tea and dunked his biscuit. "Oh, OK. I do have one idea. It strikes me that if he's not prepared to listen, we should play on his vulnerability. He's a stickler for the rules and order. What if we turn his world upside down?"

"How so?"

"I thought for starters we could deny him his work. That would be hell for him. Then we make things hell at home as well. Once he realises that the afterlife isn't all it's cracked up to be, he may decide to throw in the towel."

"Go on, I'm all ears," came the reply.

Death cupped his finger bones at the side of his skull in a parody of straining to listen. "First I need to ask; is it possible to make a ghost poster? You know, something that can only be read by ghosts? What I'm thinking of would be a bit odd if it could be read by anyone and it'd probably be pulled down or taken as a souvenir."

"Sort of a ghost it note, eh? I'm sure that could be arranged. Just tell me what you want it to say."

"So," began Gaspard once the details had been worked out, "do you think you could give me a little hand with Deidre Pargeter? I hate to do it to her but I can't see any other way of convincing her."

"Not necessary for me to get involved. We had a meeting the other day and it was decided that it's a bit unfair on you making you do all this as a complete mortal. No way of really getting the point across and so forth, so we got you this." From nowhere, Death produced a black hooded robe similar to his own. "Not very fetching I know but working wear seldom is. Try it on."

Grudgingly, Gaspard donned the garment. "I don't see how this is going to help. It may disguise me but people will still be able to see the exposed bits as human and Deidre may even recognise my voice."

"Look in the mirror."

Gaspard did as he'd been bidden. "Stretch out your hand." Gaspard emitted a sort of strangled yelp. "Those whom you appear before will see you thusly. A sort of smaller version of myself. They will not doubt you. To them you will be The Collector. The collector of souls."

"Can I take it off it off now? I'm not sure that I can take seeing myself as a skeleton."

"Of course but I suggest you get used to it, you're dead a lot longer than you're alive. Now, there's something else before you take it off. You'll need this." He handed Gaspard what looked remarkably like a set of garden shears. "Sorry about this but it's the best we could come up with."

"You expect me to menace them with a set of bloody garden shears? Why not a scythe like you? This wouldn't frighten a toddler."

"It's all in the presentation. You'll have to work on it. I know it's a bit disappointing but the scythe is my trade mark. Out of bounds for you."

"Alright, I suppose I can see that but what about a sickle? Same sort of image and just as deadly in the right hands."

"We did think of that but someone objected on the grounds that it may have political connotations. Believe me, we gave it a lot of thought. There aren't that many agricultural implements that are suitable."

"OK, but there must be something less bloody ridiculous. I look like a demonic hedge trimmer. How about a pitchfork?"

"Too American gothic. Plus, there's the other chap…you know."

"Why does it have to be agricultural? How about a sword?" Gaspard gabbled desperately, still hoping to keep his dignity as the Collector.

"Sorry, there's a few others have first dibs on those. You just have to accept that the committee examined all the options. Anyway, it's just a badge of office really," Death pronounced with an air of finality.

"Oh great, why not give me a set of moose antlers or something then? I doubt I'd look any more ridiculous," Gaspard fired back testily. He may have had a last shot at keeping his dignity but with the word 'committee' Gaspard knew he was beaten. Nothing good ever came out of a committee except perhaps expenses payments for the members. The amazing thing was that it had come to a decision at all, even with eternity to play with.

"One other thing, the committee have decided that it might be an idea to give the new outfit a trial run. There's a chap we think you can deal with by way of cutting your teeth. He shouldn't be too much bother. Spot of on the job training so to speak. Tonight would be a good time. Don't worry about gaining entrance, you'll find the robe will see you right. Just walk straight in."

"But what if someone sees me?"

"No worries there. The living can only see you if you want them to." He turned to leave. "Oh, one last thing, how are you getting on with Maud? A right terror is she not?"

"She's…unpleasant. I don't suppose…you know…now that you're here? She's just in the next room. Wouldn't take you a moment," whispered Gaspard pleadingly.

"Sorry, wish I could help but the new rules you know. More than my job's worth. I'm sure you'll learn how to handle her with time. Think of it as good training for your police people skills. Then of course she will provide you with a bit of a challenge in gathering her up eventually. She will be a client if we take your employment further."

The series of excuses immediately led Gaspard to the inescapable belief that Death was relieved he didn't have to deal with the late Mrs D'Unstable.

Gaspard's decision to wear the robe to his destination was to have unfortunate ramifications. The first to become a victim of his temporary new persona was Maud. "Aaaah! What are you doing here you bony sod? Leave me alone."

"It's alright Maud, it's only me," quickly retorted Gaspard, wondering even as he did why he was bothered by her discomfiture. Serve her bloody right.

"I know it's you bony, that's why I said to leave me alone." She paused, looked him up and down and asked with guarded curiosity, "haven't you shrunk?" She peered closer. "Is that a set of garden shears?"

Recovering herself she continued rapidly, "bugger off. I don't care what gardening implements you bring, you didn't get me before and you won't get me now."

With that, she vanished. *Well, well,* thought Gaspard happily, *I've got you now Maud D'Unstable.* He was so thrilled at having the means to best her that he deliberately left off the apostrophe. Had he thought a bit harder about his live-in ghost's reaction, Gaspard may have realised that his appearance, or in some circumstances lack of it, could cause consternation in the world at large. Unfortunately, his only thought was that since there would be few ghosts about to see him, there would be no harm done. He might have been correct had he not been driving.

It was a chilly evening so there weren't too many people about the place to see him, which is to say that there were few not to see him. Distressingly for those not seeing him, what they didn't see him doing was driving his car; or rather they did see him driving they just didn't see him. It was lucky there were so few because it saved the Mental Health Service a few bob. Most of those seeing an apparently driverless vehicle proceeding down the High Street simply shook their heads and decided they were just imagining things. The real damage was done when he arrived at his destination.

Those in the vicinity saw a driverless vehicle that most reported as being an older model Ford Focus pull up and then perform a commendable reverse parking procedure. It came to a standstill. The lights were extinguished, the driver's door opened and then closed again, seemingly of its own volition. The alarm beeped cheerily as the doors locked. A couple of brave souls approached and peered through the windows then wished devoutly they hadn't. One individual was stoic enough to feel the bonnet and confirm that the engine was warm and foolish enough to report the incident to the police.

He was treated as he should have expected which is to say that the officer spoke to him very slowly and carefully and promised an investigation with only a trace of mockery. Mrs Agnes Threadneedle of 3 The Close, was the least fortunate, she having a slight and hitherto unknown psychic ability. She saw not only what others had but swore that a shadowy figure had exited the car, floated across the pavement and up the garden path of number 28, where it paused momentarily before vanishing through the closed front door. Unsurprisingly, the others decided she was deluded.

Agnes was not aided by her insistence that the figure was carrying a set of garden shears. Her psychiatric treatment would extend for some time thereafter. In a happier turn of events, the occupant of number 48, a widower by the name of Theodore Scuttle, would hear nothing of Mrs Threadneedle's claims. Theodore would spend a peaceful and undisturbed night despite the events occurring under his very nose.

This whole soul collecting business being new to Gaspard it was probably not all that surprising that in the few hours he'd had to think about it, he had focussed exclusively on his intended victim. It was only as he was about to enter the house that certain salient thoughts struck him.

The first, not so much a strike as a full body check, was that he would have to walk through a solid door. He paused, summoned up his courage and tentatively stuck out a foot that disappeared into the dwelling; or at least he hoped it did. Never one to take undue risks he withdrew his foot which had at least returned to the exterior similar in appearance to when it went in and substituted a hand. He felt around for the door knob, found it, gave it a jiggle, noticed that the outside portion was wobbling about a bit and thereby assumed his mitt was actually in the house and not somehow trapped within the door.

Muttering quiet prayers, he took a deep breath, closed his eyes, bravely stepped through and arrived somewhat surprised and utterly relieved in a small lobby, completely unharmed. The second thought which until his passage through the door had been playing second fiddle, was that there would probably be people living here, it not being likely that the late occupant still had exclusive residency some years after his demise. That should cause him no difficulty but it nonetheless made him uneasy. It was trespass after all. Even had he not had that additional thought, the fact would have been immediately apparent by the disorder.

Theo Scuttle was after all a widower which in housekeeping terms is generally at the level of or even a step or two below that of bachelor, depending on the degree of coddling by one's late spouse and of one's social interactions. The widower Scuttle did occasionally have visitors so the place was clean enough to satisfy the average male, meaning that it was a grade or two above a wolf's lair but tidiness was not high on the agenda, as witnessed by haphazardly kicked off shoes in the hallway, unemptied ashtrays and the odd beer bottle. This general untidiness was no shock to Gaspard, a bachelor both by status and inclination towards housekeeping chores, although those attitudes were currently under severe strain from one Maud D'Unstable.

Nor was he shocked when he entered the living room to find that Theo was slumped on the couch in his underwear sucking on a bottle of ale. Not being used to walking into someone's living room uninvited, particularly via a closed front door, his first inclination was to apologise, despite being aware that he was invisible to mortals. That sort of behaviour is so ingrained in us it's very hard to ignore. "Sorry to intrude," he said in his most apologetic manner. Theo Scuttle, clearly unaware of his presence said nothing, took another swig from his bottle, belched and scratched himself in a semi intimate location. Gaspard averted his eyes and turned his attention to the second figure in the room who was seated on the other end of the couch staring at him in wide eyed horror.

"What are you doing here," croaked the spectre, too terrified to move.

"Ah, interesting question that…" responded Gaspard, who really hadn't thought much about how the conversation might run. "Are you Dr Smallpiece?"

"Yes." The reply came only after a little thought and ended with an upward inflection as though the ghost had considered lying.

"Dr Ivor Smallpiece?"

"Yes! No need to rub it in. And it's pronounced Smalpas."

"My apologies yet again." At this awkward moment, Theo scratched an armpit, broke wind loudly, sighed, muttered: "God that's better" then arose and trudged off to the kitchen to find another beer.

"Who are you?" queried Smallpiece pronounced Smalpas with suspicion dripping from every syllable. "I thought I knew you but you're too short." He edged away slightly.

"Um, I am the Collector," retorted Gaspard in a slightly tremulous and wholly unconvincing manner that gave his pretension to authority no assistance at all. He cleared his throat.

"Collector of what?" The good doctor edged further back and Gaspard was becoming fearful of him doing a Maud and vanishing. He frantically began reassessing the situation and opted for the non-confrontational approach.

"Please, take a seat, you have nothing to be afraid of. I'm here to discuss your ah, current status." The good doctor didn't budge. "You didn't answer me; collector of what?"

"Um...those who may have thought better of the manner in which they're spending the afterlife. I am here to enquire whether you may reconsider your decision to spend eternity in the manner you have chosen." The words were intoned dolorously in the hope the delivery would lend him some credibility.

"I don't follow. Wait...are those bloody garden shears? What the hell are you doing with garden shears?"

"Look, the garden shears don't matter," fired back Gaspard rudely, beginning to seriously doubt the efficacy of the implement in providing him with any authority. "They're just a symbol of office."

"What office? Chief hedge pruner?" Smallpiece sniggered offensively.

"No, bloody collector of souls if you really must know," was the answer in a voice a lot louder and more abrasive than Gaspard would have wished.

"The other one had a scythe. Now that is a symbol that leaves you in no doubt. That bloody thing of yours is just a joke," Ivor said condescendingly.

"It won't be if I shove it up your..." shouted Gaspard, now totally out of his depth and realising that the quarry had the upper hand. He managed to cut himself short and took a deep breath.

"Look, sorry. Like I say, they're just a symbol; forget them please." He took a steadying pause and continued as caringly as he could manage: "I'm here to discuss if you're happy in your present situation and whether you might prefer to explore other options."

"Such as?" The other asked, clearly deeply mistrustful and thinking that this intruder was sounding every bit like a door to door insurance salesman. At this point, Theo Scuttle re-entered the room. Conversation stopped briefly while they waited for him to settle. He scratched his backside, took a swig of his new beer, flopped onto the sofa, readjusted his conjugal appendages, sighed and belched loudly before reaching for a crisp packet.

"Oh, bloody hell" muttered a clearly exasperated Smallpiece, "not the crisps. Every bloody night it's the crisps. Rustle, rustle, crinkle, crinkle. It's like being forever in a cinema next to one of those inconsiderate slobs who spends the whole film rustling bloody bags."

He shook his head ruefully. "Although I don't suppose you have any experience of that?"

"I know only too well," replied Gaspard with a note of frustration, "I seem to attract the irritating bastards like a magnet." This was good. Common ground was a good old police ploy when trying to talk people around.

"You go to the pictures?"

"Oh yes. Just between you and me, I'm only part time. In fact, if I'm to be honest, this is my first job. I hope it doesn't show too much." Another good old police ploy. Establish a rapport. "No, no," muttered the quarry unconvincingly. "I'd have thought you'd been doing it for ages. It was just that…you know…that thing. Why would they give you that?"

"All the good ones were taken," sighed Gaspard, hoping they could soon get off the subject and on to what really mattered. It seemed even spooks focussed on trivia rather than the important issues. "I asked them if I could have a sword," he continued plaintively, knowing he shouldn't but giving in to his still smouldering outrage.

Ivor Smallpiece shook his head sympathetically.

"Already taken they said. I suppose they mean some of the fierier angels but who knows? I mean, a sickle or a pitchfork I said. Oh no, not the right thing at all. Adverse connotations or already taken. I know I look bloody ridiculous. How I am supposed to do my job, which by the way I didn't want in the first bloody place, when people are laughing at me?"

This last query was quite literally a cry of despair, Gaspard having given in to self-pity in the face of his client's obvious contempt for his implement. His misery was no doubt compounded by the occasional nightmares he had in which young ladies had contempt for…well, his implement to put it delicately. "No, no, not at all. Not laughing at you. Let's forget it, eh? Get on with what you were saying." He moved closer and perched gingerly on the arm of the couch.

"For Christ's sake, stop rustling that bloody packet!" he shouted at his unwitting host. "Sorry. Drives me bloody spare. What were you saying again?"

"Right, so here's the position; we've been finding that many who have chosen to remain on after…you know…soon regret their decision. The chip packet is a case in point. They begin to realise that they're stuck with a bunch of slobs for eternity and being forced to witness them getting up to all sorts of unacceptable behaviour and able to do bugger all about it. I mean, it's no wonder some of them turn to haunting. Then of course there is the whole eternity bit as well. It's a long time to spend idle unless you've been a public servant during your life and even then, there's the lack of a good cup of tea. Frankly many go mad. I notice your housemate there is watching a reality show. What is it, The Kardashians? I mean, how long could you take that without losing your marbles?"

Gaspard thought the madness argument an inspired one, particularly in the light of the resident mortal's taste in entertainment. He'd not been told this by Death but he was forced by circumstances to wing it and it did seem a pretty fair bet.

"You know," began Ivor, who had been growing progressively uneasy throughout, "I thought I had all this death business sussed. Of course, your…ah, colleague turning up with his scythe was a bit of a shock but I thought that was about the limit and he had always existed in myth, so it didn't take too much adjustment. On the other hand, the last thing I expected was a sort of Death Incorporated. I don't mind telling you the whole business has me questioning my beliefs. I mean…is God the chairman of the board or is there something else I should know about?"

"Look Ivor, if I may call you that, you've touched upon a bit of a nerve there. I'm afraid I'm not permitted to either confirm or deny the existence of a supreme being which is probably just as well because they won't tell me either. About all I can tell you is that they don't seem to have chocolate Hobnobs." The doctor opened his mouth to speak, his eyes wide with shocked surprise, then shook his head and decided, quite wisely you would think, to ignore the Hobnob reference. He had the decided opinion that in the matter of baked goods, the road may possibly lead to madness.

"Really, they don't seem to have done much to prepare you for this do they?" he half croaked before pulling himself together. "No reflection on you of course but they don't seem very efficient if you don't mind me saying."

"I believe it was organised by the time and motion department," replied Gaspard by way of explanation.

"Ah, well that explains it I suppose. Who'd have thought? All very puzzling. Between you and me, if you weren't obviously a pile of bones, I'd have thought this was some sort of massive hoax. Forgive the pile of bones bit but…well…oh, and while we're on the subject of bones has anybody told you that you have a bit of arthritis in that left wrist? Best have a chat to your G.P. if you have one. I'm assuming that all else considered you have some sort of medical plan?"

"I don't know that either," replied Gaspard miserably. Great, premature arthritis, that was all he needed. "Look as long as we're on the subject of medical matters, I've had this dry cough for a while…"

"Sorry," interjected Ivor quickly, "no consultations outside the surgery. I might say though that since you have no obvious lungs there should be no real cause for concern. Now, look, to get back to the subject, I find myself forced to ask how a change in status might benefit me? After all, were you to tell me that I'd trade this for flitting about in the clouds playing a harp and supping on ambrosia I might well be tempted but what seems to be on offer is what's always been on offer, a jump into the unknown. A leap of faith so to speak and a bloody big one."

"That's true unfortunately. But doesn't it give you some peace of mind to know there is much more to it all than you thought? Whether or not it's God or a Chairman or whatever, at least you know there's something more than nothingness."

"Not exactly. Just because there's some sort of cosmic corporation with someone controlling it all doesn't mean I don't just get snuffed out." Smallpiece stared broodingly across at the television set and rubbed his chin thoughtfully. It was a gesture born of habit because he was unable to feel it.

"I really wish I could be more helpful," said Gaspard sincerely, "but they've rather thrown me in at the deep end. Deep end? More like the bloody Marianas Trench. Not even on the job training. You'd think they'd have a bloody course of some sort."

"Bastards!" Ivor exclaimed emphatically. "Oh, hell, I suppose I shouldn't say that should I? Not now I know what I know. Might get someone in some department somewhere upset."

"Mm, you can always repent just in case. It might work, though I wouldn't really know."

"I didn't really want this you know?" Ivor sighed moodily. "It's just that when I realised I could run for it and exist as a spirit I thought I might have a chance to finally get back at my parents. I predeceased them you see? I mean wouldn't you if you were saddled with a name like mine? What were they thinking? You can imagine the hell I copped at school. But what I didn't realise was that there was almost nothing I could do. I believe some spirits manage a bit of manifestation and that but I could never get the hang of it. If I could, I'd sort this slob here out for a start. Anyway, when they eventually died I thought I had a chance. I tried to convince them to stick around. Built it all up you know? Thought then I could make their death as bloody miserable as they'd made my life but they were too savvy."

He sighed desparingly. "You know what? Bugger it. This is a wretched existence anyway. If nothingness is all there is, it's probably better than this. Take me up or whatever it is you do."

"Are you sure? I mean I wouldn't want to persuade you to do something you might regret." As a means of performing his task this last remark was probably not the best approach. "Well, if there's nothing then I won't be able to regret it will I? On the other hand, if there is something it has to be better than this."

Gaspard thought of Death's remark when he'd suggested using a pitchfork but wisely said nothing. It was then another factor that he should have clarified beforehand came to mind. "Um…you know, I'm not sure I know how. I rather thought that you agreeing would be enough but nothing seems to be happening does it? You'd have thought the buggers would have mentioned it. Always the same with committees."

The pair looked at each uneasily for a moment or two before the doctor could resist no longer. "Committee?" They talked for hours trying everything they could think of but without success.

Dr Ivor Smallpiece remained unwillingly in place. "Look," said Gaspard eventually with a note of frustration, "why don't you come back to my place. De…my colleague will pop up sooner or later and he has loads of experience.

58

I'm sure we can work it out. I might even be able to convince him to arrange employment for you on the other side."

"Your place?"

Constable Tweedle of Traffic Unit was unfortunate enough to receive the call from Sergeant Watt about Gaspard's driverless car. Despite being lumbered with the sobriquet Tweedledum, he was really quite bright, as was his friend Constable Arkwright who had been most unfairly dubbed Tweedledummer. When the call came warning them to be on the lookout for a driverless white Ford Focus, licence number supplied, they knew that it was a wind up. Unfortunately for them, they spotted that vehicle several hours later just as they were about to finish their shift.

In a shared moment of poor judgement, they would both forever regret, they decided to pull the car over. Gaspard was only a few blocks from home when he saw the police car behind him and heard the short blip of the siren. As a responsible driver he pulled to the kerb, extinguished his lights and waited. Constable Tweedle approached the car already preparing himself to apologise for the inconvenience. "Excuse me sir but…oh shit!" He leaped back as though stung but then steadied himself and moved back to the car to examine its contents. Or rather lack thereof. He was unaware that inside in the passenger seat Dr Smallpiece, who by the way had been somewhat mystified that Death's colleague got about in an elderly hatchback, was doubled up with mirth. This was the best thing to have happened to him since his passing. For the first time, he was finding death enjoyable. "Fred! You have to see this." Fred Arkwright shuffled over and followed his fellow officer's direction to examine the vehicle.

"Bloody hell!"

"We did pull it over didn't we Fred?" Fred nodded dumbly.

"And no one got out? I mean, I saw nobody." This time Fred shook his head, still mute with disbelief. Inside the car Ivor Smallpiece was almost in hysterics while Gaspard was wondering what in the blazes to do. "It couldn't be one of them new driverless things could it? Not supposed to be on the road but you never know do you?"

"Yeah but it'd still have a bloody passenger and anyway, it's old."

"Oh, right."

"The way I see it we have two choices. The smart one is to bugger off and pretend it never happened. The other one is to call it in."

"No choice mate. I've entered the stop into the computer. Will you call Watt, or will I? Actually, forget I said that. You call him."

"Sarge?"

"What is Tweedle?"

"You know that driverless car?"

"What about it Tweedle?" Watt came back suspiciously. "We just pulled it over and…um…it's driverless."

"Driverless cars usually are Tweedle. That's why they call them driverless," chuckled Watt. "Come on Tweedle. If you're going to try and wind me up, you can do better than that. Get off the bloody air."

"I know you're not going to believe this Sarge," whined Tweedle, "but it's not a wind up. Fred has verified it. There's no one in the bloody thing Sarge. It's spooky."

"You're right. I'm not going to believe it. You're imaging things the pair of you. The driver must have got out and done a runner."

"No Sarge. We ran back the camera. Nobody got out and it's as empty as the super's head. I don't like it Sarge."

"You'll like it even bloody less if the super hears you saying things like that and that will be as nothing if I come out there and find you've been having me on. Do you really want to risk that lad? I kid you not, you and Tweedledummer will both be for the high jump if you're wasting my precious time."

While the two constables were nervously awaiting the arrival of Sergeant Watt, Gaspard was beginning to panic. "What the hell do I do Ivor? This is a bloody nightmare."

"Why don't you just drive off? They can't see you. Just tell them someone nicked your car. They can't prove you were driving. Why are you driving a car anyway? Surely…?"

"No, I can't do that," shot back Gaspard cutting him off before things began to get out of hand. "Can't explain why but believe me it would create problems." Why had he brought Smallpiece? If he were alone, he could simply shed his robe and appear as good old Constable Feeblebunny going about his lawful business. This thought lasted only until he remembered that he was naked beneath the robe. Flowing robes had something going for them in the comfort department and he'd decided to go without. What was the point in being restricted?

He supposed he could still do that but somehow, he had the feeling that exposing his identity, as well as certain bits that may raise questions could cause the odd problem. He was in enough trouble as it was without being done for being naked in charge of a motor vehicle. He was really regretting his invitation and only now realised that he would have to remain in character until such time as Death turned up to sort things out. Maud was going to be really unhappy.

"Hey Sarge."

"What…what?" Growled Sergeant Watt to a smirk from Tweedledummer who knew irony when he heard it. "I think this has to be some sort of sophisticated prank. I just ran the car's licence details and it's purportedly registered to a bloke called Gaspard Feeblebunny."

"Feeblebunny you say?"

"Yeah. With a name like that, it has to be a hoax," Constable Tweedle replied in a slightly disappointed tone because he'd just wasted his word for the day.

"Well, well," came the curious reply.

This time it was Tweedledummer who was disappointed because he'd hoped for another couple of whats. Sergeant Watt placed a finger to his chin and adopted a thoughtful pose. "You don't know the name constable?" The mystified pair both shook their heads silently. "You've heard of the Phantom Speeder incident?"

"Course Sarge, everyone has. Complete bloody mystery."

"Well my doughty lads, the operator of the speed camera in that little fiasco was…any guesses?"

"Gaspard Feeblebunny?" Hazarded Constable Arkwright who was just a little faster on the uptake than his colleague.

"Bingo! Quite a coincidence eh? One might say mystery upon mystery eh? Methinks our young Feeblebunny is up to no good."

The group wandered over to Gaspard's vehicle and took another peer inside. "Keys still in the ignition. If nothing else, we can charge him for that."

"Should one of us drive it back to the station, Sarge?" Hearing this, Gaspard started nervously. As opposed to the car starting in any fashion.

"Don't think that would be wise young Tweedle. Who knows how it's rigged? No, best call for the tow wagon." The sergeant paused thoughtfully. "And maybe the bomb squad to be on the safe side." He chortled evilly. He was not particularly amused but he was aware of both his rank and reputation. It was what sergeants were supposed to do. "Let's see how he explains this away."

The sergeant's decision had two effects on Gaspard. The first was to put a major stress upon his bladder and cause him to fear that he was about to soil his new robe and the second to wish devoutly that he could be seen. So that's exactly what happened. The second one that is. Luckily, he was able to just hang on in the other department. In situations such as this, we are seldom allotted more than one piece of luck and in being able to gain control over his bladder Gaspard had used up his. He materialised just as Sergeant Watt was poking his head through the window for a last thorough look about.

"Aaaah," shrieked Watt in a decidedly un-sergeant like manner. He staggered back several paces completely unnerved.

"What, what, what?" he jabbered to Arkwright's later delight. For a moment or two, pandemonium reigned until Watt managed to gain control of himself because the robed and hooded figure wasn't really doing anything but sit there. "Where the hell…what are…how? I mean to say, who…?"

"It's alright Sarge."

"How did you get there?" Watt queried, finally managing to gain control of his tongue although his vocal cords were still being a bit treacherous because the question came out more a squeak.

"Well, believe it or not…shut up doctor!…I've been here all the time."

"I don't believe it." There was a pause for thought. "What do you mean shut up doctor and where the hell did you get that costume?"

"Sorry, Dr Smallpiece here," he gestured with a bony hand to the passenger's seat, "is laughing so hard I can't hear myself think. For God's sake, shut up! This isn't funny!" The doctor was by now so convulsed with mirth that he unable to correct Gaspard's pronunciation.

"There's no one there."

"You just can't see him, he's a ghost," responded Gaspard, only too aware that he was making the situation worse by the minute. Sergeant Watt steeled himself. "Please remove your hood, driver," he commanded.

"I don't think you want me to do that, Sarge."

"Do it now or I'll run you in. Do it!" Watt was at last getting control. It wasn't very good control because all he could think of was to act like a bully but at least it was control of sorts.

"Please?" Gaspard wheedled.

"Do it or I'll bloody rip it off!"

"Well, it's your funeral."

"Aaaah!"

"I told you. Shut up doctor." The doctor was laughing so hard he could barely manage to splutter out: "Christ, they really didn't prepare you for this did they?" Before again dissolving into incontinent mirth.

"Have some sympathy for the poor man," shot back Gaspard, who was beginning to get a little tired of the spectre's sense of humour. "What, what, what?" Ivor choked amidst guffaws. "Oh God, it's good to be dead."

"Take off that mask, driver," Watt croaked, more in hope than belief.

"You know it's not a mask, don't you?"

"I know nothing of the sort. Take it off."

"What if I were to do this?" Gaspard responded, rolling up a sleeve and then putting his hand through the car roof. "Aaaah!" This time the scream came from three throats simultaneously leading Gaspard to suspect that he'd perhaps gone a little too far in his demonstration. "You see. For Christ's sake, doctor won't you please shut up!"

"I...I...want your driver's licence, your name and address," gabbled the unlucky sergeant, still in policemen mode but realising that what he was dealing with was most decidedly not in any training manual anywhere on the planet.

"No you don't." To Gaspard's immense surprise the words had an immediate effect.

"I don't do I?" Could it really be this simple?

"No. I have done nothing wrong," hazarded Gaspard, taking the cue.

"You have done nothing wrong sir."

"I'm free to go." Good lord, the power is in the robe.

"You're free to go sir. My apologies for the inconvenience." The sergeant was about to salute but managed to stop himself in time. He was suddenly at a loss as to what he was doing here and feeling kindly disposed towards the driver.

"Hope you don't mind me mentioning it sir but I noticed the garden shears. Keen gardener, are you?"

"More a harvester, Sergeant."

"And a fine pastime it is sir. Good evening to you and drive carefully."

"Thank you sergeant and a good evening to you all. Shut up doctor."

"Nice chap," said Sergeant Watt, clapping Constable Tweedle on the shoulder.

"One in a million," agreed Tweedle. Arkwright nodded his agreement.

"What am I doing here?" enquired Watt, totally baffled.

63

4

"Maud are you there?" called Gaspard, quite literally putting his head through the door. He turned to Dr Smallpiece feeling somewhat abashed. "Look, I suppose I should have said something earlier but there's another here…ah…in your situation. Name of Maud."

"I rather gathered that from the little clue you just gave. You know, sticking your head through the door and calling Maud?" fired back the doctor facetiously. "Forgive me for asking but by any chance are you running a boarding establishment for the not currently alive?"

Gaspard forced an unconvincing laugh. "Ha, ha. You might think eh? She's actually the resident spirit. I'm sort of borrowing this place from the mortal who lives here. Needed a base you see?"

"You need a base? Forgive me but the way you operate doesn't seem to fit in with the traditional view of the deathly angel and his cohorts. I thought you chaps just sort of popped up when and where you felt like. The idea of you chuffing about in elderly Ford hatchbacks; you need to have your clutch looked at by the way; and lurking in borrowed high rise apartments somehow doesn't quite fit the image."

"I'm new," replied Gaspard feebly.

"Aaaah! What are you doing back here? I'm not budging if you're hoping for anything different."

"It's alright Mrs D'Unstable. You have nothing to worry about." If only he could smile to put her at her ease. Being a skeleton had its limitations when it came to body language.

"Says you," she said suspiciously. "Who's this oik with you?" she enquired nastily, finally noticing the doctor.

"Ah, yes, please forgive my poor manners both of you. Maud this is the late Doctor Smallpiece. Doctor, this is, or rather was, Maud D'Unstable, with an apostrophe."

The doctor wisely ignored the apostrophe reference.

"Pleased to meet you Mrs Dunstable" he said, making a hash of the pronunciation.

"Pleased to meet you doctor and as you're a professional gentleman, please call me Maud," she said coyly.

"And you may call me Ivor," offered the good doctor, "and the surname is pronounced Smalpas," he proclaimed, glaring at Gaspard.

It took a while for it to register with Maud but when she finally managed to put the two names together, she valiantly fought down her natural urge to snicker. Gaspard found her new found pleasantness confusing, as to this point, he had only ever seen her as a mean old bat.

Clearly the pleasantness was only going to extend to the doctor because she instantly returned to type when she addressed Gaspard again.

"What are you are you doing here again bony and what have you done with himself?"

"I take it you mean Mr Feeblebunny?"

The doctor coughed in order to suppress a chuckle.

"I…er…I believe he's going to be away on some work-related matter for a while. Don't worry, he's not been harmed."

"Harm him or not, doesn't worry me," she said viciously, "I just need him to work the tele."

She turned to the doctor, suddenly all sugar and spice. "I don't suppose you've acquired the knack, have you Ivor? It's a right bugger being at the mercy of the soppy little wanker who lives here. I have to keep chasing him just to read me the program guide."

"Alas, madam, I have not been so fortunate. I have also been at the mercy of the pillock living in my domicile." He smiled ruefully but then twigged to the implications of what she had said. "Good lord, does that mean that Mister…er…that the gentleman can see you? That must be very convenient."

"You'd think, wouldn't you?" She grumbled but then immediately relented, not wishing to appear too sour to the newcomer. "Well…I suppose it does have its advantages," she conceded grudgingly. "At least, for me. Though since he's been able to see me it's put a right cramp in his lifestyle." She cackled unnervingly.

Immediately attempting to undo any damage done by the cackle, she smiled winsomely. "So, doctor, old bony here hasn't had the manners to say why you're here. Can I take it you'll be joining us for a while?"

"Well it certainly would appear that way Maud. I must admit that I wasn't planning to be around for long, thought I'd had enough, you know? Now that I've met you though, I might just change my mind."

"That would be wonderful Ivor," twittered Maud, now as flirtatious as a young girl.

"It's just a pity you can't change the channel. I've been suffering through a bloody Adam Sandler marathon. What sort of fiend would subject people to that, I mean, how many backward, dirty minded fourteen-year olds does he think are watching?"

"Well, fear no more Maud. If bony here can drive a car, he can certainly change a channel, right bony?" He chortled. "Anyway Maud, with what I have to tell you about the trip over you won't need the tele. I'm telling you; I've never laughed so much in my death."

It was to be a bad few days for Gaspard while he waited for Death to come, although he didn't like to think of it in those terms. He decided that when he finally did arrive, he'd demand a first name to make things a little less chillingly formal.

In the meantime, Ivor and Maud were yucking it up and driving him to distraction.

From time to time, the doctor's raised voice could be heard and phrases such as 'what, what, what?' and 'I asked them for a bloody sword', left him in no doubt that he was being mocked. The longer he waited, the more his authority was eroded because unlike the ghosts, he still had to sleep and what sort of unearthly being has to sneak off for a quick snooze? He had no choice but to sleep in his robe since he was never sure whether or not one or both of them would enter his bedroom at night. Then of course there was the problem of having to get up in the night for a pee. Talk about loss of credibility.

And let's not talk about the problems of peeing in the skeletal state. Certain important bits in the urinary process having no bones meant everything had to done by feel. Aside from that, it made aiming a bit hazardous.

When Death finally arrived, he came as a great relief but also as a chance for Gaspard to get his own back. He could hardly wait to see the look on Maud's face.

"You took your bloody time," said Gaspard when he found Death sitting on the end of his bed after he'd just been doing his best not to make a noise in the toilet. "Sorry, major algal bloom in the Amazon. Lot of fish. Couple of nasty pandemics, you know the sort of thing, or at least you will. So, how did the job go?"

"Well and not well. He agreed to leave but I couldn't work out how to make him go. You could have given me some instructions. Anyway, he's in the spare room with Maud."

"Really? Sorry but I thought it was obvious. What did you think the shears were for? Just goes to show eh, never take anything for granted."

"I tried the shears, it was the first thing I thought of, I'm not a twit. Even the doctor pitched in. We tried everything we could think of."

"He was that cooperative, eh? Well, that's a good sign in any case. I'd say that apart from failing to take him up you did a pretty good job. The department will be pleased. Now you'd better give me a look at those shears, we've had a problem or two of late."

"A problem or two?"

"Mm, sloppy workmanship. I suppose we should have field tested them before we gave them to you but rushed job and all that." Death examined and fiddled with the shears for a while before throwing them onto the bed in disgust. "Bugger. Sorry about this. Sloppy bloody work again. I warned them not to use the same people as last time. The backup scythe they magicked up for me a while back was a real piece of crap. Bloody thing was in the shop more often than it was out. Anyway, don't worry, I'll get it serviced for you, shouldn't take more than a few days. Can't get a replacement unfortunately, one off job, you see."

Gaspard's head was swimming as he tried to process the idea of a half arsed heavenly service department but at least it was nice to know that some things on the other side were the same as in the mortal realm, even if it was by way of buggering things up. It took a while but he finally managed to put some words together in a coherent sentence.

"Well, I suppose if that's what you have to do," he said, not too unhappy at being parted from the hated implement. "So, in the meantime I suppose you can do the necessary with the doctor?"

"That's still a no, no. Your job. Can't interfere. Don't worry, I'll do my best to get things moving. It's all the manufacturer's fault after all. They have to honour the guarantee. He's no trouble, is he? I'd have thought he could keep Maud from being a nuisance."

"Well, yes, after a fashion I suppose," sighed Gaspard defeatedly. Then he brightened a little.

"Listen, I don't suppose before you go you could throw a fright into Maud, could you?"

"It'd make me feel a lot better."

"Happy to. Just don't tell anyone."

Death vanished. Gaspard heard a door creak open with agonising slowness, quite a feat since the hinges were recently oiled, and this was followed by 'Boo' and a loud feminine shriek.

Death reappeared. "Tea and bikkies?"

"So, look" ventured Gaspard, finally plucking up his courage. "It's a bit awkward always having to think of you as Death. I mean, not even Mister Death sounds right and the whole thing is a bit uncomfortable, you know, me being a mortal and all? I was wondering since we're into taking tea together and such, if I could…well…call you by your first name if you have one?"

"Certainly old chap. Sorry I didn't think of it myself. It's Mort. What else did you think it would be?"

"Hm…I suppose I was hoping for something a little less threatening. I mean, you already appear as a skeleton with a bloody great scythe, which by the way is a bit over the top. After all, your clients are already dead. Surely you don't have to scare them further. No wonder some of them decide to do a runner."

"And you think if I were called something else it'd be different? We're not exactly on first name terms at that moment you realise?"

"Point taken, but while we're on the subject, why do you have to appear in such a sinister form? Couldn't you make it a bit easier on them? Show up as an angel or something?"

"But I am an angel of sorts. Not in the same way you may think but an angel nonetheless."

"Well, something pleasant then. A cute animal maybe" said Gaspard beginning to struggle.

"So you think that being confronted by a talking llama would make it less confrontational? Rather adding insult to injury don't you think? Look Gaspard, this is pointless, I am what I am and I have no choice in the matter. Would I present differently if I had a choice? Possibly. But let's just say that the powers that be have a flair for the dramatic. You've read the Old Testament?"

"Of course" said Gaspard, lying through his teeth, his main familiarity with things biblical being via the films of Cecil B. DeMille.

"There you go. They like drama." Death paused meaningfully. "And just entre-nous you should take what you read with a large pinch of salt. I was there but those clever dicks in publishing based most of it on second hand accounts. Would they listen? Would they buggery. Based most of it on the ramblings of mad hermits. Bloody typical."

"Um, yeah" Gaspard replied distractedly. "An angel you say?"

"Oh blast it Gaspard, stop trying to catch me out. I was just using an image you might understand."

There followed a protracted silence while both mulled over what had passed between them.

"So, it has to be Mort then?" Gaspard said at length.

"For goodness' sake, why not? It's a perfectly acceptable name in most cultures as well as being the root for many words to do with mortality. There's one right there."

"Yeah but it's a bit sinister. Why not…I don't know…Todd. Unthreatening but still having a deathy sort of vibe in the Germanic."

"A deathy vibe?" Death queried aghast. "Where did that come from? And might I ask why you think having a name like a B movie actor would improve matters?" He held up a hand to stave off any further protest. "Look Gaspard, I've already told you it's a lot to do with the drama and if you don't like it call me Mister Death, okay? Of course, you could call me any of the names I have around the world but let me assure you that they're all equally sinister FOR I AM DEATH THE DESTROYER OF WORLDS AND MY NAMES ARE LEGION."

The voice that Gaspard heard in his head seemed to swell up from some abysmal pit and not a nice abysmal pit either but a really abysmal one. One filled with such unimaginable horrors that they were truly, well, unimaginable. A cold shiver that felt as though he'd been dragged across the entire Ross ice shelf ran up Gaspard's spine. It began at his toe tips and didn't finish until it reached his hair follicles. There it clung for a while enjoying the fun, an enjoyment not shared by its recipient.

"Jesus Christ, did you have to do that?"

"Sorry. Did I frighten you? Just a joke, bit of graveyard humour as they say."

Gaspard shuddered, his skin still icy. "Okay Mort, I suppose I deserved that. I'll let it drop. No hard feelings."

"None at all. I just hope you understand. Um…any more Hobnobs are there?"

Fred Arkwright was sitting disconsolately in the staff canteen having spent another fitful night. He was on his third cup of extra strong tea and it wasn't helping one little bit, in fact quite the opposite, he was now suffering chronic heartburn and his bladder was considering offering him an ultimatum. He was giving serious consideration to throwing a sick day and heading for the pub when his colleague, Jack Tweedle, suddenly pulled up a chair and slumped down heavily beside him, almost upsetting his own tea in the process.

Arkwright gave a start but his knees thought better of it and declined to finish. He slumped back and regarded his partner with an appropriately haunted expression. "Hell's bells, Fred, you look like I feel," he exclaimed dolefully, raising his cup with a trembling hand.

"And if you feel like you look I'd say we're both in trouble," sighed Fred. "I don't know what's eating you but I haven't been sleeping. Keep having the weirdest bloody dreams. Well…not so much dreams as full-blown flaming nightmares."

"You too? What about?"

"Well you might ask mate. Dare I say spectral figures? Skeletons in black hooded robes. That sort of thing." The eyes that settled on his friend were troubled. Possibly in the same way that those of a day release asylum inmate might be. He did his best to take a nonchalant sip of his tea but having to raise his cup in both hands to still the trembling sort of defeated the aim.

"Bloody hell, you too?" Jack muttered, shocked.

"When did they start? Was it after we pulled over that supposedly driverless car? The one owned by that bloke Feeblebunny?" At a nearby table Sergeant Hardcastle put down his tea and pricked up his ears. The terrier had heard the rat. "Funny you should ask. Yes, it was."

"Bleeding heck mate, that's weird. I was just talking to the Sarge and he's been having the same sort of nightmares. He looks even worse than you. Said last night he dreamed about a skeleton trimming his front hedge and then chasing

70

him around the house with garden shears. *And*…they all started after the Feeblebunny thing. But…I mean…there was nothing to that was there? You know…it was all a joke or something. Bloke was just going about his business."

"I know. It has to be something else doesn't it? But what? It can't just be coincidence that we're all having the same sort of nightmares that started at the same time." He paused for a moment before adding thoughtfully: "Funny thing though isn't it? The Sarge dreaming about garden shears when Feeblebunny had a set on his backseat."

They both jumped when a third party slid unheralded into a chair at their table. "Oh, it was no coincidence, let me assure you," purred Sergeant Hardcastle mysteriously, "no coincidence at all. Why don't you chaps tell me everything you know about the incident?"

He pulled out his notebook with a flourish that went a little way to disguise the newly acquired tremor. "And do not miss a single detail no matter how seemingly insignificant."

"It's a funny thing," said Hardcastle after hearing the constables' recounting of events, "but Feeblebunny seems to attract mysteries like crap attracts flies. He's at the centre of them but it always turns out that the whole business is completely ordinary after all. He just takes off on his little fly wings and leaves the shit behind."

He drummed his fingers on the table in irritation and ran them through his prematurely greying hair, a recent phenomenon at which he was not at all thrilled. "I tell you, there's something not right about that bloke. Do me a favour and keep an eye on him if and when you can and in the meantime search your memories and try to remember any details of that night that may have slipped your mind. There has to be something, I'm sure of that."

He pushed his chair back noisily from the table and stood. "I'd suggest that you sleep on it but under the circumstances that might be a bit counterproductive." He chuckled cruelly.

Gaspard was feeling a lot better about his life at the moment. For a while, Maud and Ivor had driven him nuts with their television bingeing and accompanying late night chatter. The television had been running hot twenty-four hours a day and just about driving him to distraction, or at least to the outskirts thereof. In the end, the solution was simple. He merely turned off the set and refused to turn it back on again except during allotted hours. Ignoring the

71

complaints took a bit of doing but he managed to outlast them and now all was…well, not exactly tranquil but at least bearable.

He settled comfortably in his chair with his book and third tumbler of nerve balm and prepared for a peaceful evening. If he concentrated, he could soon filter out the voices from the spare room. Gaspard was just reaching the bottom of the glass and was in that blissful state of alcoholic torpor when one has the luxury of deciding whether another glass is really necessary, or even if it comes to that; wise, when something caught the corner of his eye. He looked up to see the television remote control rising slowly and a little unsteadily from the table next to him. At that moment, there was a triumphant cry from the next room.

"That's it! It's working! Concentrate!" The remote hovered for a second or two and then began to move towards the spare room door, gaining momentum as it went.

"Yes! Hurrah, we've done it!" For a brief period there was only the sounds of muttering. The near silence was soon broken however when the television burst into life accompanied by more cheering from the ghosts. Gaspard moaned pitiably. They'd learned to combine forces and produce kinetic energy. Within a very brief period, there was the sound of raised voices. "Look, it was my idea. I want to watch University Challenge."

"That old cobblers. A pack of overprivileged smart arses showing off. Not bloody likely. It's Escape to the Continent night. We're watching that!"

"Oh, for God's sake. Why would you want to watch that? It's not as if you can go anywhere."

"And why not? If we can manage the telly we can manage other things. We just have to work up to it."

"Bloody hell Maud, you're right. We could find a nice chateau somewhere that's in need of a ghost or two. Haunted home stays are all the rage right now. We could do rather nicely. Maybe even something on the Loire? Chenonçeau perhaps? I've always liked that place. I think Mary Tudor stayed there for a while. You could play her if she's not already in residence. Though first, we need to get you out of that nightdress."

"Oh no you don't mister! No one's getting me out of anything. I'm not one of your slappers!"

"No, no Maud, please don't misunderstand, I wasn't suggesting anything improper. It's just that in your present state it wouldn't be so much a case of

Escape to the Continent as escape of the incontinent. We'd need to posh you up a bit."

"Oh," came Maud's response, which to Gaspard's ears sounded as though she was slightly disappointed that her worst fears weren't being realised, "I suppose."

The pair planned, dreamed and bickered for ages, completely forgetting about the television but that wasn't much of a consolation to Gaspard who was unable to put his mind to anything other than their conversation. On the plus side, it made that decision about the fourth drink a no-brainer. And the fifth. And the sixth. And…At about three in the morning Gaspard fell into the merciful arms of Morpheus and slept until late the next day. Alright, he actually fell face first onto the bedroom floor and awoke half frozen, dehydrated, nauseous and briefly wondering why he'd been attacked by the floor but it was still the best night he'd had in ages. As long as one forgets the initial puking.

When he eventually shambled into the living room, he could hear the pair of ghosts still chattering excitedly about their future prospects. It came as an immense relief because it probably meant they'd not heard him yarking in the bathroom earlier on. Something that would most assuredly reduce his already poor authority to just about zero. From the sounds of things, the new found powers had induced a certain intimacy between the pair which had been missing the night before and he was left in no doubt that a suggestion about getting Maud out of her nighty would be met with an entirely different response to that previously.

The pairs' newfound closeness left him in two minds. On the one hand, it may make life a little easier for everyone for the time being but on the other he now had two ghosts that would be quite a task to round up. He was under no illusion that the doctor's decision to render up his immortal soul was well and truly reversed and as for Maud…well, she'd be more difficult than ever. At the moment, his fondest hope was that they'd both disappear off to Chenonçeau and leave him in peace.

Death was uninclined to talk about much until he'd had his tea and chocolate Hobnob but having satisfied his craving, he became much more amenable.

"You appear to be a great deal more morose than your hung over state would normally be responsible for young Gaspard. Might I be so bold as to enquire of the reason?" He cocked his head in his usual manner of expressing emotion.

"They've learned to do things," moaned Gaspard. "It seems that the two of them together are able to summon more power. Last night they learned to levitate the telly remote and work the set."

"Ah, yes, I suppose I should have warned you that might happen. When it comes to unquiet spirits, two heads is definitely better than one. Unless…" he paused thoughtfully for a brief moment. "Unless one is like poor old Anne Boleyn. It seems that having to walk around with your head under the arm puts somewhat of a dampener on one's abilities, whether or not in concert with others. The poor girl has a hell of a time. Still adamant she won't leave the tower though. Stubborn streak a mile wide. Between you and me she's still convinced Henry will come back for her."

"Really?" Gaspard said, unable to completely hide the note of disinterest in his voice.

"Yup, I wouldn't worry too much though, I shouldn't think they can get up too much, a few ghostly parlour tricks should be about their limit…although you never can tell. Determination can overcome a lot of obstacles. Unlikely to cause you any serious problems but if they ever manage to join up with a third…look out. It's exponential you see."

"Thanks a lot for easing my mind," growled Gaspard. "Oh, and maybe you should know they're planning to do a runner. They've been talking all night about tripping off to France and haunting a chateau. They seem to think they can get themselves in league with a hotelier and do haunted house stays."

"Aw, that's really quite cute in a way isn't it? They really have formed a bond, haven't they? Could make things hard for you in future of course. A shame the good doctor has reneged but it was always on the cards once he found a companion. As for running off, I wouldn't despair, wraiths are strongly held by place and sometimes circumstances, their powers are nowhere near what they'd require to pull that one off."

"Oh, what a relief," responded Gaspard sarcastically. "The thought that I wouldn't have them making my life a bloody misery was keeping me awake at nights."

He glared moodily about the room. "Wait a minute, if they're so firmly tied, how come the doctor is here?"

"Well, I would have thought that was obvious, you brought him. He'd never have been able to manage it on his own but your temporary powers are able to override the normal." Gaspard sighed heavily by way of accepting the point. "I notice that you haven't brought my…symbol back," he grumbled, unable to bring himself to say the hated words.

"That? Ah, no. I'm afraid the contractor is really quite busy and the staff member that did the original design is working on another project. He did promise he'd have it ready soon though. Just as well eh? I bet you can't wait to come to grips with Pargeter now that you have more experience?"

"Raring to go," drawled Gaspard in a voice heavy with sarcasm. "And while we're on the subject, any sign of my…uh…sign?" Gaspard was in no hurry but being in a bit of a snit couldn't help but enquire. His mood had him half hoping that something had gone wrong there as well.

"Great, great, knew you'd be up for it. We really do have every confidence in you, you know. A real tryer that one, I tell the committee. You won't let me down, will you? No, of course you won't. Now…um…any more Hobnobs?"

"The sign? You seem to be ignoring my question."

"No, no, of course not. Look, it slipped my mind okay? Had a lot to think about. I'll make sure it's taken care of ASAP." He was doing his best to sound contrite but it was coming off as slightly impatient. The reason revealed itself with his next utterance. "Now, about the Hobnobs…?"

During the ensuing silence; Death being a surprisingly delicate eater; whispering could be heard originating in the spare room. Most believe that whispering is quiet but it's generally easily detectable because despite what people think, whispers can carry quite a long way. Especially if one whispers like Maud whose attempt at quiet, secretive conversation could only be described as stentorian. "He's talking to someone again. It has to be old bony, nobody else ever comes near the place."

"Didn't you say there was someone else here? A policeman, I think you said."

"Could be I suppose but we would have heard him come him in, wouldn't we? No, it's that bony creep. Whatever you do, don't go out there."

"You really should give them something to keep themselves occupied you know," Death said to Gaspard, having heard the conversation.

"With Maud's temperament, they could start getting up to mischief. Do you have any board games? Cards? Something like that? Now that they can manipulate things it may help to keep them out of trouble. Stop them squabbling and getting up to no good. Try to think of them as children on a wet day but without the runny noses and cat torture."

"I've a couple of things but wouldn't that only help them to develop their power more? We don't want them getting too dexterous, do we?"

"No, but whatever you do they're going to start practicing. Better they perform simple tasks that keep them occupied rather than learning how to throw furniture about the room. You don't want a pair of poltergeists in residence, do you?"

"Hell, I hadn't thought of that. Could it really go that far?" Death nodded sombrely which was a bit of a feat since being a black cowled skeleton it was difficult to be anything but sombre. Upgrading it would be quite difficult but he managed to put it across quite well. "I'll get out the Monopoly then."

"There's no need to be cruel."

"Mr Slingsby?"

"Who wants to know?"

"Forgive me sir. I'm DS Hardcastle from the Downer Road police station. You are Casper Slingsby?"

"Yeees. What's this all about?"

"Nothing to be concerned about sir, I assure you. Simply a follow up on a report you made vis a vis a certain driverless vehicle on the evening of the twenty first. Might I come in for a moment?"

"Oh, bloody hell. I knew I shouldn't have rung it in. I could tell by the tone in your mate's voice that he thought I was nuts. It wasn't just me you know? Plenty of others saw it too." Slingsby backed slowly down the hallway as he spoke, casting his eyes from side to side as though seeking something to lend him support.

"It really is alright sir. I'm simply trying to put together the events of the night."

"Wasting police time. That's what the others said. I'm going to be charged, aren't I?"

"No sir. Most definitely not. In fact, we owe you a debt of thanks. While I'm not free to discuss the matter, I don't mind saying that there is much more to this than meets the eye." Hardcastle smiled his most winning smile which as winning smiles went was never going to do better than a ninth place in a field of ten.

Nonetheless it seemed to appease Slingsby who had been less than thrilled at the prospect of being cast into durance vile, or even durance mildly unpleasant, if it came to that, so he was prepared to take what was on offer. The smile may have come across as something offered up by a kindly disposed hangman but it was still a smile. Of sorts.

"Oh, well…good. You best have a seat. Cup of tea?"

"So, that's it then?" Slingsby nodded. "Just like I told 'em on the phone. Car pulled up…parked…doors opened then shut and locked. Oh! I just thought of something. The car definitely moved on its springs after the door opened. You know, like someone was getting out." Slingsby smiled triumphantly at bringing the point to mind.

"Excellent sir. That will help a lot. There's nothing else though? You don't, for instance remember…oh, I don't know…a sort of icy blast washing over you?" Hardcastle shivered involuntarily.

"No, nothing like that I'm afraid. Although you should perhaps talk to Mrs Threadneedle down the road. She swears she saw a dark figure leave the car and slip through the front door of number 48. And I mean; through. Course she's a mad old bat but after what we all saw…well, who knows, eh?"

Mrs Threadneedle's house was the home of a professional widow. It was over furnished with heavy period pieces, chintz covered chairs, oriental rugs and lots and lots of small but in contradiction to that general description, largely ugly porcelain figures. Hardcastle doubted the windows had been opened in a decade because the air smelled as though it had been recycled through a musty lavender oil factory. The overall aroma was not aided by the slight whiff of soiled cat litter. The good lady herself was clad all in black and in a fashion that must have been obtained from the wardrobe department of a Jane Austen movie. He hoped desperately that she'd never be needed in court because her credibility would be seriously in question. As would her sanity.

"Cup of tea, Sergeant?" She asked sweetly, albeit a trifle nervously. She gestured towards a chair, presently occupied by a very large and even at first glance, obviously evilly disposed cat.

"Thank you Mrs Threadneedle but I shan't trouble you," said Hardcastle, wisely eschewing any attempt to dislodge the feline and opting instead to perch on a small stool nearby. "Just need to ask you a few questions about the incident of the driverless car on the twenty first. I understand you saw something the others did not?"

"Oh, dear. I knew there'd be trouble if that Mr Slingsby reported it. We all told him not to you know? They won't believe it I said, especially as it was being driven by…well, I don't know what by." She glanced adoringly at the cat.

"But I bet Mister Tiddles knows, don't you, Mister Tiddles?" Her adoring look suddenly dropped and she anxiously twisted the little handkerchief she was holding.

"There's no trouble Mrs Threadneedle and Mr Slingsby did the right thing. It may well help to bring a miscreant to justice."

"Really? Well in that case," Mrs Threadneedle's shoulders dropped noticeably and the handkerchief was temporarily forgotten. Her eyes settled on the cat again and a beatific smile immediately adorned her lips.

"So, might I ask you what exactly you observed?"

"Well...you'll probably think me a stupid old woman..."

"Not at all, not at all."

"...but I'm sure I saw a figure get out of the car but not a person mind. It was sort of...I don't know...is spectral the right word? I think it is. Yes, definitely spectral; all wispy and spectral. All in black it was. One of them cowled robes they wear in those horror films. Like what monks wear. It passed right next to me and I felt this terrible chill but they all said it was just my nerves. It was more than that though wasn't it? Yes, I'm sure it was. Anyway, it paused for a little while at the door to number forty-eight and then just passed right through the woodwork. Well! You can imagine how I felt, I nearly died. I haven't slept so much as a wink ever since."

Agnes paused breathlessly and began wringing her handkerchief again.

"I'm sure it was most upsetting Mrs Threadneedle but don't worry, we'll get to the bottom of things. With what we're learning about the events, we'll soon have the case sewn up."

Mrs Threadneedle raised one eyebrow and pursed her lips until they bore a passable resemblance to a cat's backside. "I hope that wasn't meant to be funny, Sergeant?" she enquired haughtily, rather in the manner of a stage dowager duchess. Some might see her reaction as over the top but they would probably not be people who'd suffered the japes of others who thought they were being humorously original.

"No, no, of course not madam. Just a figure of speech."

"Well I hope not because it wasn't," said Mrs Threadneedle acidly.

"So, then" began Hardcastle doing his best to syrup coat his words, "was there anything else that struck you as unusual?"

Agnes eyed him suspiciously because the coating was coming off more as saccharine. The last time anyone had spoken to her like this was when her late husband had sworn undying love after that sordid little incident. "Well, it only struck me afterwards, so of course I didn't mention it to the others but I'm sure…you'll really think me a crazy old woman…but I'm sure that he was carrying a set of garden shears."

Mrs Threadneedle decided to forgive the nice policeman which was a hell of lot more than she'd done for her husband which was the reason he was now the late Mr Threadneedle. If Hardcastle did but know, a trace of the unlamented gentleman was even now part of the musty odour that was filling his nostrils and his restless shade was jumping up and down inches from Hardcastle's nose trying to gain his attention. And justice. The cat looked up, noticed the spectre, hissed and fled from the room. "Garden shears!" Hardcastle exclaimed, causing the delicate lady to jump several inches off her seat. "Sorry dear lady, I didn't mean to alarm you…or your lovely moggy…but you've just provided a vital piece of information. You are sure it was garden shears?"

"Oh yes, sure as you're sitting there. I keep having nightmares about prowling topiary."

"I have a problem."

"Oh yes, of what magnitude might I enquire?"

"About a nine on the bollocks-up scale of ten," replied Gaspard miserably. "Bloody Hardcastle telephoned and he's coming over. Says he has some important new information to discuss with me which of course means that he's going to give me a bloody hard time."

"I shouldn't think there's much he can know of any significance. Just play dumb. There can hardly be anything to harm you and let's face it, even if he knew the facts no one would believe it. He'd be laughed off the force."

"I suppose, but in the meantime, he'll put me through the wringer. There's another thing though isn't there? I can't meet him as Napoleon, how the hell do I manage suddenly reverting to my real self. The pair in the spare room might twig."

"Sorry, did you say Napoleon?"

"Oh, yeah, it's what Maud has started calling me. Because I'm all bony parts you see? Big bloody joke."

"Mm, a trifle stale but at least it shows she's a little more light hearted than in the past. Now, as to the other business, I really can't see the problem. Just leave as…Napoleon and come back a while later as Gaspard."

"You mean like Clark Kent leaving hurriedly and turning up seconds later as Superman? Don't you think they may get a little suspicious? I mean, I have to follow that up with a reverse switcheroo after Hardcastle leaves. One coincidence they may swallow but two?"

"No option though is there? Not unless you head him off at the pass as I believe the saying goes and go into the station to confront him there."

"Can't, I'm on stress leave."

"Well, nothing for it but to do and hope, eh? *Fac et spera* as the Latin motto goes. Not a course of action I'd normally recommend, never liked leaving things to chance but sometimes there's just no choice."

"Well, I don't suppose it really matters all that much anyway does it? I couldn't have much less authority over that pair than I do now," mused Gaspard moodily. "And talking about authority, you still haven't returned my bloody shears."

"Mix up in the warehouse I'm afraid. Some silly bugger ordered the wrong parts. Apologies and all that but it shouldn't be much longer. I've really read them the riot act this time."

"Oh, it's you, Gaspard," exclaimed Maud in a voice that for once was not vitriolic. It came as a total surprise to Gaspard who wasn't used to being on first name terms or being spoken too in a half human manner. Doctor Smallpiece was definitely making a difference to her temperament. "Old Napoleon had to buzz off somewhere and left us without a third player. You can take his place."

"Napoleon? What in the blue blazes are you talking about Maud?"

"Oh, of course, you don't know. Well…"

"Later, Maud," piped up the doctor to Gaspard's considerable relief. "We'll brief him later. Let's just get on with the game."

"I don't really like Monopoly Maud," said Gaspard warily, hoping he didn't upset the apple cart in his attempt to avoid playing. "Anyway, I'm expecting a visitor."

"Come now," piped up Smallpiece, "do the decent thing and fill in for the other bloke. It can't be that bad surely?"

"Why do you think the bloody thing was stuffed away at the back of the closet," snapped Gaspard but then realising what the consequences may be if he did not participate, reluctantly seated himself and rolled the dice.

"Good lad. You'll get to enjoy it once you give it a proper try," said the doctor jovially. The trio had been playing for an hour or so which in Monopoly terms is no more than a split second when the knock came at the door.

"Excuse me but this is my visitor. Perhaps you'd suspend the game for a while? If he notices you playing it might just raise a few questions," pleaded Gaspard with just the necessary amount of sarcasm but judging by the look of determination on Maud's face his pleas were going to be ignored.

"We'll behave," she said with a trace of mirth in her voice, then winked at the doctor who winked back. "Better hurry up and answer the door. Don't want to keep your visitor waiting."

"Who were you talking to?" Hardcastle enquired rudely as he entered.

"No one," replied Gaspard innocently. "As you can see there's nobody here but me. Maybe I was muttering to myself, you know what it's like when you're alone. I sometimes have quite lengthy conversations with myself when I'm distracted." The look on the sergeant's face showed that not only did he not indulge in that particular foible but he strongly doubted Gaspard did either. "Have a seat Sarge. No! Not there! Um…sorry, don't know why I said that. Sit anywhere you like."

"Just not on my bloody lap," grumbled Maud as she moved over.

"So Sarge, what's up? What did you want to talk to me about?"

"Your turn Gaspard. Doc just bought a hotel on Park Lane. You're for it now," cackled Maud. Gaspard waved his hand for her to shut up while doing his best to make it seem as though he were shooing a fly. "Have your go Gaspard or I might start throwing things," warned Maud. "You know I'll do it."

"Um…excuse me a minute Sarge, I just have to have my turn," mumbled Gaspard, desperately hoping he wouldn't be asked why.

"Why?" Hardcastle enquired. "There's no one else playing." The penny dropped. "You said there was nobody else here. How come there are three markers on the board?"

"What? Oh, yes, had some friends over earlier. They've gone now."

"Then why do you need to have a turn? Hang on. That hotel wasn't on Park lane a minute ago. Was it?" He began confidently enough but his voice trailed off uncertainly at the end.

"Must have been Sarge. Not unless a ghost moved it, ha, ha. Now you were going to ask…?"

"Yes, ah…why did you need to have a go again?"

"Um…bit difficult to explain Sarge…technical and all that…playing online."

"Oh, come now, I…Jesus!…the dice just rolled themselves!" Hardcastle sat goggle eyed as the dice levitated, rattled about and then spilled into the board. As one of the markers began to move the number showing on the dice he leaped from his chair, wild eyed.

"At bloody last," growled Maud, "bloody cheek sitting all over a person."

"What the hell is going on here Feeblebunny?"

"What do you mean, Sarge?" Gaspard enquired innocently enough and hoping the perspiration didn't show. "Would you like a glass of water or something, you seem agitated."

"You saw that Feeblebunny, I bloody know you did!" At that very moment the doctor had his turn and to make matters worse he was passing go, so money began to disappear from the bank and reappear on the other side of the table. "Aaaah! There it is again! What in God's name is going on here!"

"Just a game of Monopoly Sarge," retorted Gaspard suddenly feeling reckless and deciding that rather than deny the obvious he'd try to make it seem mundane. "I really don't know why you're taking on so. Perhaps you should go home and have a bit of a lie down?"

Hardcastle looked about wildly. "Oh, my go I think," said Gaspard calmly, before rolling the dice. The pair of ghosts were beginning to enjoy themselves hugely at Hardcastle's discomfiture and Gaspard was finding himself caught up in the merriment. "Oh, look, I can buy Oxford street. That completes the set," he told Hardcastle. Bugger it; if he had to suffer then bloody Hardcastle could suffer along with him. It was his own fault for being such a prat.

"Your move, I think doctor," urged Gaspard, seemingly to thin air. The dice lifted into the air, shook and rolled.

"Aaaah," was about all Hardcastle could manage at first but eventually summoned up a 'what?'

"Isn't technology amazing," purred Gaspard, now enjoying himself hugely and thinking it would no harm to thoroughly confuse his nemesis.

"Technology?" croaked Hardcastle, no longer quite himself. "That's impossible. There's no technology in the world…"

"Oh, I assure you there is. The proof is right under your eyes isn't it? Unless you think I'm playing with spooks. Now, I really think you should toddle off and

have a good lie down. The super tells me you've been a bit poorly lately."
Gaspard stood and ushered a thoroughly bewildered sergeant to the door.

"Yes, yes, few things been getting on top of me lately. Odd events. Sure it'll
pass," mumbled Hardcastle, now close to catatonia.

In the background, the dice clattered onto the table. Hardcastle's eyes opened
wide in panic. "Technology…?"

"Quite so," said Gaspard kindly and unkindly shut the door in the sergeant's
face.

5

"You still don't have it do you?" Gaspard accused Death wearily. "Why don't you just admit that this isn't meant to be and let me go back to being a copper?"

"Look, it's just an administrative error. You remember me saying that I'd given them a bollocking? Well, my complaint reminded them that under the legislation, goods must be fit for purpose. It was just bad luck that the clerk who received it misread it as being fit for porpoise." Death was hoping that he wouldn't have to admit that it was he who typed the letter.

Gaspard groaned loudly. "The good news though is that it's actually working now."

"And the not so good news?" Gaspard sneered, canny enough to hear the unspoken negative proviso. "Umm, yes…well…the not so good news is that it was shipped off to the marine section but look, I'm almost sure we'll find it soon and have it recalibrated."

Gaspard groaned theatrically. "In the meantime though," continued Death with a brightness he probably wasn't feeling, "I've managed to have your notice printed up. Why don't we pay a visit to Pargeter's place of employ and see if it does the trick?"

Gaspard and Death stood admiring the poster that Death had just tacked to the factory door. Alright, to be perfectly accurate, Death was admiring it and Gaspard was staring at it while grinding his teeth and positively seething with annoyance, although annoyance is probably a pallid term for what he was experiencing. "You didn't have it proofread did you?" Gaspard growled in a shaking voice that positively oozed exasperation.

"Ah, I have to admit that I didn't," replied Death, sounding uncharacteristically chastened. "They got it mostly right though, didn't they?" he continued hopefully.

"Restricted Entry," Gaspard read. "For health and safety reasons, these premises are restricted to present employees of a corporeal nature. Entry is forbidden to non-employees or those of a non-corporeal status such as goats."

He glared balefully at his companion. "Goats? Surely even the dim-witted bastards that seem to infest wherever it is you come from could have seen that was wrong?"

"Well look, if you're going to be pedantic about it I'll admit they could have done a bit better but it still says those of a non-corporeal nature, doesn't it? It should still do the trick.

Signed. The mangerment. Hardly puts the stamp of authority onto it does it?"

"Maybe he won't notice," said Death without much conviction but then brightening a little added: "had a chap the other day…geologist who committed suicide over missing a dreadful error in his report. It should have read something like 'derived from a weathered parent rock' but the typist had used a spell checker and it ended up 'derived from a weathered pair of socks'. Poor chap was a laughingstock and ended it all."

"Don't tell me he actually went with you?" enquired Gaspard a little nastily. Before Death could answer, he added: "Anyway, we'll soon see what his comprehension skills are like, that's his car coming now. Knowing his type, he'll not only spot the error, but he'll also use it as a loophole. After all, goats are not of the same species as ghosts are they? And mangerment? Ye gods, any barrack room lawyer would ignore that and I'm pretty sure we're dealing with one here."

Death hung his head and kicked at a stone that ended up lodging between his toe bones. It was probably the first time he'd shown any real embarrassment. In the short period before Percy's arrival, he did his best to surreptitiously dislodge the offending pebble without Gaspard noticing. It was proving to be an awkward evening. Luckily the other hims that we're even now going about their business in a multitude of locations throughout the world were faring a little better. Percy's car sped into the parking lot and skidded to a halt. The driver leaped from the seat and ran towards the entrance where he checked just as he was about to enter.

"He's seen the sign," whispered Gaspard. Pargeter's lips could be seen moving as he tried to make sense of the document. For a heart stopping moment, he stood motionless, obviously in deep thought. Then to the dismay of both the watchers, he threw back his head and laughed before disappearing through the door. Mere moments later his head emerged through the woodwork and he looked around, clearly trying to spot whether the notice posters were still somewhere about.

"You'll have to do a bloody sight better than that!" He eventually shouted, facing in the wrong direction. "I know you're out there somewhere! Just bugger off and leave me be!"

The head immediately withdrew and the failed venture was ended. "I was wondering," pondered Gaspard moodily, "did you ever meet a chap by the name of John Donne?"

"Probably met thousands," Death replied cautiously, "why do you ask?"

"Let me be more specific. English metaphysical poet. Seventeenth century. I was wondering if perhaps you might have met him before he died?"

"Not a regular part of my routine, so no but I seem to recall taking him up. Again, why?"

"Well, not trying to be critical you understand," began Gaspard in a tone that gave the lie to his claim, "but he wrote a poem that began: 'Death, be not proud, though some have called thee mighty and dreadful for though art not so.' It occurred to me that going by your performances to date he might have had more than a passing acquaintance with your good self."

"I say, steady on. We all have our off days," responded Death with a slight quaver in his voice, "and that business about being proud is certainly unfair. I've never pretended to be anything more than what I am. Think of me as a sort of copper like you. In your case, chap commits a crime, you feel his collar. In mine, chap dies, I appear and do much the same, comparatively speaking, nothing more than that. Sometimes your folk do a runner, so it is with my chaps." Death sounded decidedly hurt.

There was an embarrassed silence before Gaspard replied. "Sorry Mort, I'm just frustrated. Shouldn't take it out on you. I suppose it must be getting harder all the time for you, just as it is for us?"

"You said it. The days of, 'it's a fair cop guv, I'll come quietly' are well and truly over. The old villains and dearly departed had respect for authority, these days that's well and truly gone. I blame it on all this personal liberties rubbish. People just have no feelings of obligation to society anymore."

"Should we give it another try do you think?"

"Hm, he's warned now though isn't he. Knows it's us, or at least me. He'd probably just ignore it as the ploy it is."

"Yes but there's still that part of his nature that makes him a rule follower. Even his doing a runner was following rules when you get down to it. His need to get to work on time overrode his inclination to accept that he was dead. What if we make the notice more official? Actually have it signed by the manager?"

"Good idea except for one thing. The manager can't actually sign a phantom document. Don't worry though, I can knock up a pretty good forgery. It's certainly worth a try."

Gaspard and Death had been discussing strategy and imbibing a little more malt whisky than was good for them when Gaspard suddenly threw up his hands in exasperation. Death paused in the middle of taking a nibble at his Hobnob that he found went well with the booze and cocked his head quizzically. "I've bloody well had it," growled Gaspard, trying but failing to keep the tremor from his voice.

"Need I ask, had what, dear chap?"

"No. Listen to that pair bickering in the spare room. I want to watch this, I want to watch that, it's my move, it's your move and it it's bloody endless. All day, all bloody night. I've had enough, I'm getting rid of them whatever it takes."

"Please don't be rash," Death counselled. "There are correct procedures you know. If you start going off half-cocked, you could end up making your situation decidedly worse. Just hang in there a bit longer and we'll get it all sorted out."

"That's easy for you to say, you don't have to put up with this pair of chattering bloody parakeets and now that they have some powers it's all so much harder. I'm bloody sick of finding Monopoly pieces scattered around the place and even worse, having to play the wretched game whenever they feel inclined."

He passed a hand over his face distractedly. "You know, yesterday I dozed off for five minutes as myself and they ran a hose up my trouser leg. I just woke up in time."

"Dear me, most unpleasant," muttered Death who despite his occupation was really averse to any sort of conflict. He pulled a small crystal hourglass from somewhere within the folds of his robe. "Good Lord, is that the time, must be off." He hung his head a trifle guiltily then added: "Just remember, no good can come of letting your temper get the better of you."

He slipped the hourglass back into his robe while deftly scooping up the packet of Hobnobs and secreting them about his person. Gaspard opened his mouth to argue but suddenly he was talking to thin air or at least air that was temporarily thinner as a result of the sudden disappearance.

"Right you two, I have an important guest coming shortly and I'd be grateful for a bit of privacy." Gaspard was appearing as his mortal self and doing his best to sound forceful but as usual it didn't do anything to win over Maud. "Why should we? We live here too. What's so bleeding important that we can't know what it is?"

"Please, Maud…doctor. It's quite important and I don't want to be distracted by your presence. It'd be…awkward."

"Only if you tell us what it's all about. For all we know, you could be plotting."

Gaspard sighed an exasperated sigh. He didn't have to fake it. "If you must know, I have an appointment with my priest," he began but was forced to pause when Maud brayed with amusement.

"You…a priest?" Maud spluttered, barely able to control her mirth.

"Things have been getting on top of me lately," mumbled the wretched young man.

"I didn't know that was your thing," giggled Maud, thoroughly enjoying herself.

Gaspard blushed. "Please…give me a little privacy…and if it comes to that, a bit of dignity." He sniffed and stuck out his chin in a vain attempt to appear in control of himself.

"I don't think there's any harm Maud," broke in the doctor in his best bedside voice. "You must see that he's been going through a lot." He nodded to Gaspard. "Of course we'll keep out of the way."

"Gaspard is it?" enquired the priest.

Gaspard nodded. "Good afternoon. I'm Father O'Flatus from St Saviour. I believe you said that you're in need of counselling my son?"

"Definitely father, although it may not be the kind you usually deal with. Come in please." The priest entered, already feeling concern for his parishioner, who was casting furtive looks about the room as though he expected assailants to be lurking behind the drapes. Father O'Flatus beamed his best hail fellow well met look and bustled into the room. "Ah, I see you're a chess player Gaspard," exclaimed the priest, hovering over the board. He was a firm believer in establishing a little rapport before getting down to the sometimes unpleasant business of hearing the woes of his flock. In addition, when it came to the game of chess, which was his passion, he could be a right pain in the fundament.

"Not exactly."

"No? I was led to believe that you live alone. Someone else here plays?"

"That's partly what I need to see you about father."

"Really? Well that sounds intriguing," replied Father O'Flatus, looking appropriately interested. "Almost as intriguing as this position here." He looked up and smiled benignly. "It looks a little like the Bugovsky defence but then, not quite." He continued to stare intently at the board, unconsciously scratching his head as he did.

In the spare room, Maud was edgy. "I don't trust him. He's up to something." This came as no surprise to the doctor who'd quickly learned that Maud didn't trust anybody, ever. She put her head through the door which anyone who knows anything about spirits can tell you is not just a figure of speech.

"It's a bloody priest," she almost bellowed at a startled doctor.

"Well…that is what he told us Maud," responded Smallpiece reasonably.

"He's lurking around our chess board," she grumbled.

"Well, I'm sure he means no harm. Maybe he's a player. Just casting his eye over things. Appreciating the situation as it were."

"Let him appreciate something else," Maud muttered, glaring at her companion and adopting her most pugnacious expression. It was clear that she was spoiling for a fight, although why, the doctor had no real idea. That was something else about her that he'd learned early on. She didn't need much to set her off.

"Whoever's playing black could be in a spot of bother here, I think," pondered aloud the good father to himself, so lost in his appreciation of the board that Gaspard had almost slipped to the back of his mind. "Might I enquire who's playing it?"

"Maud, I think," replied Gaspard, wishing the priest would get his mind off chess and lend him the assistance he was hoping for. He jumped suddenly as Maud's head appeared through the woodwork of the bedroom door.

"Tell the bleeding God botherer to stay away from my game!" she shouted rudely. It was a distinct pity that Father O'Flatus was unable to hear her outcry, both because it would have made explanations easier for Gaspard and saved the priest some discomfort.

"Maud, eh? Well, if she were to move her knight...so...it may just save her from being mated in three moves," mused the father, moving the piece across the board then standing back to admire his work.

"I'm not being mated by anybody, you bible bashing creep!" shrieked Maud, "and leave my game alone!"

"No! Maud! Don't!" At first Father O'Flatus was just startled at Gaspard's sudden and inappropriate outburst. It was shortly thereafter that he was next terrified as the board before him exploded upwards, then horrified and severely discomfited as the bishop was rammed firmly up his left nostril. "Jesus, Mary and Joseph!" Howled the distraught man of the cloth, vainly trying to make sense of what was happening. He staggered about the room wrestling with the chessman that was somehow resisting all attempts at removal.

After blundering into one or two pieces of furniture, he eventually fell onto the couch where he was finally able to remove the offending piece from his hooter. The uncontrolled trembling probably assisted in vibrating the piece out. His petrified gaze fell accusingly on Gaspard as he enquired: "Whaa?"

"That's rather what I'd hoped to talk to you about," said Gaspard, a lot more calmly than he felt, particularly because Ivor and Maud were now standing next to him howling with mirth.

The good Father arose shakily from his seat and glancing wildly about began to edge towards the door. "Ah, yes, I see my boy.... Well...ah...make an appointment and I'll see what I can do. Right now, I have an urgent...christening in ten minutes...or funeral...or something. I'll let myself out." With that, he flung open the door and fled into the corridor.

"That's right, piss off you bible bashing twerp," Maud shouted gleefully.

The doctor shook his head sorrowfully. "Shameful behaviour for a man of the cloth," he said lugubriously. "You'd think this sort of thing should be his bread and butter. Sorting out his parishioner's woes. I'm very sorry Gaspard but who'd have thought he'd be such a dreadful coward."

He called after the fleeing priest, "shame on you father, I've a good mind to write to the bishop." Gaspard shot an accusatory look at both of the spectral miscreants and left hurriedly in pursuit of his erstwhile visitor but not before snarling over his shoulder that he would make them regret their actions. It was a hollow threat of course because they all knew by now that the pair were in almost total control.

Maud giggled at the threat. "It'll be the other way around boyo, I'm going to want a friendly word with you."

"You really should try to be a bit kinder to our host you know Maud," said the doctor, although he couldn't hide the amusement in his voice. Maud cackled.

Gaspard caught the priest before he could summon the elevator. "Look father, I'm sorry that happened," he said hurriedly, "I just needed to unload my concerns on someone. I knew nobody would believe me and as a priest what I said to you wouldn't come back to haunt me." At the word 'haunt', Father O'Flatus flinched visibly. "Sorry father, didn't mean to sound flippant."

"By the holy mother and all the saints, Gaspard," quavered the man of the cloth, "what in the name of the almighty is happening. It's demons from the very pit of hell that your entertaining."

"Hardly entertaining father, although they seem to get vast amusement at my discomfiture and not demons, although I suppose after what happened you could be excused for thinking so. They're just ordinary spooks father, albeit bloody troublesome ones."

"Ah, so is it an exorcism that you're after?" queried the good father nervously.

"Not so loud father," hissed Gaspard, "if they think that they'll really make my life hell. No, it's as I said, I just needed to talk to someone but it seems to have been a terrible lapse of judgement. Don't worry on my account, I know how to placate them. Most of the time. It's just that they get bored easily and play practical jokes if I don't manage to keep them amused." He gazed piteously into the priest's eyes. "They force me to play Monopoly," he sobbed.

"Like I said, demons from the very pits of hell," responded O'Flatus sympathetically as he placed a fatherly hand on Gaspard's shoulder. "Are you sure it's not an e...x...o..."

Gaspard cut him off before he could spell more of the word.

"They're not children, father, they can spell. No, it's not that." He considered if he should say more. What the hell, in for a penny. "What you've seen is not the worst of it father." He paused, sure that he was being foolish but unable to help himself. He needed to tell someone. He took a deep breath. "I'm being visited by Death." He watched as the look of disbelief spread across his priest's face and try frantically to transform itself into an expression of curiosity.

"I'm not sure what it is you're meaning my son. When you say death...?"

91

"I mean just that father. The bloke in the black robe with the scythe. He wants me to be his off-sider…or rather the committee does."

"Committee…?"

"The time and motion department I think it is. They say he has too much on his plate and needs to subcontract out some of his difficult cases. Spirits that refuse to admit they're dead mainly." He knew he was sounding crazily absurd but having started had to continue. "I've got a robe and everything but the garden shears are broken."

He looked pleadingly at the priest, desperately hoping to be believed. "I can show you if you like. The robe at least. It makes me invisible. The shears are in the repair shop." Seeing the look of incredulity on Father O'Flatus' countenance he began to babble. "Really, I can be invisible and walk through walls and everything." He rambled on incoherently and by the time he'd finished his voice was more of a controlled sob. Father O'Flatus began to reach behind him frantically trying to locate the elevator call button.

As if matters weren't bad enough, Mort suddenly appeared beside him.

"What are you doing Gaspard? Are you losing your senses? For heaven's sake stop babbling and give the poor man a break. You must know that by now he thinks you're certifiable?"

"I know Mort, I know, it's just getting on top of me you know."

The priest looked startled at this remark, seemingly apropos of nothing and also apparently addressed to the fire extinguisher. "Of course my son, I can see how it would upset you." He finally found the button and began pushing frantically.

"You know if the committee found out about you spouting off, they'd be most upset. You're breaking all the rules by speaking to mortals about the mysteries."

"I'm sorry Mort. I'm just not cut out for this."

Father O'Flatus watched nervously as Gaspard continued to address a piece of firefighting equipment. "Mort…?"

"Ah, yes. He's here."

"Gaspard!"

"Oh bugger, forget I said that." The priest didn't want to continue but he was fascinated where the conversation might turn, even though he was petrified that the direction may well be a violent one. Truth to tell the only direction he was really interested in at the moment was the one generally known as far away.

"Mort? Is that what you call...?" began O'Flatus, unable to help himself, caught in the sort of horrified fascination that one feels watching a tarantula crawl up someone's trouser leg.

"Please father, forget I said anything."

At this point, the priest was only too willing to forget, although he already had a sneaking suspicion that this one was going to keep him awake for a long time to come. There was no way the details of this visit were going any further because he knew only too well that his superiors would write it off as probably a hoax or failing that the ravings of a disturbed mind. Neither of which was the concern of the church. Not strictly speaking anyway and certainly not as long as they could easily ignore it. At that point, the elevator doors opened and the father stepped into it with unnecessary alacrity.

Well, unnecessary from Gaspard's point of view but a bloody good idea from the priest's. "Sorry Gaspard, have to run. Put your faith in the Lord and all will be well. Don't hesitate to call should you need more counselling." The last words were necessarily muffled as the elevator doors had already shut, not aided in the task by O'Flatus' frantic pressing of the door close button.

"You know you didn't help the situation; I hope. Why in the name of all that's holy did you turn up like that?"

"Sorry Gaspard, I suppose I'm not very good in social situations. Not very well acquainted with the living you see. Come along let's have a nice cup of tea and you can calm down. You'll be pleased to know that I have a pleasant surprise for you."

Gaspard's recovery was a lot faster than that of Father O'Flatus whose housekeeper would from time to time over the coming months find him giggling hysterically. She wondered if she should inform the bishop about Father O'Flatus' sudden interest in demonology and psychic phenomenon. She was particularly worried that he'd begun sleeping within a pentangle and occasionally sacrificing chickens.

"So, don't tell me, you've finally had the shears returned?"

"Well, no," replied Death somewhat guiltily. "The work's been done but it seems to have been lost in the post. I'm sure it's just a matter of time now. Slight delay and everything." He avoided Gaspard's doubting gaze but continued happily. "No shears but I've got you this." He produced a package from within the voluminous folds of his robe. "Ta da!"

"What is it?"

"This my dear Collector, is a new robe. Not just any new robe either. We realised that you were being hampered by having to chug about everywhere in your car. Should have seen it immediately but you know how it is."

"I'm certainly beginning to," responded Gaspard sarcastically.

"This one will give the same powers as the rest of us. You just need to imagine where you want to be and presto changeo, there you are. Take a gander." Mort was clearly excited about the whole thing. He ripped open the package and threw the new robe across to Gaspard. "Try it on," he urged excitedly.

"Why not," said Gaspard, beginning to feel just a little bit thrilled despite his best attempts not to be. Who could resist such a power after all? He didn't dare think of the endless possibilities so held up the robe for a cursory inspection by way of self-distraction. Then something caught his attention in the region of the garment's breast. "Umm, is that an alligator?"

Gaspard could have sworn that Mort blushed. "Bugger. I was rather hoping you wouldn't notice. Alright, so I'll come clean. Our regular supplier was busy making a new shipment of gowns for the fiery angels. It's a really time-consuming business now that they've banned asbestos, so I had to use a knock off shop. Don't worry, the workmanship is as good as anybody's but they have the unfortunate habit (no pun intended) of adding these little adornments. Their stock in trade you see? By the way they do a very nice Rolex hourglass if you're ever interested."

He waggled his head ingratiatingly. "I mean, really, it's not too obtrusive is it? It was either this or the Tommy Hilfiger." Gaspard's response was a heartfelt sigh that must have just about drained every molecule of air from his body. Death looked on alarmed at the extent of the reaction, half expecting the wretched young man to cough up a toenail. Gaspard shook his head dizzily. He opened his mouth to voice his disappointment but then thought better of it. What in the name of blazes was the point? Everything so far had been a total bollocks up so why should this be any different. He'd never been much of a deep thinker but he was beginning to reach the conclusion that if this was the way the afterlife was run, it was no small wonder that the mortal world was such a bloody shambles.

"Oh well, maybe people won't notice" he sighed. "Although…I don't suppose I could sew a patch over it?" he asked a little more brightly.

"Hmm, wish that were possible but it's not like you're sewing on a button with this stuff. You've heard the expression, 'the fabric of time and space'?"

"What…come on…you don't mean…?"

"Voila."

"But…but…that's just an expression surely. It's not really fabric."

"How else do you think it works? OK the factory has to do a bit of hocus pocus to get it to look like this but take my word for it…this is like no other fabric in the universe. You're quite privileged. Now shall we give it a test run?"

"I suppose," ventured Gaspard nervously. "It's not going to drop me in the middle of a bloody motorway somewhere is it? I mean…without wishing to be too critical, the record of your people hasn't exactly been stellar."

"Nothing to worry about. It has been thoroughly tested and as long as you focus on your desired destination, you'll have no problems. Now what say we pop along to the factory and see if Percival has had a change of heart? Come on, last one there's a gorilla's uncle." With that minor challenge, Mort vanished. Rather unfairly thought Gaspard who was still holding the garment at arm's length mesmerised by the alligator; or was it a crocodile?

The reluctant traveller donned the garment, envisioned the car park at the factory and screwing his eyes tightly shut; vanished. He opened his eyes and saw only blackness. He looked frantically about with no better result. His heart began to hammer in panic. Was he trapped in some galactic limbo or was this some bloody tomb? Gaspard was about to scream and give himself over to complete hysteria when he began to make out dismal shapes in the gloom as his eyes began to adjust to the lack of direct light.

He moved cautiously closer to the shapes and realised that the objects he could discern were dark grey clothing lockers. He looked about and noticed what appeared to be benches. Exercising a courage he didn't know he possessed, he shuffled along the line of lockers and came to a room with a sign reading 'ladies' showers'. A whiff of chlorine assaulted his nostrils and it was in that moment he realised that he was in the ladies' locker room of the local swimming pool. Thank God it was after hours.

Or maybe not. For a moment, he toyed with the idea of trying to find a way out and walking home but soon abandoned the thought. He held his breath, thought of the car park and instantly found himself standing next to Mort.

"What kept you?"

"What kept me…what kept me?" Gaspard seethed. "I thought you said it had been tested? I ended up at the local swimming pool. Thank Christ the place was closed."

Mort thought for a moment. "Precisely which part of the local pool, may I ask?"

"That isn't relevant," mumbled Gaspard, blushing furiously.

"Not perchance the ladies' changing rooms?"

"Since you must know; yes. But that's irrelevant. The thing's bloody faulty," Gaspard said aggressively, ashamed of what Mort must be thinking.

"Look my friend, what happened is I suppose a fairly natural result of you being young and mortal. I suppose I should have warned you that sometimes the garment might pick up on a strong signal from the subconscious. Given a power such as you have been gifted it's only human to toy with the possibilities. You'll just have to fight down any such unworthy thoughts and hope it doesn't happen again. I'm sure that you'll get better with practice."

Gaspard, feeling completely mortified hung his head, cheeks burning with shame, not knowing what to say. He was saved from the possibility of making matters worse with half arsed attempts at self-defence when Mort gave a cry of surprise. "Good grief! Look! Is that Percival sitting on the doorstep?"

Gaspard raised his head and sure enough, there sat Percival, head in his hands and looking thoroughly despondent. "He looks wretched. I wonder what's happened?"

"No doubt the down side of his choice of afterlife is beginning to come home to him. Maybe you should wander over and have a chat. Be careful you don't spook him though." Death chuckled. "Sorry couldn't resist."

At that moment, Percy looked up and to the joint surprise of Gaspard and Death, he began to walk in their direction. Appropriately enough he was looking haunted. Gaspard watched with growing concern as Pargeter moved towards them. He'd never thought that a ghost was capable of plodding but Percy was doing a pathetically passable impression. He couldn't help but think that Percy was the most dispirited spirit imaginable.

"This looks likes it might be a matter for you Gaspard. Probably best if I make myself scarce. Nothing I can add to affairs."

Death vanished just as Percy arrived. Percy now looked offended and even more dispirited if that were possible. "Well, I say, at very least he could have said hello. It's not as if we're not acquainted," complained Percy with obvious pique. Gaspard opened his mouth to reply but was headed off.

"Sorry," said Death, suddenly appearing at Gaspard's shoulder, to the latter's discomfiture.

"Hell's bells Mort, do you have to keep doing that?" grumbled Gaspard who was becoming thoroughly fed up with the whole disappearing and reappearing business. Percy on the other hand merely looked on glumly, completely unmoved by Death's antics. He really was in a bad state.

"Rude of me," apologised Mort, ignoring Gaspard's protest.

"Sudden call you know, chili eating contest in Santa Fe. Please accept my apologies Mr Pargeter but I can't stay. My colleague here will attend to you." With that, he vanished again.

"Rum sort," sniffed Percy, casting a mournful glance at Gaspard. "Anyway, I take it we won't need him?"

"That depends I suppose. What is it we won't be needing him for?"

"Well, I'm sure you can tell by my body language." He paused and chuckled bitterly. "Or at least my demeanour, that I am little thrilled at the moment. It was all an accident you know," another bitter chuckle, "the running away I mean. I really didn't know I was dead at first and then, well it all seemed a bit of fun trying to outwit you. Now though, I'm beginning to see the downside."

Gaspard murmured a knowing sort of murmur without actually saying anything, thinking it better that Percy be permitted to get it all out of system without prompting. Anyway, he needed the break for his heart to stop racing after Death's recent little shock to his system. "The work isn't satisfying any more you know," Percival sniffled. "Can't actually make anything and there's a hopeless git on my machine. It makes me furious watching his sloppy work and there's nothing I can bloody do about it."

He looked up with a hopeful expression. "I don't suppose you could arrange for me to haunt him? That would be something I could really get my teeth into. He deserves to suffer." Gaspard shook his head sadly. "Thought not. So, there's all that but it's far from the worst. If it were just the job, I might adjust, you know. I was beginning to be able to move little things about. Once I even managed to change the setting on the machine so that the new git buggered up a whole batch. Almost had him sacked." Percy cackled evilly at the memory and Gaspard was beginning to feel a little less sympathetic towards him.

"But there's the house. I find myself there every day whether I want to be there or not. I'm locked in to the same ritual day after day. My sister's rented the house to the local council while my will is being settled and they've let it as low-cost housing for the needy. Needn't be a problem you might say. Sharing the place with some poor old geezers short of a crust. If only that were the case.

Single mother, five kids, all under eight years old. I can't tell you the bleeding racket. All hours of the night it goes on, squabbling, screeching, crying, bed wetting. And the noses. My God you've never seen so much bloody phlegm. Dirty nappies of course. Then she has her thuggish boyfriend over; do you know he even has tattoos? Then there's more yelling and squawking."

He stopped suddenly, gazing pathetically into Gaspard's eyes. "I need to be really dead. I'm ready to go with you," he slumped.

Belatedly, Gaspard realised the real reason why Mort had decided not to stick around. He wondered whether it would be a plus or a minus if Percy could see him blush. "Well Percy, I'm really so sorry for all your troubles and I know they're not your fault. It's really quite common for folk of your, er, degree of commitment to not realise they've passed. As for your present situation, it really sounds horrible and for that I'm truly sorry. More so as…umm…I'm afraid that for the moment I can do nothing to help."

He reflexively stepped back a pace as though Pargeter might take a swing at him, before pulling himself up to his full height in a last-minute attempt to restore some lost dignity. He hurried on. "You see, there's an implement I need in order to fulfil your wish and I'm afraid…well…I'm afraid it's broken."

He held his hands forth despairingly. "I'm really sorry, Mort tells me it'll be fixed soon."

"You've got to be joking. I thought you pair were sort of bloody demigods or something. How the hell could you have broken implements? This is outrageous, I shall complain to the appropriate authorities." Percival was positively vibrating with rage. He was about to continue his tirade but then came to the realisation that he had absolutely no idea who the appropriate authorities were. He could hardly write a letter to God, or rather he could but the postage would be exorbitant.

"Er, who are the appropriate authorities by the way? Just for further reference of course," he added slyly.

"Well, just between the two of us Percival, that is the problem," volunteered Gaspard unwisely. "I'm not at liberty to say too much but let's just say that the whole shebang is in the hands of something very like the civil service." He shrugged helplessly, only too aware that once again he'd opened his big trap.

"Then I'm totally buggered, that's what you're saying?" Percy said, his shoulders slumping resignedly.

"In a nutshell, yes. On the other hand, I'm told that the implement…alright, my garden shears, let's call a spade a spade as ridiculous as that is, have been repaired but are missing in transit. So maybe your present misery may be short lived. Yet, going on past performance I have to be honest with you and say that if I were you, I wouldn't hold my breath. Rest assured though that I'll do everything I can." Bugger his native candour.

"Far be it from me to correct someone of your exalted status but don't you think that advising the dead to hold their breath might be the ultimate in useless bleeding advice? Perhaps just a little redundant?" Percy enquired with no little degree of asperity. Pargeter was silent for a brief moment, apparently distracted or wrestling with some conundrum or something of great import.

At length, he asked, "Umm, is that an alligator on your robe?" Gaspard jumped as though he'd been hit by a cattle prod. He was about to spit out a pithy rebuke but then sighed and nodded despairingly. "It's either that or a crocodile, I really don't know anything about fashion."

"Obviously," responded Percy rudely. "Then, I clearly don't either because I had no idea the fashion trade designed for the afterlife. I mean it doesn't make sense. As far as I can see they generally come up with designs nobody would be seen dead in." He chortled in a self-satisfied way, clearly pleased with his joke.

"I'm sure you won't be surprised when I tell you it was organised by our admin. They said it was either this or Tommy Hilfiger," the probationary collector of souls, aka Gaspard sighed despairingly. "They're not originals."

"Ye gods! Am I making a mistake? I mean…God and his angels, yes, I was rather looking forward to that but some jumped up bunch of bloody clerks running the show and handing out fashion knock offs? It sounds more like hell than heaven."

"It does I know, put that way, but that's just admin, it's not something you'd be involved with. I'm sure your afterlife will be pleasant and free from strife."

"Well…if you say so…I suppose you'd know. You do know, don't you?" Percy queried suspiciously. "I mean you said a while ago the whole thing was in their hands."

"No, no, just the admin side. You'll be taken to the bosom of the…" in his desperation Gaspard had plumbed the depths of his subconscious and taken his cue from the 'in memoriam' pages of the local press and was about to say Lord. He was now in a fine mess. "Ah, the bosom of…of creation, the bosom of all life, of…"

"That doesn't sound too genuine to me if you don't mind my saying so. Here am I committing myself to you totally and your waffling on about spending eternity with a great tit. I mean, am I doing the right thing or not?"

"Of course, of course, take my word for it, you won't regret it. After all, you've never heard any complaints, have you?" Gaspard said desperately with an unconvincing forced chuckle. He was feeling unutterably guilty knowing that he was being about as straightforward as a shonky salesman. In earlier times, Percy would no doubt have put up a spirited argument but he was thoroughly defeated by his present circumstances and Gaspard was able to mollify his client with visions of being able to make life misery for his replacement while awaiting his being taken up. They parted on reasonably amicable terms after Gaspard promised, somewhat recklessly given past performances, that his implement would soon be available and that Percy would soon be enjoying his death.

"I don't like it, doc," grumbled Maud. "That little bastard is up to something. Getting in a priest indeed." She adopted a vicious impersonation of Gaspard. "Oh, poor little me, all stressed out by these terrible spirits. Help me father. As if. You know what he's up to don't you? He wants a bloody exorcism. Well, I've got news for him."

"Now, now, Maud. Don't you think you're being hard on the boy? After all, we did make things difficult for him occasionally. Especially when that other copper turned up. I know he entered into the spirit of it after a while but I rather think he's regretting that by now."

"He's up to something I'm sure of it," growled Maud, unconvinced. "When he gets back, I'm going to give him a good bloody seeing to."

"Well, I wouldn't worry about it anyway. If they sent someone like the last bible basher, he'd be out the door and shitting his pants a minute after he turned up. Just shove another chess piece up his nose. I thought using the bishop was an act of genius."

They both dissolved into mirth. "Better yet," spluttered Maud eventually, "I'll shove a real bishop up his nose."

When the mirth had eventually subsided, Maud sniffed the air suspiciously. "Smell that?"

"Smell what?"

"Can't you notice it. It smells like swimming pools. Don't tell me he's managed to sneak in without us noticing?" Maud crept warily to Gaspard's bedroom door and cautiously put her head into his room. She withdrew a lot more hastily emitting a stifled shriek.

"What is, it, Maud?" Queried the doctor, alarmed.

"It's that other one. The little bugger." She suddenly looked puzzled. "At least, I think it is. Hard to tell with skellingtons. His robe's different. It's got a bloody alligator on it like them poncy shirts the blokes wear. Hope the bloody thing craps in his armpit."

"I see what you mean by the smell," whispered the doctor as the pair, deciding that discretion was definitely called for, disappeared, "definitely swimming pools."

In the next room, Gaspard sat upon his bed concerned at having yet again made an involuntarily detour on his way home. At least, this time it had been the local pub which under the circumstances…

Sergeant Hardcastle was one of the old school of coppers. The type that felt that the word 'force' on the end of 'police force' had been put there for a very obvious reason. Although it was frowned upon these days, he had in the past delivered swift justice to the odd little neighbourhood toenail by means of fists and boots around the back of the local and was firmly convinced that in their heart of hearts the miscreants were appreciative of the summary punishment that saved the inconvenience of court appointments.

And who wouldn't settle for a short spell in intensive care if it meant avoiding a stretch in the Scrubs? If the crim gave as good as he got then that was all part of the job and Hardcastle had accepted the scars as part of his chosen profession. In other words, he was a hard bastard. It really messed with his head therefore that this little shit Feeblebunny was engaged in something that seemed to turn the sergeant's knees to jelly.

6

"So, Gaspard, how are we feeling after our break?" queried Dr Coombs in the time-honoured timbre and insincerity of his profession.

"Well, sir, judging by the way you look and the way I feel, I'd say we're both hunky dory sir," shot back Gaspard lightly, in an attempt to sound just that. He prayed that he'd carried it off. Coombs forced a chuckle at the unoriginal response, thinking as he did so that if he really looked as he felt then he'd frighten children, the elderly and horses. If he didn't get away from all these loonies pretty soon, he'd end up barking mad himself. Why had no one told him that the profession of psychiatry was an open door to self-medication? "Good, good. So, am I to suppose that the rest and medication have done the trick? No more…er…phantoms, wasn't it?"

"Yes sir. It was the stress sir but things are definitely on the right track." He paused, struggling with the fact that he was about to grass on a fellow officer, albeit a thoroughly unpleasant one. "Although…"

"Although?"

"Well doctor, I don't like to snitch but…well…I don't think that Professional Standards are going to take things lying down sir. I…er…um…had a visit at home from Sergeant Hardcastle. He was behaving very strangely."

"Really? And this was after our last meeting?" Coombs scribbled a note on his pad.

"Yes sir."

"You say, strangely. How so?"

"Mm, he began accusing me of…well, I don't know what, to be frank doctor. I'd been playing a game of Monopoly with friends and he seemed to become obsessed with the board and screaming that weird and unnatural things were occurring. He claimed that he could see the pieces moving of their own volition. I tried to calm him but he eventually ran out of flat and…well…if I'm to be perfectly frank sir…sort of jabbering." Gaspard had grassed so he might as well do it right.

"Really? That extreme? And you have no idea what may have set him off?"

"None at all. He started out being quite aggressive but then when he saw the Monopoly board, he just lost it."

"Understandable in some ways I suppose," said Coombs light-heartedly, "I've been forced to play myself on occasion." He forced a chuckle to indicate his little joke. "Seriously though Gaspard, you don't think that this incident may have set you back at all?"

"No, no sir," responded Gaspard hurriedly. "I'll admit that at the time it was quite stressful but I followed some of the stress relief techniques outlined in the pamphlet you gave me and they were most helpful. I only wish that I'd been able to share them with poor Hardcastle. I'm sure he could benefit from something of the sort." That last was probably putting in the boot but it was a case of 'him or me' and if he were frank with himself, he was beginning to enjoy getting one over on his nemesis.

We all have our dark side. Gaspard thought it best not to share that his real stress relief technique had been to throw away his pills and drink himself into a state of floor hugging inebriation. As a long-term method, it left a bit to be desired but humans are adaptable creatures and he was already beginning to accept his situation. A species that can survive rap, hip hop, reality television and so-called social media has already shown the ability to deal with anything up to and including the apocalypse, so his present situation just needed a bit of getting used to.

Accordingly, his drinking was becoming more that of an enthusiastic amateur than a seasoned professional and he was well on his way to becoming an also ran, recent detours notwithstanding. The session ran pretty much the way that Gaspard had envisioned and at its climax, Dr Coombs was more than happy to release him to light desk duty for another two week period on reduced medication. It was unfortunate for Hardcastle that he was in the waiting room as Gaspard left the doctor's office.

His first reaction was to snarl like a pit-bull at the first sight of the man that was making his life a misery but as Gaspard neared, he whimpered pitifully and cringed against the wall. Gaspard gave him a cheery greeting in passing, mainly for the benefit of the psychiatrist watching from his doorway but partly from a sense of guilt. It was also an act of monumental hypocrisy.

"So, Sergeant Hardcastle, I assume you know why you're here?" Coombs folded his hands in the approved medical manner and peered over the top of his conjoined fingers, his spectacles sitting in their best inquisitorial position on the end of his nose. He couldn't see a bloody thing that way but he was convinced it gave him an aura of wisdom and perspicacity. Most patients thought it made him look like a short-sighted old fart.

"Not exactly, doc," rasped Hardcastle, still shaken at being confronted by the man he thought of as 'that bastard Feeblebunny' and wielder of supernatural powers, "the super instructed me to attend but why exactly, I've no idea. He muttered some crap about being concerned at my mental state. Total bollocks of course. I've never been better."

He tried to summon an attitude of healthy cynicism of the type reasonably to be expected by one wronged by his superiors but succeeded only in giving the impression of one bearing an unhealthy grudge.

"I see. Fish should have perhaps ensured that you were clear as to the reasons for his concern. I'm really quite surprised he didn't, Fish is usually very good when the chips are down. It appears, sergeant, that not just the super but many of your colleagues have been concerned about you. It has been noted that you have undergone radical physical changes including severe and sudden …weight loss…"

"Been on a diet," interjected Hardcastle with a surly air. The doctor continued on, unperturbed, "hair loss and tremors. I have been informed that the departmental physician can find no medical reason for that decline which is why I have been brought in. Of further concern is what some have characterised as an obsession with one of your colleagues. Any comment on that latter observation?"

Coombs rested his chin on his steepled fingers and waited for a reply.

"Ah…no idea, doc," Hardcastle replied, managing to keep his voice even only with great effort. One eye was twitching madly which let the side down a bit.

"No? Perhaps if I were to mention that the colleague concerned is the one that appeared to have disturbed you in the waiting room a moment ago?"

"Feeblebunny!" Hardcastle screeched, almost leaping from his seat in agitation. "No," he continued, in a voice that sounded a little like a leaky whoopee cushion, while hastily regaining his seated posture and desperately attempting to control himself, "no, not all. Um, perhaps they, whoever they may be, have simply misread my commitment to my investigation into what I believe may be improprieties concerning that…ah…officer."

He may have carried it off with a less canny professional but the fact that he followed up this reasonable sounding defence by suddenly pounding the desk and shouting, "bastard!" sort of gave the game away. His eyes began to bulge and his body shook as he fought to control himself.

"I see. Um…was it simply professional commitment that took you to his flat after being told to drop your investigations?"

"So, the little turd…sorry…the constable has mentioned that, has he. I was just tying up loose ends sir," the voice was letting him down and his hands were beginning to shake. He dropped them beneath the level of the desk top, although he was further betrayed when the corner of his mouth began to spasm. "I see. And perhaps looking for a game of Monopoly?" The last query was not according to the psychiatrist's play book but it was worth the hazard, or so he thought at the time.

"Mon…op…?" moaned Hardcastle, unable to finish the word. His head twitched a couple of times before dropping strangely to one side. His eyes bulged alarmingly as he fell into a state of near catatonia. He began to drool slightly, his eyes staring fixedly into space. "Oh, shit" cursed Coombs, reaching for his phone.

"Nurse, a patient for you. Best come quickly…oh and bring a couple of burly constables with you. They may be needed." He drummed his fingers on the desk in thought, "and you'd best have the wheel chair with the restraints. Ready the cot too of course. I'll pop down once he's strapped in and give him a shot."

The bloody lift was out of order again and Gaspard was puffing furiously by the time he reached his floor. Thank heavens he wasn't due a fitness test any time soon. He leant against the wall for a while to recover, still sucking in the big ones as the sports commentators would say and couldn't help thinking that the new robe was going to be a godsend, even with the detour glitch. No more trudging, stair climbing and traffic jams. If only he could use it all the time. What a boon to a copper that would be. Instantly arriving at the scene—'you're nicked mate'. Aaaah! He'd be Feeblebunny of the yard in no time. Of course, he'd have to be careful that it didn't reduce his fitness level.

There still existed unwanted memories of his school days when in his early teens he had been dubbed gasp-hard by his sports master. A name taken up eagerly by his class mates who in the way of teens everywhere had made his life a bloody misery for a while. A long while. Even that memory could do nothing to dull his spirits however. After all, he was going back to work and work, unless he was severely mistaken, without the unwelcome attention of a certain sergeant. He began to whistle cheerfully as he strolled towards his door, still entertaining thoughts of terrorising villains.

Being of a generally kindly disposition he may not have been quite so cheerful had he known of Hardcastle's immediate problems. Although that was probably debatable. He burst through his front door with a cheery cry of, "hi kids, I'm home!" and was brought to an immediate halt with a concomitant plunge of his good humour by the sight of Maud and the doctor standing, or at least hovering, immediately inside the door and looking decidedly miffed. When Maud was miffed, and that was most of the time, it was time to duck in the general direction of out.

This particular miff however, had all the makings of a category ten which meant that he may well be caught up before he had a chance to run for it. "Oh…hi Maud, hi doc" he offered uncertainly, readying himself to select reverse.

"What's that other bastard doing here," hissed Maud even before Gaspard had finished his feeble greeting. "What? Who?"

"You know who, the other one."

"Umm, the one with the…you know…scythe?"

"Not him, the little shit, the one with the bloody lizard on his outfit. Smells like a swimming pool." Gaspard was momentarily stumped. It was pretty obvious that Maud had meant him in his other form but how could that be? The only logical explanation was that the pair had been in hiding when he had left for his interview with the psychiatrist. "He's here? I didn't know."

"I don't care whether you knew or not, get him out. Whenever he's here the other one is never far away. Plus, he gives me the creeps." Maud was gesturing angrily towards the door to Gaspard's bedroom. "Right. I'll sort him, turning up and scaring my friends." It hadn't taken long for Gaspard to realise that this was a blessing, even though he was a bit hurt at having been categorised as a creep.

As far as the ghosts were concerned, he and the Collector were now definitely two different entities. He stormed towards the door then held up a steadying hand. "You'd best stay back," he warned, "you never know how he may react." Gaspard flung open the door bellowing at the non-existent visitor to leave and hastily closing the door behind him. "What are you doing here?" he shouted angrily. "I didn't invite you, get out, you're frightening my friends."

Then in an attempt to put the tin lid on the exercise he roared: "Be gone foul fiend." The last time anyone had overegged a pudding to this extent was when Escoffier had experimented with his super souffle and blown up the oven.

In an attempt to recover credibility, he added: "Please." He turned to see a head peeking cautiously through the door. No prizes for guessing it was Maud. Gaspard jumped. "For Christ's sake Maud, please don't do that, you frightened the crap out of me. Anyway, I thought we'd agreed that you'd respect my privacy."

"Sorry Gaspard," she responded in an uncharacteristic show of remorse, "it won't happen again." She appeared to struggle for a while before uttering the next words that came close to choking her. "Thank you."

Maud being Maud, could never sustain the contrition for long. So, while Gaspard was seated on his bed having a joint celebratory and nerve settling glass of mother's ruin, she was reverting to her mean spirited and suspicious self. "You know Ivor, that business just now all seemed quite good on the face of it but now that I think about it, we still didn't see them together. We've never seen them together. One leaves, the other arrives."

"We did hear him though, Maud."

"But we heard no replies, did we? And that 'be gone foul fiend', I mean...please. There's something not quite right about all this."

"Surely you're not saying that they're one and the same? After all, you've known him for years before he could see you and you never saw anything that'd suggest he was the other one. I mean, it's a bit ridiculous to even contemplate surely. A local copper turning into...well...whatever it is."

"I certainly saw some things I'd rather not think about but that, no. Anyway, that's as maybe," sniffed Maud, "but the bony bastard was never hanging around before. "Everything has changed since he turned up. Gaspard may be no superman but I'm no Lois Lane either. Nobody pulls the wool over these eyes. I'm keeping a closer watch on him from now on."

Doctor Smallpiece (who by the way was in full agreement that she was no Lois Lane) was about to put up a further argument when he recollected a small detail that gave him pause. "You know Maud, now that I think of it, I'm sure I heard his toilet flush the other night when Napoleon was supposed to be there. Why would a skeleton need the loo?"

There was no sign of the shears being delivered over the coming weeks and Death was keeping his distance, no doubt out of embarrassment. Although Gaspard was still not sold on his involuntary role as the Collector, he still felt a minor obligation towards Percy Pargeter, who was still hanging about, more alone and miserable than ever.

Percy had never been a social type but in a weird sort of way he had enjoyed being in the presence of others so that he could ignore them. It probably wasn't completely correct to say that he was lonely but it was close enough, considering that the English language didn't have a word for what he was feeling. It was probably only those parts of the psychiatric profession that dealt with aberrant social behaviour that had a word or words to adequately describe Percy's character at all. The rest of us had to make do with 'miserable bastard'.

Gaspard waited until he could hear his unwelcome guests talking in what was now the TV room before removing his robe from its hiding place. He made sure that the bickering over the choice of programme was at its height before donning the garment and imagining the carpark at Percy's place of employment. To his amazement, there was no detour of a concerning nature but he did find himself for a while at the local supermarket where he made the best of things and picked up a supply of toilet rolls and some extra chocolate Hobnobs just in case.

"Hello again Gaspard, how's it hanging? Oh, yes, sorry, silly of me." Percy could never be accused of being overly sensitive as his snigger ably demonstrated. "So, still no news I take it?" There was no trace of hope in the enquiry.

"Sorry Percy. I've not seen hide nor hair of Mort for ages. It can't be much longer."

"If you're waiting to see hide or hair, you'll be waiting a bloody long time," said Percy, always happy to state the bleeding obvious. "And you've said that the last few times. Anyway, at least it's giving me time to develop my powers. You should see what I can do now. That bugger at home is on the verge of having himself committed. When he's not looking, I move things that he has to hand. Put them in the fridge, in the kid's doll's house, things like that. Sometimes I levitate the TV remote when no one else can see. It's quite fun." The tone of Percy's voice was anything but amused but that was Percy after all.

"Isn't that a bit, well, I hesitate to say mean…but mean."

"He's a nasty piece of work," shot back Percy self-righteously. "He puts his feet on the coffee table."

"You're not having second thoughts, are you?" Gaspard asked rather timidly, always concerned that the delays would scotch the whole deal. He didn't worry for himself but he did worry about the sort of havoc that Pargeter could wreak if forced to stay around forever.

"No, no. Even though I'm keeping myself amused and doing good work sorting out some of those who deserve it, I can't imagine spending eternity that way. I'm ready whenever you are."

Even in the after-life people's characters stay true to form, so it never took long before Percy was fed up with company. That suited Gaspard fine because he could never think of anything to say in any case but felt obligated to keep in touch. "See you later then. Keep up the good work," said Gaspard, knowing that the sarcasm would be lost on Percy.

"My oath," replied Percy cheerily, or at least less morosely than usual. "You should see what I have in store for that shit on my machine tonight. If he's not sacked within the week, I'm a horse's arse."

"He's a horse's arse either way," thought Gaspard as he took his leave. Finding himself again in the supermarket, Gaspard decided he may as well make the best of a bad lot and pick up a few extra items. After all, his subconscious had brought him here so he must need things. He picked up some more essentials, a bottle of single malt. Let's make that two, after all he would pay for them later. How, he was not quite sure. A packet of frozen fish fingers; he was a bit peckish and on a sudden and rather bizarre whim; a packet of condoms.

He had absolutely no chance of ever putting them to use the way his life was proceeding but he was always embarrassed to purchase them, so why not? To save any future mental discomfort he selected the giant pack. Talk about wishful thinking. For a while, he browsed the aisles, picking up the odd minor item and completely lost in the sensation of freedom he was experiencing. So lost was he in fact that he saw no need to go to the trouble of remaining invisible. In an inexcusable lapse for a rozzer, he'd forgotten about the security cameras.

It was only when he was back in his room that he realised a load of shopping might be difficult to explain, it being the middle of the night.

He stashed the unperishable items and waited impatiently for the sound of bickering from the TV room. Fortunately, there was a haunted house movie marathon so the two ghosts were seated spellbound before the set occasionally calling out facetious remarks and frequently bursting into gales of laughter. When the coast was clear, he crept to the kitchen where he made a fish finger sandwich and a glass of warm milk. He left a generous portion of the glass empty to accommodate a belt of the single malt, its purpose being to act as a soporific. "What the hell are you doing up at this time of night?" Maud's head protruded through the connecting wall. "Don't you have work in the morning?"

Her voice wasn't exactly caring but it was as close as she was ever going to get. "Oh, hello Maud. Thanks for the concern but I was a bit peckish and I needed the milk to help me sleep. I'm going on to full duties tomorrow so I'm a bit excited as you can imagine."

"I can imagine a number of ways a young man can get excited in the middle of the night and not many of them agreeable to a lady like myself. I'll try to believe you mean about work." When it came to young men's ways, Maud may not be an expert but she'd had years of observing Gaspard, a thought that he continually fought to keep in the back of his mind. Maud was obviously still giving him some credit for his phoney intervention because she immediately apologised in a roundabout sort of way.

"Careful eating that this late, you'll get indigestion. And remember that warm milk makes you fart. Keep a window open." With that, she disappeared.

Gaspard heard the doctor's voice loud and clear. "Did I just hear you tell him that milk makes him fart?" He enquired in slightly shocked voice.

"Well it does," rejoined Maud aggressively. "I was only thinking of his comfort."

Somehow Gaspard was not surprised to find Mort sitting on his bed next to an open packet of Hobnobs and a generous glass of Glenfiddich.

"Hello, Mort. Make yourself at home."

"Now, now, no need for sarcasm. I just dropped by to offer you a belated congratulation on being cleared for duty. I hope you realise how much it hurts me to say that because it may well interfere with your duties on my behalf but I know how much it means to you, so congratulations. I'm happy that your happy."

"Thank you Mort, nice of you to say so. Have another Hob…oh you are. Well take as many as you like and enjoy." The silence hung heavy between them for a while until Gaspard finally worked up the nerve to ask the question that both knew had to be asked. "So, the…"

"Still not ready. Or not found more like. I have everybody going through the dead letter office at this very moment. Won't be long now I'm sure. And I'm sure you'll be pleased to know that I've commissioned a spare. It might take a while but at least when it arrives there should be no more problems like we've had to date."

"That's nice to know Mort but in the meantime we're stuck. I'm worried that Percy has started making mischief and even more worried that he may eventually change his mind. He's an unpleasant bugger and he's well capable of deciding that he has to crusade against everything he disapproves of, which is just about everything others don't."

"We are doing our best. I'm sure it won't be long now."

"That's what I have to keep telling Percy and you know what? It doesn't sound any more convincing when you say it. What I don't understand, is how an organisation which exists outside of time can take so bloody long." Gaspard was clearly exasperated.

"I know it's difficult to comprehend. After all, we operate in what to you is a heavenly plane, not subject to the rules of physics as humans understand them. A world where time is meaningless. Am I not correct? We're omniscient, omnipresent and too some extent omnipotent. Unfortunately when we deal with you; humans that is, we're still bound by some rules that work against you. So that even though events that occur in our world happen in the blink of an eye in your terms, it means that that blink can be a hundred years to you." He held up his hands helplessly. "Think of Einstein."

"Are you saying that I may never get the bloody things?" Gaspard asked incredulously, ignoring the Einstein reference because he hadn't the foggiest what Mort meant by it. He also had more than a slight suspicion that Mort didn't either and was using the Einstein reference to bamboozle him.

"Not at all, no. I told you it's hard to explain. Without wishing to sound patronising it's beyond you." He shrugged. "You'll just have to trust me."

"Just one more thing then Mort, if you don't mind an ignorant half-witted mortal asking what's no doubt a stupid bloody question?"

"Look, I didn't mean to imply anything…you know. Sorry if it came across like that. What's the question?"

"If you lot are…let me get it right, now…ah, yes…omniscient, omnipresent and omnipotent and exist outside of time…I have got that correct?"

"Umm, yes," responded Death warily. "Then why do you always make such a monumental cock up of everything? Or is that just part of the things we mortals could not understand?"

"Hi, Sarge, how are you feeling?" The greeting came simultaneously from constables Tweedle and Arkright, who despite the apparently caring nature of the enquiry, hoped that he felt as rotten as he looked. Impossible as that may seem to some. It might not have been a particularly humanitarian hope but then humanity and Sergeant Hardcastle had never really been on the best of terms. He was universally regarded as the worst type of bully who had no place in the modern police force, or if it came down to that, in the company of any species that walked upright and had opposable thumbs. Even his mother had once opined that he would have been more at home living in a time when males had names like Og and went around braining each with clubs, although she couldn't help adding that even then he would have been regarded as an overbearing sod.

The pair would have been only too happy to have kept their distance but they were mixed up in something weird that they knew was only being taken seriously by one man and that was the man lying restrained in the bed before them. It was unfortunate that his need to solve the mystery was based more on a personal vendetta than good policing but what the hell. That was life; or at least life for one poor bastard and as long as that poor bastard wasn't them they could live with it.

"Well, what do you twerps want? Come to see the evil professional standards sergeant tied down like some bloody loony?" He emitted what could only be described as a demonic growl. "If I ever find that bloody quack in a dark alley..."

The pair never discovered what would occur in the dark alley because Hardcastle became so overwhelmed with visions of castration and evisceration, not to mention unpleasant items being inserted in places only meant by nature to be exits that he began to froth at the mouth and quiver alarmingly. "Take it easy, Sarge," quavered an unsettled Tweedle. "We're following up on that request about Feeblebunny."

At the mention of the name, Hardcastle' right eye began to twitch madly. "Tell me," he eventually managed to wheeze out. "Tell me everything."

"Well, we don't have anything new on the incident with his car," at this Hardcastle growled horribly and thrashed against his restaints, "but!" shouted Tweedle, thoroughly terrified, "there's something new."

Hardcastle's eyes narrowed slyly and for just a moment ceased their wild twitching. "Cough it up," he rasped, "and you'd better not be buggering me about."

"OK, so a few days ago we had a report of a break-in at a supermarket. You probably know the one. It's the Park and Spend on Old Cobbler's Way."

"So bloody what, get on with it man," roared Hardcastle, "I don't care if it's bloody Chylde Harold's on Buggerer's Boulevard. What's it got to do with Feeblebunny?"

"Sorry, sorry, Sarge," blurted Tweedle, thoroughly cowed, "but if you let me finish, I think you'll find it might have everything to do with him." Hardcastle gave what may have been a conciliatory grunt, although later Arkwright swore that he'd broken wind. "Right, well, they had video of the break-in, yeah? I saw it. Bloody weird isn't the word. At first, all you could see was things lifting off shelves by themselves. At first glance, it seemed they were just falling off but then some of them went back. Levitating like. Then, after a while this figure suddenly appeared. Popped out of bloody nowhere and just like the one that old lady described. Mrs Threadneedle wasn't it mate?"

Arkwright nodded. "It looked like a bloke in one of them cowled robes, like monks wear yeah? So, at first, we just thought it was a disguise but I swear Sarge, the bloody thing walked right through a row of shelves. More than once."

Hardcastle froze, his eyes wide with excitement. "Go on," he rasped.

"That wasn't all, when he put his hand up to grab something it was just bloody bones. I know it sounds mad Sarge but it's all there on video, clear as crystal. He was just like the thing we've all been dreaming about since the last business."

"Tell him about the other thing," urged Arkwright. "Oh, yeah, well, the weirdest thing, right, was one of the things he took was a packet of rubber Johnnies. I mean, willies don't have bones do they Sarge? It's just an expression. Nobody can figure out how he'd use the bloody things."

"I think you'll find that speculation on that matter may prove unfruitful, constable. Let's stick to the bloody salient points, shall we?" Hardcastle growled, his eyes flashing dangerously. "Was there any surveillance of the car park? Any sign of his car?"

"Yeah there was, Sarge, but no car at all," said Arkwright butting in on seeing his partner struggling.

"Pity. The bastard's upping his game."

"Anyway Sarge, after we'd seen the video, we took a copy to that old lady Threadneedle and asked her if she recognised the…the thing. She almost had a stroke. Started screaming. 'That's him, that's him' she was squawkin' 'he's the

113

one that got out of the car and walked right through the door.' Took us a while to calm her I can tell you." He lifted his eyes to Hardcastle's with the sort of look that the family dog gives when it's expecting a 'good boy' and a pat.

"Oh, Feeblebunny, we've got you now," crooned Hardcastle in a seriously disturbing manner. "Tell me, that original incident did lead directly to that little shite's car did it not?"

"Uh huh."

"And correct me if I'm wrong but the supermarket that was done over would be the closest shop to his flat?"

"Just around the corner, Sarge." Hardcastle's eyes took on a lunatic gleam. So mad were they that both constables instinctively took a backward step.

"Alright, so here's what you do. You go back and do all the interviews again. Don't miss anybody and show them all the video. You've checked the timelines? No discrepancies?"

"None, Sarge."

"Right. Make 'em watch it a few times. With any luck if they see it enough, they might all 'remember' seeing him get out of the car. Not that it matters."

"Yeah, but Sarge, it's only circumstantial innit," said Tweedle unwisely, "I mean we know it's probably him but it wouldn't make it in court."

"In bloody court? What sort of puddin' brained nincompoop are you constable? You think we could go to the Crown with stories of ghosts and ghoulies? No, me bucko, this is for personal satisfaction only. And satisfaction we shall have. Starting with having him kicked off the force. The beaks may not be able to believe it but I rather think that Fish may see things our way and if not, there are ways. After that, we shall proceed to kicking his arse right royally." Here he chuckled so evilly that it made the blood of the two constables nearly freeze.

Arkwright who liked the occasional bit of culture found himself trying to remember the ghost's speech from Hamlet. Something about harrowing up souls, freezing blood and making hair to stand on end. He reckoned he had a fair idea how Hamlet might have felt if subjected to the ghost's story.

"Did you bring any stills from the surveillance camera?"

"Sure, Sarge," said Tweedle subserviently, hastily rummaging in his case. He held out a sheaf of stills giving the best and clearest angles. Hardcastle snarled. "Oh shit, sorry Sarge, forgot about the…you know."

"Of course I bloody know. I'm the one that's tied up like a Christmas Goose. Hold them up for me." Tweedle tried valiantly to hold them without shaking. "You didn't mention that constable."

"What, Sarge?"

"Did nobody notice the decoration on his robe? Are you all bloody incompetent?" Both constables glanced at the photo that Hardcastle had been examining.

"Oh, you mean that lizard on his chest? Yeah, we noticed that but it didn't seem important."

"Really?" enquired Hardcastle in what was instantly recognisable as a dangerously mild tone. "Let me tell you that it is bloody important and if you don't recognise that you should be mopping out khazis. That lizard is in fact an alligator, or maybe a crocodile, who the bloody hell cares. It is the logo of some bloody fashion ponce, who I suspect, would make few such garments. You will scour the city for outlets of his brand and ascertain who has bought such a garment recently. Do you understand?" The pair nodded abjectly. "Then piss off and get to work."

Tweedle and Arkwright fled the room to begin the wild goose chase that would put other matters on hold for a while and give Gaspard a little more time before the ultimate confrontation.

"Hello Sergeant Hardcastle, how are we today?" Nurse Winsome enquired with some difficulty, since Hardcastle had all the appearance of one suffering demonic possession. He was in fact, smiling, although she could be forgiven for her doubt since it wasn't an expression that sat naturally on his countenance. She held her breath half expecting him to reply in tongues.

"All the better for seeing you nurse," replied Hardcastle winningly, thoroughly buoyed by the recent news and contorting his face into a broader smile that made him look even more like a model that Bruegel would have killed for. Or perhaps a sitter for a gargoyle sculptor. "Wonderful. You sound much cheerier today." Nurse Winsome fussed about to avoid having to view that face any more than was strictly necessary.

"Marvellous what a visit from friends can do."

"So true. Now we have a nice surprise for you. Doctor said if your blood pressure is down and you take your medication without a fuss, we can take off those nasty restraints. He thinks you're over the worst of things, and another little surprise, because your private, we can lend you this tablet. It has all sorts of games on it if you're into that sort of thing. I think it has backgammon and solitaire and that sort of stuff. I think it even has online Monopoly."

Hardcastle's seizure was enough to bring the crash cart at pace although as Arkwright said, it couldn't have been a heart attack because for that to happen you first needed a heart. The restraints stayed pending Monopoly therapy and an increase in his medication.

Police stations are subject to rumour just like any other work place, particularly when it concerns one of their own being involved in something shady. Quite naturally none of the rumour concerning Gaspard had reached his ears but he didn't need to be omniscient to work out that he was being talked about. It was the whispered conversations that ceased on his approach and the furtive glances above all else that tipped him off. He was completely mystified until the day he heard of the mysterious supermarket break-in.

Only those close to the case knew just how mysterious but the rumour mill was cranking out wild speculation. At first, he told himself he was being paranoid, he could not have been seen. It wasn't exactly a rare occurrence in the area; this despite the constant surmise indicating that it was far from the usual snatch and grab. It was only when Theodore Scuttle was brought in by officer's investigating the case that he began to worry. At first, he could not place Scuttle's face. He knew him vaguely from somewhere but was unable to say where or in what context. He may well have dismissed the sighting had not a colleague rustled a crisp packet as Theodore was leaving and enabled Gaspard to place him as Doctor Smallpiece's unwitting landlord.

He ran various scenarios through his mind in an attempt to ascertain the potential danger to himself but could see no way in which he might be in peril of discovery. Scuttle had clearly not seen him on the night he had visited the doctor and even if the worst had happened and he'd been captured on camera at the supermarket, there was absolutely no way he could be identified. Could there? Why then, had the investigating team linked the two incidents as they apparently had? Had the robe failed? He thought not. Had he been caught in his human form he would have been immediately questioned. Had he been seen as the Collector, that was too bad but hardly a disaster.

No one could possibly link him with his skeletal other form. All he had to do was to keep schtum, act normal and if necessary, deny everything. It was then he heard that the first constables on the scene were visiting Hardcastle.

"Come on, chin up Gaspard. It's not as bad as all that. It's the weekend. Take it easy, have a couple of drinks, watch some TV."

"I can't relax Mort, you don't know Hardcastle. He's got it in for me and he won't give up. He'll just keep worrying away like a pitbull until he's either won or he's dead and frankly I'm not sure even being dead would stop him."

"Well, if he's worrying, there's no sense you both doing it," chuckled Mort. "The test match is on, why don't you put your feet up and watch a bit of cricket. Do you good. Unless the Aussie quicks are on form of course and then you may have even more to feel miserable about." He gave Gaspard a playful poke in the ribs.

"You follow cricket?"

"Naturally. I shouldn't say this I suppose but you know that some people call it the game played in heaven? Well…nudge, nudge, wink, wink."

"You have to be joking?" Gaspard replied disbelievingly.

"I haven't said anything," said Mort innocently, "but let's just say that if we did, you wouldn't have to worry about copping one in the cobblers. Now, why don't you grab a glass of something relaxing and turn on the telly."

Gaspard slumped. "It's no good Mort. They won't let me. They say I gave it to them and they can watch what they want."

"But surely they'd want to watch the test. I mean it's the Ashes. They're two all! This is the decider!"

"You'd think eh? At least the doctor anyway. Maud's addicted to soaps. She doesn't enjoy them mind. Just likes to make rude comments. Anyway, when I mentioned it to doc he said that watching cricket was the only activity that would make eternity seem brief by comparison. He was quite cutting."

"Phillistine. Bet if he watches any sport it's something like basketball. Anyway, probably best you don't mention about my little hint then. The thought of spending eternity with W.G.Grace might put him off a trifle. To be frank spending five minutes with him would put most off. He can be very difficult. Just between you and me I'm surprised he didn't do a runner when I turned up. He doesn't like being told he's out." He shook his head despairingly. "Tell you what, why don't you slip on the robe and we can whip down to that sports bar off the High Street? I've got an appointment there in about half an hour anyway."

"They'd been watching the match for twenty minutes or so, with Death playfully pinching drinks when nobody was watching, thereby causing not only confusion but deep suspicion between the patrons, when he nudged Gaspard and pointed to an individulal at the bar." "See that chubby cove over there? The one on his third bag of pork scratchings? I have to go and say hullo in a minute. What's the bet I'll miss a wicket. Never bloody fails."

He moved across to the man who suddenly sat bolt upright, pointed at Death with bulging eyes, shrieked and dropped to the floor.

"Jesus you gave me a bloody fright. Where the hell did you get that costume?"

"Well, not there I can assure you. Are you ready?"

"Ready for what"

"Please look down." The spirit looked down and quickly looked up again with a crestfallen expression. "That's…shit."

"Yes but don't feel bad. It happens quite often. Nobody will think less of you for it."

"No, I mean…I'm dead." He thought for a moment. "Doesn't feel any different."

"You're not used to it yet. I won't spoil the surprises for you. Are you ready?"

"I suppose. Not much point hanging about. Don't suppose I could have a last bag of Porkies?"

"No. I'm being kind. Think what they just did to you."

"OK, what do I do?"

"Just follow me." Death waved at Gaspard. "Back in a sec. There'll be a wicket just you wait."

"There's two of you?"

"My apprentice."

"Really? I don't suppose you have any other openings?"

"Sorry." It was an instant later that Death was again seated beside Gaspard. "Well?"

"Smith run out for 114. His mate ballsed up the run."

"Tosser. Bet wassaname will cop it in the sheds. Bloody told you didn't I?" A little while later they were standing in the street outside the pub having decided to leave before the violence became too pronounced. Death's sneaking of drinks may have been a bit of fun for him but for the bunch of inebriates that frequented the place it was deadly. They began a liesurely stroll up the High Street just as the first police car arrived. Shouts of 'the bastard stole my drink' and the like were fading into the background as they rounded the corner into Gaspard's street.

Death stopped suddenly and placed a bony hand on Gaspard's shoulder. "Look, I've been thinking. If you're so worried about this Hardcastle and what he's found out, why don't you just nip down to the station tonight and take a look at the files. If you don't like what you see, you can always nick the evidence." It seemed like a good idea at the time. The station was quiet at this time of night which was a mild surprise because one could usually count on the area's young folk being well into their end of week drunk and disorderly training.

Most of the station's weekend complement were on patrol anyway, awaiting the inevitable calls to deal with drunken brawls and legless young ladies, that latter description being more behaviour than anatomical specific, so there was only a skeleton staff about the place.

One of the skeletons was Gaspard, although he wasn't officially rostered on. He really didn't need to be too careful as long as he remembered to remain invisible and not go opening doors out of force of habit. The force of his habit made doors unnecessary because it enabled him to simply walk through things. One of the things he walked through was Constable Maypole who had upset Gaspard a week or two back. It was perhaps a silly thing to do but there were no consequences, the constable merely remarking that it was suddenly chilly. The nightmares would come later. Gaspard had no problem finding the evidence files.

On the file relating to the supposed supermarket break-in, a senior officer had appended a memo: "Clearly a hoax. No sign of forced entry. Skeletal figures walking through walls. Either this is the first real proof of an after life or someone is pissing us about. Possible case for wasting our time but otherwise no further action. 'See me'. A perusal of Theodore Scuttle's file proved that he knew absolutely nothing about anything and was not worth worrying about. Agnes Threadneedle's was annotated to the effect that she had been undergoing psychiatric treatment since first claiming that she had seen a cowled figure walk through a door and was clearly not a credible witness.

The other witnesses' files held nothing new and certainly nothing that could tie Gaspard to actionable activities. The same senior officer as had commented on the supermarket case had scribbled a note which read: 'The link between this event and the supposed break-in at Park and Spend is tenuous at best. The only common thread is the mysterious figure and for that we have to rely on the word of a mad old bat.'

Gaspard breathed a sigh of relief. It was followed by a quick intake as he read on. 'Despite the foregoing, it is apparent that someone has been wasting police time with an elaborate hoax. I have viewed the footage from the patrol vehicle attending the supposedly driverless vehicle on the night in question and have concluded there is reason to consider investigating the waste of our resources. It would appear that in this instance Constable Feeblebunny must be interviewed to ascertain how his vehicle was involved. See me.' The conversation between the senior officer; DSI Hannibal Forcemeat and the officer in charge of the case, DC Oscar Kindervater, had already taken place, though of course Gaspard was not to be aware of that.

"I've been reviewing the case Detective Constable and clearly there is no point in proceeding with the investigation into the supermarket thefts. No sign of forced entry, only a few quids' worth of stock taken, if indeed it was taken and what would seem to be a doctored surveillance video. What do you think?"

"I agree sir," responded the DC, always happy to have official sanction for doing bugger all.

"Excellent. More seriously there's the question of wasting police resources. In the case of the supermarket, I can only conclude that it has to be an inside job. We could go after the culprit but it's likely to waste even more time and will probably prove inconclusive. Your opinion?"

"I think your right sir. We'd have to interview all the staff, about eighty or so mainly part timers on different shifts. Trace their movements. A massive job out of all proportion to the offence sir. There's also the possibility that the system was hacked and that's a real can of worms."

"Right. We're agreed. No further action. More concerning however is this business with the driverless vehicle, in that it in may involve a member of the force. Feeblebunny is it?" Kindervater nodded. "Not…I don't know…Philby or something?" Kindervater shook his head. "As spelled sir."

"Christ, what sort of name is that," marvelled Forcemeat, before continuing, "I've seen the patrol car footage and there definitely does not appear to be a driver, but Sergeant Watt is later seen in conversation with someone, so perhaps just a trick of the light or something? I've had a word with him and he remembers very little, only that he spoke to a very nice chap who was into hedge trimming of all things."

The DSI shook his head as though the information was hard to process. "A topiarist sir," said The DC, unable to resist showing off.

"Quite so," shot back Forcemeat, glaring at the DC and making a mental note to keep on eye on this cleverdick. "Anyway, even though the car did belong to wassisname, he does not seem to have been the driver. It all seems to be some colossal balls up but I suppose it may be worth speaking to…ah…the owner, and finding out who had his car that night, etc, etc." He waved a hand vaguely about, trusting the DC to get on with it.

"Yes, sir. Sergeant Hardcastle has been following up sir."

"Really? Professional Standards. Isn't that a little over the top?"

"He's got a bit of bee in his bonnet about the constable sir. Seems to think there may be more to it."

"Oh, well, I suppose he knows what he's doing. Have him fill you in, will you? I suppose since action's already underway there's no need you troubling yourself further. Just pass anything you have on to him." The DSI sounded relieved. Another irksome chore palmed off.

"One thing though sir, Hardcastle is, as they say, hors de combat, sir. Presently in the psych ward. Some sort of nervous breadown. I believe it has something to do with Feeblebunny sir," said the DC smugly, always happy to have one up on the boss.

"Good lord, really?"

"Mmm, the lads say he was muttering something about ghosts and telekinesis sir. That's when he wasn't screaming. He also seems to have developed an intense dread of Monopoly sir. Doctors think he may be off for some time"

"The screaming and muttering sounds serious, poor blighter but at least the dread of Monopoly indicates he still maintains some degree of sanity, what? Still, one of the hazards of the job eh," he enquired jovially. "Well, on the face of it there's nothing serious to worry about. Not unless you're Hardcastle, of course. Nothing that can't await his return to duty."

"No, sir."

Had Gaspard been privy to that conversation he would have been a lot happier. Instead he was in the privy, seated on the commode where these days he did most of his thinking, it being about the only place he felt sure Maud wouldn't intrude. He was fairly sure that the supermarket fiasco was a non-starter and even that he was fairly safe on the other business but it never did to be too casual about this sort of thing. Particularly as his career was involved. It didn't take too much of an odour before one's name began to really stink. Perhaps if

Agnes were a little less sure? Perhaps if the others were to begin to doubt their memory? It had been a while after all and in circumstances such as this it was only natural for people to begin to question their recollections.

Maybe he should just a have word. Plant a seed of doubt just in case. It couldn't hurt, could it? With passage of time the men had begun to doubt the evidence of their eyes. After all, it was an absurd propostion. It took only a little gentle questioning to have them begin to throw in the maybe's and possibly's. A chance remark, instantly regretted by Gaspard followed by a 'please forget I said that', concerning Sergeant Hardcastle's parlous mental state was then enough to have the gentlemen seriously wondering whether they might also end up wearing coats with funny sleeves if they persisted in their certainty. Job done.

He had the feeling that Agnes would be another case entirely. She was but not for the reasons that he'd imagined. In the event, Mrs Threadneedle didn't need a lot of persuasion to, if not change her story then to express doubts. She had recently begun to worry about how her psychiatrist may view her sticking to the original tale and it only took a remark from Gaspard that he would no doubt be called for the defence in any possible court case that had her backtracking faster than an escapee trying to confuse the hounds. There was another reason that Gaspard could not be aware of presently and that was that Agnes had begun to wonder just how wise it was to become entangled with the forces of law and order, or at least the forces of law, when her husband's corporeal remains were currently residing in a space under the floor boards, although since he'd been dead for some time they were now taking a lot less space than originally.

The rest of him, that being the non-corporeal part, was at the time of Gaspard's visit, sittting on the couch trying to frighten the cat. It was luck for Agnes that her psychic powers were not attuned to her late husband except for sometimes experiencing some odd feeling in his presence. Or non-presence depending on how you look at it. It was bad luck for her husband who had done a runner from Mort in the hope of torturing his late wife for eternity but who'd managed nothing more than the odd chill and occasional look over her shoulder, although she did worry sometimes about what the cat was so terrified of from time to time. It was the way it would suddenly stop what it was doing and gaze at nothing which was somehow eerier than the sudden hiss.

Gaspard was not so fortunate and had a difficult time trying to ignore both the presence of Bert Threadneedle and his mournful monologue when he'd realised that Gaspard was a policemen. "She killed me you know," said Bert forlornly. "Buried me under the floor boards. Right where she's standing. She always stands there when people come in. It's as is she's frightened I'll pop up from my tomb and give her away. I don't think she even realises what she's doing."

Gaspard was struggling to keep his attention on what Agnes was saying, while at the same time listening to Bert and doing his best not to get excited about the fact that he had her dead to rights which was ironic in a way because the reason that he had her dead to rights was that her husband was right dead at her hands. '*There was little point in reporting the crime,*' he thought. Agnes wasn't exactly knocking on death's door but she was well past the receptionist and on her way to the waiting room. An expensive trial would be in nobody's interests and she'd be unlikely to spend much time if found guilty. He decided he'd only mention it if she became fractious. "Killed me a with cricket bat," droned Bert. "Killing me was bad enough but it was one of Len Hutton's. He'd even signed it. Worth a bloody fortune of course but more than that, it was a piece of history. You know what she did after she'd bashed my brains in with it? Burned it, that's what. Bitch. Never appreciated the finer things. Look at all this crap."

He slumped back with a resigned sigh which took some effort since being a phantom he did not breath. Gaspard thought that he must have been working on it for a while which was pretty sad considering that it was only for his own benefit. Bert went back to trying to frighten the cat which eventually arched its back, hissed and departed the scene. Bert smiled for the first time.

Agnes was a traditional English matron when it came to guests of any sort and probably husbands too, so had put the kettle on for tea immediately after Gaspard had arrived. It was when she went off to the kitchen that Gaspard took his chance, an act of mercy he was soon to regret. "Mr Threadneedle," he whispered. Bert looked up, shocked to the core. "Bloody hell, you can see me?"

"I can. Look, we can't talk now. Tonight someone will come to you. His appearance may be a little…disturbing. Don't be frightened. His job is to help those in your condition."

"Bloody hell," Mrs Threadneedle returned at that moment barely managing to balance a rattling tray of tea cups. Gaspard leaped up to assist. "You know constable, I keep thinking I've seen you before. I haven't have I?" Gaspard shook his head rapidly.

"No, I'm sure we've not met Mrs Threadneedle," responded Gaspard, struggling to pick up his cup which had a tiny and completely impractical handle.

"No. Just remind me of someone perhaps. I think maybe it's the way you carry yourself."

"I'm off to the pub," announced Gaspard to the doctor and Maud, loudly. "Probably be gone a while."

"So?" Maud retorted rudely.

"Alright, Gaspard, have a nice time," said the doctor quickly, clearly embarrassed at Maud's shortness. Gaspard had stashed his cloak beneath his jacket and planned to change in the stair well. "What do you think he had under his coat?"

"Ah, so you noticed it too?"

"Hello Mr Threadneedle."

"Holy…bloody…no wonder the copper said you looked disturbing. I haven't seen anything like you since the one with the scythe. Your not him are you? You seem shorter."

"No, his job is to escort the spirits of the recently departed, mine is to speak to those who for one reason or another didn't go with him and to see if they've changed their minds." He smiled encouragingly.

The cat trotted into the room, saw Gaspard, arched its back, spat and fled. "Good one," exalted Bert.

"So, Mr threadneedle…"

"Call me Bert."

"So, Bert, I'm here to see whether you've had enough of continued existence and would like to finally depart this earth. It can't be very nice spending all your days with the person who murdered you."

"You reckon?" Bert asked rhetorically. "You know, it's been bloody frustrating knowing that I've hung on all these years and been unable to haunt her. Just having to watch her day after day, hating her guts and unable to do anything about it. All I've had to look forward to is the day she drops dead so that in her last moment she'll see me and know she's stuck with me for eternity but now I'm not so sure. I still can't forgive her but I've come to realise that she's in a prison of her own making. It's a miserable bloody life for both of us, or in my case what passes for life, and no doubt the bitch will probably croak in

124

hospital where I can't reach her. My desire for vengeance has dried up because she's pretty much punishing herself, so, yeah, I think I'm ready to depart."

"That's good Bert. I'm sure you won't regret it. Now, for reasons that are a bit difficult to explain, I can't organise it right at this moment but as soon as I can I'll return and help you out. OK?"

Bert looked even more crestfallen than usual. "You're kidding?"

"No, sorry, but it shouldn't be long."

"Can't you just take me with you, I won't be any trouble."

"There'd be no point. You'd be exchanging hanging on here for hanging on somewhere else," said Gaspard, putting his foot in it as usual. Why the hell didn't he just say no? Because he was incapable that's why, he thought, mentally castigating himself.

"I wouldn't mind that," replied Bert desperately, anywhere would be better than here. "Please."

Gaspard steeled himself. "No. I'm sorry Bert but no."

"Nice bedroom," opined Bert, "is this your place?"

"Not exactly, the owner let's me use it. It's a temporary situation. Now before we go into the other room, I need to tell you about the others."

"Others?"

"Mmm. They're in a similar situation to yourself."

"Ghosts you mean?"

"Uh, yes. There's Maud, I suppose you'd call her the resident ghost. This used to be her flat. I should tell you that she's intent on staying put. Then there's the doctor. Ivor. He's in a similar situation to yourself, waiting for…the final call, although if I'm frank I think he may be having second thoughts. Something else you should know is that Mort occasionally pays a visit. No need to fear, he's really quite a nice chap."

"Mort?"

"You may know him as Death. Chap with the scythe. We're colleagues."

"I see," responded Bert strangely, "and you use this place as a…let's say business address?"

"I suppose you could say that," chuckled Gaspard. "A funny old business though, eh?"

Bert had clearly been mulling things over. "This doctor, Ivor, you said?"

125

Gaspard nodded. "He wouldn't by any chance be Doctor Smallpiece? Topped himself some time back?"

"It's Smalpas," replied Gaspard hurriedly. "Best you don't call him that. It's a bit of a sore point."

"Right, right. I think I may have consulted him once or twice when I was still in a position to require medical services. He doesn't still practice does he? It's just that…well, one thing they don't tell you is that some of the aches and pains carry over. I suppose you'd call them phantom pains, eh?"

Bert suddenly brayed with mirth. He'd been saving this one up for a long time. "Joking aside the bloody sciatica gives me gyp sometimes."

"I don't think he consults outside of surgery," replied Gaspard sympathetically, "but you could always ask. It's not as if he can be struck off, is it?"

"Ha, ha, no. Oh, speaking of names it strikes me that I don't know what to call you?"

"Well, I don't really have a name, more a title but Maud calls me Napoleon so I suppose that would serve."

"I see. Poor joke I take it?" Gaspard nodded. "No last name then?" Gaspard shook his head. "Very well. Now, Napoleon, it pains me to say this, you having been so nice to me but I have to inform you that you, Mort and the gentleman who owns this place…who is?"

"Umm, Gaspard Feeblebunny," replied Gaspard, somewhat overwhelmed by Bert's suddenly officious demeanour. "That you, Napoleon, no last name, Mr Gaspard Feeblebunny…really?…and one known as Mort, are in breach of council regualtions under the Residential and Business Premises Ordinance, paragraph 14, subsection 8c, in that you are operating a business from a premises zoned as residential. Do you have any explanation?"

Gaspard laughed. "Good one. I see your sense of humour is already coming back."

"I'm sorry Napoleon…do you mind if I call you Nappy…Napoleon sounds so bloody formal and it sounds a bit insulting in a way. So, I repeat, sorry but no joke. It would seem that you are presently using these premises to house those not related to you, which under council regs constitutes a business under the definition of Bed and Breakfast establishments."

"But they don't have breakfast," was all that Gaspard could think of saying. "Not relevant I'm afraid. Does anyone here type? I'm afraid I shall have to make a report to the council."

"No!" Gaspard roared, thoroughly amazed and infuriated. "No one but me and if you expect me to do it for you, you are even more deluded than I'm beginning to think."

"Please, Mr...please Nappy..."

"And don't call me bloody Nappy!"

"Very well, if that's your attitude but being unpleasant is not going to change anything. I'm just doing my job," said Bert prissily.

"You job? You've been dead for twenty years you mad bastard!"

"That's no excuse for dereliction of duty," Threadneedle sniffed haughtily. He rubbed his chin as though pondering some weighty problem. "Look, I shouldn't say this perhaps because it's not my job to offer advice but there may be a solution. Even in residential premises it is permissable to run an AirBnB. It's just a matter of lodging an application. I could always hold back my report until you've submitted the necessary paperwork." He smiled winningly.

"I see now why your wife killed you," growled Gaspard, before he could stop himself.

"Oh, I say, that's a bit below the belt," whined Bert, choking on the words.

"I'm sorry. I really am but I'm doing you a favour for Christ's sake. I'm doing them a favour too."

"You're not suggesting that I am accepting a bribe?" Threadneedle asked in a shocked tone.

"Of course not. Look, we'll apply for the necessary papers, alright? Make you happy?" Gaspard said in his best conciliatory manner and with absolutely no intention of doing anything of the sort.

"Great. Just let me run over them before you put in the submission. Now, could I be introduced to my fellow lodgers by any chance?"

"He's got somebody with him. Napoleon I mean. What's he up to? That's not Gaspard's voice...the other one." She and the doctor were soon to find out.

"Here, you pair, get in here, I've got someone for you to meet."

"Do you think it's safe? He sounds murderous."

"I think we'll be OK," responded the doctor warily, "I don't think he's allowed to take us against our will." He slipped his head through the adjoining wall. "It's another one of us," he whispered, clearly astonished.

"Bloody cheek," spat Maud. "Bringing strangers into my home." In so far as a ghost could storm, she stormed into the next room, leaving little doubt as to her displeasure. "What right have you got bringing strangers here? Does himself know about this?"

"No, but he soon bloody will," shot back Gaspard, in such a manner that it even checked Maud. "This is Bert Threadneedle. He'll be staying with you until my…my…implement has been repaired."

"Forever you mean?"

"Oh, bloody hell."

"That's enough. Mort's doing his best," shouted Gaspard both unconvincingly and unconvinced. "I'm going and you lot can introduce yourselves and God help the lot of you."

Despite the rocky start, not made easier by Bert's insistence on receiving medical advice, things eventually settled down to a friendly chat between the three. Bert was almost delerious, having not spoken to anybody (he didn't count the cat) for years and the two longer term residents had just about dredged up all the interesting conversation they were likely to, which Maud being a housebound singleminded ratbag had taken all of five minutes.

"You know what I really miss?" Bert said rhetorically, " being able to eat. I used to have a really nice pub lunch every Sunday, down by the river."

"Oh, God yes," replied the doctor, "and a good pint of real ale to go with it." Both men emitted contented noises which were totally lost on Maud.

"I never got out much," she interjected. "Can't remember ever eating out. Not even in a pub." The two men ignored her plaintive remark.

"Did you ever go to the Old Butt Inn?" Enquired the doctor.

"Regularly. What a great place."

"Old Butt Inn? Why'd they call it that?" Maud enquired, interested despite herself. "You don't know? It's a part of the local history," said the doctor didactically. "This area used to be famous for the number of its butts. That's archery ranges, you know? That was in the middle ages of course. We supplied the king's armies with some of the best archers in the country. Our men fought at Cressy, Agincourt, all the famous battles."

"That's right," added Threadneedle, "we had some really famous butts, you can still find them mentioned in the local histories. Let's see; there was the King's Butt of course, Hollow Butt, Misty Butt and…"

"Lady Penelope's Butt," interjected Ivor, finding it hard to contain his delight at finding one who was quite literally a kindred spirit.

"That's right, she was the lady of the manor around the 1340s. And of course there were the one's that still exist as the three Butt villages," said Bert, nodding happily.

"The three Butt villages? I don't think I know them," said Maud.

"Really? They're quite near and as Bert said, named after three of the original and most popular of the Butts. There's Lower Butt, Middle Butt and…the other one," he finished lamely.

"The other one? I don't understand," said Maud, plainly baffled.

"Umm, well, think about it. Lower, Middle and…"

"Lower, middle and…oh, upper," cried Maud, happily. "Upper Bu…." She flushed a bright pink.

"Precisely dear lady," said the doctor, cringing slightly.

"For God's sake, why don't they change it?" Maud queried when she'd found her voice. "Surely people must be embarrassed to say where they live?"

"Some yes, but mainly the Johnny come latelies," answered Bert. "The older residents are used to it and really quite proud of its historical connotations. There was a move recently to have it changed but it was defeated. The council and the local business owners were all for keeping the name because it's begun bringing in a lot of money to the district, foreign visitors you know. Mainly American of course. They have such a peurile sense of humour."

"That's right," put in the doctor, "the last I heard was that far from changing the name they're thinking of resurrecting some of the old sites. I think the King's and Lady Penepolope's are first on the list, for obvious reasons."

"Obvious? I see nothing obvious," huffed Maud. "Excuse me but I'm going to watch some TV."

Gaspard did his best to saunter in unconcernedly and to express concern and mild surprise when swooped upon by Maud at the front door, vigorously complaining about his alter ego.

"That's very high handed of him Maud, I have to agree with you. Don't worry, I'll have a stern word when I next see him. Bloody cheek that's what it is. Rest assured that it won't happen again." He fled into his bedroom where he had some hope of being spared a further verbal assault.

"You don't learn do you? How could you have been so bloody stupid. They've been getting along like a house on fire and you know what that means?"

"I know, I know. I'm weak. He just seemed so pathetic. Then it turned out he was…well, what he was."

"The fact that he's a crank is neither here nor there. They now have another companion which will only strengthen them. I thought that Ivor was beginning to weaken but now that he has another history buff to talk to he may well be a lost cause. They've been chatting away for hours. It's like some old boys club and even Maud has been expressing some occasional interest. Just listen to them." Death actually opened the door. They both strained to listen to Bert who was in full flow. "…and then I said to him…mnk…mnk…you silly beggar, that's a form 22, you need a 16B."

Bert could hardly finish the sentence, being almost overcome with mirth. He was the only one laughing. "Oh, oh, I have to tell you this one. Phil…that's the one I was just telling you about, put in an order for some paper clips, we were almost out you see. He should have done it ages before because we'd past the lower limit which is set at a dozen boxes, anyway…"

Death closed the door. On the other hand…

The following morning there was a hell of a racket. Bert was insisting on watching the test match and the other two were standing their ground. The situation was made worse when Bert insisted on drawing up a TV watching schedule in which they were each granted two days a week on a rotating basis with the seventh day being divided into three lots of eight hours. The argument went on for hours in a vitriolic fashion and Gaspard was beginning to congratulate himself on bringing the three together. Maud, who had a daily soap watching schedule would never be happy whatever the suggestion from the other two. The next activity to spark conflict was playing board games. It was impossible for the three to last more than a few minutes without accusations of cheating and general bastardry and one party going off in a huff. Things were looking up.

7

"Good morning Marion," Dr Coombs said cheerily as he entered Hardcastle's room. Hardcastle was less than thrilled and although that was more often than not his default state, this time he had a reason.

"For Christ's sake, don't call me that," he hissed urgently, "someone may overhear."

"Oh, sorry. I take it you are not enamoured of your given name?"

"That, doctor, is putting it bloody mildly and if you'd grown up on the coalfields with a name like that, you'd have a good idea why." He rolled his eyes wildly. "Still, I suppose I have it to thank for growing up hard."

"You had a tough childhood then?"

"Perhaps a little harder than most but none of us had exactly what you'd call a soft life. My problem was that mam had ideas above her station. Either that or she was a John Wayne fan. I never found out."

"John…? Never mind. Now, how are you getting on? Been using that little solitaire set I gave you?"

"Um, a little bit," retorted Hardcastle, looking decidedly shifty.

"You really must use it you know. It's part of your therapy. In any case, it's about time to move up the scale a bit."

"It's not…that, is it?" quavered Hardcastle nervously.

"Monopoly you mean?" Enquired the doctor, studying the sergeant's reaction.

Hardcastle shivered slightly at the word and one eye began to twitch.

"No, no. It's far too early for that. I've brought a nice game of snakes and ladders. Something simple to ease you into the whole board game scene. I suppose you played as a child?"

"Maybe once or twice. We couldn't afford to waste our money on stuff like that. I think I may have played it at school when I was really young. Always hated it. If I recall, I always went down the last bloody snake every time I was just about home. Bloody frustrating it was."

"Well, I'm sure you'll enjoy it now you're a bit older. Do you think you could manage to shake the dice?"

Hardcastle's face took on a look of dismay and he began to hyperventilate. "That's alright, I'll shake them for you until you're a bit more used to it," soothed Coombs.

Life is a journey full of twists and turns that most of us negotiate with little or no damage. Up until recently, Gaspard had thought he'd been doing rather well. Not spectacularly perhaps but at least avoiding life's fender benders and mostly coming away with just the odd scratch to the paintwork. Since his meeting with Mort and the spectres however, he was beginning to feel that perhaps when it came to life's road network, someone had suddenly switched his map over for one drawn by an idiot. It was probably done by the same bloke who put a whole non-existent mountain range into Africa because he thought it looked nice.

He was mournfully pondering this fact when Death turned up. "How, now, young Gaspard," Mort greeted him sunnily. "Dare I say that you're looking somewhat downcast this fine evening?"

"You dare, because I bloody well am."

"Then gloom no more my young amigo because I come bearing glad tidings."

"You're not going to tell me…?"

"I most certainly am. Your device has been recovered and is, at this very moment undergoing pre-delivery checks. I told you it wouldn't take long. Happy?"

"Oh, bloody ecstatic. I presume when you say, 'not long' you're talking in terms of continental drift?" Gaspard was not to be uplifted by Death's cheeriness, not only because the shears were yet to be delivered but because he was becoming less and less delighted with the role that had been forced upon him.

"Please, don't be like that. I've done my best. You really should be happy. Now you can begin your work in earnest."

"I'd rather begin in Bert," sulked Gaspard. "The bastard is driving us all nuts."

"Then you should be filled with joy my moody friend. As soon as they've finished checking the new programme you can have done with him."

"New programme?" queried Gaspard, suddenly both alert and wary. "You know the unfortunate record your people have with this sort of thing?"

"Not to worry, it won't affect the operation. It's just a little bit of code to make sure it can't go missing again. Now, chin up and have faith." Gaspard really did do his best but for some reason found it difficult to get his chin off his chest, because when people talk about faith it's usually that they're unable to offer up any assurance that things won't go tits up.

"Can I ask just what this code is?" he enquired, after a couple of deep breaths to steady himself.

"Certainly. It's just a simple add on to ensure the device can't go missing in the post again. A return to sender direction if it can't be delivered or gets misdirected. Nothing that should be cause for concern."

"Mm sounds simple enough. I suppose even your lot would be hard pressed to bugger that up." He thought for a moment. "I take it that it'll now be suitable for use on humans? As I recall it was destined for the marine section at one stage."

"Absatively," shot back Death. He was now so cheerful that he was on the verge of capering about the room.

"OK. I suppose it sounds alright. Just as long as that lot out there," he jerked his head in the direction of the sitting room, "don't end up in a school of haddock after the job is done."

Death chortled. "No way old son."

"Right, well I suppose I should break the good news to the others," mused Gaspard, still a trifle wary of Death's ultra-sunny disposition. Just at that moment the sounds of a ferocious argument arose in the television room. "Beginning with Percy I think," he added hurriedly. "Care to join me?"

"Join you there. I just want to pop back home and see how things are getting on. Never know, our luck might be in." In an instant, Gaspard found himself alone listening to the seemingly incessant bickering.

"No, no, sergeant, it's down the snakes and up the ladders."

"I know, I know. For some reason, I have a mental block. I keep remembering that bloody morning at Feeblebunny's. It's all the bloody dice shaking that's doing it." Hardcastle slumped miserably. "I don't understand doc,

I've stood up to gorillas armed with bloody machetes and it hasn't phased me a bit. I've had my head half bashed in with a brick, been knifed and set upon by gangs of tough nuts and until now I've slept like a babe. Why does this bother me? Am I turning soft?"

Hardcastle was struggling not to weep.

"All that, horrible as it is, is in your realm of experience. You said that you had a tough childhood. I expect that sort of thing was quite common growing up and certainly after you joined the force. I'm told that you have a reputation as a bit of a scrapper." For the first time, Hardcastle's eyes brightened. The memory of some epic punch-ups seemed to be doing him good.

"More than a bit, doc. It does the bloody dregs I have to deal with no end of good to have their bottom's smacked occasionally. Better than any bleedin' community service order that's for sure. That's just a giggle to that scum." Hardcastle was beginning to look a lot healthier as his head filled with memories of arse kickings past.

"Quite so," murmured the doctor, feeling just a bit concerned, "so what you experienced at…wassaname's, was so totally outside your ken that it's upset your equilibrium. Of course, all that other business hasn't helped. Driverless cars, hooded spectres and the like. Possibly a little overwork?" he hazarded finally.

Possibly a deep-seated psychosis, he thought without a change of facial expression. Hardcastle's lip began to tremble again. "I tell you what," went on Coombs hurriedly, "maybe snakes and ladders was a poor choice; tomorrow I'll bring the Ludo and the automatic dice shaker."

At the words 'dice shaker', Sergeant Marion Hardcastle began hyperventilating.

The car park always left Gaspard feeling a little depressed. The vast windswept space, surrounded by rusted wire fencing in which the rubbish of years had caught and tangled had a distinctly dystopian feel, an impression not aided by the grim bulk of the factory. Like most factories its appearance gave no hint of its purpose and could equally well have been a chocolate manufactory or a chemical weapons plant. Or in some parts of the country a school. Gaspard looked about for Percy, half expecting to find him seated on the step.

There was no sign of the man, if that description could still be used of a departed soul but his car was in its usual spot, on top of a small and battered

Peugeot. That meant he was in the factory. Gaspard wandered in through the door and looked over to Percy's bench. Sure enough, Percy was there and screaming furiously and uselessly at a spotty youth who was having obvious difficulties in managing his tasks. *'By the look of him,'* thought Gaspard, *'he may also have difficulty in avoiding his knuckles dragging on the ground and saying "good morning" without careful thought and a short rehearsal.'*

"Oh, hullo Gaspard," greeted Percy, sounding intensely irritable, "come to give me more bad news?"

"Hi, Percy. No, just the opposite. The whatsit's been found and will be with us any time. You can start looking forward to the rest of your death."

"Would that I could. Do you see this nincompoop? I really regret having that last one fired. At least, he was a cut above a Neanderthal. This bugger couldn't find his arse if you gave him a map." He paused momentarily. "I was almost going to say that he couldn't find his own dick but as you can see, he manages that quite well," sneered Percy as the youth vigorously scratched at his crotch. "I'm almost of a mind to stay here and make sure he doesn't screw things up completely. A bugger like this could have the boss on his knees, financially speaking." He shook his head dolefully. Ironically, at that very moment the boss was on his knees and financial transactions were involved but of the sort that would have diminished him considerably in Percy's esteem.

"He's a grown man, Percy and he's been in business a long time. I don't think that he needs you to hold his hand. It's time to accept that you can't protect him from the world's problems and allow him to take the consequences for his own actions. Loyalty is a fine thing but there's a limit and dare I suggest that limit is death?"

"I suppose you're right. It's just that this place has been my life you know? It's hard to let go."

"I understand perfectly Perce but you said it. It's been your life. It shouldn't also be your afterlife. Let go with a light heart. I'm sure the future holds more for you than the past ever did," argued Gaspard, crossing his fingers behind his back. "Look, by way of a first small step, why not let this pillock get on with it and come outside for a chat? Just walk away with never a backward glance as they say. Postlethwaite will survive, believe me."

"I suppose…" began Pargeter, not completely sure that he would be able to manage it but then, at Gaspard's urging began to move reluctantly towards the exit.

"Aha! There you are," called Death triumphantly, "look what I have." He held the shears aloft.

"Hello Percy. Sorry about you having to wait but the best things in life are worth it, eh?" He handed the shears to Gaspard.

"Not that I've noticed," murmured Percy, unhappily. "And it's not exactly life we're talking about is it?"

"Cheer up, Perce. You'll soon be enjoying your new future," soothed Gaspard. "Think of today as the first day of the rest of your…er…death," he ended lamely.

Percy threw back his head and pushed out his chest in a display of decisiveness. "I've always hated that bloody saying. It'll be worth moving on not to hear it again."

He straightened his shoulders. "Right. Let's get on with on it. Goodbye Gaspard. Goodbye Mort, I don't suppose we'll meet again?"

Both shook their heads. Gaspard sadly, Mort abruptly. "Do it now please."

Holding his breath, Gaspard snapped the blades. To his immense relief Pargeter vanished. He may not have been quite as sanguine had he known the fate of a porpoise that up to that moment had been swimming happily some seventy miles offshore and thinking expectantly of his next meal. "What'll it be I wonder? The herring are pretty good around here. Not the squid. Had that last night. Wow! Where did she come from? Don't remember seeing her in the pod before. Maybe I'll just…aaargh."

"Well," said Gaspard, breathing a sigh of relief, "that went pretty well."

"Didn't it just," replied Death, looking about uncomfortably. "Look, sorry to leave you so abruptly but something has just been brought to my attention. Won't take long. See you at yours. And have the celebratory glasses ready, eh?"

Death being omniscient, had been instantly aware that something was not right. There had been a tear in the fabric of the universe caused by the death of a mortal creature before its allotted span. That could spell trouble if he didn't get it sorted bloody quick.

Most creatures other than humans are quite philosophical about death. They are surrounded by it pretty much constantly and many species deal it out to others without remorse. Death is very much a part of life, so when Spinner departed this life he was quite sanguine about it, other than to be a bit miffed at having had a massive heart attack in the prime of life.

"So much for the benefits of a fish diet," he said to himself looking about this strange new environment. It wasn't right at all. The afterlife was supposed to be a crystal-clear ocean filled with tuna and devoid of predators, or at least that's what he'd been taught as a juvenile. Plus, he was fairly sure he should have been taken up by the Black Orca. The only other being he could see was a wispy looking sod in the form of one of those peculiar creatures that made strange noises at him from watercraft. And why in the name of the great dolphin was he on dry land? What the hell, he'd better make the most of it. He had no choice after all.

"Hi, I'm Spinner. I suppose you're death? Have to say this is not entirely what I was expecting. A bit confined if I'm to be brutally frank. Unless of course this is just some sort of way station," he concluded, suddenly brightening at the idea.

What Percy heard was a series of squeaks. Immediately on his arrival, Percy had been no less bemused. He was pretty sure that St Peter's waiting room would not be a bedroom with several empty whisky bottles, a dodgy magazine sticking out from under the mattress and a tennis racket in the corner. Not to mention a pair of soiled underpants hanging from a doorknob. Turning around he was equally sure it would not contain a porpoise. Or was it a dolphin? The creature chittered at him as though expecting some sort of reply. The two stood staring at each other, or rather Pargeter sort of stood and the porpoise floated in mid-air. Before things became embarrassing, a third figure appeared.

"Gaspard?"

"Eek?"

"Oh, bloody hell!"

"So, where are the…? Oh, bloody hell!" cried Mort suddenly arriving on the scene.

"Look, look, I'll sort it OK," gabbled Death, more flustered that Gaspard had ever seen him. "The porpoise has to have priority though. He's not supposed to be dead. I've checked."

"Eek?"

"Why should he have priority?" roared Percy aggressively. "I've been hanging about for ages. And I think you'll find it's a dolphin." Percy neither knew nor cared what the creature was, he just wanted to be bloody awkward.

"Because Mr Pargeter," said Death dangerously, sounding menacing for the first time since any had known him, "the death of any creature before its time can seriously screw up the workings of the universe. A butterfly effect, if you will. Now shut your gob or I shall make bloody sure the rest of your death is as uncomfortable as can be managed. And that, I can assure you is uncomfortable indeed."

Percy opened his mouth to speak but then retreated to a corner mumbling viciously to himself. Death explained matters to the porpoise in a series of squeaks and trills. To Gaspard the responding squeaks and trills appeared to have a note of outrage. "So just how do you intend restoring me and what do I do in the meantime? It's a bleeding liberty, that's what it is. I was just about to chat up that new bird when bang and not the sort of bang I was hoping for. Now you tell me I shouldn't be dead?"

Spinner seethed quietly for a while before another thought struck him like a thunderbolt. "And what if I am restored? Are you saying that I have to die again down the line? That means I have to die twice and it's bloody painful. Why should I suffer for your balls up? It's a load of bloody octopus shit, that's what it is."

"I know, I know, but it's a genuine accident Spinner. I mean, it's not as if we did it on porpoise," stammered Death, thus proving that Freudian slips were a universal phenomenon. "We'll make it up to you Spinner. Rest assured that your final passing will be quick and pain free, which is not what was originally on the cards for you I might add. It'll take a bit of doing but you deserve it in compensation. As to the meantime, I am afraid that you're stuck with this lot for a short while but we'll do everything to make sure it's as short as possible. I don't mind telling you that much depends on us getting it done quickly. Oh, and I should warn you that there's a few more of this lot here as well. Sorry."

"Not half as sorry as I am but I suppose one has to make the best of a bad lot. You promise you'll be quick?" Death nodded in the affirmative. "Alright then. Now, where do I find the fish?"

"I'm afraid you don't. You're dead, you don't eat."

"But I'm starving. I haven't had so much as a prawn for hours."

"That will pass. It's just a left over from your living state."

"I'd settle for leftovers," squeaked Spinner lugubriously, his dorsal fin drooping alarmingly, "not even a ghost shrimp, eh?"

"Sorry."

Spinner sighed tragically and looked about the room. "Um, I'll be alright with this bloke will I?" He enquired after a brief inspection. "Why do you ask?"

"Well, to be honest the place looks a bit chintzy, if you know what I mean."

"Oh that, it all came with the place. He's just too lazy to get rid of it."

"What was all that about?" Gaspard enquired, doing his best to stifle his anger.

"Just explaining his situation to him. Be kind to him while he's here and probably best you don't cook any fish for a while."

"You mean he's staying? God's teeth Mort, things are bad enough as it is without adding a bloody cetacean to the mix. Though I hesitate to ask, how long is he likely to be here?"

"How long is a piece of string," responded Mort gnomically, "it'll be as fast as we can possibly make it. This could seriously fu…muck things up."

Gaspard couldn't help but notice that for the first time since he'd known him, Death was seriously worried.

"OK. Look, I don't want to add to your worries but what about the shears? Obviously, they have to be put right but could you please let me know why Percy ended up here? As far as the porpoise is concerned, I'm assuming that they hadn't completely removed all the marine programming?"

"Quite so. As far as both Percy and Spinner being here…"

"Spinner? Should I assume that's our pelagic friend over there?"

"Uh huh. Now, I hasten to add that this is a guess on my part but I think in coding the return programme they may have got a thing or two jumbled and it's been read as the particular soul being returned to the home address and not the item itself. Could be wrong of course." Mort gave an apologetic shrug.

"Oh, I think that on past performance you're pretty much on the ball," said Gaspard through gritted teeth. There was no point in taking it out on Mort, as much as he'd like to vent his anger on someone. There was a slight pause while the two stood looking at one another at a loss for the moment as to what to say. "Not even the rest of the fish fingers?"

"Eh?"

"Eek?"

In the next room Bert suddenly called for silence, thus ending, temporarily at least a furious argument about whether they should be watching The Real Housewives of Striding in the Marsh, University Challenge or a rerun of a particularly dreary investigation into the National Health Service. "Listen. There's a whole bloody tribe of them in there." Bert cocked his head. "That's Napoleon; that's a new voice…"

"And that's the bony sod," chipped in Maud. "And that, if I'm not mistaken is some form of cetacean," whispered the doctor disbelievingly.

"Perhaps he's bought another TV and they're all watching a wildlife doco," ventured Bert.

The speculation was ended by Gaspard as Napoleon suddenly appearing in their midst. "Hi guys," he greeted them nervously. "I have someone and…er, something for you to meet."

Humans have long thought cetaceans to be relatively smart. We don't really know how smart though because we don't have the foggiest idea how to test the level of intelligence of creatures with cultures and languages we cannot comprehend. Consider this. We put the average man in the street into a laboratory maze. If the test relied upon a food reward at the end, most would starve to death. If he were eventually successful and required to repeat the procedure, he would no doubt still be bloody hopeless. A mouse on the other hand will breeze through and be able to remember the correct route after the first success. In laboratory terms, we are dumber than mice. It's all about method. When it comes to porpoises, they should have thought about chess.

"I suppose there's been no progress towards restoring Spinner," said Gaspard in what was more a statement that a question. His tone was world weary, a note that was becoming almost habitual when it came to any dealings with admin.

"I wish you wouldn't take on that tone," responded Mort, "cynicism ill becomes you. In fact, there has been progress." He cast a shifty look about the room, clearly uncomfortable. Gaspard noted that he was looking somewhat downcast and not really sounding as though he believed what he was saying.

"You wouldn't make a very good politician, Mort. You lack the ability to lie through your teeth. What's really happening?"

"Well, the last time I checked there'd been an exchange of memos between the relevant departments."

Death sighed wearily and threw up his hands. "I know it doesn't sound like much but in bureaucratic terms it's a significant step. Would I wish it to be more? Of course, but you have to bear in mind that this is a unique situation."

Gaspard thought that Mort was sounding thoroughly miserable. The last time he'd heard such a forlorn note was when his father announced that the laxatives weren't working. Although in that instance, there had actually been two forlorn notes. Only one of them vocal. "But you said that the situation was urgent. That it could be a cosmic catastrophe."

"I did and it could. Unfortunately, the bureaucratic mind set is such that people would rather a disaster than be caught making a wrong decision. Bureaucracies almost never punish anyone for making no decision, if only because they're so complex that the final decision can always be laid at someone else's door. Plus of course, bureaucracy will always reward you for solving a catastrophe even if it's one of your own making."

"But it's been weeks. Surely we must be running out of time?"

"Yes and no. It's been weeks to you but fortunately in cosmic terms it's been nothing. That said, there's not a lot left, cosmic or otherwise. I'm doing all I can believe me but getting anyone to agree they have any responsibility at all is almost impossible."

"Can't you go over their heads? There must be someone who's not scared to make a decision?"

"Well, now you're talking but it's not easy getting an appointment and frankly, it will make things difficult for me in future if I succeed. I am trying for heaven's sake but don't let on."

Death looked nervously over his shoulder. "Anything I can do to make things easier in the meantime?"

"Maybe a bit of translation. Spinner's settling in well but the language problem causes occasional difficulties and he's having a lot of trouble understanding Monopoly."

It was no surprise that the arrival of the newcomers had resulted in cries of outrage from the established pair. What was surprising was the manner and speed with which Spinner managed to win them over. He was an engaging and social creature who, an early unfortunate incident involving fishfingers aside, was patient and amenable in a challenging situation. Despite the obvious language problems, he was accepted much more readily than either Percy or Bert. Those worthies eventually paired off and did an excellent job of disrupting harmony at every opportunity, having had their noses put severely out of joint at having to take second place to; as Bert put it; a squid scoffing, fin flapper who by rights wasn't even truly dead.

Maud and the doctor on the other hand were delighted that Spinner was happy to watch anything on TV, even if it was because he had no idea what it was all about and did occasionally attempt to eat images of fish. Attempts at teaching him games had mixed results. Monopoly was a complete failure because even with Mort's assistance as translator it was difficult to instil an appreciation of business, property or even houses. Chess on the other hand was a great success, dolphins having a tactical ability honed over millennia of fish wrangling. Once he'd grasped the basic concepts, he was a formidable opponent who beat the doctor eight out of ten times.

All this, as you may gather, took place over an extended period which only meant that the administration was performing at their usual level of inefficiency. Not only had they not solved the Spinner problem but Gaspard's shears were 'still in the shop' whenever the subject was mentioned. In fact, they had again gone missing in the post on their way to the marine section whose staff were supposed to fix the deprogramming glitch. Or at least that was their story.

8

"So, that's it Sarge. Case closed. No further investigation by order of upper management. They're going to question Feeblebunny about the use of his car…eventually…but no one's really interested." Tweedle looked as apologetic as is possible for one completely blameless but aware that their interlocutor is close to being a raving psychopath. Hardcastle drummed his fingers menacingly, his disordered mind racing and bouncing between outrage and desire for revenge. Think of that schoolmaster who was caught out giving the class a wrong answer by the class clever dick. Eventually he settled for revenge. "Is Fee…that bastard on duty today, constable?" he enquired with a disturbingly canny note.

"I think so Sarge. Can I ask why?"

"Why? Because I intend to search his flat, that's why."

"But Sarge, aren't you confined to the ward? They took your clothes away and everything."

"In that, you are correct young Tweedle but where there's a will…?" smirked Hardcastle. "Tell me, have you ever read The Wind in the Willows?"

"You mean Ratty and Mole and all that stuff?"

"Mm, hm."

"Of course, Sarge. Great book."

"Good. Done any clothes washing lately constable?" Hardcastle enquired gnomically.

"Um…do I get you right Sarge…clothes washing? Uh, yes but what…?"

"You, constable, are to be the washerwoman to my Toad," sniggered Hardcastle.

"I don't get it Sarge."

Hardcastle sighed the sigh of one deploring another's slowness of intellect. "You will recall, constable, that Toad escaped prison in the guise of a washwoman. You will assist me with that guise."

"Uh, you want me to bring you clothes, is that it?"

"Only in so far as that you have already brought them. I intend to use yours."

"But…"

"But me no buts, Tweedle. The plan is flawless. Here, as in every hospital in this land, there exist the shower Nazis. Their obsession means that even should I be in the shower for a prolonged period, they will be sanguine. In fact, they will be delighted. You shall divest yourself of your clothing and enter the shower until I return. No need to start until someone enters and then you shall splash and sing both loudly and appallingly, a task that I am convinced you will manage splendidly on all counts. Are we on the same wavelength, as they say?"

Tweedle sagged. He did not have to do this. It was an outrageous request that could only land him in severely hot water. On the other hand, Hardcastle was a psychotic who would have no qualms in punishing any hint of disloyalty and where Hardcastle was concerned the punishment could take a multitude of forms. All of them unpleasant.

"Sure, Sarge," sighed Tweedle disconsolately as he began to disrobe.

Superintendent Fish looked over his steepled fingers at Doctor Coombs.

"And how is our patient progressing, doctor?"

"Slowly, Superintendent. I'm afraid that the trauma he suffered will not easily be dispelled."

"Amazing thing the human mind, what? Hardcastle is a man of formidable reputation. I have personally seen him walk into the midst of a fractious mob with a smile and face them down. He is the most feared of our officers and yet…" He spread his hands in a gesture of helplessness.

"Indeed. It's often the way. Men like him are more likely than some to suffer as he's doing now. They have such a narrow vision of life that the slightest challenge to their concept of the way things work can send then into a spin. But you know, there has to be more to this than just the driverless car business and all that. His obsession with Feeblebunny is severe, almost amounting to a fixation. I only wish I knew what it is that really happened at Feeblebunny's flat. I'm convinced there's more to this than meets the eye."

He ran his fingers through his rapidly thinning locks. "One thing that might help. Perhaps you could tell me why a man of his reputation is working in Professional Standards. Did something happen that may shed some light on his current state of mind?"

"No, not really. We had to take him off the street because of the complaints about his propensity towards…er, over zealousness."

"I take it by that you mean violence?"

Fish nodded. "I suppose some would say that but not, I hasten to add, the general populace. Most were rather happy that he was keeping the riff raff under control, the odd civil libertarian notwithstanding. It was the staff at the local hospital that kept complaining. Said that he was overtaxing their emergency ward." He smiled grimly.

It was no problem for a copper with Hardcastle's experience to slip the lock to Gaspard's apartment. He entered in an uncharacteristically subdued and wary manner and glanced apprehensively towards the games table. Mercifully, the Monopoly set had been put away and the chess set put in its place. He breathed a sigh of relief but then quickly took his eyes from the chess set just in case any of the pieces had a mind to go cavorting about the board of its own volition. He moved cautiously into the centre of the room, only twitching a little as he did so.

He immediately noticed that despite it being a warm day and sunlight flooding in through the large windows, that the room was chillier than one might expect. There was also an odd feeling of dampness, so much so that he was tempted to wipe his brow which was feeling rather clammy. Or maybe oystery, he wasn't really sure. There was that odd fishy quality to the atmosphere that he couldn't quite place. Or perhaps it was plaice. All this was not surprising because he was standing not only in the middle of the room but also the middle of Spinner.

"Eek!" The residents watched as Hardcastle made his way from room to room, carefully searching as he went. He snooped in drawers, cupboards and wardrobes, he peered behind furniture, even the refrigerator was given a thorough examination. He wasn't quite sure what he hoped to find other than a set of garden shears but he would know it when he found it. Perhaps a black robe.

Please let it be. When it came to the shears, he knew their discovery would mean nothing to the powers that be but they would mean a lot to him. They could mean nothing less than Gaspard's being in the phantom vehicle because he lived in a flat completely devoid of vegetation of any sort and that meant that unless Gaspard had very tough toenails, he was discovered.

It was a good thing for Gaspard that the admin people had managed to do something right for a change.

Knowing the propensity of young male mortals to leave garments lying wherever they'd been shed, they had ensured the garment was only visible to the owner. It was a pity they hadn't bothered to go any further, because true to type, Gaspard had discarded it on the floor. So, in accordance with Murphy's law, Hardcastle tripped over it. He arose rather shaken, convinced that something was tangled around his ankles. He shivered, both at the sudden chill that seemed to have invaded the room and at the feeling of an unseen presence. Maybe even more than one. Hardcastle attempted to shrug off the sensation.

He was a lot more successful at that than shrugging off the robe which remained stubbornly wrapped about his ankles, so his attempt at rising saw him immediately fall over again. The second fall loosened not only the offending item but also his upper denture. He scrambled hurriedly to his feet, his blood running cold. Some…thing…had been seizing his ankles. He looked wildly about…there was nothing to be seen. Terrified, he rescued his dentures, now covered in carpet fluff and crumbs. After rapidly wiping them with Tweedle's distressingly grubby handkerchief, he began to back away from the vicinity of those cold grasping hands.

He was now in an increasingly chilled and agitated state and with a peculiar taste in his mouth. Hardcastle did his best to steady his nerves and logically examine the situation. Clearly, he told himself without believing a bit of it, he'd merely tripped. The rest had been his imagination. Unfortunately, he knew himself to be an inveterate liar when it suited him so it was difficult to credit what he was telling himself. Nonetheless he put a brave face on things and prayed that nothing would jump out of a closet. It was time to leave anyway. He'd used all his wiles, searched all the sneakier hiding places and nothing.

There was nothing cowardly in his departure, it was just that he'd done all he could. Hardcastle forced himself to examine the results of his search by way of steadying his nerves. He'd be damned if he was going to flee the premises like some trembling little girl. After due but hasty reflexion, the only conclusion he was able to draw, was that Feeblebunny had very strange tastes for a young single male.

He had found dainty China cups, porcelain figurines and stacks of quality linen that were completely at odds with the sort of thing the average bachelor would possess, that being more of the order of empty beer cans, crisp packets and dodgy magazines. He began to wonder if perhaps Gaspard was leading a hidden life. Not that it mattered. He was a dead man anyway. What Hardcastle was not to know was that Maud had died with no one to inherit her estate, if it could be called that and so her flat had been sold lock, stock and barrel. Although in this case maybe more stock pot and biscuit barrel. Being a confirmed bachelor he knew little of women's propensities to keep things for 'best', a habit that invariably means that those inheriting have something to either pack up and give away to charity or fight over with the relatives.

He was gloomily preparing to leave when something hit his shoulder. He leaped and turned in one motion, heart pounding and fists raised. There was no one. There was however a frozen fishfinger on the carpet at his feet. Hardcastle shook his head in disbelief, certain the item had not been there previously but unwilling to believe that someone had thrown it at him. He tried not to think that the someone might be some thing, bent down and picked it up. Still frozen solid.

He shuddered involuntarily, summoned his courage and began advancing cautiously back the way he had come and in the general direction from which frozen produce may have emanated when he was struck again. He yelped and looked wildly about. A kipper lay at his feet. Very slowly he began to edge towards the safety of the exit.

Another fishfinger struck him, this time just below the eye. He had seen nothing but clearly it had come from directly if front. "Maud! Stop it," hissed the doctor, "you're causing trouble. You know who this is?"

"Of course I know. That copper we frightened the crap out of. Nasty beggar. I may not be all that fond of himself but this horrible piece of work has broken in trying to get him into trouble. I'm just protecting our best interests. What happens if Gaspard has to leave? We might end up with some total prat." She glanced meaningfully in the general direction of Bert.

"Hm, I suppose you're right. Let's give it to the bastard." A horrified Hardcastle fled the premises cowering under a rain of fishfingers, kippers and the odd overripe piece of fruit.

"I suppose that was a bit wasteful," mused Bert to the others.

"Not at all rejoined Maud. "Himself is under orders not to eat fish while Spinner is here and those bananas were past it. With that, she hurled a can of sardines that struck Hardcastle behind the ear at the very moment he thought he was safe. "Sardines?"

"Well, they're still fish, isn't they?" Maud humphed, forgetting herself in her self-righteousness.

Hardcastle was never sure how he returned to the hospital and Tweedle, when he eventually poked his well-watered head through the bathroom door was completely unable to understand what Hardcastle was gibbering. He managed to get Hardcastle back into bed and was doing his best to calm the sergeant when lunch arrived. Fortunately, this time it was on a plate and not airborne. A little less fortunately, lunch was fishfingers.

It would remain a mystery to all what had set the patient off, all they knew was that as lunch was put before him, Hardcastle began to scream. And scream. But silently, which made it all the worse. Almost as mysterious to the medical staff was the question of how the patient managed to incur a massive lump behind one ear and a possible concussion while confined to his room.

"There's something you said when that copper was here Maud that I don't quite understand," said Percy sounding baffled. "Why would you say Gaspard could be in trouble? I mean, surely he's not of this world. There's nothing a copper could do to him."

Maud's face suddenly took on a cannily triumphant look. She nudged the doctor which just meant that her elbow passed through him but he received the message nonetheless. "Why would you say that Perce?" she asked slyly.

"Why? Because he's just like Death, isn't he? Only smaller and got those silly bloody shears instead of a proper reaping tool." Percy sniggered involuntarily at the image.

"Yes, they are a bit of a non-secateur, aren't they?" Giggled the doctor, unable to resist the witticism. His attempt at high humour was ignored by Maud, mainly because she didn't understand it. "Non-secateur, Maud? Garden shears? Not a secateur? Non-sequitur?" Mumbled the doctor pathetically.

"It doesn't work," sneered Bert, unkindly.

"Keep to the point doc. This is important," growled Maud. Then addressing Pargeter: " You say that the little bony sod is called Gaspard? You're sure?"

"Of course. I've always called him that because that's what Mort calls him. Why? Should I call him something else?"

"We've always called him Napoleon. Obvious reasons." Percy pulled the sort of face that meant it was not at all obvious to him but said nothing. "But you see, Gaspard is the name of himself what owns the place. We've never known the other one's name," retorted Maud, still with that sly note to her voice.

"Does it matter?" enquired Percy, a little perplexed by it all.

"Oh, yes. It matters a lot. It means that as we sometimes suspected, himself and Napoleon are one and the same," she smirked, "and that means I suspect, that if he had any real power over us, he'd have used it by now."

"It was always my understanding that he needed our permission," said Percy.

"Really?" Percy nodded.

"That was my understanding too," added the doctor.

"Then why in God's name did no one tell me?" shrieked Maud. "I've been terrified of that bony little git." She paused, seething quietly to herself before adding: "Well, I suppose that puts us in the driver's seat?"

"You're forgetting that his non-secateurs have been broken though," said the doctor, unwilling to give up his joke. "Once they're fixed…who knows? Then too there's the other one."

"I haven't forgotten the other one. But look, he's been here a lot and we've become quite used to him haven't we? Hardly bother to hide these days. If he could take us, he would have done before now. I think he's given his powers, or some of them at least, to Gaspard and Gaspard without his shears is buggered. Not that they seemed to work anyway."

Maud grinned, which was something none of the others wanted to see on a regular, or for that matter even occasional, basis.

"I understand you've been to see Sergeant Hardcastle recently, Doctor. I hope he's coming on?"

"Afraid not sir, he's actually a good deal worse. More going off than coming on, if you'll excuse the levity."

"Oh, I'm sorry to hear that. Am I to assume that his fear of Monopoly has grown worse?"

"Not exactly. He is still afraid of it and for that matter, any game involving dice but he now has a terror of fish fingers." Coombs shook his head sadly.

"Good Lord, fish fingers you say? I suppose a degree of repulsion is understable to some extent but terror? How in the blue blazes did that come about?"

"No one has any idea Superindent. They turned up yesterday for lunch and he just started screaming…well, not exactly screaming…more of a seizure from what I've been told. I believe the phobia also extends to other fish products as well. Tinned sardines in particular." Coombs shrugged helplessly. "I don't mind telling you that it's the most severe case of its type I've ever encountered."

"And what type would that be?" asked Fish, sitting forward with interest. Doctor Coombs was instantly uncomfortable. "Ah, well, I don't actually know because I've never encountered anything like this before. That's…um…why it's the severest case," he finished lamely.

"I've consulted others you know," he blurted in an attempt to regain some credibility. "No one else has any idea either."

Which just went to prove Fish's long held belief that the whole profession was a pack of nincompoops and charlatans. "Hm, I suppose I should pop along and speak to the poor chap. Familiar face and all that. Plus the news of his indefinite disability leave may be better coming from a senior officer. Tried and true methods, old hand at breaking bad news and so on and so forth. Yes. I think I'll do that."

"If you think it best Superindendent. It can certainly do no harm." The Superintendent may not have seen the obvious pitfall but Doctor Coombs certainly should.

The nurse stepped brightly into the room. "A Superintendent Fish to see you, Sergeant." Fish had barely managed the first syllable of his greeting before the emergengy medical team was required.

Tweedle's gaze flicked to the chart at the end of Hardcastle's bed. In the notes section, in large letters, were the words 'nil board games except under medical supervision'. Below that the doctor had scrawled: 'nil seafoods by mouth' and 'nil mention of seafoods of any form'. After that, an even more hastily scrawled addition warned: 'nil visits permitted for Superintendent Fish'. Another, perhaps somewhat redundant, warned: 'no perfumes of a fishy character'. These notes were bound to put unbidden thoughts in visitor's minds. "You're looking well, Sarge."

To an extent that was true. Hardcastle was presently so doped up that he wore what could only be described as a beatific smile, an expression that did not fit comfortably on his battered visage which was grotesque at the best of times. Not that Hardcastle was having any good times lately. "Thank you Tweedle," responded Hardcastle dreamily.

"I hear you've been given extended leave, Sarge."

"Hm, so they say. Not that I need it but at least it gives me time to hunt down that…" For all the medication, the sergeant began to tremble violently.

"You should forget about…him, Sarge. Focus on recovery. Perhaps plan a nice get away. Lots of sun, nice local pub, that sort of thing."

"A loaf of bread beneath the bough, a jug of wine, a book of verse and thou, eh Tweedle?" Hardcastle murmured alarmingly.

"Yeah, well, sort of I suppose Sarge." He cleared his throat nervously. "The bread and wine bit anyway."

Tweedle was fairly sure that the 'thou' bit was definitely a non-starter.

"Visions of paradise, young Tweedle. But maybe more like; a Feeblebunny hanging from a bough, his eyeballs bulging in the wilderness and wilderness would be paradise enow." He began to giggle.

It was becoming only too apparent that no matter how much giggle juice the doctors pumped into Hardcastle his obsession would remain. Sedating the sergeant was like raising an umbrella to ward off a falling asteroid. "I'll get him you know, constable. Even though they're watching. I'll outsmart them all. I'll hang his liver and lights from a lamppost. For starters. The doctors don't know what he's up to. Nobody does. Nobody but me." He stared in a befuddled manner at the unhappy Tweedle. "Things of a demonic nature are afoot. You believe me though, don't you constable? You and your mate."

"Uh, yeah Sarge. There's definitely something fishy going on," responded Tweedle, finally falling into the mental trap set by the doctor's notes. Hardcastle said nothing. His eyes sort of rolled back into his head, he twitched violently several times and then he was still. Constable Tweedle looked about guiltily. He was about to ring for assistance when Hardcastle revived. "Oh, hello Tweedle, nice to see you. Been here long? I must have dozed off. These bloody drugs you know."

"No, not long Sarge," replied Tweedle with relief.

"They think they can control me you know?" Hardcastle whispered slyly. "But they can't. I'll have the last laugh." He began to cackle. "Just wait and see." Later that night, anyone in a position to see, would have observed a wraithlike figure flitting along the deserted corridor.

Admittedly, we're stretching the term 'wraithlike' a little but as long as we're prepared to accept that the wraith in question is wearing a hospital gown and exposing a considerable area of hairy bum as it bends to slip past the nurse's station, we'll be apples. 'Flitting' may also be a stretch. Having gained the relative security of the outdoors, the figure slipped into the car park, sidled along a wall and disappeared into a vacant lot, cannily avoiding surveillance cameras.

From that point on, he would seldom be seen until his desire for vengeance would again bring him into the light.

Maud was bouncing about with excitement as Gaspard's key turned in the lock. "Hello Gaspard, good to see you home unharmed," she greeted him, barely able to control her urge to blurt out everything.

"Oh, thank you Maud," responded Gaspard suspiciously. "Very kind of you."

"Have a good night? I've often thought it must be…shear…murder, patrolling in the…dead…of night." This was said in such a baldly meaningful manner that Gaspard had absolutely no doubt that she was up to something and he already had a sneaking supsicion what it might be. Anyway, Maud did not do nice.

"Oh, it has its moments. Sometimes it can be bloody awful, like when the drunks are about and looking for trouble. On the other hand, it can be terribly dull too." Gaspard tried edging towards his bedroom but Maud intercepted him.

"Really, so from shear terror to shear boredom then," she said smirking and doing her best to stifle a cackle.

"I suppose you could say that," murmured Gaspard, now thoroughly convinced that she was playing games at his expense.

"Must be bad on cold nights too?"

"Mm, hm."

"You must get chilled to the bones sometimes. Pity you can't wear a robe. One of those ones with a hood. Keep you ears warm."

"Yes. A bit impractical though, eh?"

"Seems to work for some. You know, monks, Death." She watched him closely. "And comfortable of course. No need for undies even if you're that way inclined. Shear heaven I should think," she smirked.

"What is it you want to say Maud?" Gaspard queried, tiring of the game. It was now pretty obvious what she was up to.

"Funny you should ask," she retorted triumphantly, "we've been having a bit of a chat to one of our new arrivals. Did you know that Napoleon's real name is Gaspard? Some coincidence, eh?"

This time she gave in to mirth, emitting a demented bray of laughter. Gaspard did a rapid assessment. No point in denying it, it was always bound to come out.

The best course of action was to defuse the situation and do his best to take away Maud's mental advantage.

"So, you know. I am indeed Napoleon and bloody unhappy about it too if you must know. You know what though? It's a relief that you've found out. I've been sick and tired of having to creep about when I'm that character. It's not easy being quiet using the loo for a start. The worst part though is having to hold everything in when you're around."

With that, he strained deliberately and emitted a thunderous fart by way of illustrating his point. With Maud's shocked gasp and the doctor's hoots of mirth following, he stalked into his bedroom and slammed the door.

"Really!" ejaculated Percy, shaking his head in disbelief.

"Thoroughly abhorrent behaviour," echoed Bert, although the struggle to maintain a straight face was saying something entirely different.

"Yes, yes, quite unacceptable," sniggered the doctor.

Maud sniffed with outrage but then immediately regretted the urge. Both deflated and enflatussed she stormed off to watch The Young and The Restless which in itself was an indicator of how bad she was feeling. In a toss up between watching the show and staying in a room smelling of farts, it would be a close run thing for most people. In the bedroom, Gaspard flung himself onto the bed and breathed a sigh of relief, only part of which was linked to his recent expellation of gas.

Nearby, a sinister creature, clad only in a filthy and wide agape hospital gown lurked in the shadows. With a singular obsession, it watched the bedroom curtains close. Eyes that were more like windows into bedlam had watched Gaspard's progress that night and now settled unblinkingly on the windows of his apartment.

Hardcastle's home was the first place the police looked for their missing officer. There was no sign of him and no evidence that he'd been there recently. Certainly none of the neighbours had seen anything of him, which considering his current state of undress was a blessing.

It was the sort of place one might expect someone like the sergeant to occupy, sparsely furnished without a single feminine touch. Unless of course one counted the pink stuffed toy rabbit, strangely out of place in the spartan accommodation. The officer who found it didn't mention the toy to anyone and knowing nothing of Hardcastle's obsession with Gaston Feeblebunny merely wondered why the bunny had a knife through its head and showed every sign of having been stabbed multiple times. He figured it was a stress relief of some sort.

Hospital staff were questioned and re-questioned. The area around the hospital was searched and tracker dogs used to try to trace his steps. Surveillance cameras were checked.

Colleagues and friends (the latter category unsurprisingly short in number) were appealed to and his haunts visited time and again. Of Hardcastle there was not a sign. The only probable sighting was from a lady who spent her evenings visiting the homeless and distributing meals. She remembered someone who could only have been Hardcastle, although she was unable to categorically identify him from his police photograph.

"Well dear, it could be him I suppose but the man I saw looked much wilder." She shuddered involuntarily at the memory. "All my usuals were come and gone when he just seemed to appear in front of me. Now, don't get me wrong but he wasn't like the usual folk I deal with."

She thought for a moment. "I called him Tom the Ostler, 'cause he reminded me of that poem we did at school. I said to our Judith later, I said, he was just like that mad one in The Highwayman. Do you know it?"

The officer sighed and shook his head. "Well there's a bit about his face being all white and peaked and that was this one for sure. But it's the next bit that really put me in mind. The bit where it goes that his eyes were hollows of madness and his hair like mouldy hay. That's just how I'd describe how he looked if I had that way about me." She paused momentarily. "Except of course the bit about his hair 'cause it weren't straw coloured. More white but it were all matted and greasy like."

"You're sure you can't identify him from the photo?"

"Wish I could help love. Like I say, it could be him but if it is you'd best find him quick. Fair give me the creeps. I offered him a nice tuna and mayonnaise sandwich and he just run off, sort of gibbering to himself like. Oh, and that reminds me. He had on one of them hospital gowns that open at the back. I know that 'cause I could see his bum." She shuddered again at the mental image.

The super really didn't want to be bothered with all this palaver surrounding Hardcastle but he was old fashioned enough to believe that a policeman's primary function was to protect the community. He was also cautious enough of his reputation to believe in not leaving his bum exposed (a precaution that

154

Hardcastle might have done well to emulate) and from what Dr Coombs had said it appeared that it was presently exposed to a possibly psychotic sergeant. "What do you think, Tweedle? You've spoken to him more than most of late. Where do you think he might be headed?"

"Well sir, I wouldn't want to make things more difficult for a man in his fragile condition but I think it may be a good idea to keep on eye on Constable Feeblebunny."

'Fragile' is a term often used when describing mental states but in this case Hardcastle's psychosis was so entrenched that it was about as fragile as an anvil.

"Really? Why would that be?"

"Because he's obsessed with him sir." Tweedle's head dropped for a moment as he weighed up what he was about to say next. He looked up. "I really think he might want to do him harm sir," he said sadly.

"Harm constable? What makes you think that?"

"Because sir, the last thing he said to me was that he'd hang Feeblebunny's liver and lights from a lamppost sir. For starters. I think he meant it sir."

The madman moved stealthily through the streets and alleys that he'd known for decades, easily avoiding cameras. He no longer walked, he slid. Sometimes he appeared to float from one cover to another. He was a little more decently attired now, having managed to scavenge an old windbreaker and a pair of tattered bedroom slippers from someone's garbage.

His legs were still bare and occasionally a malicious breeze would lift the filthy gown he still wore and expose his nether regions. There was no one to see which was just as well for both Hardcastle and the observer. It was however bloody chilly.

He barely noticed. Or perhaps noticed barely.

In the darkness, he visited the waste areas of stores and restaurants and raided their leavings, carefully avoiding the other homeless as he did so. He had begun to think of himself as a ghost and he left as little trace as one as he stalked his quarry. At night, he dogged Gaspard awaiting an opportunity when the young constable would be truly alone and unobserved. In the day, he slept in a vacant house within a stones throw of Gaspard's flat. Hardcastle was becoming increasingly frustrated.

A while after what Hardcastle considered to be his escape, Gaspard's duties changed. He no longer walked the beat at night, having been transferred to days and paired with another officer in a squad car. Things had altered in other ways too. At night, a police car would slowly pass Gaspard's block at irregular intervals, obviously on the lookout for something and Hardcastle had a pretty fair idea what that something might be. The greater wariness didn't worry the sergeant unduly. It was the shift shift that made things very awkward. It meant that he'd probably have to take Gaspard at home. If it had to be, then so be it but the thought of that chill and eerie residence sometimes went close to weakening his resolve.

Often he awoke panicked and sweating in fear having dreamed of ghostly hands clutching at his ankles or being bombarded by flying kippers.

Not surprisingly the changes made Gaspard nervous of his safety. He couldn't understand why Hardcastle would wish him harm but neither could he understand why the man would break into his flat and when it came to his personal safety he wasn't about to take any chances. At the first opportunity, he fitted both a stout bolt and a safety chain to his front door. As an added precaution he began sleeping in his robe. What Hardcastle couldn't see, he couldn't harm.

9

As Death had warned at the beginning, the presence of the new ghosts had enabled them all to increase their abilities exponentially and Gaspard was already tired of the various manifestations those new powers were taking. On a recent evening, he'd had to dodge the fridge as it rumbled sedately past. Almost as annoying in that case was that the phantom residents had yet to learn how to plug it back in which meant that he came home that night to warm beer. Their excuse was that they were just practicing.

"I think we need a new television Gaspard," crooned Maud unnervingly. "There are just too many arguments and it's even worse now that Spinner has figured it out and realises there aren't tiny people living inside it. One for the bedroom and one for the living room."

"And what about if someone wants to play board games in the living room and the others want to watch the TV there?"

"Oh, that's easy. They can play in your room," fired back Maud casually.

"Like hell, they can. You lot already infest every other bit of the flat. My room is my sanctuary."

"They're all here because of you, or don't you remember?" sneered Maud. "Anyway, we'd only use it when you're not here. Most of the time."

"No, no and thrice no. To both propositions. You can't have my room and you can't have a new TV. I can't afford it. You'll just have to learn to get along."

"You know that's impossible. Bert and Percy are bloody difficult to get along with. Bert, by the way is working on a method to send a complaint to the council about you running a business from the flat. God knows how he'll manage it but the vicious little sod is nothing if not determined." She smiled a warning. "Perhaps with a little help he'll manage it."

"Bloody hell," groaned Gaspard.

"So new TV, then?"

"No!"

"We wouldn't like to get unpleasant, Gaspard," murmured Maud in a manner which said anything but.

"No. Do your worst."

"I don't think you mean that but have it your way." Maud turned to go. "See you later tonight," she said meaningfully as she vanished through the door.

Gaspard listened nervously to the whispered conversation taking place in the bedroom. He couldn't make out what they were saying but the evil chuckles that arose from time to time already had him checking his bank balance and researching sales at electronics shops. The switch from night shift to day was playing merry hell with Gaspard's sleep patterns but he eventually fell into a fitful slumber in the early morning hours. The fitful nature of his sleep was also resulting in strange and disturbing dreams. The dream he was now experiencing was one such. Police woman Bullock was attempting to engage him in some acts of a nature that could be categorised as distinctly friendly and her long and drawn out moans could certainly be described as disturbing. She had begun to rattle her handcuffs at him suggestively when he suddenly awoke. And cried out in alarm.

"Whoooo."

"For God's sake Maud, what in the blue blazes do you think you're doing?" Gaspard growled at the moaning figure floating above his bed. He was feeling particularly peevish because not only had he not long fallen asleep after a serious struggle but the dream had most definitely reached an interesting part. A fact that had not been lost on Maud, though she gamely kept in character.

"We warned you, Gaspard, whoooo," moaned Maud, giving her chains a rattle for good measure.

"And where in the name of all that's holy did you get those bloody chains?" he barked, thoroughly unsettled and belatedly gathering the sheets about his person.

"I told you we had ways, Gaspard. The television: give us the television and all will be well," she wailed. "If not, before the cock crows, you shall be visited by three ghosts."

Maud was now hamming it up unmercifully, although it was spoiled a bit when she sniggered after saying the word 'cock'.

"Oh, Christ, we're doing Dickens are we? Well I've got news for you; this isn't Christmas and I'm not Scrooge. Bugger off Maud and let me sleep."

"Beware, beware," moaned Maud as she slid through the door. "Remember; three spirits shalt thou receive. Threeee."

It's not easy to get back to sleep after such an interlude but sleep eventually claimed him again. He awoke to find Bert sitting by his bed. He'd obviously been chatting away in full flow for some time.

"…And then of course there's regulation 197. The Keeping of Pets on Council Premises. That's pets as defined under paragraph 3 subclause (b) of course. As you probably know, that covers pets (domestic) and includes birds and fish but not exotics such as arachnids and reptiles. No…mnk…they're covered under subclause (c) except that it doesn't cover arachnids and reptiles of a venomous nature which are of course forbidden under paragraph 198. Venomous being defined as…"

Bert droned on until Gaspard shot bolt upright thoroughly enraged. "Get out you miserable bastard!"

The next awakening was no better. "…he had the most repellent case of fungus I've ever seen. That wasn't the worst of it though. Poor chap didn't know he had a broken penis, although of course he had been a bit worried about the bend. You wouldn't think you could break your willy, would you? Well I'm here to tell you it's possible. Poor chap went quite pale when I told him the only cure was to shorten his love life. Of course, it usually only happens to chaps who are somewhat overendowed, so he was being a bit greedy I thought…"

"Doctor?"

"Yes?"

"Piss off!"

"I say Gaspard that's not like you. Most uncivil."

"Get out!"

"Do we get the TV?"

"No!"

"…Eek, eek eek, eek…"

"*Et tu* Spinner?"

"Eek!"

Gaspard was exhausted but he was also stubborn. Stubbornness is seen by some as a useful, even an admirable trait but most of the time it's a distinct handicap. He knew that he must eventually give in to the nightly harassment but he would be damned if he'd give them an easy victory.

There was also the matter of face. One in his position couldn't be seen to be a walk over. Furthermore, he clung to the hope that something might occur to him that would force the spirits to cease their relentless campaign. Hope can be a real bastard. Optimism can also be a heavy cross to bear, particularly when it is unwarranted.

The envelope bore the letter heading of The Hamm on Wye Borough Council and in view of recent events and past threats, Gaspard examined it with some trepidation.

"I warned you Gaspard," said Maud smugly.

"I distinctly told you that you were in breach of council ordinances," sniffed Bert prissily. "I gave you every chance to make things right but you wouldn't be told. I have to say that I'm extremely disappointed that it has come to this."

"How did you manage…? Forget it," sighed Gaspard defeatedly. "Remind me to send your wife a thank you card for ridding the community of a pestilence." He instantly regretted the unkindness of course but his attempts at mollifying Bert were met with a distinct lack of success. His regret was genuine enough, not only because it had severely hurt Bert's feelings but because in killing him, his wife had inadvertently lumbered Gaspard with him.

Mr G. Febblebinny,

Dear Sir,

Business and Residential Premises Ordinance, Clause 141. It has been brought to our attention that you may be in breach of subsection 8 (c) of the above ordinance in that you are using your private dwelling, currently zoned as residential, as a rental property, to whit, a Bed and Breakfast establishment. Council Inspector Philbert Worthy will call at your property at 0800 on Thursday next. Please note that under the provisions of the Ordinance, it is incumbent upon you to make yourself available at that time and date.

Sincerely Yours,
P. Worthy
For Hamm on Wye Borough Council.

Gaspard emitted a roar of rage and screwed the letter into a ball. "You total bloody nincompoop Bert. Can't you see that this is just wasting everybody's time? He can't possibly find other than that I am the only one living here." Gaspard seethed.

"We shall see, shan't we?" Bert said mysteriously.

A weary Gaspard was not surprised to awaken with Bert sitting by his bed. The harassment had now been going on for almost a week and he was seriously considering asking for lodgings at the station house so that he could get a good night's sleep. He had so far avoided breaking and buying the second TV but he was rapidly wearing down. The sleep deprivation was the worst tactic being employed so far but even his waking hours had been disrupted by such things as the ghosts throwing things at him and watching him in the bathroom.

When he was finally awake enough to focus on what Bert was rabbiting on about, he realised that he was animatedly explaining the rules of cricket. "...and then of course there's dismissal off a no ball. How many ways do you think a batsman can be out from a no ball delivery?"

"Piss off Bert."

"No, no, this is interesting...mnk...I tell you what, I'll go if you can tell me."

"You promise?" Bert nodded.

"OK, let's see," said Gaspard, barely able to suppress his anger. "Uh, run out; that's one and...uh...interfering with the field maybe?"

"Good, good. Is that your answer; two?"

"Um, yes, I suppose."

"Aha. You forgot rule 34," said Bert triumphantly.

"Oh, how could I?"

"No need to tell you what that is, I suppose?" Bert asked, ignoring the heavy sarcasm. "No. Please leave now."

"What is it?"

"Alright I don't bloody know and I don't care. Just leave. You promised." Gaspard was pleading wearily.

"Hit the ball twice," piped up Bert brightly. "Everyone forgets that. Not surprising really, I don't think the rule's been used in decades. Now, next question."

"You promised," whined Gaspard.

"If you could tell me the three ways. And you couldn't. Tell you what. If you can tell me all the ways a batsman can get out, I'll definitely go, it's Percy's turn soon anyway. I'll give you a bit of help. There are eleven if you don't include mankading as a separate form of dismissal."

161

"Oh, I'd never do that," moaned Gaspard. By the time of Percy's shift, Gaspard was so exhausted that he drifted in and out of sleep despite the constant droning. In some ways, the boring nature of the monologue was helpful.

"…And he always forgot to reset the screebling knob after he'd…"

"Glumph."

"…And as you no doubt know, aluminium alloy is particularly…"

"Znorx."

When the alarm rang, Gaspard slept straight through. It was only the pounding on the front door that woke him. It was Thursday. Gaspard sat bolt upright with that dreadful sense of confusion and nausea that one experiences having been awoken from a deep though insufficient slumber. For a moment, he didn't know what day it was, what time it was or even where he was. He was even unsure of what had awoken him until the pounding began again. He staggered towards the door trying to think who the persistent visitor could be.

As his mind cleared fractionally, he prayed that it was not Hardcastle. After a second of two, he rethought that. It would be good if it were Hardcastle. He really needed to strangle somebody. From somewhere behind him came the sounds of sniggering. Then he heard the doctor's whispered query. "Do you think we should tell him?"

"Where would be the fun in that?" Gaspard could only wonder vaguely what they were on about as he pulled open the door. The man before the door was one of those creatures who could only be a civil servant He was dapper, oiled and exuded a prissy self-righteousness. He could have been a poor clone of Bert. Something jogged Gaspard's memory. Oh, shit, it was Thursday. This was the man from the council. What the hell was his name? Why had he thrown out the letter? Why couldn't he die? Philbert Worthy gazed down at the folder in his hand in that minor league form of intimidation favoured by petty officials.

"Mr Feeblebunny?" he enquired without looking up, secure in the knowledge that official letters always did the trick, "my name is…" He stopped abruptly as he looked up. "Hello?"

"Hello," responded Gaspard a little perplexed at the delivery. "Hello?" said Worthy again, somewhat warily this time. "Anybody there?"

"Yes me. Right here," replied Gaspard, even more perplexed. From behind him came the sound of guffaws. "Is there anybody there?" Ventured Worthy in a raised voice.

"Look, I'm not sure what you're playing at but yes, there is. Right under your bloody nose." The lack of sleep was beginning to tell. More laughter from the ghosts added to Gaspard's frustration and annoyance.

"Look, um, I can hear you but I can't see you," said Worthy nervously. "Do you mind if I come in?"

"Oh, shit! Sorry. Yes, do come in," cried Gaspard, suddenly aware of what all the laughter was about. He'd awaken in such a confused state he'd forgotten he was wearing his robe.

"Um, just a second, I'll be right out," he said apologetically, fleeing into the bedroom. "Hello," he began, a minute or so later to hoots of mirth. "You must be from the council?"

"Um, yes. How do you do that?"

"Do what?"

"Open the front door from the bedroom? Some sort of electronic gizmo?"

"Something like that yes."

"And the voice? Speaker?"

"Mm, hm."

"Well, well. It's very good. I can't see a sign of anything. Bit confusing though if I'm to be brutally frank," he said, looking about.

"My fault. Now what can I do for you?" Behind him he heard Maud's voice. "Everybody ready?"

"As explained in my letter Mr Feeblebunny, we've received a complaint that you're running a B and B contrary to council ordinances. I have to perform an inspection to ascertain whether allegations are true." He compressed his lips in a slightly disapproving way.

"Inspect away old fruit," offered Gaspard in his best cavalier manner.

"You won't find another body here. Check the wardrobes if you will. Only my clothes in the flat and those are in my room. The second room I use for the TV. Don't like it in the living room. Frankly I don't know who told you this load of bollocks but whoever they are, they're either nuts or a bloody trouble maker. You know I'm a policeman? Possibly some creep with a grudge?"

"Possible," murmured Worthy. "Now if I might?" The inspection took little more than a minute. "Terribly sorry to inconvenience you Mr Feeblebunny…"

"Constable."

"Er, constable. It's a very strange case if I'm to be frank. You see, the original complaint was from someone who worked for us years ago, or at least we thought it was. That's why we acted so quickly, although we did think it a little strange. Most of us assumed the chap was dead. Hadn't been heard of in years."

"Really?"

"Go!" Maud shouted.

"Hm, looks like some sort of hoax. Again, our apologies, I…Jesus Christ!"

"What, what?" gabbled Gaspard alarmed and unable to see what the inspector was seeing.

"A bloody porpoise! What the hell are you doing with a porpoise in your flat?" Gaspard turned and there sure enough floated Spinner. Gaspard did his best to compose his features. "Um, are you alright, Mr Worthy?" he enquired solicitously.

"Of course I'm…well…there's a porpoise in the hallway…isn't there?" his voice trailed off uncertainly. "That's against regulations…exotic pet…um?"

"I think you'd best sit down, sir. I'll get you a drink of water."

"Floating," muttered Worthy, "in mid-air."

"Bloody hell how did that happen?" grumbled Maud. "What were you thinking Spinner? It was supposed to be Bert."

"Eek." ("You're cock up.")

"Alright, try again?" Maud urged.

"Hello?"

"Jesus, Mary and Joseph where did you come from?" Worthy sat staring goggle eyed at Bert. "What happened to the porpoise?" Then as recognition took over. "Bert?"

"Hello," said Bert again, still struggling with the ability to give his manifestation voice.

"Um, who are you speaking to?" asked Gaspard of the inspector, gambling on the big lie.

"Don't you see him? It's Threadneedle, the chap who wrote the letter." He suddenly seemed unsure. "Bert? Good lord you haven't aged a bit. How…?"

"I really think you need to lie down Mr Worthy," counselled Gaspard, even as Bert was beginning to fade.

"Bugger. Can't you do better than that?" Bert demanded of the others. "It's your fault Spinner. You sucked up all the energy."

"Eek!" ("It's not my bloody fault if you can't get it right.")

"One last concerted effort."

"What the buggery?" This last exclamation came from an extremely disconcerted Worthy who was frantically clutching onto his chair as the flat began to shake. Chess pieces scattered across the table under his nose. "It's a bloody earthquake," exclaimed Worthy Then, remembering his training he added, "don't use the lift."

"I'm sorry, I don't know what you're talking about. You really should see a doctor, I think."

"That lamp just fell off the table!" shouted the inspector, now utterly panicked. "It always does that," claimed Gaspard, thoroughly unconvincingly. It may have been a bit more believable if the light fitting under which he'd been standing was not now resting on his head and giving him an appearance somewhat akin to an Asian peasant farmer. Philbert Worthy fled.

In his panic, he barely noticed the bizarre figure that had been lurking outside the front door. Had he, he may have wondered why it had obviously been listening at the keyhole. He may also have wondered why it was wearing a hospital gown and sheltering beneath a tattered umbrella covered in aluminium foil.

"Well you lot ballsed that up," growled Bert. "I didn't have the chance to tell him anything."

"You can't blame others for your short comings," sniffed Percy. "You were bloody tongue tied and as for that last little fiasco…" The argument raged for hours which at least meant that Gaspard was able to ring in sick and sneak some much-needed rest, although it did take a while to shake off the effects of the morning's events.

It particularly troubled him that the near destruction of the flat had been described as a little fiasco.

In almost any other employment, Philbert Worthy would no doubt have been placed on immediate and indefinite stress leave after spilling his garbled story and insisting on filing a precise account of events. This was the local council however and their primary function was to make things as intolerable as possible for their constituents after lining their own pockets and pursuing their individual mad agendas.

Naturally therefore, the bit about the shaking residence had them immediately summoning the structural engineer. In line with their primary objective, they did give momentary consideration to calling the animal control inspector but even the most hardened official considered that to be a bridge too far. Now had he said the porpoise was in the bath…

Shortly after the unfortunate events of Thursday morning, Philbert Worthy entered a monastery.

Gaspard trudged wearily towards home. He was exhausted and it was beginning to tell on his wellbeing both mental and physical.

Despite his exhaustion, he was still alert enough to be on the lookout for Hardcastle, even though he could not bring himself to believe that the sergeant meant him actual physical harm. He noted the bizarrely accoutred figure lurking in the bushes near the front door of his apartment block but immediately dismissed the thought that the obviously disturbed individual posed any threat. The creature (sex indeterminate) was clad in a filthy and tattered windbreaker and a ruined woman's skirt. On its feet was a pair of threadbare carpet slippers and it was sheltering beneath a wreck of an umbrella that had been covered in aluminium foil. On its head was what appeared to be a large saucepan lid that had been roughly battered to fit.

He slipped past undetected which would not otherwise have happened had not Hardcastle's main intention been to use the bushes as a latrine. At the front door to his flat, Gaspard paused and listened quietly for some time before easing open the door and slipping cautiously inside.

No one about. There was a possibility he may be able to grab some sleep before the nightly torture began again. As he gained his bedroom door, he heard Maud's voice from the spare room. "Alright, again. And this time doctor, try to keep up with the others. And Percy, try a bit more vibrato."

With that, to Gaspard's utter astonishment, the three men broke into a falsetto rendition of Three Little Maids, from the Mikado.

Gaspard awoke in the early hours to find the entire collection of ghosts floating near his bed. To his bewilderment they were all in costume. Maud wore an old-fashioned bonnet and was clutching a small wicker basket while the men were all clad in what seemed to be sailor's uniforms. Spinner had a sailor's cap adorned with a pompom perched jauntily on his brow. "Good God. How did you…never mind," finished Gaspard wearily. "What the blazes have you lot dreamed up to torture me now?"

"We've come to entertain you Gaspard. We thought that we've been rather mean of late, chattering away in the night, so we've come to make it up to you," said Maud unconvincingly.

"Please Maud. The best thing you can do for me is to let me sleep."

"Are we ready?" Maud asked the group, ignoring Gaspard's protests. The doctor raised a pitch pipe to his lips and blew a single note. Toot. Maud burst into song. "I'm called little Buttercup, dear little Buttercup, Though I could never tell why…"

"Jesus Christ! Gilbert and Sullivan? You have to be bloody well joking!" screamed Gaspard. "The only buttercup I want to see is your buttock up and out of here. That goes for all of you. I've had enough!"

"It ill behoves you Gaspard Feeblebunny to use such vulgarity in the presence of a lady and I might add that you're showing a very poor attitude. We've worked very hard at this. Bert is really proud of his Modern Major General number and has been really excited at the prospect of performing it for you. Even Spinner has been practicing. Now, sit back and enjoy the performance before things get nasty." She flashed a look that more than adequately backed up the threat.

"You remember Thursday? Well there's a lot more where that came from. Ready gents?" Toot. "I'm called…"

"Alright! You have the TV!"

"Oh, that's very kind Gaspard. We hardly know what to say."

Toot.

"I'm called little Buttercup…"

"Look, I've given in. Can't you let me sleep now? No more harassment?"

"Well! I think it's very unkind of you to characterise all our hard work as harassment. We've come to entertain you." Maud gritted her teeth. "And entertain you we will." Toot. "I'm called little Buttercup…"

"Look, sorry to interrupt again but how many numbers did you have planned?" Gaspard asked, finally accepting that resistance was futile "You know, just in case I might need to get a bag of crisps or something?"

"Well, we haven't really counted but there couldn't be more than seventeen or so. Not counting the prepared encores of course. We were pretty certain you'd want more at the end. Ready, are we?" Toot. "I'm called little Buttercup…" It was a long night made even longer by frequent costume changes which Spinner was not quite able to get the hang of. Gaspard did indeed need a packet of crisps plus any number of beers.

His frequent toilet breaks didn't make the night any shorter. By the time the performance was ended, Gaspard was so well lubricated that he did indeed call for an encore. Considering the number of beers that he'd imbibed the phantom's forgave him for passing out in the middle of the last. The next morning Gaspard was in for a surprise. "Guess what Gaspard?"

"What?" He responded with immediate and deep suspicion.

"We've had a meeting and we're agreed that you don't have to buy the second TV," said Maud proudly. "We've had so much fun with the singing that we're going to keep it up."

"So after torturing me for ages you're just going to change your minds. Just like that." Gaspard snapped his fingers.

"We can change our minds if we want," said Maud defensively. "We thought you'd be pleased, being as cheap as you are." Maud sniffed haughtily. "Anyway, we all really enjoy it. A lot better that pickling our brains watching that rubbish on television. The doctor is really excited. He thinks after we've done a couple of G&S productions, we could maybe try something a bit more challenging. He thinks we should have a go at Aida, although Bert thinks that may be a bit over the top. He wants to do a Rogers and Hammerstein selection."

Was this a wind up? No. Gaspard could see the genuine enthusiasm. Was he happy? Like hell. He silently cursed himself for not giving in to the request for another TV immediately. At least, then he'd have been spared having to sit through their concerts. Worse was to come. "The trouble is Gaspard," said the doctor in that reasonable tone that always presages bad news, "we reckon we're short a voice or two. In particular, we're in need of a good baritone. Bert and I can do the tenor roles and Perce can just about manage a base, we can even throw in Spinner as a counter tenor provided you don't care about the words but we really are missing a baritone."

He fixed Gaspard with an expectant stare. "So?" enquired Gaspard nervously but he had a pretty fair idea where this was heading.

"We've heard you in the shower. You could pass with a bit of practice."

"I always thought he sounded as though he was trying to pass something," sniggered Bert rudely. "Probably a bladder stone."

"And what if I don't want to practice?" Gaspard growled, a little more aggressively than he would have liked but upset by Bert's mockery. He didn't want to sing but he didn't want to be dismissed as lacking the talent either. Humans, eh?

"We wouldn't like to contemplate that, would we doctor?" piped up Maud with more than a hint of menace. "We'll give you a list of the sheet music you'll need to buy. Don't worry about costumes, we throw something together for the performances."

"Performances?"

"Of course," said the doctor. "We're known as The Free Spirits, by the way. Best lose that attitude and get with the joie de vivre that the name implies. First rehearsal will be tonight after work. Don't be late."

"But what if…I don't know…want to go to the pub or something?"

"Bring home a bottle."

"Well, what if I want to go out on a date. There's this girl…" Before he could finish the thought, the group dissolved into what is often described as incontinent mirth.

It was the doctor who spoke first. "You know, that might just work out for us," he quavered, unable to completely keep the amusement from his voice. "We're in need of a contralto." Gaspard stormed from the room to unkind hoots of mirth.

The knock at the front door was totally unexpected. Gaspard was alarmed. Early morning visitors were not welcome at the best of times and after the episode with Worthy he was not inclined to entertain any more snoops. Then there was Hardcastle. Would he knock? There was a second knock. It sounded a trifle tentative; so not Hardcastle.

Gaspard peeked through the spyhole. It was an attractive young woman. He stood uncertainly, wondering whether he should open the door. It was too early for religious nuts. Perhaps a neighbour? That could mean a request for a favour. Would he look after her cat? That sort of thing. Potential bother.

"Who is it?" Queried the doctor, unhappy with Gaspard's dithering.

"I don't know. Never seen her before. Neighbour perhaps? I don't know many of the others in the building."

"Ask her if she's a contralto," said the doctor excitedly. "A soprano would do as well," interjected Bert, casting a meaningful glance at Maud who seethed at the perceived insult but said nothing. Maud would bide her time. She was good at that.

"Best open the door, she must have heard you. You don't want your neighbours to think you're a rude git." That was great coming from Bert who was arguably nothing but.

"No just a loon who has one-sided conversations with himself," said Gaspard. He sighed defeatedly and opened the door. He would have done it without Bert's urging. A young man of his age would never miss the opportunity of being in proximity to an attractive young woman. You never knew. Although he had a pretty fair idea. Still, it was always worth a shot.

"Oh, good morning. I hope I'm not disturbing you?" There was a slight flicker of fear across her face that said she'd heard him talking and was fairly sure she couldn't disturb him any more than he already was.

"Not at all but I am just about to leave for work." That should give him some wiggle room.

"That's alright, I shan't take much of your time. I'm Monica Goonhilly from the Hamm on Wye Borough Council. I presume you're Mr Feeblebunny?"

"Yes, that's right. Goonhilly did you say?" asked Gaspard uncertainly.

"Mm, it's an old Celtic name. Not many of us about," replied the caller.

"I'm not bloody surprised," murmured Bert who was shamelessly eaves dropping. Meanwhile Miss Goonhilly was thinking that it was a bit rich that someone called Feeblebunny should show surprise at her surname.

"Um, what can I do for you, Miss…er…Ms…Goonhilly?" The delivery was a bit shaky because Gaspard was already beginning to fall under the spell of his visitor who was just about his ideal of perfect womanhood. She was a little above average height, slender but well-proportioned and her long golden hair framed slightly elfin features.

"Monica will do Mr Feeblebunny. I'm the council's structural engineer. I've been informed that there was an event here, Thursday last. Our Mr Worthy says he experienced a severe instability."

"You can say that again," cackled Maud who was also listening in.

"Shut up Maud."

"I beg your pardon?"

"Oh, sorry…er…not directed at you, I…er…thought I heard the cat squawking."

"Meow."

"Shu…and what can I do for you…er, Monica?"

"Well, if it's convenient I'd like to do a survey some time very soon. Even now, if that wouldn't be a problem. Mr Worthy's experience was such that we have grave fears for the stability of your flat."

"Look, Monica, if I might be frank…"

"You can be earnest if you like," interjected Bert with a guffaw. "…er, if there is any instability it's in Mr Worthy. He was screaming that there'd been an earthquake. All in all, he was behaving very strangely." He shook his head sadly. "Claimed he saw a porpoise in the hallway." Miss Goonhilly showed no signs of backing down. "On the other hand, I suppose you have your job to do, so if it won't take too long…?" He ushered her in.

"Thank you Mr Feeblebunny."

"Gaspard, please."

"Um, thank you, Gaspard. It shouldn't take long. We're aware that Mr Worthy wasn't, ah, quite himself that day but once a report has been filed, we do have to follow up, you understand?"

"Of course. Red tape and all that. Inspect away, Monica."

"I've already spoken to many of your neighbours and they've noticed nothing untoward."

"Unsurprising in the circumstances."

"Hm. Is it always this cold in here?"

"Is it? I hadn't noticed." Gaspard looked about nervously having just noticed that the ghosts were missing. It was suspicious considering there earlier intrusive behaviour. His concerns were soon made real when singing broke out from the spare room. This time audible to all.

"Oh. Is that Gilbert and Sullivan? Where's it coming from?"

"Oh…um…probably the tape of my choral group. Must have slipped off pause somehow."

"Wow, it has such a realistic quality. So, you sing?"

"A little. I'm more a reluctant fill in if I'm to be truthful."

"Ask her if she likes Gilbert and Sullivan," whispered the doctor unnecessarily, suddenly appearing at Gaspard's elbow. "Um, do you like Gilbert and Sullivan, Monica?" Gaspard enquired reluctantly, praying that the answer would be no.

"I do rather. I used to be in a G&S society before I moved here. I always keep meaning to look for a group in Hamm but never get around to it somehow."

"Bingo!" Exalted the doctor. "Ask her if she's a contralto."

Miss Goonhilly's inspection was cursory by any standards which was no surprise considering that the originator of the report was currently gibbering uncontrollably in a remote monastery. It made evensong a real bugger. Gaspard bade her a sad farewell at the door, longing to establish an acquaintance but lacking the courage. Or for that matter the technique. "Well, it was nice meeting you Gaspard."

171

She shook his hand in a perfectly innocent manner that still almost made Gaspard swoon. "Perhaps if you know of any G&S group looking for members you might let me know," she said meaningfully, handing him her business card. She was beginning to think that despite his somewhat questionable behaviour initially that he might be someone she'd like to know. Six feet tall or so, slim but well-muscled and that blond tousled hair had a rather boyish appeal if she were to be honest. Faint smell of stale booze but that wasn't always a bad sign.

"Oh, yes of course. Um, I most certainly will."

"Ask her!" clamoured the ghosts.

"Eek."

"Why didn't you ask her? She'd be perfect," probed the doctor angrily.

"Why? Why? Don't you think that might take a bit of working up too it?" responded Gaspard savagely. "And how would you like to join our little group Miss Goonhilly? There's me, four spooks and a phantom porpoise. You'll fit right in."

"Well…"

"Yes, well. Think about it. I'm going to work."

10

Sergeant Hardcastle had so far been spectacularly unsuccessful in attaining his goal. That being quite simply the elimination of one Gaspard Feeblebunny. His mental state had deteriorated to the point that simply discovering what Gaspard had been up to was no longer the issue. No indeed. The issue was now solely Hardcastle's suffering at the hands of the conspirators. A conspiracy centred around one person. Gaspard. He had no real idea what the object of the conspiracy might be, other than to make him suffer but he knew that it was big and possibly something to do with board games. And almost certainly fish. They had a lot of resources and those resources included his one-time colleagues in the force. Or was it the service now? So far, he had fooled them. The saucepan lid and foil shielded him from their tracking beams but he was too wise in the ways of the establishment not to know that he was on borrowed time. He must act soon. He had come close a couple of times.

The first chance had unfortunately come when in the act of evacuation in the bushes outside Gaspard's building. His diet had been such that he was not able to rapidly give chase, his movements of one sort making immediate movement of another sort impossible, or at least very messy. Ironically both acts had something to do with the runs. Then by the time he had completed his ease and adjusted his garments Gaspard had long gone. He was disappointed of course but managed to console himself on the grounds that while he had failed on that occasion at least he was still off the radar.

As far as he could gather, no one was keeping a track of his movements. The second opportunity had come outside a music store when by mere chance their paths happened to coincide. Luck had again been with Gaspard because as he departed the store he had been joined at the exit by his colleague and Hardcastle had barely escaped detection. After serious thought, Hardcastle had at last concluded that his only chance was to gain entrance to the flat and await Gaspard's return. That had its obvious risks but how many fish fingers could one person have? It would be an anxious wait but he reasoned that if the best the forces of evil could summon up was to hurl tinned and frozen fish products, he could take it. He'd survived worse. If only he had known what was in store. Gaspard had left for the day and Hardcastle had begun to warily make his way towards his flat when the police car came out of nowhere. By now, the sergeant was of an appearance that no copper worth the name would ignore, certainly not in a quiet residential area. Hardcastle froze.

"Good morning, sir. Do you mind if I ask where you're going?" The constable greeted him with false bonhomie.

"I don't mind you asking as long as you don't mind me not answering," sneered Hardcastle.

"It was a reasonable question, sir. Do you live near here?" The tone of voice said that the officer was doubtful there were too many wombat burrows in the vicinity.

"No. Just out for a walk. I live with my brother in Middle Butt if you must know."

"And you would have proof of that, sir?"

"Well, not on me, no. I don't believe I need to under the law."

Hardcastle peered at the constable suspiciously. "What station are you from constable?"

"Downer Road, sir. Might I ask, sir, why you're wearing a hospital gown beneath your coat?"

"It's comfortable."

"Excuse me sir, but don't I know you?" The constable didn't actually know Hardcastle but he'd seen a rather bad photograph of him in the information he'd received. Or maybe not such a bad photo, more a pre-Gaspard one.

Things were suddenly beginning to piece together for the young policeman. Hospital gown, bad attitude, features that may be those of the missing sergeant.

Or for that matter a gargoyle but most likely the sergeant. He signalled to his colleague and whispered his suspicions. His colleague nodded agreement.

"Perhaps sir you'd better come with us. In the best interests of your own welfare." He smiled benignly.

"I don't know you. You're not a copper at all are you? You're one of them."

Hardcastle readied himself to flee. "I assure you I am sir. I'm Constable Salmon and my colleague here is Constable Periwinkle." Hardcastle's jaw dropped and his eyes bulged alarmingly. Salmon thought he may have murmured the word 'fish' but couldn't be sure.

"Are you all right sir?" enquired Salmon, immediately concerned that his collar was looking like someone with the world's worst case of constipation.

"You're one of them. Both of you," hissed Hardcastle.

"That's right sir, both of us are one of them. Now if you'll just accompany us?" Salmon responded, completely misunderstanding but trying to keep things reasonable in light of Hardcastle's overall demeanour and suddenly bizarre countenance.

"Why? Why would I go with the fish people? So you can put me away and force me to play Monopoly? Feed me (he shuddered) fishfingers?"

"We're policemen sir. Not sadists," said Periwinkle kindly. "Look sir, we believe that you might be our missing colleague, Sergeant Hardcastle. You are, aren't you sir?"

"You're better than I thought. How have you been tracking me? Microwaves? GPS trackers? Death Rays?" Hardcastle didn't wait for a reply, he turned and bolted, catching the two policemen off guard. Salmon tripped over Hardcastle's hastily discarded umbrella, which was clearly no longer of use and Periwinkle lost ground after narrowly avoiding a frisbeed saucepan lid.

The chase was soon aborted. It would have been better for all had it succeeded.

For the second time, Hardcastle slipped the lock to Gaspard's flat. If his previous entry had been wary, this one was with a distinct hint of terror. It was a feeling that had been foreign to the sergeant for most of his life but then he'd never before had kippers appear out of thin air and wrap around his lughole. He tentatively sniffed the air, praying there was no fishy odour. Nothing. Well, perhaps a slight and inexplicable brininess but nothing redolent of the missiles from his earlier visit. He relaxed slightly. Where to hide?

"Gaspard's home early," opined the doctor.

He poked his head through the door. "Oh, bugger, it's him again. The copper."

"How are we off for sardines?" Maud enquired evilly. Bert and Percy chuckled. Spinner looked distraught at the potential waste. "Wait on a minute," exclaimed the doctor. "Don't you see this is a perfect chance? Gaspard won't be home for hours but that copper sounded to me as though he may be a baritone. It's worth a shot, don't you think?"

Maud was the first to agree if only because it was probably a much eviller thing to do than what she'd had in mind. For the same reason, Bert and Percy weren't far behind.

"OK, who wants to manifest?"

"Ooh, me, me," cried Bert, as eager as a schoolboy who has the right answer for the first time in his life. Oddly enough, Bert had always had the right answers most of his life. Bert was a clever Dick, which meant that while he had the right answers, they usually came at the wrong time as far as others were concerned. This often meant either a thick ear or a hasty retreat. It always meant someone calling him a smart arse. "Eek!" piped Spinner feeling neglected and hoping to get in on the act.

"I don't think so Spinner. Communication could be a problem," said the doctor gently, "but you can guard the front door. How's that?"

"Eek!"

"Great. Off you go. Bert, reel him in. Oh, sorry Spinner."

"Hello sergeant Hardcastle," said Bert dolorously.

"Aaaah! What…who…?" Hardcastle stammered, dropping the jumbo pack of condoms he'd just fished from Gaspard's bedside table. A product identical to those filched by the mysterious figure on footage from the supermarket as it happened. The sergeant might have been rattled but he was tough. He gathered himself after a fashion and defensively reverted to his usual deeply suspicious state:

"This is some sort of trick…it is, isn't it?" he demanded, albeit sounding none too convinced.

"Do you really believe that? Remember our stunt with the fish fingers?"

Hardcastle almost whimpered at the memory.

"What if I were to repeat that little display? Would that convince you that I am precisely what your instincts are telling you I am?" asked Bert. Without waiting for an answer, he levitated an object from the coffee table and hurled it in the sergeant's direction. Hardcastle cried out and just managed to duck in time.

"So, you really are a…ghost, then?" He enquired tentatively, still reluctant to use the word. Despite the enquiry, he had to admit privately that even without the little demonstration it was hard not to reach that conclusion because Bert was floating a foot off the ground and semi-transparent.

"Well, I can see how you made sergeant," replied Bert drily.

Hardcastle looked around wildly. He reckoned he could make the front door before the spook could act in a more positive manner.

Or could he? The spectre had used the plural. Our, not my. How many were here? Of what hideous aspect? Last time there'd been the fish fingers from nowhere. Kippers. Sardines. How many other and possibly more repellent missiles could they summon up? For some reason he thought of tapioca pudding and shuddered. He was partially answered when he looked frantically towards the exit and saw Spinner. "Oh shit!"

"Eeeeek," warned Spinner.

"What…what do you want?" He had the odd feeling that he should have been a bit more appropriate. Something about restless and unquiet spirits perhaps but he was too shocked to respond formally.

"We require a task of thee, Sergeant Hardcastle," moaned Bert hamming it up shamelessly. There was no reason he couldn't frighten the shit out of him in the process was there? "Thou must perform a deed to expiate thy sins."

"Please. I wasn't meaning any harm. I was just…"

"But you were not just. You were unjust," interrupted Bert, hoping Hardcastle wouldn't ask him to explain what in the hell he meant. "Come. Come," moaned Bert again, beckoning in what he believed to be the best ghostly manner, which it no doubt was, he being a ghost and there not really being much to compare it against.

A quivering Hardcastle followed reluctantly, hoping for a chance to make a dash. At the front door, Spinner snapped his jaws menacingly. A heavy cloths iron floated in the air nearby him which put paid to that idea of doing a runner for the time being.

"So, introductions are in order, I suppose," said the doctor cheerily. "That's Bert Threadneedle that brought you in here. Tenor. This is Maud. Soprano, the other cove is Percy. Bass. Well, after a fashion." Perce scowled.

"I'm Ivor, also tenor. I'm sometimes called doctor because that's what I am. Not like Dr Who or something if that's what you're wondering. Ha, ha. Together we are The Free Spirits." He threw his chest out proudly although being a ghost the act lacked a degree of authenticity. "Oh, and the porpoise by the door is Spinner. Counter tenor. Sorry Spinner."

Hardcastle stood in shock, mouth agape before finally summoning up the ability to speak. Sort of. "The porpoise is a counter tenor?" Was all he could think of asking after the bizarre introduction. The question emerged as a sort of half croak.

"Ah, I see your confusion," replied the doctor light-heartedly. "We classify Spinner as a counter tenor because he can manage the falsetto rather well but of course he's unable to actually form words. He performs the melody in his own tongue however and that's sufficient for our needs. If I'm honest, a lot of the songs we do have a lot la de dah's and folderols, so it really doesn't matter."

"What the hell has all this to do with me?" Hardcastle growled, finally getting a grip on himself and reverting to type, even though he would have been just about fouling his breeches were he wearing any.

"Your voice, sergeant. Sorry, I thought it was obvious," explained Ivor, beginning to wonder whether the sergeant wasn't a bit thick. "We are in dire need of a baritone. A contralto, too of course but I doubt you can help us with the latter." He chortled.

"What?"

"A baritone. We're doing selections from the Mikado at the moment and you'd make a perfect Poo-Bah, or at least we hope you will."

"What?"

Behind Hardcastle's back Perce shrugged, pulled a face and revolved his finger near his forehead to indicate that perhaps the sergeant was a trifle doolally. "Look, sergeant. I can see you're a bit overwhelmed," persisted the doctor, a little patronisingly, "we spirits have formed a modest ensemble" (he pronounced the word in the French manner) "to entertain ourselves initially and later, we hope, others. We are short of voices. You may well fit the bill and as long as you're here…understand?" Hardcastle nodded mutely.

"Just one thing though sergeant. Perhaps a quick shower?"

"Perhaps a long shower," piped up Maud rudely, fanning her nose ineffectually.

"Alright Sarge, you have a good scrub up and we'll be ready to go. Just one thing; leave your…cloths, if we can call them that, outside the door. We wouldn't like you getting any ideas about doing a bunk. Gaspard won't mind if you filch a few things from his wardrobe afterwards I'm sure."

This last remark of Perce's was greeted by giggles from the assembled ghosts.

Reluctantly, Hardcastle discarded his garments and pushed them out the door. It had been a long time since he'd had a good shower. Or even washed for that matter. He was man enough to admit that he needed it. Almost any humiliation would be worth the luxury. The shower had a steadying effect which soon had the sergeant again contemplating an escape.

It was not that he had anything against Gilbert and Sullivan, in fact colleagues would have been surprised to learn that he had quite a collection of their works and often gave voice to the melodies in the shower. It was more that he had a disinclination to be held captive whether or not his captors had a corporeal nature.

Besides, they probably couldn't sing worth a damn. Naturally enough his first thought was a rush for the front door but his earlier fears of flying kippers and worse soon persuaded him to examine an alternative. Leaving the water running he looked out of the window. It was several floors to the ground but God be praised the building was blessed with sufficient outside plumbing to present a relatively safe descent for those brave enough or desperate enough to give it a bash and Hardcastle was both. Gaspard had a pair of bathroom slippers that though a trifle snug would do to protect the tootsies and the towel was more than ample to cover a fair portion of his anatomy.

That's fair as in ample, not attractive because the parts that most needed the coverage could scarcely be described as the latter. Unless one were of a peculiar bent that would necessarily be rare in nature. The window was adequate to allow Hardcastle's passage (and it goes without saying the rest of him) and with only a slight squeeze he managed to gain the pipes just below the window sill. It required a desperate clutching of the towel on a couple of occasions but he accomplished it with a certain aplomb and an uncertain placing of the feet.

"He's been gone a long time. You don't think…?" Perce was probably the most suspicious of the spooks but when it came to Maud and Bert it would have been a photo finish.

"Stick your head through the door. Not you Maud," exclaimed Bert hastily. "Damn. The bugger's gone. Window's open."

"Bloody hell he must have been desperate. I wonder what he has against Gilbert and Sullivan?"

"I think you might be missing the bigger picture here, Perce," said the doctor patronisingly. "Oh well, He's no doubt better off with his own kind," he continued.

"The police you mean?"

"I was thinking more of Neanderthals."

Constables Salmon and Periwinkle were on their way back for another sweep of the area when the call came in from a concerned resident. An apparently disturbed man clad only in what appeared to be a towel or possibly a skirt was attempting to descend a building via outside drainage pipes.

"Did he say Feltham Rise Apartments schnookie?" Periwinkle queried, using Salmon's hated sobriquet. Constable Salmon had for some time been known as schnook after the Chinook Salmon. He would desperately have liked to have come up with something equally hurtful for his partner but since Periwinkle was six foot five, weighed one hundred and twenty kilos and played county rugby he managed to resist the temptation.

"Yep. Feeblebunny's place. You don't think...?"

"Possible but doubtful, eh? What would Hardcastle be doing climbing down his building? Breaking in, yes?" At that moment the pair came in sight of the block where they were afforded an excellent view of Hardcastle's descent. OK. When we say excellent, we mean unobstructed because excellent in its other meaning it certainly was not, the sergeant having lost the towel about halfway down. This meant that they were not only afforded a view of his descent but other things which fell more into the category of indecent.

And when we say halfway down, we of course mean halfway down the building. As far as the anatomy was concerned it was all the way down. Hardcastle was by now in a pretty bad way. There are certain parts of the male human anatomy that at times appear to have a mind of their own. It is one of the main reasons that most choreographers worthy of the name eschew nude dancing. Unless they're after comic effect.

On this occasion, one part in particular had been quite disorderly when crossing awkward obstructions and rough or poorly finished masonry. Hardcastle was bleeding.

"Good God it is, isn't it?"

"Looks like some old bum," replied Salmon, happily feeding his partner the line.

"Yes, but the old bum belongs to Hardcastle right?" By now the pair were laughing so much it took a while to recover.

After collecting himself, Salmon radioed in their discovery. "Yes, we're at the Feltham Rise Flats. We can see the person described. From what we can make out from the car, it's just some bloody old swinger," giggled Salmon. In the passenger's seat, Periwinkle was having trouble breathing.

"You get the blanket and the first aid kit from the back, schnookie. I'll wander over and make sure he doesn't do another runner," ordered Periwinkle, suddenly regretting his choice of roles because he realised that he may have to tackle the sergeant and hold him quite close.

"Fine but if there's any bandaging to be done, you can bloody well do it," replied Salmon, only half joking. Hardcastle was not the only one discomfited at this particular time.

It had been a quiet patrol for Gaspard and his partner, when something drew Gaspard's attention to the back seat. "Aaaah! Bloody hell!"

"Christ, give over! You nearly made me go off the bleedin' road. What the hell brought that on?"

"Sorry. Nothing. Just a…a sudden pain," apologised Gaspard, trying not to look at the character now seated behind the driver. It was dressed in the same manner as Death and if it came down to it, Gaspard himself on occasion but that was as far as it went. Mainly because that *was* as far as it went. The robe was empty. Although not empty if you take the drift.

"Sorry about that," said Mort, out of sight behind Gaspard, "I should have thought. Anyway, I'd like you to meet Terrance. Don't say anything."

"As if I bloody would," responded Gaspard falling into the pit dug long ago by our natural responses.

"What's that?"

"Sorry, mate. Look, I'm feeling a bit funny. Would you mind pulling over next to that caff and getting me a coffee?"

"Of course. It must be bloody serious if you feel funny. I've never known you to crack so much as a smile," chuckled his partner, Constable Arthur Loaf, generally known as 'arfur', for reasons that should be obvious.

"So what is it Mort? And who's this? You could have given me a flamin' heart attack." Gaspard was trying his best not to look at Terrance who was somehow a lot more menacing that the skeletal Mort for all that he was not apparently present unless as an ominous garment. *"Sorry if alarmed you,"* interrupted Terrance in a strangely hollow voice, *"it was not our intention."*

"Like he said. Not our intention but you know that. I thought you must be getting concerned at the apparent lack of action on our part. Note that I say apparent. Things are progressing. Terrance here has been appointed as liaison. It was thought that my time could be better spent doing what I do best."

"And that's it? Terrance has been appointed? Nothing else?"

"It's a step," replied Death defensively, "isn't it, Terrance?"

"*Oh, most decidedly,*" piped up Terrance in a manner that positively shouted 'civil service', "*and a significant one if I do say so myself.*"

"But that's it right? Nothing to report otherwise?" enquired Gaspard, perhaps a little too caustically for Terrance's liking. "Nothing about shears for instance? Undead porpoises?"

"*I see what you mean, Mort,*" said Terrance acerbically, ignoring Gaspard completely, "*you'd have thought that as a civil servant himself he might have a bit more understanding.*"

"Oh, I understand alright, believe me. Just don't expect me to be happy about it. And for the record I'm not a civil servant, I'm a copper, which in my book is about as far from a civil servant as is possible. We actually accomplish things," said Gaspard acidly.

"*Very well then. If that's all, I'll be off. I shall report when further progress has been made,*" said Terrance, clearly unhappy, "*I hope that won't be too long to suit your majesty.*"

"Bloody hell, you've done it now, why did you have to be so hard on him?"

"Sorry Mort, I really am sorry," responded Gaspard regretfully, "it's just that sometimes this civil service rubbish gets my back up. I really didn't mean to be rude. Would you apologise for me?"

"No. It'd be pointless. He'd just think it was me trying to gloss things over. The only way is in person. *And* without delay. Get your robe on after work, I'm taking you to meet him." Mort was firm.

"You don't mean...?"

"I most certainly do, although I admit that it's highly irregular. Still, nothing else for it. We can't let him stew or he might slack off. He's really very sensitive. Even with the apology it may be too late. Remember that in the civil service the worst sort of bolloching is to tell the bollochee in a very gentle voice that he's been reprimanded. That little rant of yours was well out of order."

He sighed his disturbing sigh, redolent of zephyrs in ancient dusty lands.

"I'll do everything I can Mort. Is there anything I should know?"

"Nothing that will make a difference. Now, on another topic, how's Spinner?"

"Seems to be settling in well. He's enjoying the ensemble work. It's amazing you know; he can obviously understand everything that's said to him. Pity he can't make himself understood to others."

"Maybe. Just goes to show though doesn't it? He's learned to understand you but you can't understand him. Does that tell you something about human intelligence? Or perhaps arrogance would be a more appropriate word?"

Gaspard simply shrugged. "Oh, I suppose I should tell you while I think of it that Hardcastle broke into your flat again. Don't worry, he's gone and unlikely to be back. A couple of your colleagues picked him up after he'd climbed down the outside wall of the building to escape. Stark bollochy naked when they arrested him."

"Good God, really? I almost feel sorry for the poor bugger. Oh well, I'm sure he survived OK. He's a tough old scrote."

"Funny you should say that…"

"Look out. Her comes 'arfur. I'll see you after work."

"Count on it."

Fear of the unknown is perhaps the worst of human fears, so you'd think that Sergeant Hardcastle would feel a little better now that part of the unknown had become known. Although admittedly, what was now known was of itself unknown in that he had no idea of the spirits' powers or intentions. Nor had he solved the riddle of their link to Feeblebunny. Had he been singing one of G & S' numbers he may have chosen the one that included the words: 'a most ingenious paradox'. If he'd been capable, he would possibly have been gnawing his finger nails while he grappled with his somewhat confused thoughts but as his arms were securely fastened to the sides of his bed in the psychiatric ward that unpleasant habit was not an option. Nor for that matter were a number of equally unpleasant other habits, none of which he was partial to. Let's hope that settles any possibly slanderous speculation. He was currently still in a slightly fragile and confused state which is a medical way of saying that he was still raving. As a result, at the few times he was mentally together enough to think clearly, he could not decide whether his present position in the psychiatric ward was better or worse than the brief stint he had recently faced in the police lock-up. He lay in bed unconsciously humming 'taken from the county gaol' from the Mikado and weighing up future courses of action, which cogitation was unfortunately rendered futile both by his confinement and mental state. The only bright spot that his troubled mind could ferret out of the morass of otherwise unhappy events was that so far he'd not been charged for either unlawful entry or public nudity. A pair of offences that if put together could always be misconstrued by the popular press or the less enlightened members of the community. At the thought of the word 'members', he flinched involuntarily and mentally thanked the medical staff for the pain killers and artful bandaging.

"Hello Marion, you're looking well," lied Dr Coombs cheerily. Hardcastle growled but made no objection to the use of his hated forename. Even in his state he was cunning enough to figure that the doctor was trying it on. Hardcastle was determined not to bite. Although he'd like to have. His teeth positively itched.

"Comfortable, are we?" Continued the doctor disappointedly, thus giving the sergeant a small victory.

Hardcastle nodded. "It's a bugger sleeping on my back though," he replied, "just so's you know." He made a show of shaking his hands in their restraints.

"Hm, not the best position usually but with your injuries perhaps it's a blessing, eh?" Chuckled the doctor, before cutting the mirth short when he realised it could only antagonise his patient. The sergeant growled. If he'd been a dog, his tail would have been stiff. "So, Ma…sergeant," said Coombs, cutting the use of the name short when he saw the warning flash in Hardcastle's eyes.
"I thought if you're up to it we could have a little chat about your recent activities?" Hardcastle turned his head away and said nothing.

"I know it may be difficult sergeant but soon one of your colleagues is going to be seeking my recommendations on whether or not you should be charged. My answers could well determine your future in the force…service." He waited expectantly.

"I went to kill Feeblebunny," answered the sergeant simply after a short while.

"Oh. Really?" Stammered Coombs, completely taken aback. "And why would you want to do that?"

"He's in league with the forces of darkness. He has to die," said Hardcastle almost dreamily. "Oh, and also he's a bastard."

"So these forces of darkness," enquired the doctor, ignoring the latter remark, "might I ask what form they take?"

"I suppose you'd call them ghosts."

"And you'd also call them ghosts?"

"Of course, you bloody ninny. I just said that, didn't I?"

"You saw these ghosts in his flat?"

"Only on the last occasion," said Hardcastle with a small shudder. "It was them that threw the kippers at me before but they didn't show themselves."

"You say 'they' sergeant. How many were there?"

"Four. Three males and a female. There're probably others. Oh! And the porpoise of course. Bastard threatened to throw an iron at me." Hardcastle glared fiercely about as though he could still see them.

"A porpoise? As in a cetacean? A creature of the deep? Bit like a dolphin?"

"Mm. Could even have been a dolphin I suppose but I think the doc called it a porpoise. Not that it would make it any less bloody weird. It sang counter tenor."

"Really? Counter tenor you say? Well, well," said Coombs nervously, again taken aback. "So, it seems you were able to…ah…converse with these spirits?"

The doctor was scribbling frantically in his note book. This was one for the Institute. "Yeah. I think that's the only reason they showed themselves. They wanted me to sing baritone." Hardcastle trembled slightly at the memory.

"Sing? Ah, hence the porpoise being a counter tenor. I see."

"They had a Gilbert and Sullivan society going. They were short a baritone. A contralto too if memory serves."

"So OK, let me get this right. You broke into Feeblebunny's flat in order to kill him. There you were accosted by the ghosts of four humans and a porpoise who forced you to sing with them?" Coombs' hand was now shaking with excitement.

"The Mikado."

"Beg your pardon?"

"They were doing selections from the Mikado. They wanted me for Poo-Bah."

"Poo-Bah?" enquired Coombs more than a little bewildered by now. He'd never been much of a fan of operettas.

"Character in the Mikado of course." Hardcastle was becoming irascible now.

"Right, right, of course. Forgive me." As a police psychiatrist Coombs had often come across those who attempted to fool him with bizarre stories and behaviour in attempts to either mitigate or be exonerated from, their actions. This was the first time he'd encountered someone who seemed to be doing his best to dig himself as deep a hole as possible. He scribbled the words: 'mad as a spring ferret' and underlined them.

"Leaving the spirits for a moment, can we just examine the reason for your climbing naked out of the window of the flat," asked Coombs soothingly, thinking a change of course may have a calming effect.

"Sure. Simple. They wanted me to take a shower. I was a bit whiffy, I must admit. I suppose in a way it was a kindness of sorts, although who'd have thought ghosts had a sense of smell eh?"

"That is a surprise. Still, I suppose if they can form choral groups…"

"You have a point there. Anyway, when I went for the shower, they forced me to leave my clothes outside the door."

"I see. So obviously you had no choice but to escape naked. Might I ask why you didn't simply flee the way you'd come?" Enquired the doctor gently.

"Why? I bloody told you why. Spinner threatened to throw a bloody cloths iron at me," replied Hardcastle heatedly.

"Yes, yes, of course. Sorry, forgot. Spinner would be the porpoise?"

"Of course it was the bloody porpoise. You don't think a human would be called Spinner, do you?"

"Yes, yes, silly of me," mumbled Coombs who had actually once known a Bill Spinner but thought it wise to let it go. "And you think he would have done that on porpoise?" He asked lightly, hoping to ease the mood, only to be met with a scowl from Hardcastle. It proved yet again, if further proof were required, that absurdity had no place in psychiatry. That is of course if one were to ignore the entire premise of the speciality.

"And for the record, I didn't climb out the window naked. I had a towel. It came off half way down," growled Hardcastle.

"Right. Glad we cleared that up," replied the doctor, wisely rejecting the jest that came to mind. "Now Sarge, I think we might wrap things up for now (bugger, there goes that Freudian association again). More than enough to be going on with eh? I'll pop in and see you later on tomorrow." The doctor arose somewhat more hurriedly than was decent in the circumstances but Hardcastle had escaped once before. No point in taking chances. Fortuitously, nurse Winsome entered just as the doctor was taking his leave so he was able to draw her attention to the amended treatment chart and the requirement for increased sedation. Radically increased sedation.

As he left, a memory of his first meeting with Constable Feeblebunny came to him. Specifically, the young coppers insistence that his flat was haunted. Naturally he pushed the thought to the back of his mind. Ridiculous.

After Coombs' departure, Nurse Winsome busied herself around the bed in the manner nurses usually do, fluffing up and straightening things and trying her best to seem friendly and professional without actually having to look at her patient. She was a sociable soul and couldn't help but wonder if the sergeant were as remote as he appeared to be. Attempts at any meaningful conversation had so far been a failure, partly she supposed because she found him very difficult to look at. What to do then?

"How's the bandage sergeant? Would you like me take a look at it?"

A look of near panic crossed Hardcastle's battered visage. He mumbled something which may have been no but could equally well have been a brief cry of distress. She fussed with his blankets, steeled herself, stroked his brow kindly, bade him have a good rest, then turned and bent over as though picking up something from the floor. There was an immediate cry of pain from Hardcastle. Not that remote then. She couldn't help feeling a little guilty at what she'd done, it hadn't been very professional. On the other hand, a girl always liked to know if she still had it.

Gaspard arrived home in a state of near nervous exhaustion. He had spent all day since Mort's appearance in the car, dreading the moment he would be transported to God knew where (probably) and God knew what (also probably). The last thing he wanted, he told himself, was to be whisked away into the afterlife and have to face a literally faceless civil servant. OK, maybe not the last thing, he admitted, again to himself. The last thing he really wanted was to be attacked by a rampaging hippo or spend an evening with Hilary Clinton. Or maybe, on further reflection, be forced to eat his great aunt Bertha's goulash. As a figure of speech though it was sort of adequate in the circumstances since no hippo's, Hungarian stews or other unthinkable horrors were lurking in the near vicinity. His great aunt did only live a few blocks away but he reckoned he was safe from her gastronomic disasters for the moment, mainly because they hated each other. Always assuming one didn't explode which to his mind was not altogether impossible.

The usual unwelcome guests were gathered in the living room and staring uneasily at his bedroom door.

"What oh!" Exclaimed Gaspard cheerily, doing his best to raise his own spirits. Whether or not he raised the spirits' spirits, he didn't for the moment give a bugger.

"What are you lot looking so apprehensive about?" He knew of course.

"It's him," answered Maud unhappily, "he's in your bedroom. What's he doing here Gaspard?"

"Fear not, Maud," said Gaspard a lot more jauntily than he felt, "we have an appointment. Nothing directly related to you, I can assure you."

"Not directly?" queried Bert, who was a bit savvier than the others when it came to weasel words. "How then?"

"Nothing that need concern you. Take my word for it," replied Gaspard. The group looked from one to the other, still suspicious but eventually accepted the denial.

"Alright, just make sure he buggers off," Maud hissed. "Shall we try that bit from Pinafore again?" she asked the others as they drifted from the room.

A few minutes later, Gaspard stood nervously before Death clad in his robe.

"Ready, are we?"

"As I'll ever be, I suppose. What happens next?"

"Just take my hand and I'll do the rest."

"Must I?" Gaspard asked, eyeing Mort's bony fingers with distaste.

"Well, I suppose you could hold onto my robe," said Death, sounding hurt.

"No, that's alright," replied Gaspard, taking the proffered skeletal mitt with a well disguised shudder.

"Before we go, I should say I'm not quite sure how you will handle this. As far as I'm aware you're the first mortal to make the visit, so how you'll perceive things or how it will affect you, I can't say."

"Great! Thanks for telling me that now. I…"

A lot of things had stunned Gaspard since his first run in with Mort, their extent being anything from a metaphorical smack in the chops to a half house brick around the back of the noggin. On that scale, the sight that met him was of the piano from a great height magnitude. He was standing outside a rather picturesque, thatched cottage of the type that a London stockbroker would spend years of someone else's salary to call his weekend retreat. "This is it?"

Whether or not Mort understood the strangled query was debatable but he certainly picked up on the note of utter bewilderment. "What? Oh, sorry, didn't

I say I just had to pop home first? Need to take care of something, won't take a sec."

Gaspard stared at the cottage with mouth agape. Apparently staring back at him from within a bank of nasturtiums was a skeletal garden gnome clad in a robe and carrying a small scythe. Beneath was a plaque bearing the words 'welcome to my garden'. His gaze shifted to the front step where a large battered looking ginger cat reclined in the sun. On catching sight of Death, it leaped up and expectantly took position before a saucer set back in the shade of a small bush. "Um, you never said you had a house."

"Well of course I do. Did you think I lived under a gooseberry bush?"

"No, of course not…I just didn't think of you living anywhere truth be told. You know…well…you're not the sort of um person that um screams Tudor cottage and a moggy, what with your…er…particular attributes." He shifted uncomfortably under Death's penetrating gaze. "Um…the nasturtiums are a bit of a surprise as well. I can't say I ever thought of you as a gardener."

"Great stress relief, you should try it. The nasturtiums go great in a salad I might add. Decorative and tasty. Now if you'll…"

"The cottage is lovely, did you build it?"

"Good grief no. Bit of trans-dimensional hocus pocus if you must know. I should have thought better of it but you get lured by the charm don't you? Charm! Ha! Place creaks like the blazes. It fair gives me the willies some times. I could swear there's something there that shouldn't be and don't get me started on the thatch. Now, apologies, I'd invite you in but I must get on, pushed for time and all that. Maybe once we've sorted all this bother we can have a nice cuppa together."

With that, he disappeared into the house leaving Gaspard to ponder how it was a being that lived outside of time could be pushed for it. Those particular speculations were curtailed and replaced by another when he spotted the weathered handwritten sign pinned to the front door. In gothic script, it read:

If not at home, please leave packages with FATE at Providence Farm or Mrs Moriarty at Mill Cottage (beware of the goat). Gaspard was still struggling to absorb this bizarre information when there was a heavy plodding and a large white and somewhat depressed looking horse put its head over the small gate at the side of the cottage. Well…that should probably be pale horse. The horse fixed him with an intense expression and snorted in a manner that Gaspard could only interpret as derisive.

"So, he really does have a pale horse," mused Gaspard aloud, addressing himself to the horse and wondering why he should be conversing with a quadruped.

"Why does the bugger always turn up in my car and scare the crap out of me then? Let me guess. Formal occasions only? End of days and all that?" The horse tossed his head and favoured Gaspard with a mournful look. Clearly Gaspard knew bugger all about equine emotional states but just about any animal can look depressed if they try hard enough. Horses have a head start in that direction as many a poor joke, usually one beginning with 'a horse walked into a bar' will point out. If they can't manage it, they generally either stand about refusing to budge or failing that, bite. The animal tossed its head in a manner that almost appeared that it understood and then stared longingly at the nasturtiums. Gaspard received the message loud and clear.

Mort reappeared carrying a tin of cat food and a small crate. He scraped the contents of the tin onto the saucer which immediately became the sole focus of the cat's attention. The horse, which was still munching a bunch of nasturtiums plucked for it by Gaspard snorted as though attempting to draw Death's attention. It did the trick. "My nasturtiums! You equine bastard!" The horse whinnied triumphantly, kicked up its heels and took off at a gallop. "If you're about to apologise, you don't need to. He tries this out on everyone. The bastard knows it gets up my robe."

"Um...sorry anyway, he just looked so mournful. What do you call him?"

"Most of the time it's 'you bastard'. He doesn't really have a name. I mean think about it. Along with me the pale horse is the embodiment of death and the apocalypse. It would hardly do to call him Dobbin would it?"

He set down the little crate which bore a small dial numbered from 0 to 9 with a central panel bearing the words 'pints please' and set the dial to 2 nodding with satisfaction. "Right, are we ready?"

"That's it? You came back to feed the cat?"

"Don't forget the milk."

"I..."

Gaspard found himself standing in what may have been a vast hall. Cosmically vast. Desks stretched far into the distance in all directions and at each sat one of the faceless robed figures. Well, not just faceless but he tried not to think of that. The missing face was bad enough. "Do I have to keep holding your hand?"

190

"No. You can let go now. How are you feeling?"

"Overwhelmed I suppose would be an adequate description. And what's a word for creeped out?"

"Those two will do nicely. I presume you refer to the occupants?"

"If you can describe an empty robe as an occupant, yes." Gaspard surveyed the hall in awe. He wondered if this was the sort of thing that the ancient Scandinavians had in mind when they dreamed up the idea of Valhalla. Maybe someone had visited in the distant past and repopulated the place in his memory with the spirits of warriors. After just a brief moment's speculation, he rejected the idea as too fanciful by far.

This would be more likely someone's vision of hell than heaven, although he was willing to concede that a chartered accountant somewhere would no doubt just about wet himself with delight. The room shifted. He shook his head. Walls stretched, contracted, shimmered. The ceiling, if it was a ceiling; wobbled. For a moment, he thought he could see strange galaxies. "Oh, shit!"

"Um, best you moderate the language. You never know who may be listening. What's the matter?"

"The whole room…hall, whatever it is, sort of…I don't know…it's almost like it's breathing. It can't can it?"

"Your perceptions will be challenged here. It's not a place for mortals. That said I wouldn't rule anything out," answered Death mysteriously. "We'd better find Terrance fast and get the blazes out of here quick. Oh look, there he is!" Death grabbed Gaspard's hand in a vice like grip and began to speed along the lines of desks. Gaspard knew that they were moving because everything became a blur but at the same time, he had no real sensation of motion. He tried to comprehend how it was that Mort could recognise Terrance in a vast sea of seemingly identical robes but soon abandoned the hopeless task. How far they travelled he had no idea because there were absolutely no reference points.

It was like being in the middle of an enormous ocean. Minus the swells. Or maybe not because the whole place appeared to be in motion while at the same time seeming rock solid. It was all very confusing. "Hello Terrance."

"Oh, it's you. What the heck is he doing here? Don't you know mortals are not permitted?" asked Terrance angrily.

"Special dispensation," replied Death cagily, "he needed to speak to you."

"Tough. I'm busy," shot back Terrance unpleasantly as he bent over his work. Perhaps folded would be a better word. Or maybe creased.

"He wants to apologise."

"Yeah, right. You're forcing him to, correct?"

"Not correct," piped up Gaspard, before things became more unpleasant and while he could still summon up the courage. "I really am sorry, Terrance. I was rude, I know but I've been under a lot of strain. I know it's no excuse but what with people trying to kill me and the ghosts in my flat serenading me all night long with selections from light opera I've been just about at the end of my tether. Please. I'd like to shake your hand."

"Are you taking the mickey?"

"Oh. Sorry. Just not used to…you know. No offence meant, I assure you. I am most truly sorry," gabbled Gaspard. The hood turned in his direction as though something within was observing him.

"Very well. I can feel that you are sincere. Now for your own sake and mine bugger off before things get out of control."

"More than happy to. First though, might I ask how things are progressing?" asked Gaspard uncertainly.

"Quite well. Although it would be difficult for you to tell. There are so many departments and offices involved and their activities all have to be coordinated. Piles of paper work. Lots of memos. It's all coming together though. Gradually." The last word was by way of a reluctant admission. *"To be frank, I'm having the devil's own problems with the Office of Octopuses and Squids. How they became involved heaven only knows. I mean that literally by the way; so that's more effort."* The robe moved in such a manner that Gaspard formed the impression Terrance was throwing up his hands. *"But it is progressing. We'll get there, take my word for it."*

"Hm, well nice to hear that, Terrance," replied Gaspard, now thoroughly unconvinced that anything was going to be accomplished within his lifetime and praying that Death's warning of cosmic calamity had been a tad overstated.

"And the, ah, shears?"

"Shears? Oh yes, them. Harold is handling that for me. I believe the Marine people are having a bit of a problem with debugging the code but you can ask him if you like. Be quick mind. You should really be out of here."

"Um, perhaps you can tell me where to find him?" asked Gaspard wondering how he could find anyone in this enormous place that literally seemed to stretch into infinity.

"Mort will show you. Now if you don't mind, I'm busy." Gaspard might have been a little more convinced of that last remark had not Terrance summoned a passing tea trolley.

"You have tea trolleys?" Gaspard asked of Death disbelievingly.

"Of course. How would we get through the day otherwise?"

"But this place is vast. I mean…it's literally on a cosmic scale. How is it possible? You must have to have millions of them."

"No. Just the one. Mrs MacPherson does a wonderful job."

"Omnipresent?" enquired Gaspard, who was beginning to get a handle on the workings of the afterlife.

"Spot on."

"I'm jealous, we could do with one of those at the station. Always on hand and those Chelsea buns looked fantastic. And forgive me if I'm wrong but didn't I notice what looked like Hobnobs?" This latter observation was made with a note of suspicion.

"Ah. Looks like is the operative term. You see for obvious reasons we can't get the real thing and the local product is distinctly inferior. You really wouldn't want this particular cart at your place because to put it crudely the tea tastes like piss and most of the biscuits are lacking. How those stories of ambrosia ever got started I'll never know. I can vouch for the buns though if you fancy one."

What seemed like seconds later Gaspard found himself standing beside an empty desk. "There's no one here."

"Look underneath."

"Please don't hurt me, I'm trying my best."

"Harold?"

"I know you're angry but it's not my fault. I just pass along the instructions."

"Like goods having to be fit for porpoise?" Queried Gaspard unkindly and instantly regretting his pique.

"It was a mistake anybody could have made," whined Harold, *"I put it right didn't I?"*

Gaspard took a deep breath and ordered himself not to make the obvious response that what he'd done or permitted to be done; it really made no difference which; was far from putting matters right. He ground his teeth and adopted his most casual air. "That's alright Harold. It could happen to anyone I'm sure. Anyone here at least." He probably shouldn't have appended the last sentence but he wasn't a bloody saint.

"Thank you. I think," replied the robe that was Harold. *"I suppose you're here to enquire about progress?"*

Gaspard nodded. *"Well, not a lot is the answer. Whoever wrote that code really fu...messed it up. No one will take responsibility which makes it harder to unravel the mess. We will though,"* he finally added gamely, though the remark was let down by the stink of defeat that hung about it. *"I understand though that Mort here has requested that another be constructed?"*

"That's right. How's it coming along?"

"Um, well not really my department you understand, perhaps you could check with Phil?"

"Hello Phil, I…"

"Oh shit! Sorry, ah...can't talk...late for an appointment." Phil fled in a flurry quite ignorant of the alliteration hanging in the air.

"Time to go home?"

"I think so." They were back at the cottage. Gaspard managed to put his surprise aside and react with a certain aplomb. Alright…as aplomb goes it was more an uncertain aplomb but he managed to wing it. "Tea?"

"Thank you. This place is lovely" gushed Gaspard, taking in the wooden panelled room with its Elizabethan carved furniture and huge inglenook fireplace.

"Grant you but a few minutes on the furniture is more than enough for anyone of my build I can tell you. I really have to get some new stuff. Now, what sort of tea?"

"Sort? Well, ordinary I suppose, the sort we usually have."

"I assume you meant the floor sweepings you get in your tea bags. Sorry, we don't do that here."

"It's alright," muttered Gaspard defensively.

"Alright? If you say so." He paused reflectively. "I suppose the people who bought the stuff adulterated with sheep droppings and chimney sweepings back a couple of hundred years ago thought so too. The only difference between what you get these days and that stuff is probably that the stuff with sheep shit tasted better."

"Alright, don't get on your high horse." Death quivered noticeably.

"Nasturtium eating bastard" he muttered, clearly struggling to gain control. "I know, how about a nice Orange Pekoe, everyone likes that and I doubt that your palate, unrefined as it is would know what to do with a Russian Caravan or

Iron Buddha." It was said without rancour but Gaspard had the distinct feeling that for all that he'd said to the contrary Death was blaming him for the nasturtiums.

"Camel shit and metal filings?" enquired Gaspard innocently.

"Smart arse."

11

Father O'Flatus was not happy. The rectory was a cold and dreary sort of place at the best of times and this certainly was not the best of times for a churchman. In the old days, before the scandals, he could have expected his solitary evenings to be occasionally brightened by visitors seeking consolation or support, or even bringing him gifts of food for himself or flowers for the church. These days a knock at the door was often as not someone calling to abuse him, or if not him then to vent their spleen at the institution he represented. Either that or to deposit something unpleasant on his doorstep. Really it all amounted to pretty much the same thing. Through it all the father was expected to retain his equanimity. It was enough to try the patience of Job himself. He sometimes wondered if Job hadn't had it a bit soft.

Once, a walk down the street meant he could be greeted by parishioners wanting to chat or at least offering blessings and cheery hellos. Even sometimes inviting him in for tea and cake. Nowadays he was more likely to be followed by people accusing him of being a paedophile.

Once a child had thrown a rock at him. In short, he was more likely to be cursed than blessed; spat upon than kissed. The abuse was bad but somehow the mockery was worse. Recently someone had painted over the word 'rectory' on his house and inserted the word 'rectumry'.

Nor was that the end of the matter. When he'd requested the parish council provide a workman to reinstate the sign, one member had wondered aloud why anyone would think to do such a thing. The implication being obvious to all present. It was close to being the last straw and enough to drive a man to drink. Which it had. To be frank though it wasn't so much a drive as a short putt. On the plus side, he had lost a bit of weight. His already low spirits had slumped to rock bottom after he'd been rebuked by his bishop for a perfectly understandable use of a common phrase. In lamenting the downturn in recent attendance and the growing poor perception of the church by many of his previous flock, he had decried his inability to recruit choristers. Perhaps he should have thought a bit longer before moaning that he couldn't find boys for love nor money but you couldn't censor every word.

The bishop had not only chided him for not thinking before he spoke but had hinted darkly about investigations.

Father O'Flatus was sitting in his living room alone and miserable. This he had long since decided was to be his fate for the rest of his days. That was of course assuming that his parish didn't shut up shop completely. Something that was becoming more possible every Sunday. Should that happen he'd still be alone and miserable, just not in this rectory. No doubt it would be somewhere even more bleak and depressing. Like a retirement village. The Father reached for his bottle which these days was never very far away.

Things could have been worse. The price of whisky could go up and at least he was still using a glass. OK, so it was a big one but he did have control over how much he poured into it. Some of the time anyway. He was just taking a mood settling mouthful of his nerve balm and letting it wash blissfully around his tonsils when there was a knock on the front door. Bugger. Why hadn't he remembered to close the living room door? Whoever was outside could see his light. He arose reluctantly, took a couple of steps then instantly retraced them and took a draught of his booze. Best lower the glass to a moderate level in case he was forced to invite someone in. It was bad enough having to wear the suspicion that these days clung to church men like a particularly odiferous shroud, without getting the reputation of being a whisky priest to boot. And boot him they would given the slightest chance.

In light of recent events, he proceeded with caution and peeked warily around the door. The priest recognised the man at the door immediately. How could he not after what had happened? He still had nightmares. "Hello Gaspard. To what do I owe the…pleasure?" enquired the good father uncertainly, taking an involuntary step back.

"Hello father. I hope I'm not disturbing you, I really needed someone to talk to."

"Oh, well best come in then, I suppose," mumbled O'Flatus with no small degree of hesitancy. These days it didn't do for a priest to be observed entertaining young men alone at home. Come to think of it, it never had. He looked about so furtively that had he been being observed the observer would no doubt have thought the worst.

"I suppose you're alone?" Asked the priest sounding concerned and just a tad frightened.

"What? I...oh...I see what you mean. Yes father, although I'm not sure how long that blessed state will continue." Gaspard shook his head resignedly. "They're becoming a real trial. There's more of them now, you know?"

"The blessed Mary and all the saints preserve us, Gaspard. You must be in very hell, my boy." He gestured towards the ancient and almost springless sofa into which Gaspard sank uncomfortably with his knees in the vicinity of his chin. The father immediately regretted not having hidden the booze before answering the door because he could see the way Gaspard was fixated on the bottle. His tongue was almost hanging out. Whisky may not be going up in price but neither was it cheap.

"Would you like a cup of tea my son?" asked O'Flatus, without much hope. Gaspard declined as the priest was certain he would. It was worth a shot. Luckily for Gaspard, Father O'Flatus was an hospitable sort, a fact he often regretted. Particularly when there was booze on show. "How might I ask did all this come about my son?" He really didn't want to know. It was far too unsettling but it was his job, like it or not.

"Probably best we don't go into the details father," said Gaspard to the priest's secret relief. "Suffice it to say there are three more than there were when you visited."

Gaspard accepted a proffered glass of whisky from the father's trembling hand. The unsteadiness was only partially due to his reluctance to part with it. "Thank you, father. I find I need this more and more these days." He took an alarmingly large slurp. Alarming both for his sobriety which to be honest Father O'Flatus wasn't really in a position to comment on and for the priest's stock of single malt. It was the latter that had the holy man most concerned.

"One of them's a porpoise," sighed Gaspard, "although if I'm to be fair he's not much of a problem." He paused. "Unless of course you count the end of the world as not a problem." He chuckled bitterly.

"They're supposed to be sorting it out but nothing is happening as far as I can see. I even paid them a visit. They're just bloody hopeless. Typical civil service." Gaspard sighed tragically, leaving his host completely baffled.

"I'm afraid you've lost me, my son," said Father O'Flatus nervously, taking the opportunity to move his chair back a little when Gaspard dropped his head. That's dropped as in lowered of course. And naturally the head was his own.

Gaspard did his best to explain but like a lot of Gaspard's bests in the current circumstances it would have been better categorised as a worst. It was certainly confusing for anyone not au fait with the real after life. Meaning everyone. It was much harder for a priest.

"So, you're telling me you've been to heaven and back?" Queried the priest incredulously, suddenly realising to his great discomfort that what he'd said sounded a little salacious.

"Yes father. Although you wouldn't call it heaven, I'm sure. It was the clerical department or something and you know what those places can be like?" He paused, unsure that the priest would comprehend. "Open plan office space," he added hoping that would suffice.

Clearly it didn't because O'Flatus rapidly dropped the subject, whether from lack of understanding or discomfiture at the subject Gaspard could not be sure. It was neither. It was absolute disbelief and growing certainty that his guest was delusional at best. "So, I gather the spirits are still troubling you terribly my son?" Asked the father, having decided to ignore Gaspard's rambling explanations and change the subject before Gaspard lost his marbles completely.

"Yes and no father. They've stopped insisting I join them in board games but they're now forcing me to sing with them. If that's not bad enough, they want me to recruit others to join them. I tell them it's impossible but they won't listen. They're obsessed."

"Sing?" Queried O'Flatus disbelievingly.

"Gilbert and Sullivan mainly. And that's not the worst. If I upset them, they wake me up at night doing selections from Pinafore. Well, I say Pinafore. That was at first, lately it's been Iolanthe. To make matters worse the buggers can't sing worth a damn." He shook his head sadly. "Although I suppose to be fair, Bert isn't bad and Spinner's OK in the chorus."

"Spinner? Odd name."

"He's the porpoise. Counter tenor."

"Ah, I see," responded O'Flatus knowingly, though utterly confused and now almost certain that despite the evidence of his own eyes from his visit to Gaspard's flat, his guest was certifiably insane.

"Can you help me Father?" Gaspard pleaded.

"I'm not sure what I can do. Have you changed your mind about asking the bishop for an exorcism?" enquired the father, hoping to possibly deflect Gaspard's attention.

"Good Lord no. If they got wind of that, they'd probably start singing selections from the Pyjama Game in the middle of the night."

He shuddered involuntarily. "I was wondering if you could think of other means, you being versed in those sorts of things."

"I'm sorry to disappoint you Gaspard but all I know about haunting I've learned from 1950s Hammer horror films," explained the priest, shaking his head.

"I was wondering about…you know…pentagrams and things. Holy water…" He faded out uncertainly. "Sorry my son. I believe pentagrams are something to do with demons and possession and such if I remember my Dennis Wheatley correctly. Anyway, it's the sort of thing the novice should avoid. It can do much more harm than good." He fought down memories of his recent dalliances with pentagrams and chickens. Have you thought of looking on the interweb? Not something I know anything about but I'm told it's the way these days."

Father O'Flatus was reluctant to suggest the use of technology, not having had the happiest of acquaintances with electronic wizardry. His last attempt had been at the request of his housekeeper who suggested that he replace a broken item by shopping for a replacement on line. She assured him that it was simple and invariably cheaper than the shops. His search for 'big jugs' had produced results so alarming to the man of the cloth that he had to go to confession on three occasions to clear his conscience.

The pair was amazed at what the search produced. It seemed that ghost eradication was a major industry (at least in the USA) and along with help forums, advice columns and newspaper articles on the subject there were countless people offering their services. There was even advice on how to summon up angels. Gaspard had the distinct opinion that if he'd googled for advice on how to detect a witch that would have appeared as well.

For all the multiplicity of sites however, there was little of any use, with most of the advice being to burn sage and talk to the dead nicely. All advised strongly not to upset them under any circumstances. Gaspard didn't need to be told the last bit which had come a bit late. By the time the search was over, Gaspard was even more despondent and Father O'Flatus even readier to be rid of his guest and get back to doing what remained of his bottle, justice. It being late Gaspard departed with nothing more than the priest's best wishes, a skinful of grog and a bottle of holy water that he drank on the way home. Despite the weird nature of the conversation, Father O'Flatus' spirits had been elevated enough by the company to decide to do some work on the essay he was writing for the parish magazine.

It was a piece on the foundation of the scouting movement. Gaspard had given him a better idea of web searches and the spirits he'd imbibed had made him brave enough to do a little on line research while the computer, usually dormant, was still active. He sat down at the desk and cracked his fingers. Now what was the name of Baden Powell's book? Ah yes. With slow determination, he began to type in the words: 'scouting for boys'.

Human beings are designed to take chances which is another way of saying that we sometimes do some pretty dumb things. It's just the way our brains are wired. We just can't resist taking risks and pulling things apart to see how they work. It's probably why you tried to disassemble the cat when you were a child or put water in Dad's petrol tank to see what would happen. You should have known that what would happen was that you'd get your arse walloped.

Although you probably did know, but you just had to try anyway. It's not your fault, it's just the way you're built. But try telling the old man that. This adventurousness is why the human race no longer hunts with sticks and lives in caves. It is why we're where we are today with all our whizzbangs, spiffy transport, fabulous electronics that few really understand and medicines that have us living way beyond our use by date. Or perhaps that last one should be our best before date. You might think that a subtle difference and so it is but what it means to old codgers is rather than suddenly and mercifully dropping dead one day (use by) one can gradually and often painfully decline well beyond that date (best before).

Our adventurousness is also why the world is fast becoming a total shit hole. Sometimes our dumb sense of adventure makes us too smart for our own good. It is also why those who follow the risky path that nature intended for us sometimes die horribly when their home made rocket doesn't work the way they'd intended or they try to cross the Atlantic on a raft of beer cans. It is called skimming the gene pool. Let's face it, there are some who just shouldn't be let loose and to be brutally frank we're better off without them. Along with our adventurous spirit, there is inside each of us, that wicked little imp that tells us we should do things just for the hell of it. Even if it's the daft thing and we know it. Even if we know it's just a little bit wrong.

Gaspard's imp was beginning to stir. He knew he was doing the wrong thing in wearing the robe when he shouldn't. He knew that Mort would be extremely vexed and that Terrance and his colleagues would be incandescent. He did it anyway. In typical human fashion, he excused his behaviour on the grounds of necessity.

It started after his resident spooks began their nightly harassment. Understandably, Gaspard was exhausted and often slept later than he should. Rather than be late for work he began to don the robe and pop up in the locker room when nobody was about. Even after the nightly irritation ceased, he kept it up. It made life easy and an easy life is what we all want although unless we're very bloody lucky it's seldom what we get. More to the point he hadn't yet been caught. Sin is a heady and exotic bloom.

We may tell ourselves that it'll be just one little sniff but once we've had that first hooterful we're generally lost. One little sniff turns to another and deeper whiff until at length we're taking great lungfuls of that tantalising fragrance. Before long, we find we can't exist without it.

Maybe that image isn't quite appropriate for the wearing of a robe because to be truthful after having slept in it on numerous occasions even Gaspard wouldn't have wanted to sniff it. Particularly if he'd eaten cheese before bed. But I'm sure you get the picture. So it was that after a relatively short period it all became routine and like all routines, whether good or bad, it simply became…well…routine. Which also meant that it became a bit boring. It was time for a bigger sniff. Those who should have been keeping an eye on him hadn't caught him so far, so why not? You know how it goes.

Until that greater and more exotic whiff, Gaspard was saving a heap of money on transport, able to have a nice lie in on most mornings and profiting from a great deal more leisure time, although with the ghostly choir at it, the latter benefit was arguably not quite so beneficial as it otherwise may have been. Unless of course, he spent the extra time out of the flat and then lied about what he'd been up to. Which is precisely what he did. However, as he had no hobbies, did not participate in sports or spend time indulging in romantic diversions, that meant spending a lot of time in the pub. It was as much about lack of imagination as a desire to become legless.

After all, he could have done many things to make his extra free time pleasurable and in a sober manner to boot. There were galleries and museums in Hamm on Wye (the Mousetrap Museum was world famous according to the council) or he could have taken macramé classes at the council hall. He could, had he not minded becoming a social pariah on the same level as a mime, have learned the piano accordion or joined the local Morris dancers. The possibilities were limitless for anyone who spent a moment's thought about the options and didn't mind ridicule, social exclusion or being bored shitless.

So perhaps the extra leisure time wasn't such a great advantage, particularly as it meant he was spending all the money he'd saved on transport imbibing fermented and spirituous beverages. Separately of course. Mostly. It didn't take too long for him to realise that fact but having considered the point he came to the conclusion that you can't have everything. Admittedly the point was usually considered after about six pints so it was no small wonder that he always came to that conclusion. He did sometimes have a few doubts the next morning as he threw up in the bathroom but those doubts were then washed away down at the pub that night.

What the additional expenditure on grog did give him was time away from the stress of life with Maud and the others and that was worth a king's ransom to his way of thinking. The more relaxed state resulting from the odd pint also assisted him in fulfilling his obligation to the choir when at last he did roll in, often relaxed as a newt. Shakespeare said in the Scottish play that drink is a great provoker of lechery, sleep and urine. He might also have added bloody awful singing. A few jugs of nuclear gargle water can have even the most reticent singer belting out the score of Oklahoma like a wildly offkey Gordon McRae.

The increased pub time did give Gaspard the odd pause for thought about the wisdom of that enterprise but in typical human fashion he was able to convince himself that he was in total control and merely indulging in a little harmless social interaction. As any student of the language can tell you, drinking habits are governed by another of those peculiar English irregular verbs: I am merry; you are drunk; he is a raging alcoholic.

Gaspard had thought briefly about the manner in which his misuse of the robe may be met by Mort and co. but he had failed to think about the effect of his new means of transport on his co-workers. People notice patterns of behaviour, a truth of which he should have been acutely aware as a rozzer. So, unsurprisingly, it was not long before his colleagues began to comment on the fact that his car was no longer being seen in the parking area and remarking it passing strange that no one these days ever saw him enter or leave the building.

It was as if he just magically appeared each morning and disappeared each evening. Tongues clucked and heads were scratched but even though he began to be known as 'the phantom' behind his back, only a few thought it worth any serious consideration. Unfortunately, two of the few were constables Tweedle and Arkwright who couldn't help but speculate if this sudden mysterious behaviour was in anyway linked to the certain mysterious appearance of a figure in Gaspard's local supermarket. It seemed a preposterous proposition to be sure but preposterous things seemed to have been occurring lately.

Following much heated and often confused discussion, they decided that before they reported to Sergeant Hardcastle they'd keep a closer watch on Constable Feeblebunny. That's if they could ever find him.

Dr Coombs met Nurse Winsome in the corridor. "Just been to see the patient nurse?" Nurse Winsome nodded in the affirmative. "And how's he progressing on the reduced medication? Still improving? Any noticeable changes do you think?"

"Oh yes, doctor. He seems brighter by the day. Always whistling or humming some little tune and this morning he confided in me that he couldn't believe how badly he'd behaved. He seemed very remorseful. I do believe that he's trying hard to understand what went wrong and to deal with it." She gave Coombs the benefit of her most fetching smile; a smile that would have fetched a penitent monk from his cell at a trot.

"Excellent, excellent," muttered the doctor, wondering why it was that the temperature seemed to have elevated suddenly, "thank you nurse, I'll just pop along then." Sergeant Hardcastle was indeed humming to himself when Coombs entered. He stopped immediately that he noticed the doctor and smiled benignly. The doctor had not heard much of the tune but it seemed somehow familiar. The pair exchanged cheerful greetings. "So, Sergeant. Nurse Winsome tells me you're really bucking up."

"I do feel much better doctor. The rest seems to have been doing wonders. As much as I hate to admit it, I was totally off my trolley for a while there. It sounds trite, I know but I think I was suffering from overwork."

"It certainly seems that way doesn't it? I take it there have been no more concerns about spirits? Other than the liquid variety of course, ha, ha."

"None at all sir. I feel like such an ass. All that babbling about ghosts and ghoulies. You must have thought I'd really cracked up."

"Not at all sergeant, although you did present a bit of a challenge there for a while." Coombs scratched his head. "So, what have you been doing for entertainment? Reading, television? That little solitaire game?" Coombs eyed the sergeant cannily.

"Mainly reading and games, doc. Have you ever watched daytime television? I've been going down to the patients lounge in the afternoons and having the odd game of chess and of course there's the monopoly." Hardcastle's left eye gave only the slightest flicker of betrayal and went unnoticed by the psychiatrist.

"Monopoly eh? That is an improvement. I'd say that you're well on the road to full recovery. Well done sergeant." He picked up a weighty tome from the bedside table. "And I see your reading the librettos of Gilbert and Sullivan."

"Mm, they've always been a favourite and for some reason I've developed a renewed interest while I've been recuperating." Hardcastle favoured the doctor with a grotesque smile.

"And then there's this, doctor," he said, proffering his daily meal order. Under the evening meal he'd ticked 'boiled haddock in white sauce'. So the tick was a trifle wobbly. So what? The pair chatted amicably for half an hour or so, the doctor gently probing and Hardcastle answering freely and frankly, or at least that was how it seemed. When the sergeant's lunch arrived, the doctor took his leave, convinced beyond a doubt that his patient was on the road to a full recovery. A beaming Hardcastle sat up in bed tucking into his lunch, occasionally humming the little phrase that was the only tune running through his head these days. A number from the Mikado. Later, in the shower, he gave it full voice; "…I am the lord high executioner…"

"For God's sake, get it right!" screamed the doctor for perhaps the third or fourth time that evening.

"Sorry, got a bit muddled," slurred Gaspard by way of response. "'S'bit complicated."

"Complicated is it? I see. 'In a tree by a river' is complicated? Oh, yes. Now that I think about it I can see how you'd be confused that it's not in a tree by a bloody willow!"

"I'm tired," whined Gaspard, unable to think of any reasonable explanation and refusing to admit that he might be just a little bit tiddly. "Anyway, 's bloody crap song," he added belligerently after a little not so clear consideration.

"You're not tired you're tight. I'd think that you'd be a bit more grateful after we've given you the lead role."

"Ah yes, forgive me my ingratitude please," fired back Gaspard, not so drunk that he couldn't feel aggrieved at being forced into nightly choir sessions. "I'd forgotten what a bloody privilege it is to be compelled to spend my free time warbling with you talentless bastards."

"Talentless is it, I'll show you talentless!" screeched Maud, thoroughly incensed.

"Sorry, sorry," mumbled Gaspard, "I really didn't mean that. It's the fatigue talking. Please, just let me go to bed."

"What's the expression you professionals use for being pissed doctor?" asked Bert sarcastically. "Tired and emotional isn't it?"

"I'm not pissed. I'm tired."

"And emotional," added Bert with a chuckle.

"You're pissed Gaspard," said the doctor, not altogether unkindly, "and we're getting worried about you. You're ruining your health drinking every night. From what I can see, you exist on beer and crisps these days."

"What'd you expect. Forcing me to do things I don't want to do. I hate singing this crap."

"Oh, and you'd be much better occupied lurking in your room and goggling at mucky magazines?" sneered Maud.

Gaspard blushed and stayed silent, mainly because he was beginning to lose the thread and finding it difficult to remain upright. He'd had some bad nights recently but this was one of his worst and had more than a little do with catching sight of the tantalising Miss Goonhilly in the street.

"You might as well turn in, you're no bloody use to us," growled Percy. "Be warned though. Next time there'll be repercussions."

"Or maybe concussions," sniggered Maud. No one doubted that despite the snigger she was deadly serious.

"Hello, hope I'm not interrupting." Death's unannounced and sudden arrival was greeted with a chorus of profanity from the assembled spirits. Even Spinner managed an oath and he wasn't under threat. "Sorry about that. No need to leave on my account. I just wanted a word with Spinner," said Death hastily before the porpoise could join the others in scattering to the far corners of the flat.

"Eek?"

"Precisely," responded Death, addressing himself to the porpoise in fluent cetacean. "I just thought I'd let you in on the good news. Things have been progressing apace and it will be only a short while now before you can flip a fin at this lot and go back to your pod."

"What if I don't want to?"

"What?" Mort almost shrieked, utterly flabbergasted.

"Well, I'm not saying I definitely want to stay but I am rather beginning to enjoy myself and the doctor and I are working on a porpoise to English dictionary. It would be a shame to let all that work go to waste," said Spinner dubiously.

"But, but, what about the fish?" exclaimed Mort, unable to think of any more convincing case for the moment.

"You would think that eh? But to be honest the longer I'm here the more I realise that eating isn't all it's cracked up to be. I mean, have you ever eaten raw fish? Sure, it's alright for humans with their sushi and the like but a whole raw fish? Alive and wriggling? Scales and all? And just between the two of us some of them haven't emptied their bowels beforehand if you can imagine that."

"But you'll bugger everything up if you don't go back," argued Death desperately. "Heaven knows what would happen."

"Well, if they know what would happen, they can do something about it," replied Spinner in what seemed the logical response.

"That's not what I meant and you know it. It was a figure of speech. You could seriously mess with the orderly running of the universe," pleaded Mort urgently.

"Orderly? You call this cock up orderly?" Death dropped his head, temporarily at a loss.

"And while I think about it, I can do without the bloody sharks and orcas. I know you all think of us as fun-loving types but half the time all that leaping is just practicing to avoid being someone's dinner. And don't get me started about Humboldt squid." He thought for a moment. "And naturally I'm going to die someday, probably fairly soon, then I'd miss out on all the fun I'm having here. I'd no doubt end up in some watery afterlife in company with everyone I'd ever eaten and I can't imagine I'd be too bloody popular."

"What's going on?" Piped up the doctor, bravely peering around the door after having fled with the others on Death's arrival.

"Eek."

"Spinner is reluctant to leave. Could I impose upon you to persuade him?"

"Oh, Christ!" Ejaculated Gaspard, suddenly wide eyed as he became momentarily aware of what was going on before collapsing into a chair and passing into unconsciousness.

"That's great!" Exclaimed the doctor to Mort's dismay, totally ignoring Gaspard's little display. "He's our chorus. Without him we'd be buggered."

"Yes, but with him the universe could be buggered," shot back Death, a note of panic in his voice.

"Win a few lose a few," said Smallpiece laconically, his courage growing. "Makes no difference to us chickens."

"But don't you realise? We just don't know what might happen. It could be the end of days!"

"It won't be the end of our days. That's already happened. Anyway, nothing has happened so far from what I can see. It sounds to me that it's a bit like the Y2K fiasco. Another one of those 'the sky is falling' over reactions that we have to have every few years."

"Don't count on it. You could be heading for catastrophe," pleaded Death.

"We've only got your word for that Chicken Little and as far as I can see life is no more shit now than it's always been. Who knows, an out of place porpoise may even improve matters."

"Think about the flapping of a butterfly's wing."

"Christ, if that zen bullshit is the only argument you have…"

The argument went back and forth for some time with the others gradually joining in as they warily emerged from hiding. By the end of the evening, the ghosts were all thoroughly enjoying Mort's discomfiture and Spinner, who was having fun, had decided that he definitely wished to remain. Death departed to the assembled spirits singing 'A policeman's lot is not a happy one' with a heavy degree of sarcasm.

"You're not telling me he doesn't want to be alive again? That's bloody preposterous!"

"I am and he doesn't, Terrance. Something has to be done and fast."

"But we almost had it sorted. Isn't he aware of the hours we've had to work? The number of committees we had to form? The unprecedented cooperation between departments?"

"Any cooperation between departments would be unprecedented," replied Death, unable to resist the dig. "As far as Spinner is concerned, I believe at one stage he said something to the effect that he couldn't give a squid's fart."

"But the tea bill alone was enormous. Not to mention the extra biscuits. You have to make him understand."

Mort gave Terrance an appraising look, not quite sure that his colleague was grasping the bigger picture. Unfortunately, as far as Terrance was concerned, the working of the civil service was the only picture. "I tried, believe me but he has those buggers he lives with backing him up. Egging him on. I told him, I said his being dead meant fish not eaten, meant fish born that should never have been, meant his offspring and their offspring never existing, meant the whole...the whole plan falling apart. You know what he said? Balls. That's what he said. He's been infected by those bloody ghosts."

"Oh shit," exclaimed Terrance, finally seeming to grasp the enormity of the situation. *"All that bloody work for nothing."* OK, so maybe not.

"You have to tell the committee. Maybe our bloody Wizkid can come up with something. I'm sure I can't. I'm the wrong person for the job. Can't put things in reverse, etcetera. They need a plan and fast."

"That's easy for you to say. Do you know how many memos it would take to get the committee together for unscheduled meetings? Everybody's back with their individual departments. They have commitments!"

"Have commitments? They should BE committed. The whole lot of them. Remember the...?"

"You're going to bring up the platypus again aren't you? One little design problem and you can't let it drop. Anyway, it was the steering committee's fault. They set down the requirements."

"Well it's not my job," retorted Death stubbornly. "You need to re-form the committee and fast, platypus or no platypus."

"Fast it will never be and you know what would happen if I went running about shouting we're all doomed or the like. I'd be held responsible for the whole fiasco. It was only ever my job to sort out the initial problem and I've done that. As far as I'm concerned, the job's done. Find another bunny."

"Well it's not my job either. In fact, in terms of it not being someone's job it's a lot more not my job than it is yours. You're admin," said Death stubbornly and not a little confusingly.

"Yeah but it was your boy's balls up in the first place. Him and his bloody shears."

"That's bollocks and you know it. Gaspard has nothing to answer for. It was bloody Marine Department and your daft bloody clerk that fu…mucked everything up!" Exploded Mort. "Anybody who can't tell the difference between porpoise and purpose should be pushing the trolley for Mrs MacPherson."

"Well, find somebody who is responsible," seethed Terrance, knowing that the attack on his clerk was indirectly an attack on him. His voice trembled with rage.

"It's…not…my…bloody…job," emphasised Mort. The argument raged back and forth while those at nearby desks studiously kept their heads down and pretended not to hear and others suddenly remembered pressing appointments.

It was only concluded when a seething Mort stormed off, (if suddenly vanishing can be called storming), leaving Terrance in command of the ground but not in command of his temper or any plan to put matters right. Things would stay as they were. After all, no one was responsible. Death was not one to give up and resorted to the age-old civil service ploy of internal politics. He attempted to recruit known enemies of Terrance along with those jockeying for his job in an involved scheme to place full responsibility on him but without success. Even those hankering to fill Terrance's non-existent boots baulked lest they become embroiled in a task widely regarded as insuperable and thankless.

Better to wait and watch and hope that Terrance eventually made a mistake. Like trying to fix the problem. Terrance was too old a hand to fall into that trap although after an attack of conscience following a particularly harrowing event down below involving Humboldt squid, he did try to dupe a junior member of the Marine Department into taking on the mantle of saviour. He might have had some conscience but it didn't extend to ruining other's careers. After all, one day they may come after his job. His intended victim might have been junior but he wasn't an idiot so things remained as they were.

The marine events that soon began to occur as a result of departmental inactivity were generally unspectacular enough for admin to ignore, a task made easier by virtue of the fact that no one was responsible. That is until an occurrence some years later which was difficult for even the most hardened civil servant to pretend was anything but an abnormal and distinctly alarming event. Marine biologist Dr Orson Carte and his colleagues who had been studying porpoises near the Humber estuary were shocked when the pod was suddenly attacked by a huge school of herring, the like of which had never before been seen. The report, initially doubted by many in the field despite evidence of the savaged corpses, was only taken seriously when some weeks later a fishing trawler was attacked and capsized with serious loss of life. A Fleet Street journalist with more whimsy than empathy dubbed the tragedy the Moby kipper incident. His sense of whimsy was sorely taxed when some months afterward he was taken by a haddock while swimming off the Isle of Wight.

Relatives of the trawler's crew joked a trifle inaccurately that he'd finally been put in his plaice. Up in admin section the committee looked the other way which was just as well for their peace of mind because there were some pretty grisly incidents. Terrance took to filing those few reports that passed his desk behind his filing cabinet. With the one about the Humboldt squid on the very bottom.

12

We are assured that time passes quickly when we're enjoying ourselves. Gaspard didn't have enough experience to be able to judge whether that was true or not. All he knew was that his hours spent at home passed as though they were wading through treacle. Assuming hours could wade. Whether or not in treacle was probably irrelevant. Anyway, whatever they were doing vis a vis the act of dragging, the evening choir sessions seemed to last an eternity, maybe not so surprising considering that was what the spirits were facing. The worst wasn't the singing. He was becoming inured to the nightly warbling and though he hated to admit it, sometimes even enjoyed it, particularly when the rest of the group praised his rendition of a song. What he could never get used to was Bert's continual interruption with directions that made the late and unlamented Captain Bligh seem the very soul of moderation. The others didn't react to it, probably because he was the only target of Bert's little suggestions, as Bert himself called his intolerable bullying. It had reached the point where Gaspard no longer bothered to complain but just sat and fumed while Bert made his unwanted and often unwarranted remarks. Sometimes Gaspard would eat cheese out of spite knowing that it made him fart. Pungent farts at that. So he both fumed and fumed if you get the picture.

It could be said that he was reeking revenge. In a twist to his show of rebellion, the ghosts began to call him Gassy. When he complained, he was told that it was a mark of affection. They insisted they were bonding as a group and that use of the full Gaspard was too formal. When he continued to complain, Maud told him in no uncertain terms that if he wanted to be called something else then perhaps he should stop eating cheese. In this case, a full Gaspard was not something to be desired. And so his nights dragged on. He would often lie in bed after choir thinking of the C.G. Finney book, The Circus of Dr Lao, in which a character is told by the fortune teller that all their tomorrows, todays and yesterdays will be as one.

Certainly, that seemed to be the case for his evenings, for which he could see no end. Mort's promise of possible eternal life began to seem more a threat than a reward each evening that crawled to its bitter and lonely conclusion. His days weren't a whole lot better. Much of his duties lately had been rather humdrum and he yearned to be able to give his imp it's free reign and use his robe at work. He often found himself fantasising of superhero like adventures as he rounded up the criminal masterminds of Hamm on Wye to the plaudits of his superiors and the public at large. That was never going to happen while he had a full-time partner in the patrol car. It was probably also unlikely to happen for the simple fact that Hamm on Wye's criminal element was more likely to be pinching an unattended bike than planning the ultimate bank heist. To date, his biggest arrest, other than for traffic violations, had been a twelve-year-old girl who'd run off without paying for an ice-cream.

She'd been let off with a warning and a cuff around the earhole from her irate and seriously embarrassed mother. Despite that, he was convinced that more crime lurked in the shadows if only it could be seen and he was sure that it could only be seen if he couldn't be. Needless to say, things in the afterlife seemed to be taking their usual course which was either total inactivity or a complete bloody shambles. He sometimes wondered whether it had something to do with constipation, despite the rather obvious case against. Whatever the cause, it meant that his shears were in some sort of bureaucratic limbo. He had no idea that for the moment at least, no one on that side of the great divide separating life and death had any compulsion to be connected with a certain porpoise or the reason for his premature demise and rather embarrassing tendency to not be properly dead.

Any involvement could well spell the end of a career but only after a lengthy and terrifying interrogation. All the more terrifying because it wouldn't involve tea and biscuits.

Mort made the occasional visit, ostensibly to keep him apprised of the situation but really to stock up on Hobnobs. All the visits accomplished, other than the obvious, was to reinforce Gaspard's belief that those on the other side were all a bunch of self-interested incompetents and that Mort was beginning to push his luck. Actually, they did accomplish one other thing and that was to force him to wear his robe on regular raids to the supermarket to stockpile Hobnobs, extra tea and booze. He made a mental note to raise the question of a sub for petty cash the next time Mort visited. His only consolation was knowing that tea on the other side was piss (Mort's private stash excluded) and their biscuits not much better, along with not having to fulfil his role as the Collector. It did however mean being stuck with his increasingly annoying guests, the committee still being adamant that Death's role should not include gathering up loose spirits despite the obvious flaw in that approach. As a result, Gaspard's spirits were anything but loose. Most of the time these days they were weighed down with the iron chains of hopelessness.

Things were about to change for the better. For a short time at least.

Gladys' Caff was one of those cheap and cheerful places often found in lower rent districts of English towns. You know the sort; all day full English breakfast with lashings of baked beans and giant kettles full of hot, stewed, milky tea. Surprisingly, this one was quite close to the council chambers, albeit in a backstreet with a few dingey shops and boarded up premises. It was here that Gaspard had discovered Monica Goonhilly sometimes came for lunch, indicating to the trained investigator that even council engineers couldn't boast of sky-high salaries. Either that or they were in training for a cardiac arrest. He'd tried on a few occasions to engineer accidental meetings, an irony not lost on him but so far, he'd been unable to structure an event. Today would be his lucky day.

Once again he'd inveigled his partner; on this occasion Constable Snuffle; to pull up near the café for a break. These breaks had given Gaspard a bit of reputation with his fellow constables who could never understand why he insisted on always stopping at a place that sloshed out (served was inappropriate) what was arguably the worst coffee in the country and apparently made of wartime chicory extract. He peered hopefully in through the grimy window and his heart leaped. There at a bare chrome and formica table near the counter sat the object of his...for decency's sake let's say affections. From what he could see at a distance, she appeared to be tucking into a plate of egg and chips.

Thank Christ. Not a salad vegetable in sight. "Hello, it's Miss Goonhilly isn't?" Gaspard had gone just far enough past the young lady before pretending that he'd only belatedly registered her presence. The nonchalant air he adopted said that it was one of those chance meetings of two people who were vaguely acquainted. Certainly, the tone said, he'd not been obsessing about her from the only time they'd met and heaven forbid that he'd engineered this purely accidental meeting. Monica Goonhilly wasn't fooled in the least. For one thing, she'd seen the police car in this area far more often than one would suppose necessary for routine patrols. For another, Gaspard was a bloody awful actor. And she was a woman. If all that were not enough, he seemed to be sweating more than was strictly necessary for such a mild day, or even a moderate walk through the Sahara.

"Hello Gaspard," responded Monica, not deigning to enter into the game and subtly signalling her interest. "I see your flat hasn't collapsed yet."

"Flat? My flat what?" Gaspard stammered before hastily assessing the remark and coming to the conclusion there was little chance of it having any reference to his physiognomy.

"Oh, yes. Ah, how is your poor colleague?" he enquired, thinking that he'd recovered admirably. He didn't give two hoots about whatever his name was but thought it a good ploy to come across as caring.

"The last we heard he was still in the monastery," responded Monica, unable to suppress a smile. Whether it was out of pleasantry or her colleague's plight was anybody's guess. "I believe he's quite happy there, although some of the other monks are a little upset by his occasional bouts of gibbering. It's a silent order, you know?"

"No, I didn't. Poor fellow. I hope he's well on the road to recovery?" Damn it. How did they get onto this track? He only had ten minutes.

"The Prior is hopeful I believe. He thinks if he can rid him of his obsession with porpoises, he'll have it cracked. Anyway, how have you been? I've been thinking of your little group lately and wondering how you're getting on. I do so like G & S."

The hint for an invitation was so broad that even Gaspard couldn't miss it although the thought did strike him that it may be nothing more than wishful thinking on his part. The brief silence that followed Miss Goonhilly's query was broken by the lady herself deciding to up the ante. She'd seen the look of dismay and confusion on Gaspard's face as he struggled to come to terms with the quandary in which he found himself. He longed to have a reason to ask her out but was terrified of her learning of his unwanted guests.

"I don't suppose I could hear you one evening?" She all but purred in a manner so alluring that Gaspard began to feel a little faint.

"That snatch I heard at your flat was quite intriguing. It had a sort of haunting quality." That innocent remark was greeted with an involuntary twitch from Gaspard who couldn't help wondering if it was intentional. Her face told him it wasn't. "Um, well…ah…look…I'm not sure you'd like my group, Miss Goonhilly…ah…"

"Monica please, Gaspard," she interrupted, noting with pleasure that it made him swallow heavily. When his Adam's apple stopped bobbing, he struggled on. "You see, they're not a very nice bunch if I'm perfectly frank. A bit mean spirited." Bugger, did he really use the word spirit?

"Really? But you put up with them, so they can't be that bad?" She screwed her face up in a way she'd often practiced in the mirror. Gaspard thought it very fetching and completely disarming. It made her look so bloody cute. And desirable he thought with a faint glowing of the cheeks. Along with a little increased blood flow in other areas. The look had had its intended affect. Gaspard was completely disarmed. Later that evening he would also be dislegged when he remembered it and had to have the odd glass of tonsil wash to rid himself of unworthy thoughts.

"Well, it's hard to explain, I'm sort of stuck with them. And they really are a bit unpleasant. Bert is a bully and Maud…well…Maud is Maud. She's a bit of a crank."

"I thought Maud was the cat?" Bloody hell what a memory.

"Coincidence."

"Hm. Well, I'm really sorry to hear that. I was quite hoping to hear you. Perhaps even lend a hand if you needed it. Or I suppose I should say, a voice." She finished with an appealing and well-practiced little giggle.

"Look, I'd love to have you," began Gaspard, suddenly blushing furiously, "but I assure you, you wouldn't like it at all. Even I don't like it, even though I have them meeting at my place." He realised that he was beginning to sound a bit evasive. This wasn't going at all as he'd planned.

"Oh well. If I'd make you uncomfortable…" she said, trailing off disappointedly, allowing her lower lip to droop just enough to be almost sultry.

Bugger. He was losing her. Gaspard, never one to be able to read women, summoned his courage in one last desperate attempt to save the day, even though the signals from the other side of the table were screaming, 'ask me out, you nit'. "Um, perhaps instead you'd like to come to a performance with me?" Gaspard blurted. "The Hamm Rollers are doing The Gondoliers at the town hall this weekend." He dared to look into her eyes but with a hang dog look that displayed no confidence in a positive response.

"Oh, thank you Gaspard. Um, I think I'm free. Let me just have a look at my diary." No point in making him cocky. She made a show of examining her phone before pronouncing herself free. Arrangements were made not a moment too soon as Constable Snuffle appeared on the scene to announce they had an urgent call. Someone had pinched a bike outside the local comprehensive school and it was time to roll. After they'd left, Monica Goonhilly slumped back into her chair with a long-suffering sigh. Christ some of these boys could be hard work.

A rapturous Gaspard naturally made the ghosts suspicious. They were almost certain that his unnaturally high spirits were a result of a romantic liaison but he stubbornly refused to cop to it. The less they knew of his private life, such as it was, the better. For the ghosts, ignorance was anything but bliss. In their own interests, they had to keep Gaspard on a tight reign. It was time to take action.

"Which of you bastards has been messing about with my computer?" Fulminated Gaspard. It was the night before his date with Monica and he was on edge, so this invasion of his privacy was threatening to send him over the top. It wasn't made any better by the casual response from Bert.

"Oh, that would be all of us. You should know by now that for some things we have to work in concert." There was a chuckle around the group that Gaspard chose to ignore. "Well it's a bloody cheek and I'll thank you to leave it alone in future."

"Have something to hide have we?" Maud sniggered suggestively.

"No, I bloody well do not, it's a matter of principal." Then feeling the need for complete vindication, he added: "Feel free to look at my search history anytime."

"Oh we already have," piped up Percy. "It makes for interesting reading." There was a murmur around the group accompanied by knowing smiles.

"What the hell are you on about? There's nothing that anybody could be offended by."

"No? What about structural engineering?" queried Percy triumphantly.

"What? Ah, it's a perfectly innocent subject of interest. It was…er…it was because of the concern about the flat a while back. I just thought it was worth a bit of research," stammered Gaspard, aware that his cover had been blown.

"Nothing to do with the council engineer then? The desirable Miss Goonhilly," sneered Percy.

"Of course it was," said Maud with a cackle. "Who'd have thought structural engineering could double for pornography? I can just see you Gaspard, sitting there reading about erections and drooling over that pretty young thing. Disgusting." Gaspard didn't know whether Maud was serious or joking but knowing Maud he went with the obvious answer, that being she was an evil-minded old bat.

"Christ Maud, what is it about you prudes? You rabbit on about other's dirty minds when you can see sin where even the most prurient mind would fail. I'll bet you could find sex at a church picnic" Bert and Percy sniggered but Maud recoiled.

"It was a joke Gaspard," she spluttered, obviously offended. "I'd thought we were at last getting to know one another."

Gaspard felt as though he'd been kicked in the stomach. "Hell Maud, I'm sorry. You know I didn't mean it. I've been on edge." He knew that despite his apology it was the sort of thing from which there'd be no going back. There were some apologies that would never undo the hurt. Maud didn't make matters any easier by sniffing and turning her head away.

"Anyway," said the doctor, hurriedly seeking to divert the others' minds, "we also noted a reservation for the Hamm Rollers performance of The Gondoliers. Two tickets, no less. We shouldn't suppose that the two topics are related then? A sudden interest in engineering, an attractive engineer with an interest in G & S and two tickets to a performance? Methinks that there is romance afoot."

"I don't think it's her foot he's thinking about," sniggered Maud, doing her best to get back to her old self but looking distinctly downcast.

"Be careful, Gaspard," warned Bert prissily, "women who look like that can ruin a man." Spinner's response to Bert's caution was lost on the others' but translated roughly as, "only if he's bloody lucky."

"Of course, you'll be taking us with you?" said the doctor, in what was more a statement than a question. The others, even Spinner, nodded their heads.

"Not a chance. You think I'm bloody barmy?" Gaspard said incredulously.

"We'd be on our best behaviour."

"Which up until this moment hasn't been much to write home about, has it?" Gaspard replied with a withering sneer.

"Time for a meeting, I think," said Ivor to the others. With not a word spoken, they all five disappeared in a blink.

"So, Gaspard. Here's the situation," began the doctor who was usually the spokesman for the group. "If you don't take us, we'll make your life a bloody misery." He held up a hand as Gaspard's mouth opened to speak. "But. If you do take us, we swear that we'll not only behave at the performance but we'll also behave when you have guests. You won't know we're here." These last words were delivered with a knowing smile. "Face it my boy, if things work out with the delightful Miss Goonhilly, sooner or later she's going to expect you to invite her up. Not to do so may court suspicion and I'm sure you'd much rather court the lady concerned." The others nodded and there was the odd winning smile.

"You really think I'd bring her here? With you lot?"

"Think about it. You really have little choice. Face it Gaspard, even if you could get away with excluding the lady, which to my mind would be a dangerous path for your relationship, you can't live life as a recluse. Sooner or later you have to have people in. We can either hide away and keep schtum or start banging the pots and pans. It's your choice."

"You'll forgive me if I'm a bit suspicious but you have to admit that up until now you've taken the pots and pans option without much cause," Gaspard snapped. "I'm really not sure that I can trust you."

"Do you have a choice? Long and dare I say intimate evenings with everyone's favourite structural engineer are at stake."

"You all swear? Even you Maud?" Gaspard queried, his eyes narrowing in partial disbelief. Gaspard knew that she would be the one to break first. He could not imagine her tolerating any hint of what he thought of euphemistically as romance, under her very nose.

"I swear Gassy," retorted Maud grudgingly, making sure she got in a small dig in the process. "But," she added emphatically, "in return for my full cooperation you have to promise to stop eating cheese when we're practicing."

"Only if Bert promises to stop with his interruptions. We're not the bloody "D'Oyly Carte, Bert. Bert looked offended but nodded his assent. And you're aware Maud that there is a possibility that things may sometimes become…warm, between myself and Monica." The spectral figure that was Maud went a strange colour for a moment and shimmered slightly before she nodded. Gaspard was understandably wary but the doctor was right. He couldn't live as a recluse. Already his workmates were beginning to comment on the fact that he never invited anyone around.

"So how do we manage this?" he sighed to hoots of delight from the spooks.

"We've worked it all out mate," said Bert, taking over the mantle of group spokesman. "You take us to the theatre with your robe on, then nip home to pick up your date. After the show, we'll just hang about until you come back for us."

"And you won't get up to any mischief? No bloody phantom of the opera hi jinks while I'm gone?"

"Promise," said Bert with his fingers crossed behind his back. He hadn't thought of that but now that it had been mentioned…"And if I'm…ah, detained for a while?"

"Bloody hell, you're thinking a bit far in advance, aren't you," said Percy. "It's the first date mate. Don't go getting ahead of yourself."

"She's a nice girl," spat Maud. "How dare you think like that?"

"And you all swear you'll come home with no fuss?" asked Gaspard ignoring the outburst with difficulty and thinking that it wouldn't be such a bad thing if they did refuse. Naturally, that thought led to the unworthy consideration of just dumping them in the theatre. A little unhappily he realised that Mort and Terrance would never stand for it.

"Of course," they chorused together.

"What about you?" enquired Bert, probably the canniest of the group. "You wouldn't be considering abandoning us, would you?"

"That's a bit insulting, Bert," exclaimed Gaspard, feeling like a hypocrite but feigning outrage. To anyone with a good ear it was just the sort of outrage that said he'd been considering just that.

"That's alright then. We're all sworn. Bring on tomorrow night," exulted the doctor to a chorus of delight from the others. They vanished.

From the next room, Maud could be heard fussing. "I've absolutely nothing to wear."

"Well, we'll be going as gondoliers of course," said Bert a little slyly. "Maybe you could wear a peasant costume. One of those ones with a sort of dirndl thingy." This last sentence was emitted with a slightly husky note to his voice.

"And you can forget that right now Albert Threadneedle!" exclaimed Maud, haughtily. "The very idea!"

It was no doubt unsurprising that Gaspard had assumed he could use the powers of the new robe to transport the group to the venue. After all, hadn't he transported bags of shopping? All he had to do was…all he had to do…Bugger! He gathered the group together, which proved to be no small task in itself. Maud was still fussing with what she perceived to be a Venetian peasant outfit but looked uncomfortably like something that may have been worn by one of the less stable inmates of a Tudor era madhouse. Bert was fussily attempting to get his gondolier's hat at just the right jaunty angle and Spinner was...God alone knew what Spinner was doing but it probably had something to do with squid. "Look, hurry up. I'm not sure this is even going to work."

"Oh, great, now you tell us," came the chorused reply. "I admit that I didn't give it much thought, OK? I've just been so used to doing my own thing and it was so easy getting you all here that I just didn't take into account that this was a bit different. Anyway, maybe if we all cluster together? Right. Let's go."

Gaspard found himself standing alone in the town hall. "OK," he said to the annoyed group seconds later, "let's try holding hands."

"How the hell can we hold hands you twit? We're spirits."

"Do your best. Everybody set?" Bugger. "Look, I'll stand in the middle and you lot sort of gather round and put your arms around me. Make sure you're touching some part of the robe. Spinner, you'd better get in the middle with me."

"I'm not comfortable with this."

"You're not comfortable, Albert Threadneedle? That's a laugh. I can see your trousers."

"That's just your imagination, Maud."

"Well keep my imagination away from me then. You take my place Percy."

"Bugger that for a game of soldiers."

"Eek."

"Bugger. It looks like the car then."

"But if I drive you, I could be late for Monica. Traffic's a right bastard on Saturday nights."

"Better get a move on then. We're going whatever you say."

"Oh dear," twittered Maud nervously to the doctor as they all hurried towards the car, "this is so exciting. I'm just a bag of nerves."

"She's just a bag," whispered Percy unkindly to Bert who repaid him with a withering look.

"This is a theatre?" said Maud disappointedly. "I'd always imagined them as being really posh. This looks like...I dunno...a school hall or something."

"Well, it is sort of Maud. It's only the town hall auditorium. It's not a real theatre."

"Oh. I was hoping it'd be posh. I've never been to the theatre before, you know. I suppose I've never been anywhere really." She looked mournfully from one to the other. "Even the seats are those horrible folding things."

"You're a bloody ghost Maud, you don't need a seat," said a vexed Gaspard, who in his anxiety to be gone was being…well, a bit of a bastard if we're to be frank.

"That we can fix for you," said the doctor kindly, glaring at Gaspard who blushed to the roots of his hair and apologised humbly to Maud for his outburst. "You go and pick up your young lady, Gaspard, while we make Maud comfortable," said the doctor authoritatively. "So, Maud. What do you fancy? Red velvet plush with gilded arms? Let's do it boys!"

"A box of chocolates would be nice too, if you can manage it."

Gaspard had learned a little from his previous experience transporting Ivor, so he had been cautious about parking upon his arrival at the hall. It was impossible on a Saturday night to find a spot completely devoid of people but he did manage to find a sparsely populated area. Naturally, he did his best to park in a manner that would draw little or no attention. Which isn't all that easy when you're invisible. Unfortunately in the twenty first century there's always some prying bastard with a mobile phone. It still would have been OK if Gaspard had just taken the time to remove his robe before getting back into the car but he was a young man in a hurry.

Which is a kind way of saying that he was a young man in heat. It probably wasn't a good idea to use the car door either, since it was totally unnecessary and likely to draw attention. But then, we're all creatures of habit, aren't we? In Gaspard's case, in more ways than one.

Clyde Twimby was on his way to the performance (he always arrived well in advance of the curtain) when he saw the car arrive. Normally he would have paid it no mind but it seemed a trifle strange that nobody exited. Even after the driver's door had opened and closed. He shuffled closer. Apparently, no one had exited because there was no one to exit. He took out his phone and began to video, lingering on the licence plate then circling the vehicle to display the empty seats. Had nobody left the car? Really? Perhaps he'd just missed it. Been distracted for a moment.

He was standing a little way off now and about to put his camera away when the driver's door opened and closed again, seemingly of its own volition. The car's engine started. He moved closer, focussing on the driver's seat. Seconds later the indicators flashed and the vehicle began to move away from the kerb. The video was going viral within the hour.

Gaspard came to a screeching halt outside Monica's house. Or to more accurate the vehicle came to a screeching halt. Gaspard was the one responsible. Along with a set of crappy brake pads and lack of an anti-lock braking system. He was late but not to the point where he couldn't blame the traffic. Plus, he thought, he could always throw in Maud the cat for good measure if necessary, realising with a strange and momentary pang that he'd have to kill the non-existent cat off before Monica came to visit.

Was there such a thing as cat flu? Time to research cat disease. One had to be ahead of the game when it came to women. They were just so bloody good at sniffing out deceit. It didn't strike him that he was just no good at lying. The living room curtains twitched as he approached the front door and Monica could be seen briefly studying the street before disappearing from view. He was about to knock when he saw his skeletal hands and realised not a moment too soon that he was still wearing his robe. Hastily, he returned to his car and divested himself of the garment.

"Oh, that was you," observed Monica when she realised that the car that had drawn her attention was indeed Gaspard's. "Isn't that funny? I heard you but the car seemed to be empty. I figured that the noise must have been another car. How on earth did you manage to get to the door without me seeing you?"

"Ah…trade secret," Gaspard joked feebly, in a singularly unconvincing attempt at levity. Monica gave him one of those looks. Not a good start then.

Overall, Gaspard was happy with the way the night had developed. He and Monica had sat as close as could be and midway through the performance she had held his hand. Conversation had flowed in the car and he'd been the recipient of quite a telling good night kiss at the front door. A kiss that held promises of more to come. He'd been a bit miffed at having to turn down the invitation to come in for coffee which he was pretty sure was female code for something a lot more desirable and probably a lot hotter as well. On the whole though, he did not regret being unable to accept the invitation. This was a first date and if he'd misread simple politeness for a euphemism, things could have taken a disastrous turn.

He really didn't know women very well but his innocence had done him no harm. This gentlemanly turn of mind had surprised him almost as much as the delight he was feeling at his ghostly companions' excitement. They chattered and sang in the car on the way home and were still in high spirits as they approached the flat. Percy seemed almost sociable and Maud in particular was transformed. She clutched the lorgnette that the others had conjured up for her as though it were a talisman. They'd all had a good time, although those who had a bit more experience than Maud at theatrical evenings were aware that the performance hadn't been exactly professional. For a start, the Grand Inquisitor had been a superannuated old codger whose dentures slipped every time he opened his mouth to emit a cracked high note.

In addition, Casilda, the lovely young daughter of the Duchess of Plazatoro had been an overweight matron in her mid-fifties and her mother had been a very obvious fifteen years younger which led to some unfortunate confusion for a part of the audience. Of the two main male characters, supposedly of an age, one was a spotty seventeen-year-old and the other old enough to be his father. For all its apparent faults though, the performance was enjoyable enough for anyone familiar with the restrictions of amateur theatre. Maud was thrilled and the others were glad enough for the outing they would have put up with anything.

"So, you had a good time Maud?" Enquired Gaspard in one of those pointless questions designed to show friendly interest but really that just exhibits the fact one hasn't much to say otherwise. "Oh yes!" She followed this up by singing: "no possible probable shadow of doubt, no shadow of doubt whatever." This was followed by laughter and applause all round. When they reached the front door, she held up a hand to stay Gaspard as he was about to enter.

"I'm sorry Gaspard," she intoned seriously, "but I'm afraid we're going to have to repossess your property." Even Gaspard laughed. He went to bed that night a happy man for the first time in ages. That didn't mean he could sleep of course. His thoughts whirled between Monica and the group. The change in them all was amazing. It was almost unbelievable what a little entertainment could do. Mostly though. He thought of Monica. Was that a 'come hither' look he'd seen in those melting eyes when they kissed goodnight? Should he have risked the coffee invitation? No. Maud was correct. Monica was a nice girl and certainly wouldn't have been indulging in sexual euphemism. He had no idea that he was already falling into the error of placing Monica Goonhilly on a pedestal. For the moment though, he had no regrets which was as much a surprise to him as it would be to those who knew him. Monica meanwhile was lying awake and chewing her lip while wondering if her invitation had been a mistake. Inviting a first date 'for coffee' whether or not a lover of Gilbert and Sullivan probably looked at least desperate and at worst a bit loose. She wondered whether he would ask her out again.

Gaspard eventually drifted off in the early hours wondering if all this could possibly last. As it turned out, the truce with the ghosts lasted a night. Although even so, relations would still be a lot warmer than previously. Luckily, his relationship with Monica Goonhilly would last a lot longer despite some significant challenges.

"You've seen the morning paper?" Gaspard enquired acidly. "I thought you promised to behave yourselves?"

"I've no idea what you're talking about," replied Bert, thereby identifying himself as the guilty party.

"Look," said the doctor, butting in quickly. "It was just a bit of innocent fun. No harm done. If it helps, I apologise on behalf of the group."

"No harm done? You drew attention to yourselves. Read it!"

The headline was in the entertainment section which reduced the seriousness of the breach considerably but there was no doubt that it would still draw unwelcome commentary.

'Phantom of the Operetta?' read the headline. The following article reported a mysterious incident witnessed by the cast of the Hamm Rollers after their performance of The Gondoliers when the auditorium's piano had apparently burst into a spontaneous rendition of Shine on Harvest Moon.

This, coincidentally, was about the only tune that Bert could manage on the keys with any degree of competence. Although it was written in a light-hearted vein, the article was still enough to cause Gaspard significant disquiet. That disquiet would increase to a terrifyingly uncomfortable level a couple of days later when some smart arse put it together with the video of his car.

Hardcastle was out. Which is not to say that he'd suddenly announced he was gay, although his behaviour lately had been such that none would have been that surprised by anything he said, except…well…maybe that. No, he was out of hospital and resting at home. Resting was what the doctors called it. What others may have called it was anybody's guess but the word 'plotting' would probably have popped up there somewhere. This meant of course that Dr Coombs had pronounced him cured. What the sergeant's colleagues would have pronounced him was as mad as a rogue bull elephant in must and one lacking the cooperation of lady elephants at that.

One shouldn't think too badly of Coombs for having been taken in. After all, it was his job to cure people, so naturally his need for success in his chosen field meant that despite all evidence to the contrary he had to believe in his ability to do just that. We must remember that self-deception isn't always a conscious thing. He also had to believe in the validity of his chosen field which for anyone who'd been in the game as long as he had was a bit of a stretch but self-interest allowed him to manage it. Barely.

Then there was his professional reputation which depended on getting his patients back on their feet, psychologically speaking.

That part of the professional conundrum wasn't quite so innocent. So, Hardcastle was officially cured which as we all know means that he was still mad, just zonked out on drugs meant to mask his more extreme tendencies. That way he could be no harm to society, or so the theory had it. Unfortunately for the sergeant, it also meant that he was no longer a fully functioning member of that body. As well as no longer having a fully functioning member. Medication as a form of treatment can be a bit unfortunate when patients decide not to cooperate and reputations can be damaged severely when 'cured' patients go off the rails and have to be incarcerated or worse.

Fortunately for the profession, those reputations usually belong to someone else. Magistrates and parole boards being perennial favourites. Coombs hadn't had too many go full-on bananas in any serious way, leastwise not in any manner for which he couldn't disavow responsibility. After all, everyone knew that the occasional loon would crash and burn and at least in his branch of medicine his mistakes didn't usually result in anyone dying. Except maybe for that one highly unfortunate incident involving the bull dozer and human remains but nobody was ever able to prove anything so he was able to fool himself into feeling vindicated. Oh, and perhaps that case which the press with their usual hyperbole had reported as ending in a hail of gunfire even though the patient concerned had only been shot twenty seven times. Anyway, how could he have known that a paranoid schizophrenic couldn't be trusted to take his medication? Even the police officer in charge of the manhunt had assured the public that the patient was no more dangerous than any other criminally insane psychopath.

"Taken from the county jail. By a set of curious chances," sang Hardcastle, happily busying himself about the house not long after being released from what was somewhat euphemistically known as the rest centre. "Liberated then on bail,

On my own recognisances." At that, he laughed heartily and slung his day's dose of medication into the toilet bowl.

"My own recognisances," he chortled as he pressed the flush lever. It was now three days since the sergeant had taken any medication at all and his mind was a lot clearer. Clear enough to plan vengeance.

Clearly as mad as a Chinese clock. He picked up the pink furry bunny from a side table and turned it thoughtfully in his hands, while humming The Lord High Executioner absent-mindedly as he did. Deliberately he picked up the knife and began to stab it. Slowly and with a lot of twisting. It was only two weeks before he could return to work. If he was cleared by Coombs that is. Hardcastle had no doubt he would be. He knew how to manipulate the doctor. He'd already done so twice. Once when he was released to the rest centre and then when he was released to home rest. On his own recognizances. Which meant he alone was responsible for taking the tablets. The doctor would probably check though, which was why they were ending up down the loo. Absence meant consumption. He just had to hope there'd be no blood tests. Hardcastle knew there was nothing wrong with him.

Nothing that exacting revenge on Feeblebunny wouldn't cure anyway. He certainly didn't need the sort of medication that the doctor was giving him. The sort that made him somnolent and furry brained instead of his usual sharp and focused self. Sergeant Hardcastle hadn't quite grasped the idea that it was the focus the drugs were supposed to cure. The insane focus on one Constable Feeblebunny. Even had he, he would have pushed the idea to that part of the mind where we imprison unwanted thoughts. After all, it would have interfered with his plans. Whatever they were. He was a bit confused at the moment because while that part of the mind responsible for seeking revenge was lusting for blood, there was a still some small semblance of lucid thought trying to keep it in check.

At the moment, it was fighting a one-sided battle against a well-armed opponent and copping a right duffing up while refusing to yell Uncle. What it was yelling whenever it thought it could be heard was, 'you don't have to do it! It makes no sense!'

Hardcastle ceased his stabbing and went quiet for a moment. He didn't really need to kill Feeblebunny did he? What had he done, after all? What would it accomplish?

"Who gives a shit?" Said vengeance with a nasty poke from insanity.

"Kill the bastard anyway."

"There's somebody knocking at the door," cried Maud, in a voice so high and tremulous it made the others laugh.

"Ignore it," replied Percy, true to form.

"Maybe it's the council," piped up Bert hopefully. "They never did resolve my complaint properly."

"Of course they did. That nutter who came here said there was nothing to it."

"Yes, but his report was a travesty. They couldn't take that seriously. If it's not the council, I shall write to them again and demand proper action," huffed Bert, full of indignation. "I'll just pop to the door and take a look."

"Take a look if you must," said Ivor with a note of warning in his voice, "but if you write to the council again, we'll all have your ectoplasm for garters."

"It's the copper. The nasty one!"

"What? Why would he be knocking? He usually breaks in."

"Maybe he's come to bury the hatchet with Gaspard."

"Not unless he's changed a hell of a lot. From what I gather, the only place he'd want to bury a hatchet would be in Gaspard's bonce. Anyway, he must know he wouldn't be home, surely? What's he up to?" The doctor scratched his head. "Unless it's a ruse in case the neighbours are about. You know, knock and then slip the lock as though he's been let in?"

"Hello? I know you're all at home. I believe you're looking for a baritone." The cry from Hardcastle caused a significant raising of a number of spectral eyebrows. Except in the case of Spinner who sort of flapped a fin in surprise. "Do you think he's genuine? Should we let him in?"

"Gee, I don't know Bert. Gaspard said he's been under treatment. Maybe he's come to put things right. What do you reckon?"

"What harm can it do? Maud can always heft a large can of tuna at him," said the doctor, only half joking.

"We're out of tuna. Would a large can of baked beans do?" joked Maud in response.

"A wondering minstrel I…" emanated from a deep baritone on the other side of the door.

"That does it, let him in. We can't lose a voice like that."

"Are we sure?" Perce was still a little doubtful but being an antisocial bastard at the best of times his concern carried little weight.

"I've got a little list and I'm sure he won't be missed…" Hardcastle cut himself off realising that he might just be giving himself away with that one. The group put their minds to it and the lock disengaged.

"You can open it, it's unlocked," called the doctor, materialising beside the door. "But no funny business, we're armed," he added just in case.

"That's right," put in Perce, not to be outdone and still dubious, "we're right well tooled up."

Hardcastle's head appeared around the door, soon to be followed by the rest of him trailing behind his feet. "Hullo. I'm sergeant Hardcastle. No hard feelings about my previous visits. Not on my side anyway. Are you still looking for a baritone?"

"We are, Sarge and no hard feelings on our side either." Despite the words, the doctor sounded a little wary. Hardcastle would have to prove himself before they could forget that he had been stalking Gaspard.

"You sound a bit doubtful and I'm not surprised. I tell you freely that I had a serious breakdown. I've yet to apologise to Feeb…Gaspard but I will once I'm back on duty. In the meantime, best you don't mention my having been here. He might take it the wrong way until he's convinced of my recovery." Hardcastle favoured the group with his gargoyle smile. "Oh, and while we're on the subject of the master of the house, perhaps you should tell me what time he usually gets in. It would be a bit awkward if I were still here, I think you'd agree."

"Right, well he usually gets home about seven, give or take a few minutes," said Maud, the self-appointed official time keeper, "but it can be a bit hard to tell these days because he sometimes just pops up in his room without us knowing whether he's in or not." The doctor gave Maud a warning shake of the head.

"You mean he comes in without you hearing him?"

"Something like that," she replied, suddenly sounding a bit nervous. "Let's say six to be safe. That way you're not likely to be caught with your pants down." This unfortunate turn of phrase brought back memories of Hardcastle's less that happy previous visit. "Sorry," she added hastily, "didn't mean nothing by it."

"Not all, not at all." Interesting. Feeblebunny's shift officially finished at seven. How in God's name did he get back minutes later when he lived twenty minutes from the station?

"Come on through," said the doctor, a trifle suspiciously, "we're just about to start on The Yeoman of the Guard. Do you know it?"

"Not well but I'm happy to learn."

"Look," if we're to be friends, said Hardcastle a short time later, "or at least fellow choristers," he hastily amended on seeing the scowl cross Perce's face, "perhaps we should properly introduce ourselves." There was a general murmuring of agreement.

"Eek."

"That's Spinner, as you already know," piped up the doctor taking charge as usual, "ex-squid chomper, accident victim and unintended ghost. I'm Doctor Ivor Smalpas, one-time G.P. You can call me doc or Ivor." He ignored the sniggers from Bert and Percy at the use of his peculiar pronunciation.

"Maud is Maud D'Unstable, spinster of this parish and one-time owner of these premises. The glum looking bastard is Percy Pargeter, misanthrope and ex-machinist, sorry Perce, just joking and the one who looks like a constipated clerk is Bert Threadneedle, late council inspector and murder victim. Once you've known him for a while you won't be surprised about the latter." The doctor's smile was in stark contrast to the other spectre's glares. Snigger at me will you, you bastards.

"Pleased to meet you all," responded Hardcastle formally. "I, as you all know, am Sergeant Hardcastle. What you don't know and what nobody but my mother, the registrar for births and one or two favoured individuals knows, is my Christian name, which I loathe with a passion. It is Marion. I tell you this in the interests of friendship. Feel free to use it if you wish, although you may also call me Sarge if you'd prefer. I shall be comfortable with either." He looked directly at Maud. "So, tell me dear lady, are you responsible for the elegant furnishings of this place? It seems to be too tasteful to have been the work of a mere police constable."

Bert's sotto voce remark of: "Oh. please," was ignored by both parties to the conversation.

"Why, yes it was, Marion, thank you for asking," simpered Maud. Hardcastle winced but bravely put up with Maud's use of his hated forename. "I'm sure if it were left up to that oaf, we'd all be sitting on orange crates and sleeping on the floor." She paused momentarily. "And if you don't mind me saying sergeant, I think Marion's a lovely name, you have no need to be sensitive about it. If you'd rather, though, I shall call you Sarge, I don't wish to make you uncomfortable."

"Not all Maud, please feel free to call me anything you like. Just don't call me late for dinner, eh?" he replied jocularly. This was all going very well. He'd soon have them eating out of his hand, although Percy might be a bit of a challenge. He'd have to bone up on machining. Perhaps invent a machinist uncle. Percy seemed the type who'd only be truly comfortable talking about work. That little obstacle aside, he reckoned he was in. All he had to do now was to play it cool, enjoy himself and wait until their guard was down. Then at the appropriate moment he could pounce. Who knew? Perhaps they could even be won over as accomplices? First though he had to apologise to that bastard.

Over the coming days, Hardcastle's resolve to do Gaspard harm waxed and waned as his sanity struggled against all odds to reassert itself. It was Tweedle who brought the information that finally pushed him over the edge.

"Have you got anything for me?" Hardcastle snapped rudely. His partial confinement was beginning to tell.

"As a matter of fact I have Sarge. Really weird stuff. Not sure what to make of it. Of course, being posted on the net it's most likely to be shit but…"

"For Christ's sake, what is it, man?"

"Right. Sorry Sarge. Take a look at this video that was posted a while back. And I can tell you we've checked the plates and they belong to the car owned by Constable Feeblebunny." Hardcastle watched the video disbelievingly, or rather he did believe it, he just couldn't believe it.

"That's not all Sarge. The car was parked outside the town hall where they were having a performance of a Gilbert and Sullivan thingy. Have a gander at this." With a dramatic flourish, he handed over a copy of the article about the ghostly piano. "People are speculating that the two events are linked Sarge, although that only works if you believe in ghosts, ha, ha."

"Oh, I believe Tweedle. You would too if you knew what I know."

"Um, right Sarge. Anyway, that's it. DSI Forcemeat has decided that on the strength of that video he's not going to wait for your return. He's going to interview Feeblebunny about that and the event a while back that you were looking into. Everyone's really mystified."

"Not everyone Tweedle, not everyone."

Hardcastle had successfully inveigled the High Spirits into doing some numbers from The Gondoliers, which he'd learned had been the performance at the town hall. "That's excellent, Maud. Your Casilda is wonderful."

"Oh, not that good I'm sure, Marion," simpered Maud. Hardcastle really knew how to pull her strings.

"Don't sell yourself short, Maud. If you were alive and well you'd have a part in the Hamm Rollers any day of the week. You're streets better than that fat old bag who did the role the other night."

"Oh, no. She might have been a bit old for the part but I'm sure she was a lot better singer," Maud twittered, fishing for another compliment and missing the frantic signals from the doctor to shut up.

"Don't be modest, my dear. I was at that performance and I know of which I speak. You'd leave her floundering in your musical wake."

Maud smirked to herself but said nothing. She was too busy acting coy to speak. "So, did you all enjoy it as much as I did?" enquired Hardcastle innocently. "I thought that for a local amateur group they weren't too bad."

"It wasn't bad," replied Bert grudgingly, realising that there was little point in pretending now that Maud had blown the secret. And what harm could it do anyway? The Sarge was one of them now, in a manner of speaking.

Got you.

"Did you know that your arrival had been videoed? It's all over the internet. You're virtually stars."

"What?" They all cried simultaneously.

"How the hell did that happen?" Queried the doctor sharply, just managing to get in before the others.

"How? Somebody saw Gaspard's car and thought it was a bit strange that it didn't have a driver. Not surprising when you think about it. Everyone's a bloody journalist these days."

"I told him to take off that bloody robe!" Bert exclaimed, belatedly realising he'd put his foot in it. And there we have it. After the revelations, the singing proceeded in a rather desultory fashion as some of the ghosts struggled with the implications of what they'd let slip. Through it all though, Percy had been studying Hardcastle's face with a serious intent. At length, the coin dropped.

"You're the one at the roadside. I knew your face was familiar."

"The roadside?"

"Yes, with the radar unit. Gaspard was the first one and then you popped up. I only glimpsed you as I drove past but yours is not the sort of face one easily forgets, if you'll forgive the observation."

"You were the phantom speeder?"

"If that's what you called me, yeah. I'm sorry about breaking the speed limit but I was late for work. If it makes you feel any better, you can issue a ticket on my estate. In my defence though, I was in a bit of shock, I mean it's not every day you wake up dead at the side of the road."

"No, I should think not," murmured Hardcastle thoughtfully. "Do you mind if I ask how it was that you were able to…ah…continue? I suppose that goes for all of you really. I've never thought to ask before but how did you end up as ghosts and not…um…taken up?" enquired Hardcastle, struggling with the concept.

"Well, it's different for each of us I suppose" responded Percy, barely ahead of the others. "In my case, I couldn't believe that I was dead. Simple as that. I have to admit that I was a bit obsessed with punctuality in my mortal state and when I realised that I was going to be late I did a runner. At first, it was unintentional but then after that bony bastard with the scythe kept trying to take me up, I deliberately avoided him."

"Shit, Percy, I'm not sure we're supposed to talk about that," exclaimed the doctor urgently.

"A bit late now, isn't it?" Pargeter said aggressively. "Anyway, everyone knows about Death, right?"

"Um, I not sure I do," said the sergeant uncertainly. "Do you mean to say that there really is a skeleton with a scythe that carries off people's souls?"

"Told you," hissed the doctor. "You've put your foot in it now Percy. Mort is going to be really pissed."

"Mort?"

"Oh shit."

After that, there was really no reason not to spill the beans.

"What I don't understand though," said Hardcastle after the ghosts had all told their stories, all except Spinner, he being a special case, "is how you can continue to avoid…Mort, is it?"

"Uh, huh. Look, you have to understand that he's quite busy. He doesn't just do people you know?"

"Really?"

"Fish, lizards, spiders, you name it. It must be a right bastard. You might want to consider that the next time you squash a roach. Anyway, sooner or later he has to give up and concentrate on taking the willing ones. Of course, none of us appreciated that at first. We kept hiding when he turned up. Now, though, we realise that he has limitations. The only one we need worry about now is the Collector but he has to have our consent, or so we're led to believe. He hasn't done anything yet that would lead us to believe differently, so we're feeling quite safe."

"The Collector? Who's that?"

"Well, it might surprise you to…"

"Percy!"

"Um, well, best not to go there. Let's just say he's Mort's assistant. You might meet him if you stick around."

"Percy!"

"Look, I might be a bit thick but I still don't quite understand. You said that Mort had given up but then you intimated that he keeps visiting. I mean, why does he bother?"

"Oh, he doesn't visit us, he…"

"Percy!"

Of course the bastard's office was in the new wing. These fast-tracked junior desk jockey types always had the best of everything. Not that Hardcastle cared about his surroundings. He'd happily have worked out of a filthy chicken coop as long as it meant he could kick some arse. Truth to tell, the best wasn't much improvement on the old. Those latter wings might have looked like parts of a slightly upgraded Victorian era public lavatory (minus the cottagers) but the budget for the new part still didn't run to much more than 70s civil service.

Even though it had been built in the new century.

They really must have had to search hard for an architect bad enough to pull that off. No doubt they'd had to pay for someone who'd won prizes. The ceilings were that depressing bloody polystyrene tile stuff complete with row after row of flickering fluorescent tubes. The floors were drab coloured linoleum tile squares, already showing signs of critical wear and the walls were finished in that dreadful civil service cream. Apart from the senior officer's hidey holes the place was mainly open plan with here and there some low, vinyl covered dividers that were coloured in that particular 'I think we're going to get some rain' shade of grey designed to lower the spirits of the most optimistic.

If Hardcastle cared about his work environment, he would have been mightily depressed. As it was, he couldn't help whistling a few bars of the executioner's song as he almost skipped along the corridor to DSI Forcemeat's office.

"Morning sergeant," said Forcemeat, barely looking up from his desk and pretending that he hadn't been playing Tetrus on his mobile phone.

"No sir, very high spirits," replied Hardcastle cheerily, thereby confusing the hell out the DSI.

"Sorry, what?" responded Forcemeat irritably. "Not in mourning sir. High spirits sir. Bad joke sir. Good morning sir."

"Mm, yes, well what can I do for you sergeant? I didn't think you were due back on duty yet. All ship shape and Bristol fashion I take it?"

"I'm afraid not sir. A few days yet before I can fashion the Bristols." Christ, is this what joy did to you? He needed to be careful before he pissed the DSI off. "It was about this business with Feeblebunny sir. You know, driverless cars and all that?"

"Ah, Feeblebunny. Yes. What was it you wanted sergeant?"

"It's like this sir. I have recently had some information from confidential informants who could blow Feeblebunny out of the water sir. I can't say too much because it has yet to be verified but I was wondering sir, if the case could be held over until I'm back on duty. There are other factors that need to be taken into account that predate this recent business and without wishing to sound smug sir, I'm the only one that's fully up to scratch on all the details."

"I see. You'll report to me, of course?"

"Naturally sir," lied Hardcastle.

"Very well then. Better you handle it than having to fill in someone else for the matter of a few days. After all, it's hardly of earth-shattering consequence is it?" That did it then. Someone else got to do the groundwork and Forcemeat could take the credit. Or apportion blame if it went tits up.

"Thank you, sir, I'll let you know as soon as I have something we can stick him with."

"Hm, not sure that's the attitude sergeant. Innocent until proven guilty and all that."

"Quite so sir. My apologies sir. I assure you that he'll receive due and impartial process sir." He'd process him like a ham.

"Very good and don't forget to keep me in the loop." As Hardcastle turned to leave, the DSI called after him. "Oh, and sergeant, are you sure he doesn't pronounce his name Philby? That's what most would do. I mean, Feeblebunny? Bit of an odd one, is he?"

"You've no idea sir."

235

13

An hour before the change of shift, the somewhat reduced and now balding figure of Sergeant Hardcastle, recently permitted to return on light duties, could be seen moving shiftily around the building. He checked out the sign-in book, the briefing room, staff canteen and after satisfying himself that Gaspard was nowhere on the premises made his way to the changing rooms. There he inspected each and every toilet stall, the shower room and changing area before taking up station outside the door. He lit up a forbidden cigarette and waited.

"Morning Hardcastle, back on duty I see."

"Morning Watt, yes indeed-y. Ready and willing to wreak havoc on the ungodly."

"Um, yeah. I suppose you know that this is a no…" Watt stopped himself dead, suddenly burdened with the uncomfortable feeling, brought on by the insane gleam in Hardcastle's eyes, that if he finished his warning sentence it would be he who was stopped dead. Hardcastle took a long drag on his cigarette and looked up expectantly.

"You were saying, Watt?" enquired Hardcastle with a twisted smile. Well, more twisted than usual. His features suddenly took on a look of studied confusion. "Which is not to say 'what' in the interrogative sense, you understand? I was using your patronym. I suppose what I should have said was, what were you saying Watt? Although maybe even then…how about, what were you saying, Watt, what? It must all be very confusing for you sometimes."

Sergeant Watt was almost certain that Hardcastle's eyes rolled about in his head as he made his bizarrely challenging remark. If that were not enough to have Watt inwardly questioning Dr Coombs' diagnosis, the grotesque smile, enough to curdle water, that accompanied it, certainly would have. "Uh, nothing mate. Have a good one." With that, Watt departed in an unusual hurry. Hardcastle giggled and began humming.

Something about deferring to the lord high executioner. "Hello Gaspard."

"Aaaah! Oh, hello sergeant, you startled me. Didn't see you by the door. Back on duty then?"

"More like back on duty now. A few words with you constable."

"Sorry Sarge, no time. I have to be on patrol in a few minutes." Gaspard did his best to sidle by what was, despite the weight loss, the still formidable bulk of Sergeant Marion Hardcastle. Even had Hardcastle been an eighty-pound weakling the scarred face alone would have been enough to instil caution. The scarring wasn't just to the face of course. Hardcastle was marked from head to toe and after his abrupt escape from the ghosts a while back, the damage now extended into his trousers.

"Not to worry my boy. It's all cleared with your sergeant. I shouldn't think it will take long. Just a few questions concerning your car."

"Argh."

"Before we get into that though, I would be pleased if you could tell me how you managed to get to work this morning?" Hardcastle did his best not to leer but he was enjoying himself.

"What?"

"I've already been through that with Watt," responded Hardcastle gnomically. "Simple question. How did you come to work? Walk, drive, bus?"

"Oh, that," replied Gaspard warily. "I, uh, drove as usual Sarge."

"Yet your car is not in the parking lot."

"Um…I parked in the street, Sarge."

"Risking a parking fine. Not very smart Constable."

"I suppose not. I'll move it later. Thanks for the warning Sarge."

"Not at all. Tell you what, give me the keys and I'll have it moved for you while we talk. Can't risk a fine. Not with your career teetering on the brink." Gaspard made a pathetic display of patting himself down. "No? Really? Alright, putting the missing keys aside for the moment, if something missing can be put anywhere, perhaps you'd tell me how you gained entrance to the changing room?"

"What? I don't understand Sarge. I mean. I just walked in, ha, ha." Gaspard was now feeling distinctly uncomfortable. On a scale of one to ten, it was cactus in the underpants level. Clearly Hardcastle was playing a game at his expense and it was likely to be expensive to the point of bankruptcy. He had no idea what the rules were for starters. The only thing he did know was that Hardcastle had written them and for the moment at least was keeping them to himself.

"Really? And how is it then that I didn't see you arrive? I've been standing here for some time now."

"I, ah, suppose I must have arrived before you then. I did get here quite early."

"Yet you haven't signed in. Nor were you in the changing room when I checked it an hour ago."

"I suppose, er, I suppose that I must have been in the bog, Sarge," stumbled Gaspard, now becoming distinctly rattled.

"Constipated are you? An hour's a bloody long time for a…well, you know. Or perhaps you don't if you're that badly bound up. Eat a lot of eggs, do we?"

"What? No. I…"

"Cheese? I'm told you're partial."

"I…er…"

"Before you say anything more, let me tell you that I searched every cubicle and the shower area an hour ago. You were noticeable by your absence. Nor did I hear any straining."

"I suppose…. I suppose I must have passed you without either of us noticing Sarge…er, as unlikely as that sounds, ha, ha."

"Ah, so now you're supposing that you passed me. Not a turd then? Or are you saying I'm a turd? That's a lot of supposition you're throwing up there Gaspard. You suppose you must have come in early; you suppose you must have been in the bog; you suppose you must have walked by with neither of us seeing each other. I'll tell you what I suppose Feeblebunny. I suppose that you're lying through your teeth. I suppose that you're unaware I have been talking to your live-in friends, although as we both know that's stretching the definition of live-in, who have spilled their guts and well and truly dumped you in the ordure. What do you suppose now?"

Gaspard heaved a sigh. "I suppose I'd better ask what they've been saying Sarge."

"That's not how it works my son. Let's get this finished in the interview room."

It was a long walk through to the old section. Hardcastle led the way and Gaspard trudged dejectedly behind, wondering frantically just what he was going to say. He had no doubt that Hardcastle knew more than was easy to explain.

"He knows everything," said Death unhappily as he fell in beside Gaspard.

"Oh, shit! I wish you wouldn't keep doing that."

"What?"

"Uh, nothing Sarge, just, er, stubbed my toe."

"Do you often have conversations with your pedal appendages Feeblebunny?"

"No Sarge. Sorry Sarge."

"Room's just around the corner."

"I think you're in a spot of bother."

"Don't you think I bloody know that?"

"Don't try that with me Constable or I'll bloody-well make you regret it."

"Sorry Sarge. I don't know where that came from."

"I think your best bet is to cough up. He knows it all anyway and in his deranged state he'll accept nothing but what he believes to be true."

"Second door on the right."

"Oh, do tell," replied Gaspard to Death, unable to stop himself but instantly regretting it.

"One more smart-arse remark, Constable and I'll have you on bloody toast."

"If it helps, I can say that whatever you tell him now will make little difference."

"Really, well I suppose that's a relief."

"Are you insane, Feeblebunny?"

"Right, Constable…"

"Before you start Sarge, I intend to come clean. I'll tell you everything, so I think it's probably best if you just let me tell you how it all happened, as it happened. I'm sure once you've heard everything, you'll understand why I couldn't tell anyone. I mean, you already know about the ghosts and talking about that alone would have been enough to have had me kicked off the force and sent to a home for the permanently bewildered."

Hardcastle twitched. "Alright. Off you go. Cough."

"OK, so if you've spoken to Percy and I presume you have," Hardcastle nodded, "you'll know that he was the cause of the radar anomalies. Did he mention Death at all? That's Death as in the entity not the ultimate cessation of life?" Again, Hardcastle nodded, allowing Gaspard free flow.

"Right. So, he wakes up dead at the side of the road and being an obsessive time keeper drives off before Mort…that's Death's name in case you didn't know, can collar him. Don't ask me how in the blue blazes he was able to drive because no one has managed to explain that to me but I suppose there are stories of ghost horses pulling chariots so why not cars? This keeps up for several days because he's caught in a spiritual loop. No doubt he's already told you all this. The critical part of it all, is that while Percy is finding his way to realising that he's dead, Death is trying to catch him and take him up. That leads to the bloody photo that had you so fired up. For whatever reason, Mort thought he could jump him in his car and ended up being knocked base over apex. Somehow the camera caught it, although only a very few could see it. The problem for me was that I could not only see the photo, I could also see Death. I think that I would probably have been able to convince myself that I hadn't except for the fact that he turned up at my door that night."

"Ah. That, I wasn't told. Not directly anyway," interrupted Hardcastle.

"Not surprisingly. Even the ghosts didn't know about what Mort had me doing until a little while ago." He shook his head sadly and looked across at Mort who gave him an encouraging wave.

"You will probably find this hard to believe but he hired me as an outside contractor to take over chasing down ghosts. Well, I say hired, what I really mean is press ganged. I had no choice." He shrugged helplessly. "You wanted to know how I got to work? I used the robe he gave me that gives me similar powers to him in that I can…I suppose teleport is the closest word, and also be invisible if I choose. Obviously. He also gave me a set of…believe it or not…garden shears, in lieu of a scythe, to gather up the souls I could persuade to accompany me."

"Jesus Christ!" Hardcastle exclaimed, who was finding it difficult to assimilate, even though all of his suspicions were being confirmed. There's a big gap between suspicion and fact. "But, the question arises, why did you use your car if you had the robe?"

"The original one only allowed invisibility and passing through solid objects. The committee took a while before they realised the impractically of that and gave me a proper one."

"Committee?"

"Best not to go there Sarge. And I mean that in more ways than one."

"OK, but if you had the new powers, why did you use the car to take your ghosts to the theatre? And while we're on the subject, why in the name of all that's holy would you take them for a night out anyway?"

"Simple. The robe wouldn't transport them all and blackmail."

"Hm, I suppose the next question is why you have a flat full of ghosts anyway? And why a bloody porpoise for Christ's sake?"

The interview, if that's what it could be called, went on for most of the morning. From time to time, the sergeant called for tea in what could almost be mistaken for a sympathetic gesture. Oddly enough, finally getting to the truth seemed to have gone some way to restoring the man's grip on reality.

Perceptions can be misleading. "I suppose all that remains, Feeblebunny, is for me to view this fabulous robe of yours," ventured Hardcastle. "Purely in the interests of dotting and crossing, of course. I don't doubt you for a moment. I wouldn't, even if most of what you say hadn't been confirmed by another if slightly unusual source, although that source does help it go down a lot better." He chuckled at his little witticism. It sounded a lot like a creaky gate.

"Is it really necessary Sarge? You won't be able to see it unless I put it on and when I do you may not like it. If I didn't mention it before, I can only appear as a skeleton."

"Just for the record, if you'd be so good. Not that there will be one." He sighed tragically. "Although Bloody Forcemeat expecting a report has put me in a real carborundum."

"Don't you mean conundrum, Sarge?" Gaspard enquired diffidently.

"No constable, I mean carborundum. That's a bloody conundrum that wears you down." He emitted what Gaspard had to assume was a laugh but which sounded more as though it should have come from a deranged sea lion. Hardcastle didn't really manage humour well. What he was doing lately and doing very well, was mad.

"Holy shit!" exclaimed Hardcastle, recoiling. "I see what you meant now." He shook his head in an attempt to regain his shattered composure. "I suppose this is a bit how Death himself looks, is it?"

"Uh, huh. In fact, a lot like how he looks. Except for the scythe of course. Oh, and he's seven feet tall." There was more wasn't there? "And he has better teeth," he added grudgingly. "Really? Um, and the eyeballs? It seems a bit unnecessary and frankly once you get used to whole skeletal persona it looks a bit ridiculous. Sort of comic horror."

"Like I should know what they're bloody thinking!" snapped Gaspard, feeling oddly offended. "I have to go with what comes."

"Yeah, I suppose. Does that include the alligator?"

"Everyone's a bloody critic," grumbled Death from the shadows.

"You know Gaspard, I don't mind admitting that I really hated you before all this came to light. No doubt that doesn't surprise you one little bit." Gaspard shook his head mournfully. "Now, don't get me wrong, you still rank somewhere below Dr Crippen in my list of all-time favourites but now that I'm fully aware of the all the horrors you've faced, I have a degree of sympathy for your plight. Enough to wonder just what the hell you intend to do about all this? Though not, I hasten to add, enough to even dream of trying to help."

"Thanks Sarge…I think. What can I do? The other side has me by the short and curlies…and that's the other side if I haven't made myself clear. The ghosts have settled in as you well know and seem intent on making my life a living hell. My only hope is that someone in authority will realise that I'm a complete failure, let me off the hook, somehow get rid of my spooks and save me from a lifetime of amateur theatricals."

"When you say someone in authority…?"

Gaspard merely shrugged in response.

"One of your fellow mortals once said that you're only a failure when you start blaming others for things going wrong," mused Death, unable to let things slide. "Or words to that effect, at least."

"Oh, another bloody county heard from," snapped Gaspard. "Excuse me sergeant," he said hastily, addressing himself to Hardcastle, "but Mort over there is putting his two bob's worth in." He turned his attention back to Death. "That Mort, if I may speak freely, sounds like a crock. One of those things that comes across as clever but is total bollocks when you analyse it," spat Gaspard angrily.

"I wondered why you kept looking into the corner. Has he been here the whole time?"

"Uh, huh."

"Shit."

"So, let's assume your unnamed mortal…"

"Technically no longer a mortal. He's dead."

"…is correct," argued Gaspard, sounding almost hopeful. "That would mean since I blame the incompetent morons on the other side for screwing everything up, that I'm a failure. So, fire me."

"It's not a rule just an observation. In your particular case, I fear your apportioning of blame is entirely justified."

"Weasel."

"I say, steady on."

Hardcastle had been looking from Gaspard to the seemingly empty corner like a spectator at a very short tennis match and not surprisingly, quickly tired of being privy to only one side of the conversation. "Look, if you buggers are going to keep this up, perhaps you'd be polite enough to include me," he exclaimed irascibly.

"Oh, sorry Sarge. It's easy to get carried away. Politeness makes you answer even though it's impolite, if you get my drift." Gaspard cocked his head while looking across at where Death sat. "Mort says he's sorry but he can't do anything about it until you get physically carried away." He again addressed the corner. "Very funny Mort."

"He's making jokes? The grim reaper makes jokes?"

"No need to sound so surprised. He's really quite a nice bloke. Just doesn't have much of a social life. I'm sure you can see how the misconceptions might occur."

"Well, be that as it may, I really think he should show himself. He's the last clue in the puzzle. Not that I doubt his existence for a moment but I'm a copper after all. Seeing is proof."

"Tell him no can do but if it's any consolation he'll be seeing me a lot sooner than he might like."

"He says it's impossible Sarge. He's already overstepped the bounds in making you aware of his existence."

"Who's a weasel now?"

"OK, constable. You might as well bugger off. There's nothing more we can achieve here." Hardcastle gestured impatiently towards the door.

"Have we achieved anything at all Sarge?"

"Nothing of an official nature but my mind has been put at rest which to be frank was what it was all about in the first place." He pointed to the door. "And make sure you take your friend with you." That relatively innocent parting shot pointed towards a hugely unsettling mental struggle taking place within the sergeant's mind, more troubled than at rest, although troubled may be somewhat of an understatement. A stormy sea is said to be troubled. In marine terms, this was brewing up as a super typhoon. Just a note of caution here. When we say 'brewing up', 'we're not saying it was preparing a cup of tea, just in case you've misunderstood.

Anyway, his untreated paranoia was refusing to relent in its efforts to find Gaspard responsible for all of its manufactured woes and now that it had proof positive of dark, invisible and who knew, perhaps even saturnine forces, it used that knowledge to sink itself deeper and deeper into the foul morass of insanity. The feeble voice of reason that had from time to time managed to rise above the ooze was fast being overwhelmed. Oddly enough, it was this very paranoia which may save Gaspard, because now there was nothing to stop Hardcastle from believing that he was constantly under surveillance by ghosts and invisible skeletal entities. Possibly worse. In a real twist, the miniscule sane portion of his mind, in a last desperate attempt at survival, allied itself to his paranoia by insisting that if he were being watched, then murder would be a foolish course of action.

Even more foolish, it added sagely, gaining in confidence, because he now had proof positive of an afterlife. What horrors might await a policeman who went about knocking off colleagues? That's knocking off as in murder, it added with a faint blush. Hardcastle began to quietly hum but then stopped suddenly and looked warily about. No. No lord high executioner. They may be watching. They almost certainly would be watching. He took out his pen and began to scribe a draft of his report for DSI Forcemeat. Not that there was much to draft.

Forcemeat would be told only that a thorough investigation has discerned there was no need for matters to be taken further. If that didn't suit him, then tough. It was a matter for Professional Standards. If need be, he'd have his boss go over Forcemeat's head. Not that he expected any such unpleasantness. The DSI was one of those rapid climbers and the last thing that rapid climbers wanted was for any slippery rungs on the ladder.

Gaspard flew through the front door with a look of incandescent rage that was so intense the ghosts scattered in terror and confusion. "Check if he has the shears," squeaked Bert as he sheltered behind Maud. Only Spinner seemed largely unaffected, he only had one way to go and it wasn't the same way as the others.

"You stupid bastards!" Gaspard roared, panting with anger. "What have you been telling Hardcastle? No, don't tell me, I already know."

"Come on Gassy, calm down," said the doctor, usually the first to recover his sangfroid. The carefully modulated tone of his voice may have helped if he hadn't called Gaspard, Gassy.

"Don't bloody call me that. I haven't eaten cheese in a week." Gaspard stood looking from one face to the other, his ire slowly dissipating. It was already done wasn't it? "So, how often has he been here and why?" he asked, more calmly now.

"He came to join the group. He knew we needed a baritone," replied Maud nervously.

"Oh, and he was so nice you peached?"

"Peached?" Enquired Percy sarcastically, having realised there was no immediate danger. "Peached? Where did you park your Spitfire, Wing Commander?"

The others all sniggered and despite himself, Gaspard grinned. That's if the heavily constipated look that creased his face could be termed a grin. "Why didn't you tell me he'd been coming here? That's what I don't understand. The bastard had sworn to kill me?"

"Well, I know it sounds a bit feeble but he asked us not to. He said he was all better, going back to work and wanted to apologise to you in person so your mind would be put at ease. As far as doing you harm was concerned, we'd never have allowed that. We were well stocked with baked beans."

"Baked…? Never mind."

"Um, I take it he hasn't apologised?" The doctor wrung his hands guiltily.

"Not so as you'd notice. I think there were some words to the effect that his hatred for me exceeded that for Dr Crippen. If you can make an apology out of that, be my guest." There was a general mumbling amongst the group and scattered expressions of dismay and contrition.

"I suppose this means no more concerts for a while?" Maud asked miserably.

"No. I can't see why not." The reply was a grudging one but welcome for all that.

"We can't mend what's been done and if I'm to be honest, Mort seems to think that no lasting harm has occurred." He ran his fingers through his hair distractedly.

"You could have said that a bit earlier, growled Percy."

"OK, let's say no more about it. I'm going to grab a G and T."

"That's right, put us through the emotional ringer then go off and get rat-arsed," grumbled Percy, not altogether unreasonably.

"I don't suppose you'd like to run over the Modern Major General?" Asked Maud timidly, hoping to resolve the little spat.

"Why? Has he been blocking the road?" Gaspard enquired with an attempt at light-heartedness he hoped would put the ill feeling to rest. It may have been a bit weak but the ghosts all decided to laugh to help ease the remaining tension. Sometimes you just have to let the other guy win one. It was only a few minutes later that Gaspard rejoined the group. He was minus a G and T which was a real pity because he was also minus his composure, so it may have helped his mood. Although that's open to debate.

"Someone's been pissing about with my computer again." He glared at the group and reached for the non-existent glass of granny's ruin before silently cursing himself for neglecting to make his drink prior to changing. He emitted a frustrated groan that frightened the bejasus out of the assembled spirits, before storming off to the kitchen. There was a sound of corks squeaking and large quantities of liquid being poured. This was shortly followed by noises of what was clearly an ill-tempered attempt to extract ice cubes from the freezer tray. Damage was probably done. He returned to a sea of blank faces, one of the reasons for which was that porpoises really don't do facial expression all that well.

"Eek."

"He says it was him," translated the doctor, who knew full well who the main culprit was. Which of course meant that there were other, slightly, but only slightly, minor culprits. Four of them in fact. They were just a little better at obfuscating than Spinner, who was still a bit of an innocent in many ways.

"Why? What does a porpoise need a bloody computer for?"

"He's writing his memoirs."

"What? Are you bloody serious?" Gaspard looked wildly from one to the other. On realising they were completely serious, he gave a slightly deranged half laugh before consuming most of a very large tumbler of G and T. To be precise, it was a very large tumbler of G with a very small amount of T.

"Of course. Why shouldn't he? We need to do something to pass the time when we're not practicing and it's a worthy endeavour." The doctor who had been inspired by Spinner to begin his own autobiography felt understandably defensive of Spinner's efforts.

Gaspard was flabbergasted. "Look, far be it for me to deny him his right to tell his life story but what the hell does a porpoise have to write about? I mean; swam, ate squid, swam again, would be about the limit I should think."

"You really can be quite unfeeling you know Gaspard?" sniffed Maud, who was still nursing a grudge. She was not the sort to forget a slight and had in fact, weaned the grudge off nursing and was now feeding it solids.

"Sorry. You're right. It's doing no harm." Gaspard reluctantly backed off, although it was obvious to the seasoned Gaspard watcher that his heart wasn't in the apology. "I just wish you'd asked first."

"Eek."

"He says he's sorry but he didn't think you'd mind since you never use it for any worthwhile purposes." Gaspard forced himself not to make the obvious porpoise/purpose joke that arose unbidden despite his ill-humour.

"I don't suppose there's any chance that I could have a look over it?" enquired Gaspard in a half-baked attempt to undo his lack of empathy. "At very least, I could possibly help out with grammar and punctuation."

"Eek."

"He says thanks but you have a tendency to split infinitives so he's not sure how much real use you could be. In any case, we'd already asked him and he said that he doesn't want any distractions. He's afraid we'll all start putting in suggestions and lead him off track."

"Eek."

"Oh, and he says some of it might be a bit salacious. He doesn't want to be embarrassed."

"Eek."

"I see. Got you. When he says embarrassed, he doesn't mean that he finds what he did embarrassing. It's a natural part of porpoise existence. What he's afraid of is the human propensity to be judgemental." The doctor glanced meaningfully towards Maud. "That would embarrass the crap out of him."

It took a little time and a lot of gin but eventually things returned to what Gaspard was beginning to regard, a trifle hysterically at times, as normal. Being normal, or what had become normal of late, they were all singing and Gaspard who'd had maybe a thimbleful of gin too many, had begun eating cheese. Not out of a desire to irritate his fellow singers as had often been the case in the past, but out of a genuine craving for the stuff. That irresistible need was fuelled by alcohol which creates in us all, intense cravings for fatty food. That's the excuse anyway and a bloody good one, as anyone slobbering up a kebab at two in the morning will tell you. So great was his need that he ignored the protests of his fellow singers and not only broke his word (and so far, only his word) but dredged up a particularly stinky epoisse that had been incarcerated in the fridge for a few days more than strictly necessary and had been threatening to escape.

The only plus side was that the cheese was such a festering horror, olfactorily speaking that even had he farted no one would have noticed. Like all such festering horrors it was bloody delicious and no one was able to convince him to give its remains a decent burial. He was spooning up another tasty morsel when Bert noticed the knocking at the door. Door knocks come in a wide variety, ranging from timorous tapping to the three a.m. open up it's the police category. This one was the are you bloody deaf, I've been standing here for friggin' ages and don't think that I don't know you're home, type. For those not familiar with it, it's a grade below what the hell have you been doing with my daughter/son. Gaspard dropped his spoon which sighed with relief and swore that it would hide at the back of the drawer in future. Assuming that it ever recovered. It was already feeling distinctly tarnished.

"Who do you think it is? They sound really pissed."

"So do you, if it comes to that Gaspard. Those last few bars were distinctly wobbly. Either that or the bloody cheese is melting your vocal cords," snarled the doctor, not usually one to sound such an aggressive note but these were exceptional circumstances. The doctor had never before smelled epoisse and was beginning to think that he may never smell anything ever again after this assault on his receptors.

"It has to be bloody Hardcastle. I can't imagine anyone else making such a bleedin' racket."

"We have the beans ready," said Maud bravely.

"It's Monica," whispered Gaspard after peering through the peephole. The pair had had several recent dates but Gaspard still hadn't had the nerve to invite Monica back. It looked as though she'd decided to take matters into her own hands. Rather noisily.

"Are you going to stand there all bloody night," said Bert, sotto voce. "Let the girl in before she knocks the door down."

"Alright. You remember your promise?"

"We remember ours. It's you that didn't remember yours."

"Look, I just needed…"

"Open the bloody door!" The ghosts looked at each other and nodded almost as one in a signal indicating that all bets were off. Not as off as the cheese smelled though.

"Hello, Monica. Sorry if we…I…didn't hear you for a while. Have you been here long?"

"It depends whether we're talking twenty-four-hour clock or geological time, Gaspard," sniffed Monica, trying not altogether successfully to hide her less agreeable side. She offered up a perfunctory peck on the cheek and barged past clutching a bottle of wine that had been chilled when she started out but was now at best tepid.

"Have you got a corkscrew?" She noticed the outsized glass of G and T in his hand and drew the obvious though possibly hurtful conclusion. "Why am I asking? Of course you have. Rustle it up for me, will you?" Gaspard scooted off as though he'd been stung which metaphorically speaking he had been and Monica took the opportunity to take a few deep breaths to steady herself. It was far too early in the relationship to behave like this. It would need a couple more dates before she could really kick the shit out of him. Something in the air redolent of long unwashed body parts but probably the ghosts of meals past gave her cause to instantly regret the deep breaths.

"Um, the bottle feels like it could do with a bit more chilling. Why don't I pop it in the freezer for fifteen minutes or so and I'll do you a G and T?"

"Perfect. Can you do me a large one?" Monica asked with just the right hint of suggestiveness. It was probably a good thing that Gaspard was just a trifle too squiffy to notice, or if he did, not to believe that it was intentional. "So, where are your friends hiding?" queried Monica after her first steadying sip. Look, she's a lady, to say she gulped would be inappropriate.

"Friends? I'm alone, love."

"But I distinctly heard singing. G and S. You were virtually rattling the windows. And if I remember correctly when you opened the door you said, 'we didn't hear you'." The gaze she drilled into Gaspard would have bored through tungsten.

"Really? I must have had more than I thought." He waved his glass. "No, there's just me. What you probably heard was me singing along to a recording, I do that a lot, I'm afraid. One of the penalties of a bachelor life. Gee, I didn't realise I was that loud. Hope the neighbours weren't disturbed."

"But it sounded live."

"Believe me, it was anything but that. Other than me of course." It was nice to be able to tell the truth, even it was being stretched.

They were seated on the couch in what for the moment could not be described as intimate proximity, Monica still having her nose slightly out of joint which was just as well considering the heady aroma of cheese. "So, I'd like to see this fabulous equipment of yours Gaspard," said Monica, causing Gaspard to blush furiously, "I have to say that the reproduction is fantastic. Really true to life."

"Oh…ah…it's in the spare bedroom," Gaspard stumbled, trembling with relief. "I keep it there to avoid disturbing the neighbours." It was a stupid lie considering no such equipment existed.

"She knows you're lying, Gaspard." It was the doctor's voice coming out of nowhere.

"Eek."

"See. Even Spinner can tell and he's not even human." Gaspard narrowly avoided speaking and just managed to slowly shake his head.

"Are you feeling alright, Gaspard?"

"Mm, hm. Head just a bit fuzzy."

"If that was a new bottle tonight, I'm not surprised. Do you think the wine will be chilled by now? I'm not really a fan of gin."

"Sure, I'll open the bottle." He took up Monica's glass, not failing to notice that for someone who wasn't a fan she'd managed to do it reasonable justice and poured its remaining contents into his own. "Waste not, want not," he chortled, stumbling slightly as he headed for the kitchen and immediately regretting the act.

Christ, that was probably not the thing to do was it? With a display of courage that was bordering on the heroic he tipped the contents of his glass down the sink.

"What do you think?" Percy said to the group at large. "Should we show ourselves?"

"We promised we'd behave," responded Maud, being uncharacteristically responsible.

"Yeah, but he broke his wind…er, word, about the cheese," replied Bert, falling into one of Freud's well-planned traps. This remark was instantly followed by a chorus of snorts, sniggers and giggles from the others.

"True," managed the doctor, being the first to recover, "but it's not just about that, is it? I think we owe it to him to blow the lie."

Bert sniggered and was about to make a remark but the doctor cut him off abruptly. "It's making his life miserable," continued the doctor with a withering glance at the miscreant.

"Well, more miserable. He can't carry on a relationship with anyone while he's forced to hide our existence and it's not as if others aren't aware of us. I say we have a word with him and give him the option to come clean before we take matters into our own hands. For his own good. What say?" The others all assented in various ways, from nods to verbal affirmations. Bert was staring sulkily at his feet but managed a mumbled agreement.

"Maybe I should have a word with him?" said Death appearing suddenly in their midst.

"Must you do that?"

"Sorry but it's not as if I can do much else is it?" There's was a short and pregnant silence until Bert, who was feeling a bit stroppy after being chastened by the doctor, piped up. "You could always pop up in another room, don't you think? Make a slightly noisy entry. Maybe rattle a few things by way of warning. It's not bloody rocket science."

"You mean like clatter my rib cage perhaps? Maybe play it like a xylophone?"

"Not exactly, smart arse but it would do. How about you just cough?"

"It won't be nearly as much fun."

"So you do do it deliberately?" growled Percy, emboldened by Bert's display of surliness.

"Wouldn't you?"

"Now that you mention it, probably. It does wear a bit thin when one is on the receiving end, though."

"In my defence, I don't have many chances for distractions. Just because I look like this doesn't mean I don't have a sense humour. Put yourself in my place. It's not as if I can crack jokes with the recently departed. They tend not to be too receptive, as you all well know."

"Maybe you could come in with a bit of a warning…like a cough but wearing a false nose or something?" Maud suggested helpfully. "I'm sure that would give everyone a chuckle."

"I did try that once," reminisced Death unhappily. "On Anne Boleyn actually. I thought it might cheer her up, what with her hubby having been such a prick. You all know how that turned out. I should have known better. I'd tried it before her with Thomas Beckett. He called me a tit."

"Yes but we're already spirits. I'm sure we'd all have a good laugh."

"I suppose I could give it another try."

"That's the spirit." There was an uncomfortable silence before Death remembered what had started the conversation. "So, what do you think? About

Gaspard, I mean? I think he'd probably take it better coming from me. He's finally beginning to comprehend that I'm in a position to see the bigger picture." The ghosts looked at each other in that odd way they were beginning to exhibit, as though unspoken messages were passing between them. This was mainly because that's exactly what was happening. Death found it a bit disturbing.

"OK," they all said at once, even Spinner, though he did say it in his cetacean dialect.

"Ta da," exclaimed Mort cheerily as Gaspard was fetching Monica another drink. Gaspard was still managing to keep away from the stuff himself but his resolve was now being challenged because not only was Death standing uninvited in his kitchen but doing so wearing a red clown nose and a curly bright yellow wig.

"What the fu...?"

"You're not laughing."

"Of course I'm not laughing, you frightened the shit out of me."

"Really? The others were sure it would be hilarious, although I have to say I had my doubts. Poor Anne took it very badly and I won't tell you what Thomas said after he called me a rude name."

Gaspard emitted an exasperated sigh. "What is it Mort?"

"Well..."

"Who are you talking to, Gaspard?"

"No one love, just muttering to myself...spilled some wine. Would you like some cheese with your wine?"

"Is that what I can smell?"

"Uh, huh."

"Thank God, I was worried it was your feet!"

"It might smell a bit manky but it's really delicious."

"I'll take your word for it. Would you mind telling the name so that I can avoid it in future?"

"Epoisse. It really is delicious. Funny you should mention feet though because I think the mould on the cheese is related to mould on human feet. Who would have thought, eh?"

"Me for one. As to the delicious part, I'll take your word for it. You wouldn't have a nice piece of cheddar by any chance?"

"We need to talk," whispered Death unnecessarily, "meet me in the bathroom. I'm sure she won't be surprised if you tell her you need a pee. Not judging by the level of that gin bottle."

"You need to tell her about the others," confided Death later but only after having to turn his back while Gaspard relieved himself.

"There's no point trying to hide it. It'll just make you unhappy and she'll take it worse if it's dropped on her out of the blue."

"Look, before we go on with this, could you take off the bloody clown stuff, it makes it a bit hard to take you seriously."

"I thought it might help to keep things relaxed. You don't find it…I don't know…a little whimsical?"

"Grotesque would be more my choice of words. To be frank, Mort, it makes you look a bit of a tit."

"That's what Thomas Beckett said. It doesn't hurt any less the second time around," mumbled Death in an injured tone.

"Sorry, I didn't mean to be insensitive."

"And yet you were. Knowingly. Just saying you're sorry doesn't necessarily undo the harm done by an unfeeling remark, you know."

"You're right but what more can I say?"

"Say you'll think before you open your yap next time."

"I promise," said Gaspard, although to Mort's trained ear it sounded insincere. OK, we know Mort doesn't actually have any ears but he can hear so the expression is sort of valid. Stop trying to be such a bloody clever dick.

"You really think that it's a good idea to spill the beans," continued Gaspard a little unsurely. "The alternative is that she finds out by accident or the others make sure she discovers them and God knows how they may choose to organise that, or even worse, Hardcastle goes off the deep end and all hell breaks loose. Which do you prefer?"

"What about the rest of it? The robe and the shears and all that?"

"I presume the all that part encompasses my role?" Gaspard nodded.

"No. Definitely not. I can't believe you even thought to ask."

"I did assume not but we blabbed to Hardcastle, so to be honest I'm beginning to get mightily confused," exclaimed Gaspard somewhat touchily.

"Put it down to the exigencies of the service. Hardcastle was and is a special case. Just trust me that it won't have any deleterious effect on the workings of the scheme."

"Unlike poor Spinner?" questioned Gaspard unkindly, already forgetting his promise to think before he spoke.

"Well, we're not sure that's had any unpleasant after effects despite our original concerns. There don't seem to have been any reports." Gaspard couldn't help but notice that Mort was sounding evasive.

"No? It's just that there was that news item on the Alaskan salmon run the other day. Admittedly nobody is taking it seriously but if it's true, on at least one occasion the salmon ganged up and ate a bear."

"Obviously a load of old cods wallop."

"Or walloping salmon?"

"Gaspard, are you talking to yourself again?" asked Monica from outside the door.

"Oh, er, just singing a few bars."

"Sounds more like you've been to a few bars. For God's sake, aren't you finished yet? I'm bloody-well bursting out here."

"Sorry, I'm finished, I'll let you in right away." Under his breath to Mort he murmured: "Your will be done."

"Good oh. Mind if I grab a few Hobnobs on the way out?"

"Why not, you've never hesitated before?"

"Is that a clown nose on the floor?" enquired a clearly baffled Monica.

"Oh! That's where it got to. I had it for red nose day a while back." He bent to pick it up.

"And you wore a wig as well?"

"In for a penny, I always say."

"Right, well speaking of pennies, I have to spend one, so bugger off unless you want to watch a lady wet herself."

One imagines that broaching a difficult subject like…I don't know…let's say, that the listener is currently in a house inhabited by four ghosts and a phantom porpoise would be difficult at the best of times. How much harder would it be then, were the one breaking such news, to be three parts rat-arsed.

Paradoxically, in Gaspard's case it was both harder and easier. Easier because being lightly plastered his inhibitions were lowered; harder because it made it difficult to put more than a few words together in a sequence that made much sense. His inebriated ramblings, most of them coming to an inconclusive and often bewildering halt initially had Monica amused. As is usually the case in such circumstances, the amusement soon morphed into irritation, then rage followed by an overwhelming desire to shake the speaker by the throat. In the meantime, her attempts to make sense of the meandering gabble was coming up with scenarios ranging from the terrifying to the lewd. None of them even approximated the fact that she was in a haunted house. "For God's sake, Gaspard! What are you trying to say? Spit it out! Are you asking me to go to bed with you?"

"Good lord no."

"Oh." There was a pregnant pause. No doubt a bit ironic considering the thoughts that had been running through Monica's mind.

"What the hell is it, then? You're not proposing, are you?"

"I thought we'd just covered that."

"Very funny. Just say what you want to say without beating about the bush. I think we've already covered the two that could shock me the most. Unless of course you're going to tell me that your married." Bugger, that one just jumped in there without it having crossed her mind previously. "You're not are you?" she enquired suspiciously.

"Good heavens no. Who'd be mad enough to have me?" The words were out before he fully realised their implications and having been said necessitated another rambling apology and attempts to diminish the faux pas.

"For God's sake, just tell me!" She roared, interrupting his flow of ill contrived drivel.

"The flat's haunted!"

"Oh, is that all. What was all that beating about the bush for?"

"It doesn't bother you?"

"Why should it? I shared a bedroom with the ghost of my great grandmother until I was ten. She used to sit at the end of the bed and read me bedtime stories."

"You're kidding?"

"Perfectly serious. We Celts have a certain connection with the spirit world, you know."

"And yet you've noticed nothing here?"

"Only that the place has a certain chill. I suppose that should have been a clue but one doesn't link modern apartment blocks with spooks." She smiled, encouraging Gaspard to further explanation.

"Well, I'm glad that's out of the way but there's more. The singing you heard…"

"The recording?"

"Not a recording. The G and S group we've talked about…well it's me and the ghosts."

"Mm, hm," murmured Monica noncommittally, beginning to think that if any committing were to be done it might be of Gaspard.

Slowly and painfully, Gaspard poured out the story, naturally omitting the role of Mort and his own alter ego. Monica sat transfixed, wondering if she really stick around or make a break for it. "It would probably help if I introduced them. I realise it's a bit hard to take in. Even for someone who believes in ghosts."

Monica thought that would be a splendid idea. "OK. I'll ask them to pop up one at a time, shall I? After we've all been introduced maybe we could have a bit of a sing along. They're all very anxious to have you join the group."

"There's no catch to that is there? I don't have to be dead or anything?" she enquired nervously, perching on the edge of her seat, ready to flee.

"No, no. You should probably meet Maud first. She's the original."

And with that Maud materialised seated primly on the chair directly opposite. "I do hope you're a contralto," she said immediately.

After that, the whole business went off swimmingly, especially when Spinner was introduced. The problem with introducing the new love interest to ones friends is that apart from one or more of them trying to steal said interest away, they usually manage to spill some rather embarrassing beans that one has managed to keep the lid on. Luckily for Gaspard there was no one likely to win Monica's affections but unluckily they were all privy to a number of secrets, embarrassing foibles and downright bad habits. As is usually the case the party atmosphere that soon developed after everyone had been introduced brought forth revelations that Gaspard would rather have kept until his death bed or preferably thereafter.

Maybe not even then, it being a particularly curious human trait to be worried about one's reputation after death.

"That's why we started calling him Gassy," the doctor was chortling, having been thoroughly captivated by Monica and doing his best to be the soul of the party. Had he been mortal it would have been he who would try to win her away.

"It's not my fault that I'm lactose intolerant," whined Gaspard, struggling to get with the agenda which at the moment was Gaspard bashing. In the nicest possible way of course.

"No but it is your fault if you ignore it and make us suffer the consequences."

"I thought that smell was getting stronger," put in Monica to everyone's amusement. Everyone that is but Gaspard who was considering crawling under the carpet. What he did do was to sneak off and surreptitiously gobble a handful of Lacteze tablets. All of the embarrassment was worth it in the end though because Monica began to exhibit an increasing degree of affection as the night progressed. Right up until breakfast in fact. That night was the first in a minor idyll that had Gaspard enraptured for days to come. Monica wasn't faring too badly either. It was the death of Sergeant Hardcastle that buggered everything up.

14

For some time now, things in Hamm on Wye had been in a state of unrest. The council's interest in reviving some of the ancient butts and opening them up to tourism was widely applauded but the manner in which it was to be done was still a matter of intense disagreement. Many of the council members who were anxious to earn a few quid were in favour of allowing them to be commercially developed while a vocal minority, operating under the unfortunate name of The Butts for Sport Society, called for a tasteful reviving of the mediaeval sites. Possibly even returning them to their original purpose. Today was the day of the council vote and it was widely held that the developers would carry the day and the supporting councillors would carry off a big bag of cash.

Naturally a futile demonstration had been planned by the opponents. The usual fate of the majority of such local demonstrations is to go unnoticed by most of the country and certainly by overseas tourists. They are, after all, merely local squabbles. That it was to be otherwise in this case was partly decided by puerile humour and the headline in the Hamm on Wye Bugle, which had trumpeted the following: **OPENING UP OUR BUTTS—RECREATION OR BUSINESS?**

A headline such as that was always going to be posted on-line. Once the posts had gone viral it was up to the individual's sense of humour as to what they did with the information. Many decided it would be amusing to take part and march with banners. The two favourites were: HANDS OFF LADY PENELOPE'S BUTT and THE KING'S BUTT IS SACRED.

Sad to relate many of the protesters let the side down by totally buggering up the placement of their apostrophes or maybe more shameful still, leaving them out completely but what else could you expect from a mob that was only there to take the piss? Other less involved tourists had flocked to the area armed with cameras and a sense of ribald humour. It probably goes without saying that the vast majority were young and American. The police of Hamm on Wye were mobilised for the event, it being widely expected that the large crowd would bring in toe rags from far afield to pick pockets, snatch purses and perform other unsavoury deeds. The headline: **PUBLIC WARNED TO BEWARE OF BUTT GRABBERS,** provided fair warning to those attending the demonstration that their possessions might be at risk.

Those who thought the warning meant something else were to be sorely disappointed. Mostly. The press attention to the event soon became responsible for a few more visitors after another Bugle headline which read: **POLICE LEAVE CANCELLED FOR BUTT DEMONSTRATION** which inadvertently resulted in even more disappointments. Gaspard saw it as his chance. He would be required to wander watchfully through the crowd. Today he could finally wear his robe and feel some collars as he glided unseen through the mob.

He wasn't quite sure how he'd effect the arrests in a state of invisibility but he'd cross that bridge when the time came. At very least, he reasoned, he could scare the crap out of some nasty characters.

Being on light duties, Sergeant Hardcastle was not one of those mobilised for crowd control, and his loss was sorely felt by the upper echelons. If anyone could be counted on to crack some skulls, it was he. As it eventuated, he was involved in some skull cracking anyway. Ever since his victorious confrontation with Feeblebunny, Hardcastle had been feeling at a loss. It was over. His nemesis was conquered and there was nothing in the offing that would even come close to replacing his obsession.

From time to time, his fevered brain still toyed with the idea of vengeance but he was being watched. Every minute. Oddly enough he was also missing his singing sessions with the ghosts. It had started as a means of getting close to Gaspard in order to murder him but he'd soon found it enjoyable. He not only discovered the singing to be to his liking but he also enjoyed the company. Sure, Bert was a prissy little twerp, Percy a single-minded grouch and Maud a cantankerous old bat but they were still streets ahead of the sort of characters he'd been used to dealing with. They were also considerate enough to be dead.

So, it was on this day of potential inactivity he set off to visit Gaspard's flat, possibly to join the group in belting out a few choruses. It wasn't exactly with a song in his heart and a smile on his lips but he hoped nonetheless to convince them of his true feelings of friendship and possibly work out a rehearsal schedule acceptable to all. OK, the word friendship might be overstating the case but at least he hoped that he could convince them he meant them no harm. Things didn't start well because the lift was yet again out of order. Hardcastle puffed and panted his way up the stairs, feeling more and more lightheaded as he went.

Unfortunately, his weeks of bed rest and poor diet while on the run had told on his fitness which after a few years behind a desk wasn't all that much to write home about. He began to perspire heavily and there was a strange feeling in his left arm and neck. By the time he reached the flat, he was weak, nauseous and in a state of near collapse. He managed a feeble knock on the door that was heard by the ghosts who were taking a break. Spinner was putting the finishing touches to his memoirs and the others were having a game of Ludo. "It's Hardcastle."

"Should we let him in?"

"I think we'd better; the poor bugger looks like crap."

"Hello Sarge, are you OK? You look terrible. You're white as a sheet. Come in and sit down."

"Glass of…water," gasped Hardcastle.

"Sergeant, this is important," said the doctor urgently. "I think you may be having a heart attack. Do you have any chest pains?"

"Nothing I haven't had before," panted the sergeant, staggering towards the kitchen sink. "Just need a glass of water."

"Sit down please Sarge."

"Cough."

"Did you hear something Maud? Sounded like somebody coughing in the bathroom."

"Oh, dear me. You don't think…?" Hardcastle suddenly clutched his chest, his foot slid on the small mat kept in front of the sink and he toppled backward in a manner reminiscent of a falling pine. In his case, the pine in question would have a lot of loose squirrels in it.

Gaspard had always been an untidy bugger and this morning had been no different. After fixing a leak in the pipe beneath the sink, he'd left the large stilson spanner he'd used lying where he'd last dropped it. That being on the tiled floor exactly at the point now on a collision course with the back of Hardcastle's head.

"Hello everyone."

"Oh, no. Don't tell me," groaned the doctor. The others just looked shocked.

"Gaspard?" enquired the wraith of the sergeant, looking a bit bemused. "You look taller."

"Not Gaspard."

"Oh. The scythe. That's the give-away isn't it?"

"You could also say take away if you wanted to be flippant but I don't suppose you feel in any mood for jokes at the moment."

"You could say that. So that's me on the floor? God, I look bloody awful. I suppose that means…and forgive me if I'm jumping to conclusions here; that I'm no more?"

"Afraid so. Time to come."

As Death held up his scythe, Spinner appeared in the doorway. "Eek!"

"He says run," said the doctor, "we need your baritone."

"Oh, come on," roared Death as the spectre of sergeant Hardcastle scarpered, "I thought at least I could count on a professional to do the right thing."

"Please leave him to us Mort, we need his voice," urged the doctor reasonably. "Give the collector something to do. At your age, you should be putting your feet up."

"Another one for poor Gaspard?" Death complained, offended by the age remark but choosing to ignore it. "You'll drive the poor bastard out of his mind. And Hardcastle hates him."

"I'm sure we'll be able to sort things out. Let's not have an unseemly chase around the flat."

"I'm losing my touch you know," said Mort miserably. "There's more of the bastards on the run…no offence…these days than coming quietly. Maybe I should pack it in. Hand it over to a younger entity. There's an admin spot in Disease and Famine going at the moment. You don't think that Gaspard might…?"

"Not a chance. Not while the lovely Monica is available. He's besotted."

"I don't know, maybe I could convince Santa to swap for a while," Death pondered aloud. "He gets really bored these days with nobody believing in him. That shouldn't stop him pulling his weight of course but the idle sod can't be bothered. Imagine if I did that? Then of course there's the little problem of us hating each other's guts."

"Isn't he also a bit…portly for the job?"

"Hm. You have a point I suppose. He has to have all those sodding reindeer just to get his arse off the ground. I don't suppose the jolly fat man imagine quite fits either does it? Nor do the whiskers if it comes to that. OK, well make my apologies to himself for the mess. I doubt he'll want to see me for a while, now that I've lumbered him with Hardcastle. I really am losing my touch." He shook his head sadly. There was the sound of bones creaking. "I don't suppose you know where he's put the Hobnobs do you? I think the bugger has hidden them from me."

"Right up the back behind the sardines."

"All I can see is a jumbo family pack of condoms. Bit of an odd choice of description for condoms don't you think? I'd have thought the whole idea was to avoid family. That jumbo business could lead to a few disappointments as well."

"Behind them."

"Ah, good show. I notice the condom box is still sealed. No luck on that front then?"

"Not so as you'd notice." Mort slipped the entire packet of Hobnobs inside the folds of his robe. "Best be off then, don't forget to give him my regrets."

"On that point, Mort, don't you think you could have given us a bit of a heads up about this business? You must have known."

"Of course. It's all part of the overall scheme but letting on is against the rules, surely you must know that?"

"I'd assumed so but then Gaspard is one of yours…sort of."

"Only a civilian contractor I'm afraid. Not privy to the mysteries. In my own defence, I did give him a hint when I really shouldn't have. Not my fault if he didn't twig." The group stood around the body of Hardcastle wondering what to do.

"We mustn't interfere with anything," said Ivor sagely. "I'm afraid that the police will need to investigate. Poor Gaspard."

"What about me?" Hardcastle snapped testily. "I'm the one that's dead."

"Yes but it's over for you. You're happy. After a fashion. Poor old Gaspard has to deal with the fall out."

"Yeah, I suppose but it just seems a little premature to be worrying about somebody else while I'm still warm. Anyway, one thing we should maybe do," he added slyly, "is to hide the spanner. Trust me, I'm a copper. That looks bloody suss. The first thing I'd think is that Gaspard had crowned me with it."

"You reckon?" Percy asked. "I suppose it does look a bit damning now that you mention it."

"Definitely. It's Gaspard's flat so they'll start thinking arguments, a falling out. They'll soon discover we didn't get on."

"But it's tampering with evidence isn't it? Won't that look even worse?"

"Nothing could look as bad as it does now and if you hide the spanner away there'll be no evidence. They'll just think that I cracked my bonce on the floor. Under his mattress would be a good place. Without the spanner it'll be passed off as a fall. The autopsy will soon show I had a heart attack."

"Then why bother to change anything?"

"Because we're not completely sure it wasn't the head knock that finished me. And even if it wasn't, in the meantime he'll be put through the ringer and probably spend time inside. It can sometimes take ages to get an autopsy result."

He gave a little shudder, "You alright Sarge?"

"No. Have you ever seen a bloody autopsy? I'm soon going to be filleted."

"I think maybe we should do as he says," mused Bert.

"It would be best. Have you any idea the sort of things that can happen to a copper in prison?" Hardcastle smiled secretly to himself. If he had to die to put the bastard through the wringer, it was worth it.

"Can we do the Mikado?" he asked, "I rather fancy doing the Lord High Executioner again."

It hadn't been a good day for Gaspard who had not managed to collar a single miscreant. Either his belief that Hamm on Wye was infested with the criminal element was wrong or he just wasn't good enough to spot them. Perhaps it was that his luck wasn't in on the day. It wasn't going to get any better. Although that said, he was still one up on Hardcastle.

"Hello Gaspard, who'd have thought we'd meet up again under these circumstances?" Enquired the wraith of Hardcastle as Gaspard popped up in his own bedroom.

"What the…? Hardcastle what are doing…. dead?"

"You noticed?"

"It's hard not to. I don't believe I was able to see through you before today. Not your body anyway. Your motives were always transparent. What are you doing here? Shouldn't you be wherever it is you expired?" Gaspard sounded worried.

"Would you believe that I am?" asked Hardcastle, sounding oddly cheery for one recently departed.

"Oh, no. You don't mean to say…? How did you manage…?"

"Sorry about the mess in the kitchen. You might want to get onto emergency. Police and ambulance. I mean, the ambulance is unnecessary, obviously, but it's probably best for form's sake. It's always a bit suss when people don't."

"Sorry Gaspard. I suppose we shouldn't have let him in but he looked so ill," whined the doctor.

"Now you know why."

"It wouldn't have made much difference when you think of it," said Bert sensibly. "If he didn't die in here, he'd have dropped dead in the hallway. Either way you'd have been lumbered with the corpse and when you think of it, it's best he's here where we can exercise some control than to have him howling outside the door."

"I'm not the bloody Hound of the Baskervilles," exclaimed the sergeant reverting to his usual grumpy self. "Anyway, if I had died out there, I'd probably have gone with the reaper. It's you that convinced me to leg it." Gaspard glared at Bert, then swung his gaze slowly to encompass all members of the group.

"You convinced him to stay?" Steam wasn't quite coming out of his ears but if he put his arms just so he could have done a fair impression of a kettle.

"It wasn't me," complained Bert, "don't look at me like that. Spinner thought we should keep him because we need his voice."

"And the doctor translated," added Percy, making sure that he was also off the hook. "Without that he'd have gone."

"Well thanks a bloody million," growled Hardcastle, "it's nice to know I'm welcome." There was a chorus of apologies from the group.

"Of course you're welcome Marion," said Maud kindly, "they're all just a bit confused."

"Marion?"

"If you ever tell anybody Feeblebunny, I'll find a way to throttle you."

Unsurprisingly, Hardcastle was pronounced dead at the scene, after which the attending constables had taken Gaspard's statement. A little later, Detective Constable Pickler appeared because the powers that be had determined Hardcastle's demise to be suspicious.

"So, tell me, Constable...Philby, is it?" asked the DC, after consulting his case notes.

"As it is spelled sir, Feeblebunny."

"Really? I am sorry."

"About what?" asked Gaspard, narrowing his eyes.

"Oh, um, your circumstances constable. The incident. Do you need to ask?"

"I thought for a moment it may have been something else."

"Such as?"

"Nothing." That may have been the response but Gaspard was sounding just a tad hostile. Pickler eyed Gaspard suspiciously. The circumstances of Gaspard finding Hardcastle's body on the kitchen floor and his subsequent actions were gone through before the more intrusive questions began to be asked. "Now, constable. Preliminary findings on the time of the sergeant's death are that he died at between three and four p.m. What were you doing around those times?"

"I was on duty. I was rostered on to the butt demonstration."

"Did you at any time return home?"

"No sir. I was on duty until seven."

"And you arrived home at…?"

"Around seven ten, sir."

"And the record shows that you rang emergency at seven thirteen."

"That sounds about right."

"One little thing, constable. If you left work as you say at seven. How did you manage to arrive home ten minutes later when the station is at least a twenty-minute drive?"

"Um…er, perhaps I left a few minutes early sir. The protest was long over by then and there wasn't much to do."

"The station book shows you as signing out at three minutes past seven."

"Well, er, we do sometimes fudge it, sir."

"Did you get along with Sergeant Hardcastle constable?"

"We had a rocky relationship sir. I don't think it's a secret that he had an unhealthy obsession with me. I'm sure Dr Coombs could fill you in on the details."

"For God's sake Feeblebunny, you're making me sound like a gay stalker," railed Hardcastle.

"He was stalking you? Is that what you're saying?"

"No I bloody wasn't," screeched Hardcastle hysterically.

"Not as such. I really can't say why he was fixated with me but he is on record as having broken in on a couple of occasions."

"Really? And why do you think the sergeant may have been in your flat, if as you say, you were at work. Could it be that you met him here and an argument ensued? Perhaps he broke in and there was an understandable confrontation?"

"I was at work sir."

"If you could fudge the time book constable, maybe you could also take a little unauthorised time off."

"No sir, I was there all the time."

"You tell them Feeblebunny!" Cackled the ghost of Hardcastle, not quite as nastily as he would like because he was still worried about whether his sexuality was in question.

"Stand firm, Gaspard," advised Bert, "don't let the bastards bully you."

"Sir?" The enquiry came from Constable Entwhistle, currently standing in the doorway to Gaspard's bedroom. Pickler joined him. "I believe that you gave permission for the premises to be searched, constable?"

"Certainly sir, I have nothing to hide."

"Well, perhaps one thing, eh constable? A little matter of a blood-stained pipe wrench under your mattress?"

Gaspard stood dumfounded, his jaw hanging slack.

"Oh, dear," wailed Hardcastle theatrically, "we are in the poo now aren't we Feeblebunny?"

"Marion, how could you?"

"You bastard Hardcastle. You set him up!"

"Eek!"

"Gaspard Feeblebunny, I am detaining you on suspicion of the murder of Marion Hardcastle…"

"For Christ's sake, stop with the Marion!"

"…You don't have to say anything…"

Gaspard had never been in serious trouble before and he hadn't been a copper for long but there was one thing he knew instinctively, that being, it is not a good sign when an interrogator walks into the room smiling. He could be a friendly sort, he supposed and happy to see a fellow policeman but somehow Gaspard didn't think so. What made it worse was that one look at Detective Sergeant Aardvark made him realise that the DS didn't usually have much to smile about.

Not if one were judging by his looks. The DS was pot-bellied, bandy and balding with a physique that put most who met him in mind of a shaved orangutan. What little hair he had left was red and wispy and did little to dispel thought of the comparison. Neither did the fact that he had a bad case of duck's disease. He might be six feet three inches tall but five feet of that started above the hips. The face wasn't as ape-like but it would have been a definite improvement if it had been.

Gaspard had had plenty of time to think about his dilemma, having spent the night in the cells. The reason for his overnight stay was partly a ploy on the part of the lead detective, DI Flaxwort and partly that officer's desire to go home on time because his wife was making spotted dick and custard for afters. Whatever the reason, it had had the effect of giving Gaspard a bloody restless night. In the long hours of darkness, he did what most do in such circumstances which was to imagine the worst. It being night-time when our greatest fears surface, every imagined scenario ended with him well and truly…for modesty's sake let's just say that it involved him trouserless and bending over while clutching his ankles.

He wasn't a detective but he'd watched enough episodes of Vera to know what the investigators would do. The forensics teams would scour his flat, his colleagues would be interviewed to see if they could help determine his whereabouts during crucial times and surveillance footage would be checked. Then there would be the autopsy result. It was this last that gave him some cause for hope. If what the ghosts had said was correct, the sergeant had probably suffered a heart attack and the injury to his head might be superficial. He could only hope. He also needed to have faith that the forensics team would realise the blood evidence did not support the conclusion of a bludgeoning. On the other hand, he'd been invisible all day which would be construed as absent from duty. Why? they would ask.

In the circumstances, they would only reach the one initial conclusion. That he had absented himself from work, probably with the intention of meeting Hardcastle at his flat.

Should all the other evidence prove inconclusive it was going to be hold tightly to the waistband time. With the daylight came the usual renewed hope, soon dashed when Aardvark came into the interview room smiling. Worse, he nudged DC Pickler and winked.

The powers that be had long since decided that the use of the word interrogation was too intimidating for those whose fate decreed they should find themselves on the wrong side of the legal process. That didn't stop Gaspard's interview being about as pleasant as an unsedated colonoscopy. It was not made any better by his insistence that he did not need a solicitor, in the mistaken belief that it gave his denials credence. For the first hour, it was sheer hell. Then it got worse. None of the process was improved by Gaspard's struggles with his digestive system as a direct result of the very milky tea given him both with his mediocre breakfast and at the beginning of his examination.

His bloated stomach squeaked and gurgled severely and he found it difficult to concentrate on the questions put to him because most of his attention was directed at trying not to fart. For some strange reason that seemed to be his mind's first priority. He stumbled and stuttered his way through questions fired at him relentlessly by both of his tormentors, the only saving grace being that he stuck firmly to his story. The fact that neither Aardvark nor Pickler could break him down didn't count for much considering that Gaspard could provide no reasonable explanations. After what seemed a lifetime, the interviewers called a break. Five minutes later Constable Entwhistle entered with a large mug of milky tea for Gaspard who despite an understandable reluctance to further increase his discomfort drank it both to steady his nerves and slake his raging thirst.

Immediately after Entwhistle had left the room, Gaspard let loose with a blast that both shocked and horrified the observers on the other side of the one-way glass observation screen.

A few minutes later they would be totally mystified when he began having a conversation with himself.

"Hello Gaspard. Things going alright are they?"

"Oh, it's you. As if you bloody care. Why in the blue blazes didn't you warn me? You've landed me well and truly in it."

"Sorry. You know the rules."

"Well, I don't actually because no has ever told me. In fact, I think you buggers make them up as you go along."

"That's a bit unfair. I would have given a heads up if I could, believe you me. Chin up though, I'm sure this won't last much longer…nudge, nudge, wink, wink."

"Are you saying that things are going to work out?" Gaspard suddenly experienced a surge of hope which corresponded with another explosive emission. The two were not mutually dependent.

"You know I can't confirm that. Nor by the way am I able to hold my nose. You couldn't give a me break, could you?"

"Sorry, it's the milky tea. I've been in agony for hours. You'll just have to put up with it."

"Hm. It might be an odd question but why have you been holding it in all this time? Why should you be worried about bothering your accusers but not bothered about me?"

"You're a friend. It's different."

It was about this time that the observers were beginning to suffer some disquiet which considering that the option was to be next door suffering the flatus, wasn't such a bad deal. DI Flaxwort who'd been witnessing the interrogation turned to DS Aardvark. "Are you hearing what I'm hearing?"

"Are we talking about the one-sided conversation or the farts?"

"Do you think he's trying for an insanity defence or really nuts? There have been stories," said Flaxwort, ignoring the fart reference.

"I'd say he's either a complete loon or a candidate for the Oscar," opined Pickler, stepping out of his league but much like Gaspard, being unable to hold back.

"My thoughts exactly. I think we might get a shrink in on this as well. Pop off and see if Coombs can make himself available would you?"

Before Pickler could leave, something happened that caused jaws to drop. While those behind the screen had been discussing their suspect's sanity, the conversation in the interview room had been continuing.

"Chuffed as I am to be considered a friend, I think your emissions are best saved for your enemies," said Death, not altogether unreasonably. "I don't suppose you've considered that far from being impolite, your farts could be a useful tool? Put them on the back foot a bit? Take it from me that the pong makes it difficult to martial one's thoughts."

"You have a point I suppose, it's just so embarrassing."

"Not quite as embarrassing as being accused of murder I would imagine."

For some time, Mort had been sizing up the uneaten biscuit that had accompanied the mug of tea. It was as Pickler in the observation room was rising to leave that Mort could stand it no longer. "Look, I don't suppose you're going to eat that biscuit, are you? Not with your stomach. Lot of fibre in those. I couldn't have it could I?"

"Be my guest." And so, just as Pickler rose, so did the biscuit. It travelled a short distance through the air, a sight perplexing in itself but not as perplexing as the fact that half of it suddenly disappeared, to the visual accompaniment of a shower of crumbs.

"Did you see that?" exclaimed the DSI in absolute amazement. The only answer was dumbstruck nods. "How the bloody hell did he do that?" At which point the remaining portion of the biscuit which had been hovering awaiting its fate, suddenly vanished.

"Shit! Play it back, play it back," howled Flaxwort, pointing to the CCTV controls. The replay cast no light on the phenomenon. Not even on the tenth replay. Other eyes summoned forth to view the event were no more able to discern just what in the bloody hell had happened. The observers decided to call for another cup of tea while they pondered what they saw. For some reason that no one was willing to articulate, the interview room didn't seem a very friendly place at the moment. And not only because of the lingering aromas. When they finally did enter, it was with a certain hesitancy that Gaspard couldn't help but notice.

"So, Gaspard. How are you feeling? Need another cup of tea?" This was the first time since his arrest that he'd been called by his first name. To date he'd been at best constable, but more often Feeblebunny or you murdering bastard. Gaspard accepted the offer but with reservations.

"Do us all a favour though, eh sir? No milk."

"Whatever you say, Gaspard. Pickler? Do the honours." Pickler did not just leave the room he fled it. There was a long and uncomfortable silence pending the DC's return, during which time Aardvark continued to look apprehensively about. "Um, perhaps you could tell us about the…er…biscuit," asked Aardvark nervously after Pickler's reluctant return. Gaspard, who had been expecting a question about Hardcastle's demise was temporarily stunned. Mort however knew immediately.

"Ah, biscuit?"

"Hm. The biscuit. What happened to it exactly?"

"Wasn't I supposed to eat it?"

"Did you eat it?"

"Well, there was only me here sir, so I suppose I must have."

"That's not what the video showed constable," said Aardvark, finally regaining some degree of composure. "How the…how did you do it?"

"You have him on the ropes Gaspard, take advantage of it."

"How?"

"Yes, how?"

"What?"

"How did you make the biscuit do what it did?"

"You mean get digested?"

"I mean fly through the air and disappear bit by bit?" "Do you mean bite by bite?"

"If you insist," sighed the DS.

"I don't know, it's the sort of thing that happens around me these days," replied Gaspard, both unable and unwilling to obfuscate any further. "Like spanners hiding themselves under mattresses. I wouldn't sweat it if I were you."

"Interview suspended at ten fifteen. DS Aardvark and DC Pickler are leaving the room."

"Ask them if you can have another biscuit."

"Oh, perhaps I could have another biscuit? A Hobnob if you have them."

"Thanks."

"Don't mention it?"

"What?"

"What's all this about biscuits? I thought it was a murder enquiry, it's beginning to sound more like the Caine mutiny," said Dr Coombs when the others entered the observation room.

"You haven't seen the video?"

"No."

"Just watch, Gaspard."

"Should I, do you think? asked Death in an amused tone. "It'd be very wicked now that we know they're watching."

"It'd be fun though wouldn't it?" asked Gaspard brightly, suddenly feeling devilish, "it's all on film from before so why not? It is a Hobnob."

"Sold!" Mort answered enthusiastically, taking up the treat as Gaspard sat with his hands locked behind his head for added effect. "You're the copper, what do you think they'll do?" enquired Death, munching the biscuit.

"I haven't a clue. The video forms part of the evidence though, so it could all prove rather embarrassing when they have to give it up. No doubt they'll be asked to explain and of course they can't. I should imagine they'll get in a professional magician to try to work it out."

"Really. That would be worth seeing."

"Hang around. In the meantime though, I'm still in the poo. All this is doing is making things awkward for them."

"And providing some amusement."

"And that."

"Jesus," gasped Coombs. "How does he do that?"

"If I knew that, I'd be on the stage. I suppose we'll have to get in a professional to view the footage. I can't work it out though, none of us can. We've viewed the footage in ultra-slow motion and his hands never leave his sides."

"Or his wrists, eh," joked Coombs to scowls from the others. "So what do want from me? I can't explain it."

"You're not here for that. This talking to himself, do you think he's bunging it on or is he nuts?"

"Well, if he's bunging it on as you say, he's going about it very differently to most. He seems to be having a one-sided and rational conversation. Most people trying to appear nuts would gabble and act weird. He's either very good or completely batshit."

"There is another explanation," piped up Pickler, who was more than a little suggestible, "he might actually be having a conversation with someone." After that remark, he was sent off to make the tea.

"We've found something sir," said Pickler anxiously some hours later. His face was the colour of chalk and his hands were trembling noticeably. "Apparently Hardcastle interviewed Feeblebunny not long before his death and…well, it's very revealing to say the least."

"How so? Did one of them do a strip," chuckled the DI.

"Not that sort of reveal, sir," responded the constable who, after seeing the footage of the interview was in no mood for jokes. "I think when you see it sir, you'll not be in a mood for humour."

"Really? How did this footage come to light, constable?"

"Oddly enough sir, it was because Hardcastle attempted to destroy it. As you know sir, ever since the Loophole Lapwing affair, all interview rooms are equipped with automatic recording devices and the footage goes to a back-up hard drive. It seems that Hardcastle was so concerned about the interview being seen that he attempted to access the hard drive and destroy the footage. Ironically enough, it was that attempt that brought it to light. Had he not done so, in all likelihood, no one would have noticed."

"Well, we'd best see it, I suppose. Could you give me a short synopsis before we begin? Just so as I know what I'm looking at?"

"Believe me sir, you'll know. But then again you won't, I'm sure. I still have no bloody idea what went on in that room but I don't mind admitting that it's scared the shit out of me. Sir."

"Ah. Should we call in the others, then?"

"As many as you can, would be my advice sir. It's not the sort of thing you want to watch alone."

The assembled officers viewed the footage with varying degrees of scepticism. To begin with, most thought Hardcastle to be deranged. Not surprising, considering the subject of the interview. That all changed when Gaspard did his vanishing act and reappeared fractions of a second later as the Collector. There were various cries of surprise, most of them having something to do with excrement.

"How the bloody hell did he do that?" screeched DCI Foxglove, whom DI Flaxwort had felt compelled to brief.

"There's more, sir," said Pickler when the general hubbub had settled. Despite his discomfiture at the bizarre event, he was revelling in the attention. "I assume everyone noticed that midway through the interview a constable brought in tea?"

"What of it, man?"

"Bear with me please sir. If we roll back," here he signalled to Constable Strongarm who was operating the computer, "you will see the constable places a saucer of biscuits, three to be precise, in the middle of the table. Now if we scroll forward to the point where Feeblebunny does his…change…we will notice the biscuits are still there, uneaten."

"If they're still there, it follows logically that they're uneaten wouldn't you say? What's this sudden obsession with bloody baked goods?" Foxglove roared, one of those who believed that rampant aggression was the best form of covering ignorance.

"Well sir," continued Pickler a trifle shakily, "if you watch closely you will see that Feeblebunny is in the middle of the room away from the three biscuits. Hardcastle stands when…er…the thing, appears, at which point the biscuits are still untouched. He goes nowhere near them. Now look at the table after he seats himself again."

"Holy shit! They're gone."

"Knocked over, perhaps?" Aardvark hazarded, beginning to feel a bit left out. "We've watched it over and over sir. No one goes within three feet of the biscuits or the table."

"There's more sir," piped up Constable Strongarm, who'd been holding something back in order to grab a bit of attention. "I've zoomed in on the saucer and look." All those in the room saw the biscuits levitate from the saucer and vanish.

"It has to be a hoax," muttered Foxglove, almost to himself. "You say this biscuit trick happened at your interview of Feeblebunny?" Aardvark nodded, unwilling to trust his vocal cords not to betray him. "And...and...this bloody skeleton business. Impossible. There has to be a rational explanation."

"If it helps sir, we've had some analysis done by forensics. They superimposed Feeblebunny's face on the skull and it's a perfect match. Bone structure, teeth and eyes."

"No constable, I don't think it helps at all. Not a word of this to anyone until we can get that bastard to confess how he's orchestrated this fiasco."

Foxglove was not a man of great imagination which was fortunate for him in this instance. Unfortunately for one or two of the others they were and would spend numerous disturbed nights alternately jumping at shadows and peering behind the drapes.

After Gaspard's stonewalling and the revelations of the CCTV footages, Sergeant Aardvark was not in a good frame of mind. It would be more correct to say that he was in a mind to frame.

By now, he had managed to almost convince himself that the bizarre events he'd witnessed were a hoax and that Gaspard was playing them all for fools, an opinion reinforced by a rocket up the keester from the DCI who wanted Gaspard's naughty bits for decorations. He gathered up a reluctant Pickler and stormed towards the interview room, where sat Gaspard, having been summarily brought from his cell. The abrupt and brusque nature of his summoning had him fearing the worst and bad it would have been had not Aardvark been intercepted on his mission by a messenger bearing the latest reports from the pathologist and the forensics team. With an anticipation bordering on delight, he tore open the envelopes. The sergeant's features never made it easy for his feelings to be discerned but since in this case the sudden twisting was accompanied by a full-throated roar of disappointment, Pickler didn't have too much of a problem guessing what was up.

Or maybe, since it was related to his spirits, what was down. "Problem Sarge?" Aardvark was not an unfair man. The reports all pointed to Gaspard's innocence of murder and after a deep breath or two, he was prepared to be happy for a colleague while still being mightily pissed that all his efforts had been for nought. He threw the reports to Pickler.

"Read and weep."

"Mm…cardiac arrest…yadda, yadda…superficial injuries to the back of the head consistent with a fall…etc, etc…no blood spatter consistent with bludgeoning…yackity, yack…evidence points to death by natural causes. That's it then Sarge?"

"It looks that way. Bloody suss though, eh Cyril? No sign of him for hours, the spanner under the mattress…?"

"We can't charge him with anything though can we Sarge? The reports clear him," he stroked his chin thoughtfully. "You don't suppose…? You know that funny business when Hardcastle was interviewing him? Disappearing and all that? Could that be why he didn't show up on the surveillance footage?"

"Did you see any skeletons swanning about the place on that footage, constable?"

"No, no, course not Sarge," replied Pickler quickly. He didn't like it when the sergeant called him constable. It usually meant he'd done something wrong. He had wanted to point out that before Gaspard had metamorphosed, he'd completely vanished for a short time but since the Sarge wasn't in the best frame of mind thought better of it. As the pair strolled towards the interview room Aardvark had a thought. "You know, there's still the spanner under the mattress. Feeblebunny may not have killed Hardcastle but that's still tampering with evidence. I might just have a quiet word with the DI." DS Aardvark might have been a fair man but he wasn't that bloody fair he'd be pissed about and not want revenge. It was DCI Foxglove who gave Gaspard the news that he was to be released without charge. That was the good news.

The not so good news was that he would be required to explain his whereabouts during the butt demonstration and to also explain the phenomena recorded during his interviews. He was to report at nine the following morning and God help his career if the answers were either not forthcoming or not satisfactory. "I'm to drive you home," said Entwhistle after the DCI had departed in a flurry of veiled threats.

"Not necessary thanks, Horace," "I'll make my own way."

"They won't pay for a taxi you know?"

"I know. I'll…ah…walk."

"It's a twenty-minute drive. It'll take you forever. Let me drive you. It'll save your feet and give me a chance to skive for a while."

"No thanks, really. I know a short cut." Entwhistle watched Gaspard disappear into the changing rooms. He waited, hoping to be able to convince Gaspard to take up the offer. He could do with and hour's break. After ten minutes, he went in to look for Gaspard. Horace had a bad feeling but hoped that Gaspard may have simply decided to have a quick shower or visit the loo. The changing room was empty. Horace Entwhistle fled to report to Sergeant Aardvark, after first taking a sly nip from the bottle he kept hidden in his locker. He would have liked a long draft but somehow the locker area didn't seem a place to linger.

Relations with the group were now such that they were almost pleased at Gaspard's return and definitely pleased that he was not to be charged with murder. All save one that is. Hardcastle glowered at Gaspard as the others clustered around and did their best to make up for their folly in moving the spanner. "Out on bail, I suppose," said Hardcastle, more in hope than with any true conviction.

"Sorry to disappoint you Marion but all charges have been dropped."

"Don't call me Marion!"

"I thought it was OK," said Gaspard with more innocence in his tone than in his intent.

"For the others only. You can call me Sergeant Hardcastle or sir."

"Not going to happen Sarge. It's my home you're infesting and if you don't like it you know what you can do. Mort is still on the clock with you for a while so you only have to put your hand up."

"I'm staying."

"Then in the interests of harmony I won't call you Marion but you'll have to get used to Sarge. That's if we have anything to say to one another which I strongly doubt."

"It all worked out then? I told you not to worry" said Mort, more than a trifle unconvincingly.

"That's not what I recall. My memory is that you dropped me right in it. In fact, I'm still right in it. I have to front up to an examination in the morning and explain the inexplicable. They have the tape of the Hardcastle interview by the way, so they already have my confession. They don't believe it of course and want me to tell them how and why I did what I did. Then there's your biscuit noshing."

He fixed Mort with a studied glare.

"Shit. I need to run this past Terrance. Your confession to Hardcastle was bad enough but now that it's in the public domain so to speak it's a real can of wriggly things. This whole business is getting out of control."

"You're telling me. Maybe your Wizkid should have foreseen something like this happening, don't you think?"

"I warned them, you know," said Death sounding a little bit too pleased with himself. "Bringing in a mortal could result in all sorts of complications I said. Would they listen? Would they buggery. That's the problem with the young ones, won't listen to the voice of experience."

"Yeah, well as pleased as I am that you feel vindicated that doesn't help me one little bit does it? The question remains, what the blazes do I do tomorrow?"

"Give me half a mo." With that brief reply, Mort vanished. Briefly. "OK, so what Terrance says and I heartily agree, is that we have no option but to pull out all the stops other than to throw you to the wolves and that is not an option. It's really quite simple when you think of it. Just go in there in the robe and tell them they've seen nothing. If necessary, I'll put in an appearance."

"But there's the CCTV footage. Others will have to see my interview. The one with Flaxwort, at least. Oh and I suppose there's the demo footage as well."

"Don't worry. The tech boys are working on that."

"Oh shit. We're in trouble, aren't we?"

"Don't be so ready to accuse others of incompetence. Just because there have been one or two minor mishaps it doesn't follow that there will be this time. Remember, we've been running the world since year dot."

"And look how that's turned out. Still, I have no option but to trust them have I?"

"You can always quit the force."

"No way. However, maybe I can quit the other job. I mean, now that the committee have seen the sort of problems that can arise, surely they realise that their decision was a mistake?"

"You don't know much about how governing bodies work, do you Gaspard? Simply put, they do not make mistakes. Someone will have to be blamed for the problem of course but that will be some minor functionary who will probably be transferred somewhere unpleasant."

"But what if they can't find someone to blame?"

"Even better. They'll hold an investigation into an unfortunate miscommunication, announce that new measures have been put in place to prevent it happening again and life goes on."

"So they won't let me go?"

"That would be admitting an error."

"I'm stuffed then?"

"Right royally, my boy."

"Good morning constable. Are you prepared to offer a full explanation?"

"I am sir. May I ask sir, shouldn't Constable Entwhistle be present?"

"Constable Entwhistle is not required Feeblebunny. Constable Strongarm will handle the technical requirements. Not that it's your place to ask. Now get on with it."

"Don't worry, I'll handle it" said Mort, briefly popping up at Gaspard's side.

From somewhere in the general direction of Entwhistle came a hideous scream.

"Done."

"If you don't mind sirs, any full explanation on my part requires me to don the robe you saw me wearing on the Hardcastle interview."

Without waiting for approval, Gaspard donned the garment. The assembled officers knew what to expect but knowing didn't make it any easier to handle. There followed assorted cries ranging from the blasphemous to the downright foul. There was one cry of terror. "Now that I have your attention gentlemen, I must ask you if anyone outside of this room other that Constable Entwhistle has seen the footage of the interviews."

"Your union representitive, I believe," replied DCI Foxglove as though in a trance.

"And that would be?"

"Sergeant Trollop in traffic." Gaspard nodded at Mort although no signal was necessary.

"Consider it done." Deep in the confines of the traffic section officers were treated to a bloodcurdling shriek.

"Now gentleman, you have seen nothing out of the ordinary on any of the interview tapes and surveillance footage of the demonstration shows me going about my assigned duties."

"Of course, why would you think otherwise?" responded Foxglove.

"And it goes without saying that no one has witnessed anything untoward."

"Of course, of course. What are we doing here? Could someone remind me?"

"Yes sir. I believe that the board was going to apologise for my arrest."

"Quite so. Our most sincere apologies constable."

"I believe you were also going to offer a commendation for my sterling efforts at the demonstration, sir," added Gaspard, deciding that he might as well get all he could out of the situation. "Oh and one final thing sir, there never was a spanner under the mattress."

"What a preposterous idea, constable."

"Thank you gentleman."

"Thank you constable. You are dismissed and may I say what a pleasure it is to have such a dedicated officer as yourself in the service. You thoroughly deserve to have the commendation on your record."

"Thank you sir. I try my best."

Flaxwort turned to the others after Gaspard's departure. "What a lovely chap. Fast track for promotion I'd think."

"That went well."

"I suppose. You'll make sure the report about the spanner gets doctored?"

"We'd already thought of it. Trust us Gaspard."

"Why wouldn't I Mort?"

It was a pity that everybody had forgotten the chap in forensics who'd overlaid Gaspard's likeness on the skeletal figure. When some bright spark in the tech department did eventually remember, it was a little late. Ever since he'd done the work Fred Hopper had been having waking nightmares, if such a thing is possible. In the interests of his sanity; a decision that proved to be sadly ironic; he decided to have one last look at his copy of the footage. There had to be a rational explanation and he was the man to find it.

Shortly after again viewing the footage he was escorted from the building by two large men in white coats. It didn't really need large men because by then he'd been heavily sedated. Terrance, who'd been overseeing the tech boys in altering the evidence was not amused by the turn of events. *"Could you explain to me what just happened and why, Nigel?"*

"I can only assume that the gentleman was upset by the alterations, Terrance."

"And why do you think that might be, Nigel?"

"Um, I really don't know Terrance. I suppose any change would have been disconcerting but we couldn't just erase the footage, that would have been both suspicious and time consuming, we had to make some credible alterions so that the interview appeared less incriminating."

"I understand that Nigel but what is it about having Sergeant Hardcastle singing Putting on the Ritz that convinced you it was (a) a good substitute and (b) credible in any way?"

"We were pressed for time sir and it's hard to make things up, so we went for something existing. As you see we only just made it even then."

"Mm. And Feeblebunny responding with The Indian Love Call. Same answer?"

"Urgh."

"So, let's go to the transformation if we may? Why did having Gaspard become a fluffy bunny seem such a good idea."

"Time again sir. We couldn't erase the transformation completely and since he had to change we thought it should be something less threatening."

"Thank you, Nigel. You realise that once again a man's destiny has been altered? There will be consequences."

"For the man Terrance?"

"For the planet, the man and possibly others, Nigel. Have you ever considered a career in the Department of Insect Plagues?"

After the interview with the senior panel, things began to come together for Gaspard. At work, his star was on the rise and he actually managed to collar a couple of bike thieves and a pickpocket while clad in his robe. He couldn't take them to the station but a threat to appear in their bedrooms in the dead of night was enough to put them on the straight and narrow. In most cases anyway. One of the bike thieves was gay so in his case it was just the narrow. At home, things were going even better if that were possible. The choral evenings had brought together Hardcastle and Monica and the sergeant was entranced.

It had resulted in a much warmer atmosphere and though it couldn't be said that it also resulted in a mending of fences, at least the open animosity was no longer present. The only down side was that Hardcastle's feelings for Monica, being of a fiercely paternal nature, put a bit of a cramp in any romantic dalliance on the home front. Any open canoodling would bring wrath down upon Gaspard and had to take place at Monica's house. Gaspard reckoned the peace was worth it. At least, he didn't have to worry about Hardcastle floating above him with a carving knife while he slept. On the other hand, a night away from home or even a late return home could bring about repercussions.

"I see the romance is proceeding well, Gaspard?"

"I don't know what you mean."

"I went looking for some hobnobs the other day."

"Now I definitely don't know what you mean."

"You keep them behind the sardines…and such."

"So? What's that got to do with romance."

"Directly, nothing I admit. It's just that I couldn't help noticing that the 'and such' item has been opened. It's now not so much a family as an economy size."

15

For months, things had been progressing reasonably well. Hardcastle was being kept in check by the other spirits and they soon learned that they had to keep a particularly watchful eye on him when he deemed Gaspard's time with Monica was overly long. There had been one occasion when their vigilance failed and Gaspard awoke to find that a tin of sardines had been emptied over him but everyone including Gaspard reasoned that to be a minor discomfort considering the possible alternatives. Hardcastle it seemed, was mellowing. It was when the letter arrived that the newfound harmony was disturbed. It was addressed to: Feeblebunny, Goonhilly and Gaspard, Literary Agents, 12a Feltham Rise Apartments, Feltham Rise, Hamm on Wye. Gaspard didn't dare open it until he'd called the ghosts to explain what it was all about. He had no doubt that whatever it was, the ghosts were behind it.

The excitement exhibited by the ghosts on seeing the letter was proof positive that he was correct. When it proved to be a request for a meeting to discuss the publications of A Porpoise's Tale, the author being one A.P. Spinner, there was uproar, followed by tears. "I'm very pleased for you of course Spinner but what I don't understand is why you thought it necessary to invent a literary agent," said Gaspard, finding it difficult to control his annoyance.

"Because Gaspard," replied the doctor in a tone bordering on the patronising, "publishing houses seldom bother to read manuscripts sent on spec these days. You need an agent."

"Oh, I see. It didn't bother you that this agent didn't actually exist? Never crossed your mind that a publisher may know that it didn't exist? You didn't stop to think that in the event the manuscript was accepted you might have to actually create such a firm? No. Forget that last bit. That I might have to create the firm?"

There was a sulky silence eventually broken by Spinner. "He says we couldn't exactly deal with any existing agent. It seemed like a good idea at the time," said the doctor interpreting.

"Much like invading Russia in winter seemed a good idea, I presume?"

"No need to be sarky. Anyway, it worked didn't it?"

"I doubt that your ruse did work. You were just bloody lucky. Now though, Monica and I have to bugger about creating the firm to make you clods look good. Maybe next time you'll do me the honour of asking my opinion first."

"We knew you'd probably be against it. Face it Gaspard, you're a miserable bugger at the best of times. You'd just have cranked up the pessimism meter to ten and said we were wasting our time." It was the doctor who had spoken but the remaining spirits all nodded their agreement. That the agreement was of a type generally referred to as enthusiastic was particularly hurtful to the one on the receiving end. Gaspard felt the urge to strike back but remained silent. They were probably correct although he excused himself as having a perfect right to be, all things considered. When he did speak, it was in a more conciliatory tone.

"OK, we'll let that drop. In the interest of future harmony, however, might I enquire if any more of you intend going on the firm's books?" Despite his resolution to himself he was not quite able to rid the enquiry of a sarcastic note. He couldn't think of anywhere that it said conciliation couldn't have a bit of attitude. Not that he was inclined to look very hard.

"Um," began Hardcastle with uncharacteristic timidity, "I've been toying with doing a few lines on my early career."

"I've read some of it," interrupted Percy, "it's really quite good. Sort of early Joseph Wambaugh but with more kicks to the groin."

"Thanks Percy. Appreciated. If you're interested Gaspard," the name almost stuck in his throat, "I'm calling it 'Not a Happy One'. You know, after the song."

"A policeman's lot is not a happy one," added Bert unnecessarily.

"I did get the reference, thanks Bert," said Gaspard, sounding sharper than he intended. "Why not a policeman's lot?"

"There's nothing happy about some of the events. Most of them in fact." Hardcastle paused to ruminate briefly. "Or me for that matter. At least, at the time. It seemed more appropriate."

"Well, run it past the review panel when you're happy with it," said Gaspard, "we don't have too many clients at the moment so we'll be pleased to review your manuscript for the usual fee of bugger all. Double spaced please." The words may have dripped with sarcasm but they were taken seriously by all. Even Gaspard was beginning to think that something worthwhile may come out of it. "Any other would-be authors?"

"I've got a children's book in the pipeline," said Bert to everyone's surprise.

"That must be painful," sniggered Percy, "I'd take it out of there if I were you."

"Just one other thing, if I may," said Gaspard, ignoring Percy's obvious jibe and causing a ripple of consternation through the group. They could tell by his delivery that whatever he was about to say would be bloody awkward. "How did you intend to deal with the publishers? Pessimistic bastard that I am, I can't help wondering if they've previously dealt with any disembodied porpoises and their phantom translators."

"Well, we'd rather hoped...."

Gaspard and Monica were seated nervously in the office of Oswald Sharkey, President of Cuttlefish Press. The office was everybody's idea of what a publisher's office should look like, assuming that the everybody in question knew absolutely sod all about interior design. It was furnished in lots of leather and mahogany with massive bookshelves lining the back wall and framed award certificates and commendations hanging at eye level. While it was undoubtedly impressive in its way, it only went to show that while many of the house's authors may have been original, the management certainly was not.

It having been decided that Spinner's attendance may be a serious error, Gaspard was posing as the author of A Porpoise's Tale, penned (or more accurately typed) by one, A.P. Spinner. The A.P. standing for 'a porpoise'. Spinner hadn't thought very deeply about his choice of alias. Monica was the Goonhilly in the firm of Feeblebunny and Goonhilly, the third original member Gaspard having passed away suddenly prior to the firm's very recent registration. The firm's creation had been a chore and an expense not relished by the partners.

"I'm so very pleased to meet you Mr Spinner. And you too of course Miss Goonhilly. A new firm in the trade I presume? We looked and looked but couldn't find a record of you anywhere." This pronouncement was accompanied by a smarmy smile.

"Very new," said Gaspard, beating Monica to the punch. "I'm afraid I rather jumped the gun and embarrassed my friend Monica here. She took me on before they'd registered the firm and I fear that I was rather precipitate. Too anxious, you see? First offering and all that. I'm ashamed to admit that I got hold of some of the firm's stationary."

"No harm done," said Monica with an appropriately long-suffering air, accompanied by a little eye roll for the benefit of Sharkey. She finished it off brilliantly with a smile that said, "What do you do with these literary geniuses'?"

"And your…Mister Gaspard was it? No longer with the firm?"

"No longer with the living. A tragic incident involving a mongoose while on safari," said Monica whose sense of humour could be a bit of a trial at times.

"So sorry to hear that. My sincere condolences," replied Sharkey although his eyes were saying something else. "Are you having a laugh?" to be exact.

"My condolences again. Now, I believe that Miss Goonhilly is Monica, but I fear I am ignorant of your first name Mister Spinner?"

"This is Alan," said Monica quickly, realising by the look of panic on Gaspard's face that he'd not given the matter any thought.

"Wonderful, wonderful, call me Ossie. Now, I don't mind telling you that we're very excited about this book of yours Alan. Original concept and told with a really touching humanity. Considering that you chose to write in the first person, one could almost believe you were a porpoise." He finished with a chuckle.

"But if I were a porpoise it wouldn't be told with humanity would it? It would have to be porposity."

"Ha, ha, quite. I see your roguish sense of humour isn't limited to your writing. Tell me, do you have any qualifications in marine biology or such? I don't mind divulging that we ran the manuscript past a few experts and they were astounded by the depth of knowledge. Some even said that they were made to see a porpoise's life for the first time in their careers. They were most complimentary."

"I'm pleased to hear that but no. No qualifications whatsoever. Just general interest. For a long time now, I've felt quite close to the creatures."

"And it shows."

Monica and Gaspard left the offices of Cuttlefish Press in a state of near shock. They were too inexperienced to have negotiated any amazing deal but Oswald Sharkey had been generous in offering a little more than the standard contract terms. Following a degree of cooperative editing, mainly to cool down some of the hotter passages to make it suitable for the younger reader, A.P. Spinner would receive a generous advance for the completed work and a guarantee of an equally lucrative share of paperback rights.

He would also receive a substantial advance against a three-book deal. He'd already envisaged another porpoise-based book and his next work, with the suggested title of Sam Squid and the Tentative Tentacle, was already well advanced. It was agreed the title may be subject to revision at a later date. There was one caveat. "Ossie has asked me to assure you that there's no reflexion on Sammy, Spinner. He just thinks that from the commercial point of view, Orca! would be a better fit as a second work. The concept is more of a follow up to the memoir. He's still not sure that as a new author you could sell the idea of a squid with palsy to the reading public. He likes what he's seen of the partial first draft but still feels you need to consolidate your reputation first."

"Eek."

"He says what the hell. He can knock off Orca! in his sleep. He'll have the first draft in a couple of weeks. He'd like assurances though that Sammy will be taken seriously. He thinks it will be the great cetacean novel."

"Just a thought but as he's the only cetacean author, that might be pretty much a slam dunk."

The doctor looked severely at Gaspard. "And, just a thought from me," he began, ignoring the remark, "you might like to give some consideration to learning his lingo if you're going to be acting as his agent. Especially as he looks as if he's going to make you fabulously rich. We haven't signed a contract yet you know. There are other agents."

"Eek."

"Oh and on the point of riches he feels that now he's made you all wealthy maybe you could see your way clear to a new Ludo set and maybe a backgammon board."

"How about a couple of new laptops too," said Gaspard, suddenly feeling terribly guilty and stupidly generous. "The firm can't have you fighting over the one we have."

It was quite late when Father O'Flatus turned up unannounced at Gaspard's door. He was clutching an elderly computer protectively to his bosom. Exactly what he was trying to protect would have been anyone's guess but from what Gaspard was to discover later, it was undoubtedly his reputation and along with that, his livelihood. Possibly also his body if it fell into the wrong hands. "Sorry if I'm disturbing you Gaspard. I was just passing and wondered if you might be available to lend me a hand?"

"Of course, father," responded Gaspard reluctantly, wondering just how often it was that the good father roamed the evening streets clutching an aged laptop; although laptop was possibly a generous description for the item the priest was carrying. Gaspard's previous experience with the device had led him to ponder whether when this particular machine was sold it was more likely to have been described as a personal difference engine.

"Ask him if he remembered to bring the hand crank," said Percy rudely from behind Gaspard's left shoulder.

"Shut up Percy," snapped Gaspard, unable to stop himself. It was difficult not too reply when conversations with ghosts made up at least eighty percent of social interaction.

"What…oh…they're here?"

"They're always here father. Don't worry, they've promised to behave." When the priest was comfortably seated, at least physically, his mental comfort still being in some doubt, Gaspard enquired of the reason for his visit, although that it had something to do with the priest's encumbrance was pretty obvious.

"It's the computer. You know about these things and I was hoping you could tell me why I seem to be receiving a lot of…um…unsolicited stuff. I hesitate to bother you my son. Normally I'd have asked someone more intimately connected with the church but the…er…stuff…is such that some might wonder how I came by it. Some of it at least."

Knowing the churchman's innocence of worldly matters and in particular the pitfalls of the internet, Gaspard could well imagine the sort of problems he was having. He also couldn't help thinking that considering the troubles the church was having these days it was a good idea for the priest not to use the words intimate and church in the same sentence.

"They're not watching, are they?" enquired O'Flatus with a display of concern. "I wouldn't want any more people than necessary to know about the problems."

"It's alright father, they're working." The priest gave a blink of surprise but said nothing. It was best not to know. After the computer had wheezed its way to start up, it became immediately obvious what the problem was. The father's innocent searches had not been regarded quite so innocently by the browser he'd been using and to add to the problem, the machine was completely devoid of any software protection.

The result had been that he'd been inundated with unsolicited downloads and ads for sites such as 'raunchyboyscouts', 'boysnaughtyintents' and others with even more salacious web names. And it was not only the more dubious sites. He'd also received numerous invitations for various ghost related sites as a result of Gaspard's searches during his visit to the rectory. "I hate to say this father but you really should junk this thing and buy a new one."

"Can't you just…I don't know…get rid of what's there?"

"I can but I can't stop it happening again. You need protective software but your operating system is so old you won't find any that's compatible. In any case, if someone were to take a serious look at the thing, they'd find the stuff even though it's been deleted."

"Really? They can do that?"

"They can and do. We know that you've never intentionally surfed for the stuff that's on there," he said making a generously charitable assumption, "but you might find it hard to explain. You might just get away with 'big jugs', I really don't know but the others…well…" Gaspard scratched his head for a moment.

"Tell you what, father, I've come into a bit of money lately and I've been meaning to replace my old machine. Why don't you take that? I'll teach you the basics for keeping it updated and clearing your search history."

"That's really very generous my son."

"Not at all father. Now let me show you for a start how to clear the history. We both know that 'scouting for boys' was a perfectly innocent search but there may be some folk less charitably minded. Some people will find the devil in anything if they're intent on finding it so best get rid of everything you search for immediately, just in case. Even if it's a recipe for spotted dick. Come to think of it, especially if it's anything to do with spotted dick. You can never be too sure."

As he scrolled through the various ads, one happened to catch his eye. "I mean, would you just look at this; 'spookbooking.com.' It's a site dedicated to booking haunted hotel stays. Who'd have thought?" In the next room there were at least two who would have thought and had not completely given up the dream of making a new life…well, perhaps not life…of being resident ghosts in a stately manor somewhere. One of them, Maud D'Unstable, pricked up her ears. "That's it doctor. I've got it!"

"Well see me in the surgery tomorrow morning, Maud," replied Ivor with a chuckle.

Weeks passed and things seemed to have settled down. Spinner's book was heading for the press and there was a great deal of excitement about his second work. Even Hardcastle appeared to be in a more accepting frame of mind and hardly ever tried to punish Gaspard for spending too long in Monica's company. Once or twice he even ignored overnight stays. There had been the one incident of the spam fritter in Gaspard's shoe but it was a half-hearted assault at best. The other ghosts put it down to his immersion in his writing.

It couldn't last of course. The knock on the door came at around dinnertime. Gaspard was immediately suspicious because instead of the usual disinterest on the part of the group there was a distinct air of excitement. Maud in particular was extremely agitated and began straightening her hair and fussing over her attire, which now that Gaspard came to think of it was a bit dressy for an ordinary evening's get together. "What's going on Maud?"

"I have no idea what you mean. Hadn't you better answer the door?" She couldn't hide the eagerness in her voice. Gaspard made his way reluctantly to the door and peered through the peephole. His reluctance immediately deserted him and began running about the place in a frenzy with its tongue hanging out because on the other side of the door was a creature that would make the most dedicated celibate not only break his vows but do his best to trample the pieces into the dirt.

"Um, good evening, may I help you?" enquired Gaspard, desperately attempting to rid his mind of visions of how that might be accomplished while simultaneously struggling to control his respiration.

"Good, evening. Mister Feeblebunny is it? I'm Valeria. Your new guest." Gaspard quite literally took a step back in surprise. The thought flashed through his mind that the raven-haired goddess before him was welcome anytime. It lasted about a nanosecond before he realised that if she placed one foot over the threshold Monica would do her best to slowly eviscerate him. It took a while for the more obvious thought of 'what bloody guest?' to sluggishly push some rampant hormones aside and impress itself on his consciousness. "Guest?"

"Yes. I booked a stay through spookynook.com. I have the confirmation here if you want."

"Psst, Gaspard. Let her in. We can explain."

"Um, no, no, not necessary, please come in."

"Offer her a drink."

"Would you like a drink, Valeria? Tea, coffee, some wine perhaps?"

"No thank you Mister Feeblebunny, it's been quite a tiring trip. If I might just have a little freshen up?"

"Mm, certainly. If you wouldn't mind taking a seat for the moment, I'll just go and make sure that everything is in order for you. I've not long got home from work so I'm not sure if…er, the maid has left your towels and such."

"Sure. Perhaps I will have that glass of wine if it's OK. It'll help relax me."

"Bottle's in the fridge," said Gaspard hurriedly, "glasses in the right-hand cupboard. Make yourself at home."

"Alright you buggers. What have you let me in for now?" hissed Gaspard, trying his best not to be overheard.

"It's very simple," said the doctor soothingly, "you remember a long time back we, Maud and I that is, were talking about doing holiday hauntings; well this is a beginning. We signed on to a site called ScareBnB… where people can book haunted rooms. It'll be fun don't you think?"

"Oh, Jesus," groaned Gaspard clutching his suddenly aching head.

"Look, you don't have to do anything. Just be nice, make her breakfast, ensure she has some clean towels, toiletries and such and we'll do the rest. Just make sure you ask her what sort of haunting she'd like."

"What sort of…?"

"You don't want us to traumatise the poor girl do you? Perhaps you could hint at an old lady; sorry Maud, sitting at the end of her bed. That seems to be a common one. If she doesn't seem keen, we could do the menacing wraith slowly drifting across the room. On the other hand, if she seems a bit of a goer, we could maybe try for the distraught, bloodied spirit hovering over her wringing our hands sort of thing. Sound her out. You're a copper, you should be able to get her to say what she's expecting."

"Didn't you put it on the web site?"

"We sort of left it a bit open. We thought if we said multiple manifestations had been experience it would give us more range for theatrics."

"Eek."

"Oh and ask her what she thinks about porpoises." Gaspard was seated opposite Valeria trying to keep his hand steady as he sipped his wine. Part of the reason for the shakes was that far from sipping he wanted to guzzle and another and far larger part was that he was sitting opposite Valeria.

"So Mister Feeblebunny…that's so formal don't you think…perhaps I could call you…?"

"Um, Gaspard," said Gaspard eventually, his fascination with his guest making him a bit slow on the uptake.

"Gaspard. Not a very English name, I think. Nor I think is Feeblebunny? Quite an unusual name if I am correct?"

"Very. I think there are only one or two of us in the country. Perhaps the world if it comes to that. I'm sorry but I seem to have forgotten your surname. Forget my head if it wasn't screwed on."

"Katzarz. I'm Valeria Katzarz. Not an exotic name like yours, I'm afraid."

"Really?" said Gaspard trying not to choke and wondering in what sort of world the name Katzarz could be considered commonplace.

"Mm. It's a very common name where I come from. There are Katzarz's all over the country. It does make for nice get togethers though. We have one day a year when as many Katzarz's as can make it meet up for regional gatherings." There was a burst of incontinent mirth from the next room and even Spinner gave a few shrill whistles.

"You could have warned him you know," giggled Bert, addressing the doctor. "Did you see the look on his face?"

"Bloody priceless," said Percy. "He looks as though someone poked a pineapple up his bum."

Gaspard leaped to his feet on the pretext of looking for some snacks but really to steady himself. "I'm sorry Valeria, you must think me very rude. I haven't asked if you've eaten?"

"She looks like she could eat you alive," sniggered Percy.

"I have, thank you. It was my understanding that you only provide breakfast?"

"That's correct but I can't let my guest go hungry, can I?" He smiled winningly. "Now if you don't mind my asking, what sort of experience are you expecting tonight?"

Valeria eyed him suspiciously, obviously trying to fathom whether there might be something suggestive going on. She obviously concluded that he was either genuinely speaking of ghosts or that he was harmless.

"Oh, any manifestation would be wonderful. Can you tell me what you've noticed? You have noticed things, haven't you?"

"More than you can possibly imagine. The predominant ghost is a woman called Maud D'Unstable. She committed suicide here some years back. Frankly there's no telling what she might do. If she's in a good mood, she usually watches television or sits and reads. If not, she may throw things. That hasn't happened much though; I wouldn't want to scare you. So far, it's only been when she felt threatened."

"Oh dear. I hope she doesn't feel threatened by me." Valeria looked about the room a trifle apprehensively. "And did you say that she's the predominant ghost?"

"Um, yes. I suppose though it would be more correct to say senior as she's been here the longest."

"So there is more than one then?"

"Oh God yes. I'm tripping over the buggers."

"Now Gaspard, I think you are pulling my leg."

"You've noticed the cold?"

"Now that you mention it, yes. It is very cold in here. The ghosts? How many?"

"I wouldn't want to alarm you. Let's wait and see who turns up shall we?" He smiled reassuringly. "Just out of interest, what do you think about Gilbert and Sullivan?"

"And breakfast? What do you normally have?" asked Gaspard some while later, after the topic of historic hauntings had been exhausted and Valeria had expressed a desire to retire for the night.

"Whatever you have would be fine."

"No please, you must tell me, you're my guest," said Gaspard, whose larder was not exactly overstocked with breakfast-time comestibles. Truth to tell, the closest he came at the moment was a tin of baked beans, three stale crusts from a suspect brand of supermarket bread and the remains of a box of cereal that he'd been thinking of donating to the British Museum. He didn't count the sardines.

"Well in my country we usually have raw yoghurt and cold sausage with sometimes, hard boiled eggs. A little cheese too usually."

"No problem at all," said Gaspard whose closest relationship with yoghurt was to occasionally have a month-old bottle of milk in the fridge. He was secretly cursing that he'd have to make another raid on the supermarket but keeping up a brave face. The family size pack was getting a bit a low anyway. "Pastries?"

"Oh yes please."

"And you wouldn't prefer a bit of hot sausage first thing?" he enquired innocently, or more correctly his conscious mind enquired innocently. Behind the scenes his subconscious was getting up to tricks.

"No, I wouldn't," said Valeria a trifle too quickly for comfort and with a decided edge to her voice. If she'd heard the sniggers from the next room, she would have been even less happy.

"OK then. I'll let you get settled." Gaspard's obvious innocence of any intentional suggestiveness left Valeria feeling slightly guilty over her snappy reply. It was a pity then that he followed up with what he said next. "If you need anything, just knock on my door. Oh, by the way, would you like me to give you a bit of a poke in the morning?"

Valeria's jaw dropped. Before she could reply, Gaspard's sense of survival came to his rescue aided by the guffaws from Percy who could always be trusted to spot a double entendre, or sometimes to manufacture one where it didn't exist.

"Sorry, local lingo. That probably means nothing to you," he blurted desperately. She gave an appraising look that told him it meant a lot to her but not in the manner he claimed to have meant. "I meant; would you like me to knock you up? Aaaak. I mean…I mean, give you a call?" He blushed furiously which in company with his obvious state of embarrassed confusion went some way towards mollifying her. Anyway, she'd had quite a bit of experience of young men speaking through their subconscious.

"Thank you no. I have an alarm."

As it eventuated, she would have several alarms. It took a bit of doing but he managed to weed Bert and Percy out of the bedroom before Valeria began readying herself for bed. Hardcastle was no problem, he being a gentleman of the old school despite also being a thorough going bastard.

"OK you lot. Fill me in. How long is she booked for?"

"Just three nights, Gaspard," replied the doctor. "I think she's also here to look at the butts."

"I suppose that's only fair," interrupted Percy, seldom one to miss the chance for a sleazy remark, "there'll be plenty looking at hers."

"There has been a lot in the foreign press about it lately," continued Ivor with a glare meant to both silence and shame, "and she's a history student I believe."

"Three nights, Jesus, Monica will kill me," Gaspard moaned, unable to absorb anything other than Monica's potential wrath.

"Hm, if it helps, we can explain it to her. Let her know that you were completely unaware of her visit," said Ivor sounding a little guilty.

"I might have been unaware of her visit but I'd have to be made of bloody concrete not to be aware of her. Monica will not be pleased."

"Maybe you could keep her away?" Bert said.

"Bugger that," said Percy, who was one of the great northern school of telling it how it is. "All you need to do is to be honest." Along with the telling it how it is school Percy was also a member of the knowing bugger all about women school.

"But if she sees her…?" Gaspard said miserably.

"I wouldn't worry, Gaspard," said Percy in his most hurtful tone, "she'd never believe that a stunner like this one would give you a second look."

"Yeah but that doesn't mean she wouldn't suspect me of being hopeful."

When the first horrified cry came, Gaspard was hard boiling some eggs, one of the few culinary tasks he could just about manage as long as you didn't mind the eggs either runny or with dry and crumbly yolk. Although it was a challenge, he was simultaneously preparing a breakfast cold plate. He jumped and was about to fly to Valeria's rescue when he realised that she was experiencing what she had paid for and may resent his intrusion. He waited breathlessly for a short while before returning to his chore.

A second cry split the air. This one was more a panicked shriek and had him worrying what the neighbours might think, particularly after the suspicious death of Hardcastle on the premises. It was an event still providing endless speculation despite his having been absolved. He began to edge toward the bedroom door listening for a plea for assistance. At the third and almost unhinged shriek, he decided that enough was enough. She still hadn't called for aid so his knock was a little tentative.

"You'd best come in Gaspard," called the doctor, "I think the young lady may be somewhat traumatised."

Valeria was still in bed but sitting up and crammed as tightly as she could manage into a corner. It was apparent from the disordered nature of the bed linen that at some time she'd had it over her head. "Are you alright Valeria?" Gaspard enquired in the most comforting tone that he could manage. It had a slight tremor as a direct result of Valeria being one of those young ladies who didn't see much point in being overdressed for bed. There was no response other than to hold out a trembling hand and point at Maud who had obviously gone all out to give the girl her money's worth. Behind her floated Spinner looking concerned.

The doctor was standing at the foot of the bed and appeared completely out of his depth which was no doubt appropriate in a way because he had departed this life by drowning himself. "Valeria?" There was only a whimper in response. "Valeria, I think we'd best get you out of here. You can stay in my room tonight, the…the others know that it's out of bounds. You won't be troubled there." He turned to address the ghosts. "Could you lot vanish for a moment? I don't think it helps that she can still see you."

"Oh, right, sorry Gaspard. Sorry Valeria." Gaspard held out a hand and after a lengthy amount of persuasion managed to persuade Valeria to leave the dubious safety of her corner and edge along the wall. Once in his room she seemed a bit more at ease but still terrified. "You make yourself comfy. I assure you that they won't disturb you. They know that you didn't enjoy it and since you're paying for the experience, they'll give you what you want. OK?"

Valeria nodded dumbly before pulling the covers over her head, "I'll just have a word with them and then come back and see you're alright. Anything I can bring you? Warm milk? Whisky? Tea?"

There was a brisk movement of the bed cloths to indicate a shake of the head. Possibly. He thought he had better bring her some nerve balm anyway. "So what the hell happened?"

"Nothing that we could have expected," Maud said moodily. "It was her what wanted the haunting."

"Which took the form of…?" And so the unfolding of the evening's events was relayed to Gaspard. Maud had decided that since Valeria had been informed of her suicide; that should be the theme. She had donned a bloody night gown and appeared, hair awry and face contorted madly, hovering above the girl's bed repeatedly stabbing herself with a dagger and moaning eerily. The girl had screamed and become panicked. The doctor had attempted to calm her but when he sat on the bed and tried to take her pulse, she'd become even more terrified. At that point Spinner, being of a sympathetic nature had popped up to see if he could help. That and the doctor's bumbling attempts to calm her had elicited a second scream.

After that, Hardcastle who'd been trying to work on his book had stormed into the room shouting that he was trying to work and would all they all just bloody well shut up. The third scream followed and a state of near catatonia ensued not made any better by Maud deciding that it might help to sooth the girl's ragged nerves if she sang. The sight of a bloodied maniac singing Buttercup from *HMS Pinafore* had exactly the opposite effect to that intended and did little to improve the girl's state of mind.

"I don't get it," Maud said, twiddling her hair distractedly. She seemed so keen.

"You know the old saying Maud," said Ivor, putting his arm protectively about her shoulders, "be careful what you wish for. It might just come true."

Back in his own room Gaspard held the whisky glass to Valeria's quivering lips, steadying her with an arm about her body. He really was concerned but her proximity was intoxicating and soon it was hard to tell whether it was her that was trembling or him. It turned out to be both. "There you go. I'm so sorry about all this and I can say with certainty that the others are all most apologetic. They'd tell you themselves if they didn't think it would upset you further." Valeria snuffled. "Now, you settle down and relax. Take my word for it that you're one hundred percent safe."

"Stay with me," croaked Valeria. "Um, yes, of course. I'll be over there in the chair." It wasn't something he wanted to do but in the circumstances, he had little choice. At least, tomorrow was his rostered day off.

"No. Get in with me. Please. You must hold me." He really did protest but eventually yielded to her pleading and a wicked urge to do just that and climbed in beside her. Gaspard was struggling with the almost impossible feat of adhering to Valeria's wishes for close proximity yet avoiding any intimate contact. That is, he was adhering while desperately trying not to adhere.

Meanwhile, in the next room, the ghosts were conferring. "We didn't think it through, did we?"

The doctor aimed a guilty and partly accusatory look at Maud. "'Tweren't my fault," replied Maud somewhat belligerently. "If the girl didn't know what she wanted, she shouldn't have booked. Or at least left a note on the booking form. No stabbings or something." Maud glared sourly from one to the other of her colleagues.

"Don't look at me, it was your daft idea," said Bert with a sniff. "You and Ivor."

"Oh yeah. All our fault. I seem to recall it was you that arranged the council permit."

"Yeah, well…I was only being helpful. It's not as if I was behind it or anything."

"Weasel."

"You should probably drop it," said Hardcastle, "it's not as if we need the money and I'd bet anything it'll happen again."

"We can't drop it; we have advance bookings and it was never about money. We just wanted some fun. Maybe we can just cut it back a bit? Sit in a chair and moan or something?"

"That sounds alright on the face of it," said Percy sagely, "but people don't really know what they want, do they? It sounds like fun 'til it happens. It's like these silly bastards that think it would be great to have a fifty foot Burmese python until it eats the cat and tries to strangle the wife."

"Well I think we should keep going," said Maud petulantly, "it's only for me and the doc to say in any case."

"Bollocks," Hardcastle exclaimed, "it affects us all. We should all have a say. And as much as I hate to admit it, Gaspard should have been consulted."

"I don't think he'll worry if he can get to cuddle with the guests," chuckled Percy, "not if they're like this one."

"Maybe not but our next one is Eustace Hassenpfeffer from Minnesota. He's sixty and deals in farm machinery."

"Probably wouldn't be up for a cuddle then?" Maud giggled.

"You never know these days," said Hardcastle without the least hint of humour but being closer to the mark than he would have thought.

"There's one thing we should do, you know?" Bert said with a degree of reflexion. "Have them sign a waiver. If this carries on, Gaspard is eventually going to be sued for every penny."

"Take my advice, shut the whole stupid carry on down," said Hardcastle in his best street copper's delivery.

"We've signed a contract," confessed the doctor after a brief pause. "We've just got to work out a decent business plan. Beginning with the waiver."

"Bloody great," Hardcastle growled menacingly. "I'll never get my book finished with a load of bloody strangers gallivanting about the place. It's not as if it's ideal now."

"Eek."

"Yeah, I suppose you're right Spinner. We should have thought about how it would affect Gaspard."

Monica awoke feeling a little kittenish. She knew that it was Gaspard's day off. She also knew that he liked a long lie in. What better way to start the day then, than to slip unannounced into his room and surprise him? With any luck he might surprise her. If she turned up late for work, so what? She was employed by the council, an organisation that with a few notable exceptions, her being one, employed largely misfits, failures and incompetents. She was certainly right about the surprise.

Women are very good at instantly absorbing every detail of a rival, potential or actual and in the situation that presented itself when she entered Gaspard's room, the rival looked very real indeed. Despite her hair being awry and lacking make-up, the girl looked every inch the rival and there were a lot of inches of all sorts to rival with. Perhaps it was the absence of significant amounts of clothing. Maybe the question as to how the hair had become tousled. Perhaps just the impossibly long legs in questionable proximity to Gaspard. Of course, it was all that and more. This girl was an absolute knock-out. She'd probably have to be killed.

The one piece of luck that Gaspard had that morning, other than still being asleep, was that Monica was too shocked and angry to speak. She stood, hands on hips in that peculiar display of aggression that is particular to the female sex. Her mouth was hanging open but her lungs were working like an industrial bellows and anybody could see that her verbal release valve was about to fail big time. Fortunately for all concerned, Valeria Katzarz could read the symptoms. A girl with her looks got plenty of practice, after all. She put a finger to her lips, unwound those incredibly long legs; legs that would be cut off at the knees if Monica had her way; and moved sinuously towards Monica.

The sinuous bit didn't help matters in the least. "Please, it is the fault of the ghosts," she whispered. "You know of them, yes?" Monica tried to reply in kind but only managed to make a sound like a pit-bull about to launch a frenzied assault. Valeria bravely took her hand and led her out of the room. "The ghosts frightened me. I forced Mister Feeblebunny to stay with me. I could not sleep alone. He did not want to do it."

"Yes, I'm sure he took a lot of persuading. I'll bet it was very hard for him," sneered Monica meaningfully.

"Please, he was a perfect gentleman."

"No one's that perfect," Monica spat, looking her rival ostentatiously up and down.

"He was, please. He just hold me. For my fear," wheedled Valeria, her language skills deserting her in the heat of the skirmish.

"It's true," said the doctor, suddenly appearing. It might have caused Monica to start but it had an outstandingly galvanising effect on Valeria who not only managed a leap that would have shamed Michael Jordan but simultaneously effected a mid-air about face, worthy of the great Fonteyn. She covered several feet before her toes touched the floor. It was those toes which carried her hastily back to the bedroom where she disappeared beneath the covers and flung her arms about Gaspard. It might have looked great as an act of athleticism but in no other way did it look good at all. The not good perception was not aided by Gaspard immediately responding to her embrace.

He would later have a hard time trying to argue that it was merely a reflex action. In an act of near heroism, the doctor managed to restrain Monica from following behind and committing mayhem. He was able with some difficulty to temporarily sooth the savage breast and explain what had happened the previous evening. Eventually he was able to convince her that Gaspard had had no part to play in Valeria's presence in the flat but it would have taken Freud himself to persuade her that Gaspard had not enjoyed the evening a little too much for his own good. Come to think of it, Freud might be a bad choice considering his hang-ups about funny business. While this conversation was going on, Monica had her eyes fixed on the couple in the bed in a death ray stare that had Gaspard transfixed in a cobra/mongoose sort of way. It was the sort of stare that eloquently said, "Just wait 'til I get you alone you bastard and as for you, you bloody slinky tart…"

Fortunately for the bloody slinky tart concerned she was unable receive the force of the stare being in a position sometimes described as face down and bum up. It left her invulnerable to Monica's glare but oddly vulnerable to other forms of assault which in her terror of the ghosts she'd not properly considered. Gaspard's inability to move was nothing to do with him being less brave than the doctor, he just knew Monica a hell of a lot better.

Staying put might look bad but common sense told him that approaching her at the moment would be akin to trying to pat a crocodile on the nose and with a lot more chance of being eaten. Not that common sense had much to do with the present situation because no matter what course he took, sensible or otherwise, Monica would exact her pound of flesh. He had an unpleasantly sinking feeling that he knew exactly where it would come from. Give or take an ounce of so.

Well alright, minus several ounces. Allow a young man his fantasy. When it came down to the duration of his torment, he reckoned that remembering to let go of Valeria might count to his advantage but he had to weigh that against being clad only in his underwear. And not the boxers either. In his favour was the fact that Monica knew he did not possess pyjamas, the ones he had owned being ruined by sardine juice. On the minus side, he was in his underwear. Six of one half a dozen of the other?

Not a bloody chance. He was doomed. Luckily for all concerned, the doctor turned out to be better at diplomacy than he had been at suicide, or at least at remaining dead. He negotiated a deal which turned out to be to everyone's satisfaction except perhaps Gaspard's. Monica would stay at the flat and since Valeria had prepaid for three nights, she would stay at Monica's, taking with her the makings for her meals. As the negotiation progressed, Valeria was increasingly of two minds because she had begun to rather like the doctor and believe Gaspard's assurances that there was nothing to fear. She was also beginning to wonder whether another cuddle with Gaspard under better circumstances might not add a little missing spice to the holiday.

On the other hand, Monica was a bloody sight scarier than any ghost and there was no way on God's green earth that she would allow her to stay without blood being spilled. Eventually Valeria agreed to the proposal. It was however arranged that if she wished she could return when Monica was present to make the acquaintance of the other ghosts in a more controlled and calmer setting and experience the haunting that she'd paid for. Gaspard was the loser because although he would get to spend long nights with Monica, he would have to spend those nights with Monica in quite a mood. The mood was of the 'whatthebloodyhellwereyouthinkingGaspardFeeblebunnygettinginto bedwiththattartanddon'ttellmeyoudidn'tenjoyit' variety. Surprisingly, or maybe not depending on whether you think that names affect one's perception of an individual, she became a lot more amenable once she learned that Valeria's family name was Katzarz.

Not even the most miserable periods in our lives can last forever, always assuming we discount afternoon teas with elderly relatives and flights on certain budget airlines. Everything passes after all, a point best not dwelled upon if one wishes to maintain one's balance. So it was that eventually Monica settled but only after providing Gaspard with numerous occasions when he considered joining his spirit guests in a more permanent capacity. It helped a little that the next guest was to be a sixty-year-old tractor salesman. When it came to the next guest, the others had yet again failed to take all eventualities into account. For instance, in their enthusiasm to start up, they'd not taken into consideration who would welcome the guests and when.

So far, they'd had one happy coincidence when the guest's arrival just happened to coincide with Gaspard being home from work, although Monica would have argued the use of the word happy. As would Gaspard after Monica had finished with him. Eustace Hassenpfeffer arrived unannounced while Gaspard was at work, much to the consternation of the others. They gathered immediately inside the door, frantically discussing what they should do. He'd paid after all and it was pretty soon clear that Eustace was not a man to be denied. They were forced to admit that they had no choice but to admit. When the door mysteriously opened, seemingly of its own accord the new guest was amused. It was obviously a little joke played on the newcomers. When Maud suddenly materialised in front of him wearing the bloodied robe she used on Valeria's visit, the joke didn't seem funny any longer.

Maud rung her hands concernedly and being nervous at the unexpected situation said: "Welcome, we're happy you could join us," in a voice that was little more Boris Karloff that she might have wished. Eustace Hassenpfeffer fled and not wishing to risk waiting for the lift, headed for the stairs. He only made it as far as the third step before his high heels proved themselves unequal to the task and he tumbled with his skirt flung over his head in a display that was mercifully unwitnessed by any. Any living that is.

"Hello Eustace. Time to go."

"Oh, shit! You're real."

"If that's the way you choose to look at it."

"Why's my head at such a funny angle?"

"I think you know. It was quick and painless. You should be happy."

"You think? I'm wearing stilettos and a dress and my knickers are showing. What the hell will the wife think? I'll be a laughing stock."

"Look on the bright side. You won't be around to notice and I doubt it's something she'll want to share."

"Mort," called Ivor from the door of the flat, "I don't suppose we could have him, could we?"

"Not this time doctor, things are getting a bit out of hand. In any case, I think out friend might be just a bit embarrassed."

"You said it buster. Let's get the fu…can I say that here?"

"Best not."

"Boy, that's gonna take some getting used to. Um, before we go…?"

"Yes?"

"Any chance I could get a refund do you think?" The ghosts milled in confusion in the doorway.

"What the hell do we do now?"

"Eek!"

"What did he say?"

"He said it's time we pulled our flippers out and rethought this whole bloody business."

16

Time passed as it has an unfortunate way of doing. Guests continued to arrive; their reception being handled by a small local letting agency when Gaspard; who was building a substantial nest-egg from the business; was unavailable. In matters of the nest variety however, the eggy bit did not really compensate for the disruption to his home life. He would have much preferred the nest minus the egg and thus, minus the guests. Had he been alone, as he appeared to be to the normal mortal, the guest situation may have been tolerable but he was far from that, him having five human ghosts and one cetacean ghost to cope with as well. If the place had any rafters, it would have been packed to them.

As for his less substantial and unfortunately permanent guests, just because they were busy didn't mean they were any easier to live with. If anything, they were becoming more difficult as they all did their best to outdo their fellows on the literary front. All save Maud that is, whose life experience didn't really lend itself much to literary output, it being pretty much limited to the ending of it and even there she'd done a fair job of ballsing it up. Percy's life hadn't been that much more interesting but he insisted his work of life in a machine shop would not only be published but fly off the shelves. Gaspard and Monica dreaded the day he submitted it formally for consideration.

Maud meanwhile, managed to content herself by writing songs of a distinctly G and S character but it kept her happy. Gaspard also suspected that she was visiting some porn sites on the internet but said nothing about it, mainly because he wasn't sure. He couldn't imagine any of the others searching for 'big willies' but he wasn't prepared to bet on it.

Most of the disharmony revolved around frequent squabbles and demands for quiet. It was all beginning to tell on Gaspard who was usually forbidden any home entertainment other than reading or listening to music through headphones. The latter activity was soon abandoned because the frequent use of headphones made his ears sore and did not allow him to scratch inside them with his car keys, an unpleasant habit of which the doctor was attempting to break him with only marginal success.

This meant that when devoid of guests he was spending as much time as possible at Monica's and though she swore undying love she was frankly becoming a bit pissed off with his frequent presence and his habit of cleaning his ears with his car keys. The main reason she found his numerous visits annoying was that there are some things a girl doesn't want her lover to know about her before marriage. Once the contract is sealed there's no problem. Until then it's best he doesn't know that she farts in the bath. Or at all for that matter. For the time being, he was unaware of the plan the others had concocted, which was a positive. He had enough to deal with.

The others were biding their time. Speaking of having enough to deal with, he was having his hands full being a full-time police officer, literary agent, bed and breakfast host and posing as an author, not to be seeking a method of dealing with his problems. He also had the other role of Collector of Souls but luckily that duty was still on hold due to reluctance on the other side to become involved in the Spinner fiasco.

His lack of success in coming up with a solution left him peculiarly vulnerable to the spirit's machinations. Hardcastle had finished his tell all book. It was a work that would have any publisher unconsciously doodling dollar signs all over their note pad. It was also a work that may cause them to check carefully if they had anything to hide because the police would be far from pleased and would undoubtedly come seeking redress once the initial furore had died down. Oswald Sharkey was frankly amazed that a serving police officer would have the suicidal courage to pen such a work because it was bloody dynamite and would have senior ranks looking over their shoulders and dodging journalists and outraged citizenry for some time to come.

Which is to say, that at first he doubted the veracity of the work. "Forgive me Monica, Alan, if I seem a bit dubious but it's very difficult to believe that anyone would sink their career in such a spectacular fashion. Not to mention putting themselves in lifelong jeopardy of his soon to be ex-colleagues." Ossie smiled and looked meaningfully over his steepled his fingers. Gaspard and Monica had had a struggle coming up with an answer to this question which they knew was bound to come. Come it did however.

"I can see why you'd think that, Ossie. The answer is a simple one. Sergeant Hardcastle was in ill health and wrote the manuscript to be released only after his death. He asked me as his friend to try to publish it and set the record straight. I'm afraid that at the end he was very remorseful over some…most, of his actions while on the streets."

"Ah, so that explains your involvement, Alan. I wondered to be frank, whether you may have written it under a pseudonym. You didn't, did you?"

"Entirely blameless, I can assure you Ossie. No connection in anyway other than doing a friend a post mortem favour. Didn't even ghost write it before you ask. It's all his own work one hundred percent." At the words 'ghost writer', Monica blinked and gave him a warning look that effectively said stop being a smart arse.

"I see. It's a pity he's dead in a way," said Ossie, who'd never realise how close he'd come to categorising Hardcastle's true state of being. "The interviews and television spots would have sent sales through the roof. Even so, there'll be enough crap flying about the place to ensure this goes best seller and stays there for quite a while."

"Great news Ossie. He would have been thrilled."

"I suppose the royalties will go to his estate?"

"Sadly, he died without heirs or any living relatives. He generously signed over all rights to me as his one friend and as payment for my efforts in having it published."

Sharkey looked Gaspard in the eyes while a hint of suspicion ambled slowly across his features. "Look, I hesitate to imply anything less than complete honesty on your part Gaspard but if you did have anything to do with this, now's the time to come clean. Questions will be asked when it hits the shops and I'd hate it if it later came to light that this was a work of fiction." He attempted his best all friends together smile but not being terribly familiar with real sincerity the look crashed and burned on take-off, the wreckage later resembling more of a sneer.

"No fear of that. Hardcastle's career is a matter of record. Including some of the less savoury bits. You can also rest assured the most I've had to do with it was to read the manuscript after his death. I've not even changed the punctuation."

"Yes, speaking of that, it might be something you could profitably set your mind to before we send it to the press. I'm afraid the good sergeant's work in that regard was about as brutal as his policing methods."

"We did notice that, didn't we, Monica?"

"We most certainly did Ossie. We decided to leave it as it was written though because we had a strong feeling questions would be asked. It seemed best to leave it unedited until you'd had a chance to review it in all its rough originality." Monica and Gaspard could have been forgiven for assuming that the copious notes Ossie was making had something to do with their conversation. It was actually a list of accessories for his new Bentley.

'The moving finger writes,' as Omar said, 'and having writ moves on.' A lot of fingers had writ and moved on at Gaspard's and a lot of work produced.

Omar didn't say anything about flippers but no doubt he'd have been willing to stretch a definition. Not much of the work contained a lot of piety or wit which may have distressed the poet but it was substantial stuff by and large and just what Cuttlefish press was looking for. Ossie Sharkey was coining it and a portion of that pelf was dripping down to Gaspard. Spinner's follow up to a Porpoise's Tale, entitled Orca! The harrowing story of a porpoise pod's battle with their nemesis was just as well received as his first work and he, or to be more precise, honorary porpoise Gaspard, was being feted worldwide. It was a challenge for Gaspard who despite his efforts to shun the limelight, was expected to appear at signings and give interviews and although an unwelcome trial, after a few dismal displays he managed to get the hang of it.

As Monica said, it at least kept him out of the way in general and out of the police station in particular while the furore surrounding Hardcastle's partial autobiography was resounding. So far, his link to the sergeant's work was known only to the publishers but there was always the chance that the barracudas of the yellow press would unearth the link and hound him. Or possibly if one is to keep the metaphor correct, fish him. After that, his colleagues would no doubt have a word or two to say and his superiors who had been generous in allotting time off for his signing tours would almost certainly find interesting and marginally legal ways to punish him severely. For the moment however, he was popular as the man who might have escaped being found guilty of murdering the bastard. It was irony indeed that the whole police force of Hamm on Wye really hoped that he had committed murder and got away with it.

All of this notoriety had the unfortunate effect of unmasking Gaspard at the offices of Cuttlefish Press where he had been known as A.P. Spinner. He should have known that the charade would never last, not once the public appearances began. **'LOCAL ROZZER PENS BEST SELLING TRIOLOGY'** trumpeted the Bugle. And yes, Spinner had been forced to follow up the success of his first two works with The Inky Darkness. A book that was not, as one might imagine, about the furthest ocean depths but about a pod's encounters with the dreaded Humboldt Squid. It positively leaped off the shelves and Mister Sharkey was buying his wife a Silver Ghost to match his Bentley, completely unaware of the irony.

"And you definitely did not write Hardcastle then Al…Gaspard? Should I call you that or Alan, er, Alan?"

"Either's fine with me O.S. but I suppose now that it's all out in the open you may as well call me Gaspard."

"So why the pseudonym?"

"You've seen the crap in the press. Local copper etc, etc. You don't need that sort of notoriety as a policeman. Now that it's out I have no choice but to resign. I can't do my job being flocked by fans all day long and the alternative is desk work. I didn't sign on to be a clerk." Gaspard looked as distraught as he felt at the death of his career.

"Mm, unfortunate. And Feeblebunny and Goonhilly? Why the literary agency?"

"I simply thought it was the only way you'd take me at all seriously."

"It was lucky for all of us that I did. Now, about the children's book you're flogging."

It was at last time for the big talk. Gaspard had been corralled in the living room and surrounded by the spirits who were virtually vibrating with excitement.

"So, Gaspard. You are now an extremely wealthy man with promises of a lot more to come. I understand that negotiations are underway for an animated version of the porpoise trilogy?"

"Hm," responded Gaspard, fearful of where all this may be leading.

"No doubt that will bring in a pretty penny?"

"Ah…mmm."

"So, let's put our cards on the table," Ivor said in a meaningful manner, noting that Gaspard cringed visibly at the words. They both knew that little good came of sentences beginning that way. At least, not for the one on the receiving end. "The wealth you now enjoy; how is the Aston running by the way? came to you as the fruits of our labour. I think we can agree on that?"

"There was the b and b," Gaspard mumbled unconvincingly.

"But it was our idea, although we concede that your elbow grease was required. No doubt that would have purchased you a used Fiat Uno. No, let's face it Gaspard, your considerable wealth is also our considerable wealth. Not so? I'm not wishing to be unpleasant, just making a point as a means of speeding negotiations."

"Ah," said Gaspard, now realising that this was going to be all about how the loot was to spent, "it's about money."

"I'd have thought that was patently obvious," put in Bert.

"Now, now, Bert. Keep it pleasant," said the doctor firmly. "I won't beat about the bush, Gaspard. We want some say in how the money is used and we have a plan we wish to put to you. We hope that you'll consider carefully because we believe that it will be to all our benefit."

"Shoot," Gaspard clenched his toes and waited. (Some may realise at this point that toe clenching is not a typical activity in times of severe tension. The word toe has been used for the sake of decency. The reader is free to insert an appropriate bodily noun.) "Let me preface what we propose by stating that we all believe the present situation cannot continue. The flat is too small for all of us and before you say anything, we have no intention of passing over. Understood? Good. So, the obvious answer is to move to more suitable premises. So far so good?"

"Sounds reasonable. Does that mean we'll be dropping the b and b?"

"Not only does our plan not include dropping the hauntings, it will extend the scope."

"Oh, shit. No bloody way."

"Please, hear me out. We have located a stately home that is for sale as a going accommodation business. It has adequate space for us all and private apartments for you and Monica if she wishes to join us. It is our plan to advertise ourselves as a haunted house, the most haunted house in England in fact, offering five-star accommodations. We're certain it will be a spectacular success."

"Private apartments you say? What about management? I know bugger all about running a hotel, haunted or otherwise."

"We have already contacted an experienced gentleman who is interested. I might add that the existing staff at the manor would welcome staying on."

"Do they know about the haunting?"

"From what I gather, the place already has one or two resident spirits. The staff are used to the idea. Most of them say they've experienced something."

"They aint seen nothing yet," said Maud happily.

"OK. Now let me get this straight. I get to live there but I'm not needed to run the place or be involved in any way?"

"That's what we agreed isn't it fellas?" Asked the doctor of the others. They all nodded their agreement. "Of course, we'd be chuffed if you were to help out in any way that you see fit."

"We'll see. And the profits?"

"Yours of course and Bert will manage the accounts. Plus, we shall continue to pursue our writing. My book should be completed shortly. I'm sure Ossie will find it acceptable. I decided to drop the autobiography and do a murder mystery." The doctor had wanted to give a full description of his work which was really a mediaeval medical murder mystery but decided that his lips weren't up to the task and may have the effect of stalling negotiations.

"Well," began Gaspard cautiously, "I see no real problems with the idea. If you are willing to risk some of your own money in this venture; and I'm prepared to stipulate that it is mostly your money; who am I to stand in your way."

"Bert has checked the financials. We can make a go of it. More than a go."

"Alright then," conceded Gaspard, who'd just about reached breaking point in his current circumstances. "Where is this place?" It was a while before the doctor could continue as the ghosts celebrated with cheers and high fives. Or in one case high flippers.

"The place is not far from here. You know Burnham Down? Just near there. It's the estate of the Hardfast family. Or was, I suppose I should say."

"I don't think I know the name."

"Interesting piece of history there. The estate was granted by Edward the third to one of his knights, Cyril of Bannister, after the battle of Crecy. Cyril stood his ground against repeated attacks and was called my most true and hardfast knight by the king. He later became Earl Hardfast."

"Interesting. I've always thought it would be marvellous to have one of those ancient piles with a lot of history."

"Bert has ancient piles," butted in Percy crudely. "I don't think there's much historic about them though."

"Must you be so sodding vulgar," snapped Maud.

"So," Gaspard asked a trifle warily. "the name of the place is…?"

"Hardfast Manor. Why?"

"Oh God, I was afraid of that," moaned Gaspard.

"What's the problem. Why the funny look?"

"Why? You have to bloody ask?"

"He does," chortled Percy. "His mind just doesn't work like ours." Gaspard was offended by being linked with Percy's train of thought but tried not to show it.

"I don't get it either," said Maud querulously.

"That's just your half-arsed manner," shot back Percy, who just couldn't resist the opportunity.

The ghosts took turns in advising Gaspard of their visions for the future and it was therefore sometime before the doctor dropped the bombshell that was his next idea.

"We're going into TV production," he said as though he was stating that he was off to the shops.

"And just how, pray tell, do you intend to manage that?" asked Gaspard, sounding seriously exasperated. "Naturally we won't do it ourselves. We've contacted a production company who have tentatively accepted the premise. What we do is, we open up the hotel for hauntings and when we have enough reviews from people swearing that they've seen ghosts, we offer a challenge to anyone who thinks they can disprove their existence. When they come, we frighten the crap out of them on camera. Believe me, it'll really rake in the viewers."

"And the gelt," said Hardcastle who was beginning to like the idea of appearing on television but not as much as the prospect of putting the wind up people.

"Cough."

"He's here again."

"Stay put. There's nothing he can do."

"Evening all," said Death in a comic stage policeman's delivery, accompanying it with the traditional bending at the knees and a not so traditional creak. "What's going on 'ere then?"

"If you must know," said Maud truculently, "we're discussing the purchase of half-arsed manor." Her hand immediately flew to her mouth and she looked stricken.

"Strike one," chortled Percy. "Now that's in your minds you'll never know which is the correct way to say it ever again." He laughed evilly.

"Ah, know the place well. I've tried a few times in the past to get Lady Hardfast and Siegfried to come along quietly but they've always refused. Maybe you'll have better luck Gaspard."

"Not bloody likely," said the doctor, who'd long since lost his fear of Mort, "we need them for the hauntings."

"Oh. You're carrying on with that then."

"Not only carrying on skinny, we're upping the ante," Maud cackled.

"Well, that's a bugger. I've brought you these." Death reached beneath his robe and handed Gaspard a small object.

"Secateurs?"

"Yep, the boys are into miniaturisation. Reckoned the shears were too clumsy. Don't worry, they've been fully field tested."

"Oh, goody," said Gaspard despondently. "I take it the problems have been resolved then?"

"Hell no. These are the ones I commissioned ages back from a private firm. Things are still tits up otherwise."

"So, you said something about a person called Siegfried earlier," enquired Gaspard after he'd finished moaning about the secateurs. At least, temporarily. "Siegfried? Yes, interesting chap. Doesn't get along well with Lady Hardfast though. Not surprising I suppose, landed gentry, a bit on the stuffy side, meets a Fokke-Wulf pilot."

"You're joking?"

"Why would I? Shot down near the manor. He was taken there to save him from the locals. Seems they weren't too pleased he'd shot up their maypole. Did a runner when I turned up."

"Great. I haven't got enough ghosts, I have to inherit two others and one is a bloody Nazi."

"Three."

"What?"

"Three. You're gaining three ghosts. Lady Hardfast, aka Lady Cynthia, Siegfried and Lady Cynthia's maid Ethel."

"Oh bloody hell."

"I don't want to worry you but it's probably worse than you imagine. Lady Hardfast is a religious zealot and has a number of peculiarities. She will be extremely hard to manage, Ethel is a raving nympho when she's not trying to develop ways of strangling cats and Siegfried is certifiable."

"A great addition to the menagerie then," groaned Gaspard.

"You said it chum. Sorry to be the bearer of bad tidings but surely you wouldn't expect much else. Certainly not in Lady C's case anyway. Ethel too of course. Being around for over six hundred years can have that effect on people. Well, spirits. As for Siegfried I suspect he was always a mad bastard. Fighter pilot…what more is there to say?" He paused after a decent interval. "You look like you could do with a bracer. Any of that nice Irish stuff in the cupboard."

"I take it I don't have to ask?"

"Applaud that man. And the Hobnobs too if you have any." Death drummed his finger bones thoughtfully for a moment or two. "I don't suppose you could change it to Hardfast House? It might rid you of that Fawlty Towers vibe." A few nips of fire water soon had Gaspard brave enough to ask the question that was hanging menacingly in the air between them. If it could have banged a few pots and pans together to gain their attention it would have.

"OK Mort. The secateurs. Let's have it."

"I thought I already had," replied Death lightly, enjoying the social interaction too much to want to balls it up just yet.

"Spit it out. And I don't mean the Hobnob before you try to get cute."

"Oh well, since you seem intent on spoiling my one little bit of relaxation. I don't have days off you know? You've obviously realised that the new equipment meant that you're back on the payroll. Full time, I might add."

"You're bleedin' joking, aren't you? I mean, I figured you'd want me to try them out but full time? I'm too busy. I've got the guests, there's…"

Mort cut him off. "You'll have plenty of time for all that. Now that you're on the staff the boys have built a time chip into the…implement."

"You can't say it can you? Go on, say secateurs. You can't say it because you know it's bloody ridiculous."

"Please, don't start up. It's not my fault and anyway at least you can hide these in your robe until they're required."

Gaspard sighed an exaggerated sigh. "I suppose. Tell me how they work."

"No need, the chip will take care of everything. You'll arrive back here at exactly the same time as you departed. As for the rest, just give a little snip once they've agreed to accompany you and Mable's your aunty."

"When?"

"Soon. First one will be a doddle. Just a trial run to make sure your happy with the equipment. Maybe just a couple more drinkies first though? I won't tell if you won't."

Gaspard nodded and poured another couple of generous shots. We're talking more of canon fire than pistols here.

"I don't suppose I could impose on the group to do a couple of numbers? I do so like G and S" Mort enquired winningly.

"So's definitely been checked?" enquired Gaspard a trifle foggily.

"Take my word for it. Checked and double checked. Nothing can go wrong."

"See front page yesterday?"

"We've stopped taking the papers. You might be able to guess why. Terrance has the Times crossword photocopied for him."

"But you'd know what happened in…in…thingamy? Your job an' all."

"You're referring to the squid attack?"

When Gaspard arrived, Gladys was sitting dejectedly in a corner staring at the floor. She evinced not the least degree of surprise or shock at his precipitate appearance on the scene. "Oh, it's you. Didn't think I'd ever see you again," she said mournfully.

"Not who you think I am," said Gaspard, enunciating with some effort.

"Hm, 'course, no scythe. If you're here to prune the roses, you're a bit late."

"Not who you think I am. His assistant." This was hard. Particularly the esses for some reason.

"Well, that's a relief. Last thing the missus needs is some maniac running around spoiling her Lady Margarets. What are you doing here then?"

"Come see if you willing to…er…pass over?"

"Pass over what? Are you drunk young…are you drunk?"

"Might have had a few," Gaspard mumbled grudgingly.

"Shame on you. Drinking on the job."

"Look, do you want get out of here or not?"

"Let me get this straight. You turn up here in the dead of night posing as a gardener, drunk as a lord and then ask me if I wish to accompany you to God knows where?"

"God knows where is correct. Good one, eh?"

"As much as I wish to depart this veil of tears young…whoever you are…"

"Collector. Mmm the collector."

"What sort of collector if I may make so bold? Snuff boxes, garbage?"

"Souls. Collect souls. Subcontract. Not my fault. Makes you feel any better you don't ashually go with me. Go on your own. One snip, poof, ashually."

"Really"

"Hm. One snip."

"Go on then."

"Wah?"

"Do it."

"Oh, right. Wish I could do more. First customer, ha, ha."

"First...is that an alligator?"

"How'd it go?"

"Bloody hard work. Might be...um...instant but still tiring. Instant...heh, heh...instant soul just add Gaspard."

"Maybe you should lie down, my boy. You have a lot to do tomorrow."

"Heh, heh, maybe should fall down."

He made it to the bedroom before he did just that. "The kid's turning into a right tosspot," spat Bert, sounding disgusted.

"It's the job," sighed Death, "really takes it out of you. Did I see another bottle in the cupboard? Goodo, how about another number Maud?"

The purchase of Hardfast Manor was all a lot more difficult than Gaspard or any of the others, with the notable exception of Bert could have anticipated. It was not made any easier by having to deal with the local council's building heritage officers whose primary function seemed to be to ensure that historic structures would fall down. This they accomplished by insisting that any renovations be performed using only materials and methods available in the original century of construction and only then at a cost that would bankrupt Croesus.

Gaspard had been warned. Luckily Bert spoke fluent council and was able to grease the wheels and not a few palms against the day when such work may be needed. Naturally it was necessary to interview those staff members who wished to continue working for the new owners. He did this with the aid of Ivor and the new manager, Harold Pentecost. Some of those who'd stated a desire to stay on quickly changed their minds when subjected to the ghost test, which consisted of Maud suddenly appearing in her blood-stained rags and shrieking maniacally.

A surprising number did agree to the new terms however. Usually after a large shot of brandy. Those terms did contain a spook bonus as well as an increase in salary. The resident ghosts, who had not attempted at any time to make contact, could sometimes be seen hovering on the fringes of the interviews, obviously interested in what was occurring. They would however, flee if approached.

It was Ethel, Lady Hardfast's maid who was the first to make contact. "You can see us can't you sir?" She asked nervously, giving a clumsy curtsy. She'd had over six hundred years of practice and still couldn't manage it.

"I can Ethel," replied Gaspard watching her reaction.

As he'd predicted she started. "How did you know my name sir, if I may make so bold?"

"Death told me." This time her knees buckled and she crossed herself several times.

"There's no need to worry, he's really quite a kindly soul."

"He didn't seem that kind when he swung that by our lady great scythe at me."

"It's just his job. It's only to release your soul to the afterlife. Think of it as a favour. Do you mind if I ask why you ran away from him? Didn't you want to go to…um…didn't you want to go?"

"Well, I'd have preferred it to this, truth to tell but as her ladyship had long passed and was haunting my bedroom I thought she wanted me to carry on in her employ. As it turned out she was just watching me and his lordship playing at…well sir, I'm sure you're a man of the world."

"And the other as it turns out."

"What?"

"I am a man of the afterlife as well. If you wish, I can set you free."

"Oh, I couldn't do that to her ladyship sir, she relies on me and then there's Siegfried. He's not really as bad as they say. I'd ask you not to mention this to Lady Cynthia though sir, she wouldn't approve."

"You're having a relationship with Siegfried?" Gaspard enquired. Ethel giggled coquettishly. "Good Lord, is that even possible?"

"You'd be surprised sir," said Ethel, fluttering her lashes. Maybe not, Gaspard thought, remembering what Mort had said about her. "May I ask why you came Ethel? I assume you had a purpose?"

315

"Oh yes, sir. Her Ladyship wanted me to tell you she misses her tele sir and would you mind if she uses the second drawing room? She's already days behind in her soaps and she'll never catch up if it carries on like this."

"She watches soap operas?"

"Well, there's not much for her to do otherwise sir. Me, I've got my chores and Siegfried when he's in the mood but she's read everything in the library a hundred times over. The telly's all she has, poor thing."

"Hm, do you think she'd prefer to cross into the afterlife?"

"That's not for me to say sir but I'd doubt it. Elsie's up to her tricks again you see and she couldn't miss finding out what she's scheming. I could ask though sir if you'd like?"

"Thank you, Ethel, but I should ask her myself. Tell her that she's welcome to have the second drawing room but only if she'll come and talk to me first."

"Very good sir. Perhaps sir I should acquaint you with a little peculiarity she's acquired sir. From all that telly, sir, although I'm sure it's not my place to mention it."

"Go on."

"It's her speech sir. All that tele has sort of affected it, like."

"I'll bear that in mind and thank you Ethel. By the way, the doctor will ask you I'm sure but are you interested in haunting a few guests at all?"

"And how might I do that sir?" she asked, suddenly very interested. "However you like I should imagine. The Manor will be used in future to receive guests who wish to see ghosts."

"Well, if you like sir, I'm sure I could entertain some of the young gentleman sir."

"You wanted to see me sport?" Lady Cynthia asked in an accent that was a weird mixture of Australian and the East End with a touch of California and the North.

"Yes, thank you for coming Lady Hardfast."

"She's apples."

"Yes, well I wanted to tell you myself that you're more than welcome to the second drawing room. I understand that you enjoy the soap operas?"

"You dribbled a bibful there mate. If I don't get my fix, I'm like a snake with a burr up its bum."

316

"I assume...er don't ask me why...that you like some of the Australian soaps."

"More than that. Yank, pommy, the last lot put in pay for view, so I get twenty-four hours of it. I know it's a load of cobblers but there's bugger all else to do. Except pray of course but you can't spend all day on your knees, you have to have something else. Ethel can tell you that."

"That raises a point your ladyship. You are a pious woman. Have you considered leaving this world? I can help you know?"

"You know what? If you'd asked me that thirty years ago, I'd have been on it like a dog on a porkchop but I've got me serials now. They're bloody addictive."

"You surprise me your ladyship. Surely your religion...?"

"Yeah, yeah, I know but until you've got that lot in yer 'ead you don't know what bloody indoctrination means. It beats the Jesuits hands bloody down."

"Very well, if that's your decision but if you have a change of heart..."

"Sure, whatever. I can't go anywhere though while that gormless little berk's still on the B and B. I keep hoping someone'll kill the carrot munching little wimp. 'Course, who they should really kill's the bloody writers."

"It may seem a silly question but if you dislike it so much why watch?"

"Stupid innit? I tell you what I fink. Me late hubby once sliced up a few peasants on the front lawn. It was just so bleedin' 'orrible I couldn't look away. That's what the soaps is like. Once you start you just 'ave to look."

"Hm, I can maybe see that. Very well, the offer is always open. Maybe if you pray for guidance?"

"Yeah, uh, huh. Anyfing else."

"Mm, I understand there's another spirit here. Siegfried? Could you tell me anything about him?"

"Don't talk to me about that mad bastard. Randy sod always sniffing around my maid as if I didn't know. Miserable git acts like a proper geezer dun 'e. Finks he's the dog's bollocks. You can take him any day of the week and welcome. Ship the little git out of here. He's a bloody foreigner too. No right to be here at all. Not in my bleedin' 'ouse anyway."

"Ah, yes, well thank you your ladyship. Might I ask if you'd be interested in a little guest haunting? Just for fun sort of thing?"

"Ethel mentioned that. Nah, fanks for arxin' but that's arfter minnight's when they does the Coronation Street reruns. I bet she hopped at it though? Give 'er a chance to get into some bloke's trarsers."

"Well, if you change your mind let us know. It might be a bit of welcome amusement. You could always just pop up in someone's mirror, doesn't have to be late."

"Yer, that does sound a bit of a rort. I'll fink abart it."

It took some while yet before Siegfried put in an appearance. Or rather, until he formally contacted anyone. It all seemed odd to Gaspard and didn't appear to fit in with opinions of those who knew him that he was a bit of a self-proclaimed geezer. He had been seen occasionally floating on the fringes of gatherings and Monica complained that on one occasion he frightened her when he popped up while she was in the bath.

If Monica was to be believed and Gaspard had no reason to doubt her, the popped up part was not just a figure of speech. In fact, she'd been so incensed by the whole sordid affair that she demanded Gaspard have a stern word with the spectral peeping Tom. Gaspard said that he would but that he wouldn't use the word stern because that might set Siegfried off. Monica was not amused.

"Your name is Gaspard, nicht wahr?" asked Siegfried without preamble, suddenly appearing at Gaspard's side while he sat at his desk.

"Jesus, don't do that. I get enough of that from the others."

"My apologies. One sometimes forgets the common courtesies. Being dead will do that to one."

"Apology accepted Siegfried, just please don't do it again, particularly in bathrooms." Gaspard favoured him with a meaningful stare.

"So, the young lady complained. I apologise to her if she was discomfited. It was too hard to resist."

"Yes she said something in a similar vein."

"Bitte?"

"Nothing."

"You know my name then? I presume Ethel told you? Or that mad cow Cynthia?"

"Lady Cynthia. Yes but I knew it already. Death told me." He awaited a reaction that was not forthcoming. "You're not surprised?"

"Not at all. I've been watching you. You put on that robe, the one with the alligator. You are not of this world, mm?"

318

"The opposite actually. I'm not of the other world. Just on reluctant secondment."

"Fascinating. You must tell me what it's like."

"I think you already have a fair idea. Before you ask what it's all about, I'll tell you. My job is to collect the souls of those ghosts who are tired of this world and wish to move on. Would you be interested?"

"Only if you can tell me what I'll be letting myself in for. I have to admit all this ghosting gave me a surprise. I'd never believed in anything after…well, you know."

"Only too well."

"So, it strikes me that if some of what I'd thought was…what's the word…?"

"Bollocks?"

"That will do nicely. If it was not all bollocks, then perhaps some of the nastier bits might also be true. You know, the bits about having one's bum burned for eternity, that sort of thing."

"I know you want me to reassure you but I'm afraid I can't. I'm only a human subcontractor. They won't give me access to the mysteries."

"Sounds a bit short sighted. It's like asking you to fly a plane without first giving you some lessons."

"Exactly. I can't tell you how often I'm asked what's on the other side. It's only the really depressed spirits who agree to go when I say I can't help. Very short sighted but then, that's the civil service for you. They really go about things in a half-arsed manner."

"Aha. Just like you go about in Hardfast Manor, huh?"

"So, Siegfried, what made you run from Death in the first place?" Gaspard enquired, studiously ignoring the now tired jest.

"Are you kidding? I'd just shot up the village and some yokel turns up with a bloody great farming implement? You are telling me you wouldn't hot foot it?"

"You have a point I suppose."

"So did he, a bloody big one."

"I take it that you decline the offer to move on?"

"In the circumstances, yes but give me a bit more information and I might take you up on the offer. Meantime, I'll politely decline the opportunity to be buggered by demons. I notice that you've brought quite a retinue with you. It will be nice to have someone to talk to other than the mad cows that have been here 'til now. Have you spoken to Lady Hardcastle? Absolutely gaa, gaa. I mean, when she's not soaking up that drivel she watches on tv she's on her bloody knees. And not in any useful way."

"Hm. Has it struck you that the others might not be too keen to speak to…at the risk of giving offence…I know the war's been over a long time and all…a Nazi?"

"Nazi? Who's a Nazi? Me a Nazi? You think just because I was in uniform, I was a Nazi? Eat your tongue without mustard. You try telling no to that little shit Hitler. Anyway, for me it wasn't about the politics, or even patriotism, it was about the competition."

"Competition? You call killing people competition?"

"Of course. What else would you call it? Us against them. Fokke-Wulf against Spitfire. Your crappy sausages against ours? No contest there as you'll surely agree. Of course it was a competition. So a few people get killed. People die every day. I once killed a chap in a ping pong tournament. Lucky shot. He was up two games to love! I tell you something, it only hurts for a while. No biggy. Bit like going to a shit dentist only without the Novocain. What really hurts was that we was on top until you lot cheated."

"Cheated?"

"Sure. What else would you call putting those supercharged engines in the Spitfires. Our 190's was all over you before that. Bloody cheats. Ha! At least we can kick your arses at football. Hoo boy!"

"We don't always lose," said Gaspard who hated football but would be buggered if he'd sit and listen to his country's team be slagged off.

"Ha! See! Spirit of competition. Already you want to take me on. I bet if I put you in a Spitfire, you'd be wanting a dog fight."

"OK, OK, I can see what you're saying but in the interest of harmony it might be best to keep those ideas to yourself. In the meantime, I'll tell them you aren't a Nazi."

"Hardcastle and Percy might be disappointed, you know."

"What? You've already spoken to them?"

"No but I've been eaves dropping on their conversations. They're not exactly from the social reform movement. More like the national social reform movement if you take my point."

"I admit they are a bit, ah, right of centre but Nazi might be a bit strong."

"Have it your way, I'll let you know if they start demanding lebensraum."

"You do that. Now, I've been asking the others if they'd be interested in doing a bit of casual haunting. I suppose Ethel mentioned it?"

"More than mentioned it. She's already sizing up the younger guests. I really don't know; I suppose I could think about it. Bathrooms off limits I should think?"

"I can't see why."

"I'm in."

"Lady and gentlemen, I'd like you…"

"Eek."

"Sorry Spinner, I was actually including you as a gentleman. But if you prefer; lady, gentlemen and gentleman porpoise, I'd like you to meet Siegfried."

"Don't mention the war," Percy said loudly.

"I tell you what, you don't mention the war and I won't mention the world cup."

"Good one, Siegfried," said Maud, already smitten with the uniform, even if it did have rents in embarrassing places. Or maybe because it had rents in embarrassing places. "Do you like to sing, Ziggy?"

"Do I? I was in the Gruppe choir."

"Great," enthused the doctor, "maybe you could teach us some of your songs?"

"As long as none of them include either of the words valderee or valdera," snarled Hardcastle.

"Hah! I am with you there. You know we sometimes were forced to sing that as a marching song in training. I tell you what, three of the guys deserted on the third day. Talk about a shit song."

"I suppose we all have them though," said Maud kindly.

"You ain't kidding. If we'd had to sing A Horse with No Name, I'd have shot myself." After that first meeting, it was all downhill. The only sticking point was Siegfried's unfamiliarity and often frank contempt for Gilbert and Sullivan. Once it was pointed out that they were never going to perform Wagner he soon got used to the idea and even began to secretly enjoy it. For some reason that was never explained, he particularly enjoyed being one of the three little maids from school.

17

It didn't take much advertising before things really began to kick off. Word of mouth pretty much carried them forward from that point. The reviews on the accommodation sites were with one exception, outstanding. The exception was a widow whose husband had suffered a seizure when Lady Hardcastle appeared in the mirror while he was shaving. The widow blamed the hotel, quite unreasonably most thought since the only proof she had that it wasn't completely natural was that hubby had pointed at the mirror, eyes bulging and said 'gaaak' before collapsing.

Mort had made sure to get him out of the way before he became an embarrassment and his widow was dismissed as a litigious nuisance just angling for a pay-out. The evidence that a haunting was to blame for his demise was so slim even American lawyers refused to take her on as a client. The incident was soon forgotten and everyone was having a wonderful time performing for the guests without doing anything too scary. Even Hardcastle. Soon, it was noticed that Mort, who had to make the occasional visit was entering into the spirit of things to the point that he was becoming quite whimsical, which is a kind way of saying a pain in the bum. It would have been argued that he was experiencing a second childhood had he ever had a first.

It was a bleak and dismal afternoon when Gaspard entered the lobby to find Death manning the reception desk and checking in an American couple.

"Good afternoon sir, welcome to Hardfast Manor."

"Wow, you guys really go all out. If I didn't know that was a costume, I'd have sworn you were real."

"Very kind sir."

"Fred and Dorothy Fleegle, checking in for three nights. Did you hear the voice hun? He sounds just like Lurch from the Adams Family."

"Who ya talkin' to hun?"

"Ah, yes here we are. Fleegle party of two. The Siegfried room. Checking in for three nights, Mister Fleegle checking out in one."

"What? Oh, ha,ha, great joke fella."

"We try our best sir. I notice sir has prepaid the three nights."

"Uh, huh."

"You wouldn't like to reconsider?"

"No. Why would I?"

"Just a precaution sir. One never knows what the immediate future may have in store."

"Droll. I like it. Come on Dorothy. See you later fella."

"You shall sir. At three fourteen a.m. to be precise."

"What? Oh, yeah, see you then. What a joker huh Dorothy?"

"Who were ya talkin' to hun?"

"Would you like Percy here to take your bags, sir?"

"There's no one here."

"He's shy."

"Aha. A ghost bell boy huh? Cute. Thanks, but I'll carry them. Percy may find them a bit heavy, huh?"

"Just leave them sir. They'll be in your room when you get there."

"Ooh, spooky."

"Who ya talkin' to hun?"

As soon as the guests were out of earshot, Gaspard stormed over to the desk and collared Mort before he could do a runner. Not that Mort ran anywhere, it had a tendency to bruise his heelbones.

"Bloody hell Mort, what were you thinking?"

"Just a bit of fun. It seemed appropriate somehow. You know, bloody miserable day and all. Poor bloke's on the list for tonight. I thought I'd brighten his day a bit. The weather certainly won't do it for him."

"By telling him he was going to be dead in a few hours?"

"Part of the act. He didn't believe I was real. It amused him."

"Well please don't do it again. I thought you weren't supposed to give any advance warning?"

"Bit of harmless fun," said Death sulkily. "It won't hurt if he doesn't believe me. Can't I have some amusement too?"

"Not, I think, when you're taking undue risks with our reputation. And dare I say yours on the other side?"

"Spoil sport. Oh, and talking of reputations, best tell Siegfried not to pay a visit. We wouldn't want the widow to start jumping to conclusions."

"Phew! You mean it'll be natural causes? Thank God for that."

"I won't tell if you won't."

"What? You mean it should be ghost related? How...?"

"Trade secret. Anyway, it's bad enough the poor chap has to exit without getting a fright to boot."

"I know I shouldn't ask but does that mean the bloke last month...?"

"Shtum," said Mort, placing a finger to his lips. Or at least to his mouth. "Let's just say Hardcastle was AWOL that night."

"If you say so. Um...you will clean up afterwards?"

"Don't I always." Gaspard tried not to let Death see him roll his eyes.

Ghost Hunter Challenge, the poorly named reality show the ghosts had proposed was a locked down certainty once the producers saw the reviews from the guests. Not to mention the hysterical outpourings from the sceptics that appeared almost from minutes to minute on social media. The battle raged between the parties with the photos and videos posted by true believers being condemned as fakes by their opponents. Insults flew. It all sent bookings through the roof and soon the hotel had a six-month waiting list. Once word of the show was released, every sceptic, magician, self-proclaimed psychic and debunker of strange phenomena signed on to investigate the hotel's claims to be the world's most haunted building.

There were enough to keep the show running for years. The public clamoured for the program to be released. Already destined to be an instant success, that fate was assured when on the first show, a world-renowned sceptic, famous for his success in rooting out fraud, leaped from a second-floor window and managed to cover almost a mile despite having two broken ankles. From his hospital bed, he insisted that his experiences must have been a clever fraud but was unable to offer any proof. He declined the challenge to return and prove it beyond doubt. Over the next twelve months the money simply rolled in. Ghost Hunter Challenge sold worldwide, the hotel boomed and Feeblebunny and Gaspard had more clients than they could handle, although a great deal of its revenue still came from its in-house writers.

Hardcastle, the book, had hit the best seller list and was being made into a TV series. Monica by now had quit the council and worked full time for the agency while Gaspard was kept busy with interviews and book tours as well as the odd chore at the hotel. The task of soul gathering, while not time consuming as such, was proving exhausting when added to his already busy schedule so that on the rare occasions he and Monica had some time together he generally ended up falling asleep. He really did try his best because a distance was growing between them and while that distance increased, the distance between Monica and a certain author she was handling appeared to be diminishing.

It had reached the point where Gaspard had begun to think that the word 'handling' wasn't just a work-related term, a suspicion reinforced by the pairs' obvious pretence of having no interest in one another when he was around. Under the circumstances it was just as well for his peace of mind that he missed the news item in the Bugle headed 'Local Priest Detained. Police Impound Computer'.

"You know Mort, I'm beginning to think that all this money isn't worth it. I don't have any time to enjoy it and even worse, I don't have time for Monica." He sighed and looked soulfully at Mort, a quite appropriate expression considering his part time job.

"Really? Then what I'm about to tell you might…um…not exactly come as a relief but at least won't be quite as devastating as I'd feared." Mort said all this without looking directly at Gaspard. Gaspard felt a sudden chill. The nasty sort that starts in the vicinity of the scrotum.

"Devastating?" he queried apprehensively, feeling certain parts contracting to the point it became almost painful. His voice rose several octaves.

"Hm. Terrance called me in the other day. It seems that the committee has been discussing your situation."

"That's never good is it? On the other hand, what more can they do to me? I'm assuming the news is not that I'm off the books? You know me well enough that you would not describe that as you have."

"It's more the opposite I'm afraid. They want you full time. I know it may be a bit of a shock but it's really quite a compliment. You'll be introduced to the mysteries. It'll make your job a lot easier."

"I don't understand," quavered Gaspard, although he was rapidly beginning to fear that he was understanding only too well. "I'm already sort of full time. I go after all the runners you give me."

"I don't wish to upset you, my boy but by full time they mean no longer on contract. You remember when we first met? I mentioned if it worked out it might mean immortality for you? Well, they think it's time you came onto staff. Sorry."

Gaspard found the room no longer wanted to keep still and it was some time before he managed to control himself sufficiently to speak. He grasped at the one thing he could think of from that early conversation. "But…but…that means I'll be dead. You said my time wasn't for ages." He stared pleadingly into Death's face. Not a pleasant aspect considering the topic of conversation.

"Ah. Legal loophole I'm afraid. Maybe you should have read the fine print."

"Fine print! There was no bloody fine print. There was no contract!"

"It was held in legal. You really should have asked to see it. Please Gaspard, try and stay…try to calm down. Technically you won't be dead. Your soul will depart your corporeal shell without you actually going through the unpleasant bit."

"I'll die."

"Not as such."

"But I won't have a body. I won't be able to feel?"

"You'll still be able to enjoy Hobnobs and have the odd bevvy," Mort said, trying to sound encouraging.

"I want to see Terrance. I want to lodge an objection."

"Impossible I'm afraid. It's already cleared with personnel and legal. You start work at midnight."

"But that's only ten minutes. Can't I even say goodbye to people?"

"Sorry again. Anyway, what would you say? I'm going to die in ten minutes, see you in fifty years? You'd give the game away. You'll be able to visit afterwards. You've received a special dispensation to appear in spirit form to Monica and your old house mates. Other than that, I'm afraid you're…ah…"

"Screwed?"

"Royally. Sorry. If I were you, I'd go over to the couch and have a lie down. It won't be long."

"I might pass on that. I think my body will be getting all the rest it can handle in…oh, about ten minutes," Gaspard said venomously. "It's not fair Mort and you all know it. I've done everything asked of me and they reward me like this? Eternity as a sentient skeleton?"

"Steady on. That's me you're talking about. Look, I know it's hard at the moment but try to look on the bright side. You'll meet a lot of interesting people.

I'll introduce you to Anne Boleyn. She's got a great sense of humour as long as you don't mention her head and get her off the subject of Henry. You'll be able to help spirits in misery."

"Yeah and I'll be one of them. No chance I could do a runner I suppose?"

"Doesn't work that way, I fear. They'll get you wherever you are. Best to bite the bullet. You need friends on the other side and you could upset some if you're a baby about it. Come on, we'll be chums."

"No chance I could get the teeth fixed first, I suppose?" asked Gaspard plaintively. He'd always felt a little embarrassed about showing his choppers when in skeletal form.

"I'm glad you mentioned that. We'll handle that on the other side. Can't have you exposing your fillings now that your full time. Wouldn't do at all." Death hummed in an embarrassed fashion trying to think of a way out of an awkward situation. "I see you've still got a few minutes. If you don't want to lie down how about a quick game of snap?"

'PORPOISE TRILOGY AUTHOR FOUND DEAD'

The renowned local author A.P. Spinner whose real name was Gaspard Feeblebunny was found dead today at Halfarsed Manor the hotel he co-owned with long-time partner Monica Goonhilly. There were no suspicious circumstances. Mister Spinner became a multi-millionaire following the publishing of the bestselling porpoise trilogy. He was co-founder of Feeblebunny and Goonhilly, Literary Agents which had numerous best sellers including the controversial tell all Hardcastle. In addition to his hotel interests, he was well known as the driving force behind the spectacularly successful reality television series Ghost Hunter Challenge.

Budding local author Ernest Shumway speaking on behalf of Miss Goonhilly said that Feeblebunny will be sorely missed by all in the literary community for his tireless devotion to the arts.

"Hello fellas."

"Gaspard! You did a runner," enthused the doctor.

"No. Afraid not. I've been given special leave to come back and say goodbye."

"That's a bit weird isn't it?"

"Yeah. I didn't really die though, you see. They've taken me on full time as the Collector."

"That'll be a bit drafty," said Percy unsympathetically.

"You're not going to come hunting us, I hope?" asked Maud with a tremor.

"No, no. Although I have to warn you that now I'm full time, I no longer have to ask permission." This statement was followed by a confusion of remarks from the ghosts. All except Spinner.

"Don't worry, it's at my discretion. You're safe but do let me know if you change your mind about staying, any of you."

"There's something different about you," said Bert, always the first to notice things.

"Had the choppers fixed."

"Of course. And whitened by the looks of it."

"Yeah, well you can't have a skeletal being with dodgy fangs. Let's the side down. The clients wouldn't take me seriously. So they said. Apparently, Death's were in a right state when he first started."

"All your own then?" Percy asked suspiciously.

"Of course they're all my own. How'd I get on as a skeleton with bloody dentures?"

"Alright. No need to get the hump. Just interested."

"You know?" Hardcastle said suddenly, "for a long time I wanted to kill you. Now that you're dead I have to admit I'm not the least bit pleased. I hope you can pop back occasionally and pay us a visit. Perhaps do a couple of numbers?"

"Why not. Now that I'm of the afterlife I have the power of omnipresence. I can be belting out Ruler of the Queens Navy while simultaneously gathering up some runners and eating Hobnobs with Mort. It takes some getting used to, I can tell you. I would have to come as the Collector though."

"Don't bother."

After a prolonged goodbye, Gaspard found himself in Monica's rooms. Luckily there was no sign of Shumway other than some innocent items on the second bedside table. "Gaspard! I had a feeling you were still around. How are you feeling?"

"Dead."

"Oh, silly question. Are you back permanently?"

"Afraid not. I've been given special leave to pop in and say goodbye but I'm afraid I'm not permitted to say anything about my future situation. Not to mortals anyway. Wow, it feels weird saying that. Rest assured that I'll be fine and able to keep an eye on you."

"No need," she said a little too hastily. "So, I won't be seeing you again then?" She asked, in a tone that sounded distressingly hopeful.

"Perhaps in the very distant future. I'd like you to know that I'll have no hard feelings if you find someone else." He cast an unintentional glance at the bedside table.

"Oh, I am sorry love. You were always so busy." She favoured him with a downcast look. "I was getting dreadfully lonely," she added, utilising every cheat's excuse since the beginning of time.

"Understood," he said with a sinking feeling; no better now that he no longer had a stomach. "Now, I want you to know before the solicitors contact you, that I've left everything to you. Your set for life. Enjoy it please. I wasn't able to and it'll be great if someone can get the true benefit."

He hoped he was sounding more charitable than he felt at the moment. The thought of that conniving little bastard Shumway enjoying the money he'd not been able to, was really rankling.

"Oh, Gaspard, you really shouldn't have," protested Monica but in much the same way as one protests when another party pays the restaurant bill.

"One request though? Give a few mill to animal charities and if you marry get a pre-nup. Most importantly, I'd also like you to keep in a supply of Hobnobs and whisky. When they go missing, please replace them as soon as possible."

"Of course, anything you ask sweetheart. I'll certainly keep in the supplies, although I really don't understand why."

"I might get peckish. If we need anything else, I'll leave a note. Maybe some cheese would be nice."

"Do you think you should, with your…um…problem?"

"Ha! One of the few benefits of being dead. I no longer fart."

"Oh," she said uncertainly. "So, um…what will you do with yourself now that you're, um…no longer with us."

"Nothing. I'm dead."

"I didn't mean that."

"Oh, right."

"Doesn't seem to get in Siegfried's way though. Randy sod." There was no point in trying to embrace. The pair stood about uncomfortably for a little while making humming noises and trying to avoid saying 'well this is nice' until Gaspard decided it was time to take his leave.

"Well, best be off. I see you found the keys to the Aston?"

"Ah, mmm."

"Don't forget to keep it serviced."

"How is she taking it? Devastated I should imagine."

"Disappointingly well. I'm not one to want people to weep and wail but I've seen more show of melancholy when a pet budgie's died."

"Folk take loss in all sorts of ways. I'm sure deep down she feels it."

"I'm sure she's feeling something and it probably is deep down but I doubt it's grief," he said bitterly.

"Did you remember to ask about the Hobnobs and such?" Death though it best to change the subject pronto.

"I did. There'll be a permanent supply in the pantry cupboard."

Death placed a friendly arm about Gaspard's shoulders. There was a slight clatter as bone met bone. "Louis, I think this is the beginning of a beautiful friendship."

"Louis?"

"You've not seen Casablanca? You'd love it. Tell you what, it's on in Greenwich village at the moment. What say we pop over and catch the midnight show? After that, I'll introduce you to Bogart."

The End